P9-EMR-132

SKARRA

SKARRA

Henry V. M. Richardson

Thomas Y. Crowell Company
Established 1834 New York

Published simultaneously in Canada by Fitzhenry & Whiteside Limited, Toronto.

Designed by Ingrid Beckman

Manufactured in the United States of America

Library of Congress Cataloging in Publication Data

Richardson, Henry V. M.
Skarra.

I. Title.
PZ4.R5225Sk [PS3568.I3176] 813'.5'4 75-9739
ISBN 0-690-00909-7

1 2 3 4 5 6 7 8 9 10

To my parents
and my grandparents

BOOK I

Geness

I

A yellow shadow fell over his face and slid across the boughs of the sleigh, and Skarra saw it was evening twilight of the north country. He saw they were moving down a rude village street where two-story logged houses with very small windows, set against the white ruffled snow, peered down on them, and the windows cast brave yellow patterns onto the road.

"Cossacks!" he heard someone call out, the voice piercing with despair.

"No, he killed them all."

"He's so tall. A Scotsman?"

"Cossacks, between here and our blessed sea."

Bruce McTaggart of Skarra recognized many voices mingling in the cold gloom. The German was clear to him, but he did not understand the Finnish dialects used by Piippo and the other university students who had found him, and who were explaining to the townspeople what had happened. He saw they had picked up a large crowd. They were such short people, Skarra thought, staring from the primitive sleigh, which had stopped in front of a high logged home with a paling fence surrounding its courtyard and vegetable gardens. The snow lay everywhere.

Skarra saw short men in felt boots tumbling down the steps, dragging on bulky outer garments, their faces alive with concern.

"Sire, we counted eight Cossack bodies, nine peasant trackers, and three dead wolf dogs—"

"All dead?"

"Very frozen, sire."

Skarra saw Piippo, the Finnish student, at attention, speaking to a short officer with the same open, smooth-skinned Finnish face and the same wide-set blue eyes and short chin. The silver buttons of a tunic showed at the collar of his wolf-skin greatcoat, and Skarra saw the curved sword hanging at his thigh from his shoulder baldric.

The crowd of townspeople were around them. The soft faces of the merchants with their greedy, fearful eyes, women in shawls, and some children. The word "Cossacks" bobbed about their heads.

"His Majesty, God bless him, he has abandoned us on this frontier! Abandoned us to Cossacks!"

"No, it was a raiding party," Piippo said, "a lost raiding party driven out of Pskof, the Captain said."

"Cossacks, nonetheless," said a fat-faced man whose jowls quivered with indignation when he said it, the fear turning to scorn as he refuted the boy.

"Tame Cossacks," Piippo said. "Dead men."

"Tamed by the Englishman," another man said, pointing to Skarra, who listened to the hubbub caused by their entrance into Dorpat. Skarra had crossed from Stockholm, in 1629, on a small sailing coaster to Revel on the north coast of the Baltic peninsula. The land was frozen, and he had bought two horses, one to ride and the other to pack his Latin and Greek classics, and he had plunged into the winter forests, with his appointment from King Gustavus Adolphus of Sweden to the faculty of the University of Dorpat.

The crowd turned their attention away from the pile of Cossack boots, sabers, knives, and hatchets lying in the sleigh, and stared at Skarra.

"He'll never live," the fat fellow said. "And he drinks."

Skarra noticed they were staring at the earthen jug of Scotch in his arms, from which he had drunk all day to ease the pain in his face and body.

"A mercenary," someone said.

Skarra moved his hands over the jug of Scotch, trying to conceal it with his arms, but the gesture only made his discomfiture more obvious to the onlookers.

"Herr Doktor Skarra of Scotland," the Captain said, his mittened hand at the edge of his fur cap, "we at Dorpat are honored at so distinguished a gentleman, and our university will profit from a warrior on its faculty. Please accept my apologies for not policing our territories with more vigor."

"Seventeen dead men?" someone asked.

Skarra heard the crowd seem to breathe at the outrageous sense of carnage, and he wished to God he could go away from all these people, where he could bathe and ease his wounds, and not be a public spectacle. He nodded his head to the officer. "I am a classics scholar from the University of Edinburgh, with an appointment to the University of Dorpat from your King, Gustavus Adolphus. Some strangers set upon me and killed my pack pony. Now please show me to my quarters."

Skarra stood and the people seemed to be astonished at his height. They stopped talking as he stepped out, holding his jug.

"A drunken professor," one merchant said.

Skarra turned up the steps, nodding his head when the officer asked for the blunderbuss. He was acutely aware of how isolated the town was, on the frontier with Russia, a giant of unparalleled power and ignorance. Skarra shrugged his shoulders at the question of which would come first, murder or enlightenment. Mary Stuart, Queen of Scots, was his queen, and she long dead of religious war and family treachery, and his father calling him a Papist for saying religion mocked God.

"What's a Scot?"

"Is he to be our general?"

Skarra went unsteadily up the heavy timbered stairs to his room, leaving the people out of his hearing. She was in the room straightening the bed when he came in. He noticed her at the same time he saw his personal belongings stacked in neat piles in the middle of the room. He saw the straight flaxen hair falling across her back and in front of her shoulders, leading his eye to the cleavage between her breasts, that swelled and ducked under an embroidered bodice caught over the nipples.

"I hope you are comfortable, my lord." She curtsied to him, not lowering her eyes, which were blue and unflinching in the pale white face.

"Pretty," he said, flinging off his cloak and outer garments, and tugging loose his leggings and peeling off his leather surcoat.

"We're all sorry you were waylaid." She did not move to leave.

"It was my life, girl, what's your name?"

"Geness, my lord. My father owns the inn."

"Swedish?"

"Yes, my lord."

"I'm Bruce McTaggart. Call me Bruce, if you like."

"Thank you, my lord."

She smiled, and he saw the pale red lips part to show a double row of very even teeth that seemed to crowd her jaws. In her face it gave life to her mouth and he found it arresting.

"And I will call you Geney when I need something," he said, walking to the bed in his long wool shirt. He gestured at the door. "I want to shave and bathe. Leave me, girl, but send in your physician."

"Your face is clotted, my lord."

"I'm all but naked. . . ."

"I've seen naked men."

"But not me." He saw her clear open face as she appraised his split eyebrow, which lay in a flesh lap over his left eye. "Though I'm a cautious Scot, you're pretty enough to make me fast."

"You can lecture your students. They will love your morality." She turned and poured the earthen beakers of hot water into the wide pewter tub. "You can bathe your body and I will clean your face, my lord. You are truly a brave man."

"Lord, girl, you win."

Skarra had not meant to kill the seventeen men, and as he lay in the featherbed waiting for the physician he tried to grasp how he had managed to do it. It was really not what he believed in, and now that he had survived it seemed a nightmare. The killing itself came so fast with his life or theirs that he did not have the chance to be frightened.

The third day on the snowy trail he had realized a party of Cossacks were tracking him. The wolves which infested Livonia, and had accompanied him, staying just out of musket range and fearing the fire at night, had suddenly disappeared. He had heard their warning howls at a distance, and heard the domesticated "chop" of short-tongued dogs answer them. The tracking dogs had betrayed their masters.

He had watched the Cossacks ride slowly across the white snow-field, the trackers hissing to the dogs, their slavering noises making the little dun break its tether and run to him. The dogs came over the snow and leaped into the flanks of the dun, one burying his mouth into the hamstring, others leaping at the soft muzzle, tearing the velvet lips Skarra had fed, and he heard the horse scream in terror.

Skarra had stepped into his bow and felt the exultation of drawing against the Cossack who was laughing, showing the ivory patch of teeth that split the hair over his face.

The arrow left his arm and bow cleanly, and he saw the Cossack close his mouth and look down at the ashen shaft that stuck out of his thick chest.

"Pleasured by sorrow, are ye?" Skarra cried. Skarra was satisfied to see three Cossacks down in the snow, while riderless horses galloped about the frozen meadow.

The men were upon the dun with the hounds and Skarra saw a knife, and the horse leaped sideways into the swirling mass of dogs and footmen, leaving a bright coiling mass of green ribbon from the stomach cavity to tumble on the snow.

"Ahhee-EE-aaa!" It was the Scottish war cry. Skarra felt every hair on his body rise. The cry startled them, and they hesitated while the arrows emptied another saddle.

The dark men huddled on their saddles, their heavy shoulders and long arms flashing their sabers, while their short legs seemed to fold up under the mass of them.

Skarra sent his arrow at the skull of the lead Cossack and watched the man duck his head to take the arrow into the top of his crown. Silently, the man slid off his horse, stiff-legged and stiff-armed with a shaft in his brain, like a gingerbread man on a light string.

Skarra darted back into the green boughs and snatched up his shield and slipped it onto his forearm. The hoofbeats were close to him, the horsemen crashing into the limbs about his head.

He crouched, seeing a muscular man swing his saber with such force he stood in the stirrups to drive home the blow. "Whunk!" The brass of his shield saved him. The horse wheeled and crashed amidst the limbs of the trees as the Cossack sought to swing his arm. They were together again for an instant and Skarra drove the double-edged blade up into the soft underbelly of the chunky man, lifting him clear of the saddle. The short, booted legs with tassles on their toes kicked in the air like a frog—the angry man's face swept with disbelief just as he tried to kill his adversary. There is no justice, the dark eyes said, and Skarra flung the body clear and pulled out the claymore.

The other Cossack galloped away, and Skarra could see the dun was down by his rear quarters, the small furry head held high, seeking to drag himself clear of the boiling mass of dogs with his clawing forelegs that dug at the snow. Skarra watched the warm muzzle sink into the snow and inch ahead.

The Cossack stopped by the footmen, grunting noises to them, and he saw their bearded faces turn to the forest where he stood. They were short men, muffled in sacks and wrappings from their legs to their necks and heads. They fumbled inside their wraps, drawing blades and knives.

Skarra picked up the blunderbuss. "It worked in Stockholm, dear God, now don't let it fail me in my troubles," he said to himself.

"Come!" he shouted at the men, and he heard himself scream again the Scottish war cry, "Ahhee-EE-aaa!"

"He's alone!" he heard one of the men call out.

The Cossack rode at a walk, behind the trackers and the bristling bodies of the hounds.

"He's wounded, and can't shoot the arrows!" The men picked up their wary step toward him, as Skarra glanced down at the rotating hammer of Swedish steel.

"See him, brothers! See him!"

The men paused, raising their knives. He saw the dogs slipped free and racing toward him. With a shout the men surged in unison, their mouths open with cries of hate and death.

He felt his forefinger release the trigger, and felt his heart sink when nothing happened. He stood rigid, holding the massive belled snout aimed at the oncoming movement over the snow and out of the mist. The dogs were at him.

"Whooommm!" He felt himself doubled over his hips, saw fire blurt out away from him in a blast of noise that deafened his skull and laid him crashing backward into a tree.

He reached for his claymore as his eyes focused on the thrashing bodies alive on the snow where two dogs were spinning around, biting at their flanks. He walked clear of the woods shouting "Flee!" in High German as the single Cossack came toward him.

"Stranger!" the man said.

Skarra felt the saber clout his shield and heard his sword bell ring as he instinctively parried the dark figure who came out of a mist to rain blows on him. He stumbled over the body of a dead man whose open eyes lay under snowflakes.

"Damn you!" Skarra yelled, slamming the shield into the dark cheekbones and hooked nose. The shako went into the air and they were rolling on the snow, the Cossack inside his shield, and Skarra had his dirk in his hand.

He stabbed furiously into the greatcoat as the man's short fingers closed over his Adam's apple and he felt a thumb go into his eye socket. His loins burst as the man drove his knees into his lower belly, but he was too short to reach Skarra's genitals.

He snapped his body into a violent roll with his long legs, and rolled the thumb out of his eye socket, and managed to close both his hands over the dirk, which he drove with all his might into the violent, muscular man, as they rolled and thrashed together like a single body. He felt the blade settle into a rib. He twisted the blade free of the bone and felt it slide, up to its hilt, deep into the lung and heart cavity. The Cossack arched his muscular body convulsively in his arms, the eyes full of indignation, and he spewed a froth of blood out of the hooked nose. Skarra twisted the knife until he felt his own throat breathe. He flung the man from his body and rolled free. He lay in the snow a long time. "Lord, what have I done?" he said.

When he got to his feet he saw all the men were dead, and he walked uncertainly into the woods to his little mare, where he covered her with a blanket and wrapped himself in an eiderdown quilt, and crawled among the dry needles beneath the fir trees, with a jug of his father's whiskey. He pulled the plug from the jar and upended it, and felt the rolling fire explode in his throat and light a great warmth under his heart. His last thought was to hammer the plug into the bung to save his Scotch, and then to wrap himself, his dirk held sheathed against his breast.

"He killed them all," Skarra heard Piippo say, and woke, seeing Geney and a stranger with them. "We found him wounded."

"Poor man, he's slept like the dead," Geney said.

Skarra focused his eyes on the doctor, whose beard and mustache ran together in frozen mucus that gave his graying hair a sheen of rivulets so repulsive Skarra could not take his eyes from them, nor believe what he saw when they began to melt. "God," he said to himself. He tried to rise.

"Easy, boy," the physician said, putting a cold hand onto his chest.

"No, do my leg first," Skarra said, thrusting out a hairy thigh, which the doctor looked at and came down on with his clawlike fingers, gripping either side of the warm flesh. "Pour whiskey on it."

"Whiskey?" Skarra poured Scotch into the wound before the physician sewed it. When he sat up and saw the haphazard overlap of flesh zigzagging up his thigh, where the stitching had gone uneven, he rose, cursing, and drove the doctor from his room.

"Get snow, pack my forehead until it's numb, then get a steel needle and silk and sew this damned flap over my eye."

"Yes, Bruce," Geness said, and ran from the room. She was back in a moment with a large scullery maid, a bucket of clean snow, and the sutures. She knelt astride his chest, her knees on his shoulders, and sewed. The last thing he remembered was looking straight up through the blood at the white face beyond the smeared fingers which worked across his nose and over his eyes. When the primitive shock wore off the next morning, Skarra saw a very respectable wound running down from one eyebrow and crossing a "T" over the cheek torn by the axe. She had carefully sewn his hand so that it showed almost no scar. "When did you do that?" he said, holding up his hand, knowing only his mother knew more about him than the lovely Swedish girl.

"When you fainted," she said.

2

It was a pleasant room. It had been left unfinished and the square wood beams lay exposed in the wooden walls and vaulted ceilings. The cheerful warmth of wood in its natural tints enfolded him. In the middle of the room was the Scandinavian stove, gleaming in white pottery and blue tile, and the engine of life within his quarters. The windows were caked in ice that left fairy prints in the morning sunlight, but the stove was everything. He bathed in front of it, and Geney hung his wash to dry on racks about it, boiled his tea billie on it, and he stared in transfixed divination at the red coals in its tubby bowels when he sought some credence in life.

"I suppose I am so frightened I do not want to get up."

"Then stay in bed. I will tend to all your wishes," she had said.

The Master of the University came to call on Skarra at his quarters. The sleigh bells woke him and the innkeeper had escorted the university officials to his room.

"Herr Doktor Paul Veblen," the large man said, the wide fleshed cheeks aglow as he crossed the room to where Skarra was pulling a quilted cloak about his lank frame. Veblen was accompanied by a small Provost who wore a long blue robe that dragged on the floor.

"Thank you, sire," Skarra said, taking the hand, and feeling no response of greeting, realized he was to kiss the back of it. Skarra shook it vigorously and looked into the coarse-lidded blue eyes, past the veil of formality, and saw a gross elderly man, sure of his position, and meaning to maintain and extend every inch of it. "Bruce McTaggart of Skarra, I'm a Scotsman."

"A nobleman?"

"My father, the laird."

"Of Skarra?"

"Yes, my lord."

"In the academic and ecclesiastic world it's ability, not birth."

"Would you care to see my *curriculum vitae* and my appointment from the King of Sweden?" Skarra hoped to keep the meeting professional.

"Later. What religion?"

"What religion is there, my lord?"

The Provost shuffled his feet uneasily, making the gown sway about his small body.

"Are you Catholic or Protestant?" The jowls shook.

"Tell me the difference, sire."

"Only an atheist would ask that question," Veblen said. "Our King has been deceived."

"Sire, I'm a classical scholar. You talk of a religion founded by a man who had neither academic nor ecclesiastic standing."

"Blasphemy!" It was the innkeeper.

"Your King appointed me here, as your Professor of Classics."

"His Majesty, in his august person?"

"Yes. The King. I was staying with my kinfolk in Stockholm."

"My university?" Veblen's face had assumed a slack pallor, the eyes vacant.

"The King said it was his university, because he was the people," Skarra said.

"When men of good cheer can create an ordered society and cohese it with education, the world will be safe." He outthrust his open hands and brought them expansively to his belly.

"Men would rather be dead than admit a mistake." Skarra was tired and wanted to be rid of the officials.

"I heard of the seventeen Cossacks."

"Eight Cossacks and nine trackers," Skarra said.

"You're a sounding brass, that many dead." The jowls trembled.

"They outnumbered me, they could have run," Skarra said. "No, they put their vanity ahead of their lives."

"You are indeed an interesting young man," the Master of the

University said. He stared at Skarra, sensing that he had met a person he could not cow with religion nor threaten with dismissal, nor crush in a battle of wits.

Skarra was not aware that Geness was in the room until he saw the innkeeper's face color as he raised his thick hand. "Out! Out, you slut!" The three of them turned to see whom he meant.

"Gentlemen, excuse me," said the innkeeper, a fellow named Roglan, and Skarra was amazed to see the man seize the girl by the shoulder and twist his other hand deep into the garments across her buttocks and frog-walk her across the room toward the door. "Sorry to have a slut in the presence of gentlemen."

Skarra saw the look of humiliation and resignation in her blue eyes.

"Pretty wench, about the tits," Veblen said.

Roglan laughed, a small burst of air in his throat. "Her mother was a slut. Had to run her off when she took up with a soldier."

"Too fair to be buxom."

"Her mother was my wife. God knows who's her father."

"Not you," Geness said.

"Silence, you cheap slut!" Roglan slapped her face, making her neck and bosom flush in embarrassment.

"Don't hit the woman," Skarra said.

"You'll be civil to me, young man, you can't insult a businessman."

"Turn her loose!"

Roglan shoved her toward the door. Skarra jumped across the room, tearing Geness out of Roglan's hands, leaving the skirt still twisted in the thick grasp.

"God damn you!" Skarra shouted, clouting the innkeeper in the side of the head and sending him falling backward, still holding the dress.

"I'm naked."

"What?" Skarra was furious.

"He's got my dress."

"What in hell's the matter with these people?" He looked down at the slender, incredibly white legs seeming to sprout from the bottom of the girl's tight bodice and run down to the boarded floor, to the two slim white feet with frail sinews corded to the toes, and his eyes came up the legs to the wide hips of flesh across her loins, and his eye came to rest on the wisping strands of fine ivory hair set where the thighs faired in to support her body. It excited him to see her nude.

"A wench, look at her," Roglan said, flinging the skirt at her.

"That son of a bitch," Skarra said.

"A fine bedchamber," Veblen said, his gross-lidded eyes boldly searching the quarters, "and nice buttocks on the girl."

"The best in Dorpat, my lord."

"So they are. And your guests are well-nourished, if I may observe, for the wants of the flesh in more ways than one."

"The best in Dorpat."

"Ah, to be young again. I haven't had a bone in my codpiece in ten years."

"My lord drinks his dreams away," Roglan said, eager to ingratiate himself with the authoritative university figure, not only to assuage his vanity but for future business prospects. "Turn your ass, girl, for the gentlemen to see."

Skarra saw the three men had their attention on Geness. He watched Geness stare, unflinching, from Roglan to the corpulent eyes and coloring jowls of the Master and the narrow face of the Provost, who was breathing openly through his mouth with excitement.

"Let the gentlemen see your ass." Roglan crossed over to the girl and spun her around to show her buttocks. "You can't beat an ass like that this side of Stockholm." He slapped the near cheek of white flesh, and Skarra saw it ripple as it slid back to nestle by the other, the imprint of a thick hand and strong fingers glowing on the flawless white rounding skin.

The men laughed, and Skarra got a grip on himself that would contain his anger, which, if he lost his self-control, would demean him, knowing the men were no more and no worse than rude men, coarse among themselves with dirty jokes and vying with contempt for anything they could not devour with their bodies nor eat.

"Gentlemen, we've all had our laugh," Skarra said, drawing their attention, "but I was severely wounded." He put his hand to the strip of black stitching tied into the eyebrow. "Would you excuse me?"

"Oh, of course," Veblen said, eager to find some suggestion of pain or weakness in Skarra to dominate from solicitude. "You unfortunate young man."

"We had the physician for him."

"That man?"

"Not a bad doctor, bleeds too much," Roglan said.

"Ah, to have a bone in my codpiece," the Master said as he stroked fitfully at Geness' buttock and went out of the room.

Skarra did not leave his quarters at the inn for three weeks. His wounds had not festered. He had known the Egyptians used alcohol to purify and had sutured with fire-ants' heads, placing the pincer to the lips of the wound, then twisting the body from the head when the angry insect had closed the pincer, leaving the pincers to bind the flesh. Yet he was gripped with a terrible depression, which only Geney could relieve by puttering through the room and about his bed. He could not bear to have her out of his sight, though he did not sleep with her.

The inn, named Roglan's Hotel in the French fashion, with a heavy wooden timber bearing the carved name, was known as Roglan's, or the Inn; it was the largest and most convenient private structure in Dorpat. Like most of the buildings, it was built of massive logs, fronted with rough-sawn boards, all unpainted, and in the patina of natural wood.

Skarra could see the town from the windows of his quarters, the two hundred buildings, the University of stone, and somehow he stayed in his bed and dreamed of Scotland.

Geness sat at his bedside far into the night, after bringing him Swedish coffee and cakes, and brewing English tea instead of serving at the nightly revel they could hear in the main room of the Inn. The noise rose against the heavy floor, of curses, carousels, fights, whores' shrieks, women's goads, and the daring of university students baiting their dimwitted elders.

"That man won't mind?" he asked.

"No, your appointment from the King makes you special." Her face was matter-of-fact.

"I'm a slow Scot, not necessarily virtuous."

Geness stared through the frozen traces of the middle window. "Have you ever loved?" She turned back, seeking to look beyond his words.

"Yes, I thought so. But I recovered."

"Is that good?"

"It left me free. Love's a terrible bondage."

She looked into the open grates of the large stove, where the flame licked up and trailed off in white vapors.

"I sewed up your face out of hate."

"You did well at it."

"Yes, I liked sticking the needle in your bare skin and seeing you catch your breath. I knew I was hurting you, but when you fainted I felt sorry for you."

"That is why a woman is superior. She can change."

"It is change or die."

"If we want to live," he said.

"What is your weakness?"

"Hope." He lay his hand atop hers.

"Hope, a weakness?"

"Aye, hope. Hope for all, hope that springs anew with the air we breathe."

"It seems so simple, to hope."

"Any virtue is a burden. My hope keeps me trying when there is no hope. And it leaves me victim of any man without virtue. Have you ever loved?"

"Yes, but long ago, my father and my mother."

"Aye, someone loved you, for you are beautiful." He spun the girl into his chest and hugged her mightily, and felt her squirm within his arms then fold herself around his body.

"Do you want me?"

"God, no, you're beautiful, but all I want is quietude and silence, and to think. I had hoped that this might bring me wisdom."

3

Colonel Malmo, a tall Swede with a desiccated face traced with streaks of red from the cold, called on him, representing the Royal Governor. He and Captain Lund of the Finnish Ski Patrol had brought him eighteen silver coins and a single doubloon from the sale of the Cossack horses and equipment. The ski patrol had buried the seventeen men by tying stones to their bodies and putting them through a hole they had cut in the ice on the Emijogi River. Piippo, who was in his room, had returned the "English" arrows, quite battered and gore-encrusted, taken from the bodies before being put into the river.

"I never expected to have them back," Skarra said.

"We had to warm up the bodies to pull them out," Piippo said.

"We are a frugal people," said Colonel Malmo, noticing Skarra's dismay.

Skarra nodded. "Colonel, obviously indolence is not a vice in this country."

"Correct," said the Colonel, pursing his lips and putting the fingertips of his hands together. "Learned young man, we need officers."

"Yes, our garrison is undermanned," Lund said.

"Every garrison is undermanned, and besides, I'm a schoolteacher. . . ."

"If we could but muster our college students," Malmo said.

"With this handsome Scottish devil right in their midst, what more could we want?"

"I am a teacher," Skarra said firmly.

"Yes, it's a wonder the students aren't meaner."

"They did burn the whorehouse, sire."

"The students burnt the whorehouse?" Skarra said.

"Yes, a lark, naked girls running about all over town."

"They have no men to emulate," Colonel Malmo said. "The professors don't teach. A wonder they didn't burn the whole town."

"I hope to teach classical philosophy," Skarra said.

The two officers laughed and gathered their cloaks about their shoulders, setting the hoods over their caps so the wolf hair protected their cheeks from the cold, and went out of the quarters, talking cheerfully.

Skarra came down the wooden staircase of the inn, crossing among the massive tables and benches set at random on the rush-matted floor. The disheveled remnants from the night before lay in the slumber of drunken men. "Hey, you!" a sodden voice said to him. The smell of sour ale and vomit lingered in the chilled room.

He passed into the kitchen, where the fires were stoked in the cooking pits. A half-grown lackey with bare shanks was wiping his red nose while a vast wench in a grease-streaked dress called the boy a bastard snot and gestured with a wooden spoon. She stopped when she saw Skarra. A gleaming joint of meat, crusted in black flakes, dripped blood that sizzled each time it splashed into the fire, making a small puff of steam.

"My lord," the woman said, assuming airs.

He nodded and went out into the snow-banked cold, the white sloping up to the tall eaves from the high-palinged courtyard. Horse manure rose in rich conical heaps, steaming under the warm vapors from the fresh dung.

"Oh, sire, we've waited for you," said a boy, coming up to him.

"For me?"

"Yes, we knew you were coming. I saw it in the sky on my big wheel."

Skarra turned his eyes to the boy and saw a young man with very large ears fanning out through his dirty hair and a nose which was too massive for the head. The eyes had a surface beauty that was absolutely empty.

"Who are you?" Skarra said.

"I'm the true idiot, sire." The face opened into the purest smile of guilelessness Skarra had ever seen.

"Idiot?"

"The *true* idiot."

"Good God."

"Get, boy! Get! You will only discommode our young professor," said a thick voice that came from a burly man with a wide beard streaked with gray. "I am Voltoff, troika driver, horseman, and fund of Baltic, Swedish, and Russian knowledge." The heavy fur hat came off, and the man bowed low before Skarra, the long skirts of his overcoat opening to show his high boots.

"But the boy?" Skarra said.

"Ah, yes, the boy. He is on my staff. An idiot, to be sure, but an excellent human being, and the only creature I have ever known who truly understands horses."

Skarra stared at the Russian with the deep voice and the sad blue eyes peering from the mat of hair.

"If I did not keep him they would kill him for sport at the Inn or at the University, what does it matter, my lord?" The massive shoulders shrugged, so strange a gesture in so robust a man.

"Good God."

"Idiots are baited like animals."

"God, yes," Skarra said, catching his breath, "I know. Bedlam is the sport of fashionable London."

"At times we are all idiotic, my lord."

"And you are Russian?"

"A child of Mother Russia."

"I will need someone to show me Dorpat, I suppose."

"The lovely girl said you were different, begging forgiveness for my familiarity, my lord."

"Oh, you mean Geness?"

"Yes, the young lady."

"She calls herself a strumpet," Skarra said walking out into the courtyard.

"The young lady is a flower in sorrow—with love, she may bloom, but it will take some young man for the girl." He gestured to Skarra. "In Russia everything is understood and nothing shown."

"And you think me," Skarra said, tugging his furred mittens onto his hands.

"The girl reads Latin, my lord. Her father was anointed in the holy orders, and he was a gentleman."

"She does not tell it."

"One cannot tell what one loves without crying, my lord, but we all know her story."

Skarra hired the troika for the afternoon, to be driven about town before he made a call on the Royal Governor. Voltoff took his fancy. There was a simple virtue in the old man that made Skarra feel he had known him all his life, and to meet him was to once again share his soul with a delightful old memory.

Skarra sat in the high back seat of the troika amidst bearskins, feeling the icy air hard against his face. The troika was magnificent. The center horse, under the bow, trotted with a long floating glide, while the two wing horses galloped in a springing beat, their manes flying over the fanlike set of their arched necks and heads.

"Lulululu," Voltoff crooned softly to the horses all the while, and Polonitz, the retarded boy, sat at his feet.

They came down the main street of Dorpat, passing sleds piled high with fodder and hay, surrounded with stocky countrymen. Heavy oxen, yoked behind their swaying heads, stared balefully at the troika. Some dogs ran out from the frozen gardens of the larger homes to bark.

"Lulululu," crooned Voltoff, hunched stolidly before Skarra.

When they had reached the other edge of town, Skarra saw the stone citadel.

"I thought only the Tsar had a Kremlin," he shouted up to Voltoff.

"No, sire, every town in Russia has its Kremlin."

"This is Russia?"

"Oh, a thousand pardons." He heard the Russian laugh a contented rumble. "My lord, temporarily this is not Russia. Our gracious majesty has called it Livonia. Russia goes from the Baltic to the oceans beyond Siberia. It is all Russia."

They passed bright fires on the bank of the river, among the willow thickets that strung sparse limbs in the overcast sky. Students were sliding down the long bank and scooting out onto the river ice. Young voices filled the air, and Skarra wished to join them, particularly those sliding on wooden slats.

The troika went through the stone gate of the Kremlin, where halberdiers sagged their bodies down into their wraps, breathing into their mufflers to warm their necks and chests.

"A young gentleman for Count Bofors!" Voltoff shouted, not slowing the troika.

Skarra saw the blue eyes peek up, the heads nodding imperceptibly beneath the desolate pikes. The troika swept into the large courtyard, ringed with a walled battlement, with the snow lying atop the cannons that stared through empty slots, overlooking the white countryside. Skarra took off his tam and knocked it against his knee to clear the snow.

They glided past the large wooden church which was painted red and yellow and green, in striking color, under a bulbous Byzantine onion for a steeple. There was an aplombing grace to it. The graveyard lay between the church and the wall.

Voltoff stopped the troika before a stone building.

"The Governor's Palace, my lord."

Skarra vaulted out of the troika, eager to be courtly and gracious, but not to please the Governor so much that he would want him as a soldier.

"Herr Doktor Skarra," he said to the two soldiers holding flintlocks.

"Yes, Excellency," one of them said, looking up at Skarra's height. "We know." He gestured to the carved door.

Inside the palace Skarra was impressed with the cold. The stone floor, the gray corridors, and the very air seemed laden with a heavy chill. An officer in a bright cuirass came up.

"Captain Seversen, at your service, sire."

"The Governor wishes to see me," Skarra said.

"Does His Excellency know you are calling?" The elegant eyebrow went up, and the clipped beard appeared disdainful in the same motion.

"He sent for me," Skarra said, knowing the typical secretary outside the office of power, his vanity gnawing on small bones of triumph.

"Oh, I did not know."

Skarra came through the door of the gray office and saw the battle standards of the regiments along the walls, and at the far end was the broad desk, flanked by tables. He saw the officers looking his way as Seversen's voice rolled out in measured, self-pleased tones, "Herr Doktor, the Honorable Bruce of Skarra!"

Walking in, he noticed the floor was oak, and he saw the room was heated with white and blue porcelained stoves. It was too far away to say "Hello" to the officers, so he nodded.

"Ah, Skarra, how glad we are to have a man amidst that discontent of the mind at the University," a short, barrel-chested man said, breaking clear of the group of officers.

"Professors, too much thinking," a gray-haired officer said, shaking his head and perhaps deaf to his booming voice.

"Such stature, did you ever see the like?" It was Colonel Malmo.

"Indeed."

"What presence in a battle, we do indeed need him."

The officers spoke openly.

"I am Count Bofors," the barrel-chested man said. He had a broad red face with sharp features.

"Your Excellency." Skarra bowed.

"No, do not bow. It embarrasses His Majesty to see his officers bow."

"His officers?"

"And his professors, tut tut." Count Bofors was in a brown hunting surcoat, as were the other officers; some of the coats were trimmed in wolf fur. Bofors' eyes were blue and with a piercing, roguish quickness.

"I meant to come sooner."

"I heard you threw out the physician."

"Yes, he was drunk."

"A typical frontier doctor," Bofors said. The Count took Skarra's hand and shook it in the English fashion. The other officers followed suit, each beaming at him.

"And we hear you are well cared for at the inn," an elderly Major said.

"Yes, it is commodious enough."

"We have news from your cousin, Captain Dumaine," the Governor said.

"Oh, what news?"

"Captain Halvorsen has just arrived by ship from Stockholm." A vigorous officer in a steel cuirass decorated with marten fur across the breastplate seemed to rise slightly on his toes and strike his boot heels together with great force.

"At your service, sire, Captain Gurd Halvorsen of His Majesty's bodyguards."

Skarra looked at the coarse nose under thick eyebrows which ran together. The hand was not proffered. It held a plumed helmet, and there was an immense saber which jangled at the high boot heel. The confident blue eyes met his in a smirk of defiance. He was a big man, chestier and meatier than Skarra.

"What was the news from Dumaine, my lord?" Skarra said.

"Good news. His Majesty is to pay us a visit."

"To Dorpat?"

"Gustavus Adolphus drove the Russians out of Dorpat at the point of his own sword."

"So it is like home to him, you see," said the gray-haired officer.

"I believe the Scot does not care for Dorpat," said Halvorsen.

"No, it is a quiet town."

The officers laughed easily.

"No, it is terrible, wait until you see the mud," boomed the gray-haired officer.

"Winter is our springtime, springtime is a quagmire of ooze, and in summer the insects are like vultures."

"I do like my sleigh," Skarra said, regretting his childlike remark immediately.

"Malmo says you are not for the army?" Bofors said.

"No, my lord."

"And why not?" Bofors said.

Skarra glanced at the Swedish officers in their brown hunting coats, their clear eyes and clean figures showing their outdoor lives, and he had a desire to join them, but he wanted a life that was not an escape into a closed mind.

"You finished off seventeen men. Whether you like it or not, you are now classified as a warrior."

"I have an appointment from the King to the University. . . ."

"We can change that."

"Perhaps, my lord," Captain Halvorsen said, "our Scot has no stomach for true battle. I have heard the Scot is keen of ambuscade but fearful in pitched battle."

Skarra turned to face the Captain, feeling his neck flush, and was furious with himself that he could not hide it. He saw the studied contempt of a man who has no respect for anything except power, and who looks on other men as steps simply to advance or retard his career.

"Don't goad him, Halvorsen," Colonel Malmo said.

"Oh, these professors are always tame."

"I don't believe he is a professor," the Governor said. "I never knew a professor with brains enough to carry an English longbow." He shook his head.

"My lord, I seek something else," Skarra said.

"What do you seek, Bruce?" Malmo said.

"I don't know, sire."

"Your attention please," Count Bofors said, his voice carrying the edge of command. "Gentlemen, as we know, Dorpat is a window facing the Russia of the Tsars, so far a Russia of nomadic peasants, lecherous Boyars, and a succession of Tsars each more terrible than his predecessor. And the Cossacks of the Don, brutal men who hate the Russians but love the Tsar's gold. Bad as they may be, our true enemy is Europe, not Russia."

Skarra realized the words were for him, both as a man of classical learning and as a prospective soldier.

Getting his breath, Bofors lay his hand on top of a map of Austria. "The Holy Roman Empire, with its capital in Vienna and ruled by Hapsburg emperors, is drunk with victory over the Turks in the south, now must move north, over German states, or west, into France. Men and power seek counterforce and rebuff, and Cardinal Richelieu of France and our King, Gustavus Adolphus, are the barriers to the empire of a united Europe."

"May I ask a question, my lord?" Skarra said.

"Of course."

"Would it be so wrong to join Europe?"

"No, not at all."

There was a stir among the officers at the Governor's words.

"Has Scotland joined England?"

"No, not yet, sire."

The Governor laughed.

"If equals join there is no quarrel, but unequals always hate and fight each other because the weaker is devoured by the stronger, so there is no peace between unequals." Count Bofors pirouetted on his tall boot heel, his thick body whirling smoothly, the hands turned out to face his officers and nobles.

"A quarrel as old as Cain and Abel, and each side called the 'anti-Christ.' "

"That is the 'hate factor.' " Malmo spoke agreeably.

"Time enough for all that," Bofors said. "You must see your university."

"Yes, that I would like."

"And His Majesty will want to see you again."

"I was most impressed with your King."

"And I have Veblen's report on you. Said you were an atheist."

"Truly, my lord?"

"Excellent report. Speaks well of a man if he hates no one."

The officers laughed pleasantly, as a band of brothers. It filled the chilly room with sound. Skarra shook hands with the Count and took his leave, aware the Royal Governor was a skilled leader of men who ignored their idiosyncrasies.

Veblen was looking out his second-story window, his hood pulled up over his head and his arms thrust into the sleeves of his academic robe, watching the troika slip over the snow behind the elegant horses. "It's the Scot," he muttered, seeing the tam slanted forward over the eyebrow of a lank man lounging among the fur skins. "An insolent young buck."

The Provost came over and stared out.

"He is here to see the college."

"Shall we put him among the students?"

"God, no, he is an atheist."

"Then to sup among us?"

"Oh, yes, don't be an ass, Provost."

"My lord said he was an atheist." The voice was reproachful.

"You fool, we'll have him dine in the Vasa Commons, but he will stay at the Inn. We don't want any foreigners among our students. Bad influence." Veblen turned his gourded jowls to the small man, contented with himself, and felt his bowels move a spasm in the excitement of a prospective encounter with an enemy, and enjoyed the lightening ease within his belly as he passed out a bubble of air betwixt his buttocks that broke into the chilled room as a robust fart. He gathered his robe about him instinctively, to hold the warmth of it, and to enjoy the rich smell of it filtering up round his neck and head.

Skarra enjoyed the University. It was two buildings of stone, connected by a commons. He was surrounded with dons who spoke High German, and among them were a sprinkling of students, prankish with rapid elbow thrusts and happy jostling. He smelled the wine and realized the boys had been drinking, and from the grog-flowers on the cheeks of the professors he guessed that they roistered more than they studied.

"The buildings are grand," Skarra said.

"Two foot of stone at the base," said a young man with a splayed strawberry nose.

Skarra nodded, but avoided eye contact with the professors, to escape the ordinary hostility of inebriated men seeking to lock into a stranger to quarrel.

"His Lordship, Herr Doktor Veblen, will preside at Commons," Skarra was told as he passed through one of the two lecture rooms. He saw the students' quarters were cubicles with heavy wooden beds and washstands. Downstairs were the commodious suites of rooms where the dons lived, and where the tutoring and molding of the students' minds went on far into the night, in the sense that even while drunk, or at supper, the universal fellowship of the scholar feeds the student's mind through the master. There was no escape, except in drinking, and he saw the students well along this happy route.

Skarra sat at a bench among the dons and students while the commons roistered with sound. The wine seemed to lift the men into the laughter of good fellowship as they shuffled to their seats.

"A broad table makes good friends," said the short don beside him, slapping the boards.

"A broad wench makes a better friend," said a tall, hollow-chested don. The laughter roared about Skarra's head. It pleased him to have found young men of good humor.

A filtering silence gathered into the room as voices dropped away. Skarra noticed the wide dais, presided over by Veblen, his jowls magnificent by candlelight. At Veblen's side stood a slight man in a black surcoat who was praying. He had the slender, cadaverous look of the parson who feeds his delusions of power by vaulting his own thoughts to those of God and has no need to eat for his belly. Skarra tried to fix his face in a respectful mask.

"Wenches! Wenches!"

He heard the men call for the waitresses, but noticed as many skinny serving boys as girls running among the tables, serving the large platters of meats that steamed in rich smells.

"Your *curriculum vitae?*" said a skinny don, leaning forward, gesturing with a fork in one hand while rapping his knife handle on the table.

"Classics." Skarra carved his meat and turnips.

"Classics?" The man had a scooping jaw.

"Yes."

"What Classics?"

"Hellenic, there is no other."

A quick laugh ran through the table among the professors and students who had heard of Skarra and waited for his conversation, having been jaded with themselves.

"Catholic?"

Skarra glanced up and saw the tall man was annoyed at his answer, and was pressing him with the unanswerable.

"No, before Christianity."

"What was before Christ?"

"Life, called the *entelechy*." Skarra did not look up.

"You will not trap him," said the short don at his side whose name was Dodderhoff.

When they had eaten, the wine and lager came in large earthen pitchers, seeming to swamp the long table in the pungent froth of hops. Skarra drank sparingly, but with pleasure.

"Where did you earn your degree?" It was the scoop-jawed professor across from him.

"Edinburgh, correct?" said the hollow-chested young man called Pickereill.

"Yes, Edinburgh."

"I've never heard of the University of Edinburgh," Piippo said.

"Every woman in Scotland wants her children at the University of Edinburgh."

"How does this make it good?" another student asked.

"Any common want that elevates the soul is always good."

"Always?"

"Perhaps you know where this is not so," Skarra said, putting the conversation back onto his questioner.

"A war."

"A war degrades the soul," Skarra said.

"Do you like to teach?" the student asked him.

"Yes. It's very gratifying, if you can reach people."

"Have you ever failed?"

"Lord, yes." He spoke easily.

"Some of the professors think they are infallible," said a young man.

"Truly, why do you teach?" said the scoop jaw, still pressing Skarra.

"Oh, that is complex," Skarra said, looking into the lager foam. If he told the truth, he would have to say that he sought to teach himself; that there was a way among men where virtue was not an illusion to mask vice, and where reality was not the gorged snake strangling to death on his own conquests.

"Why do you teach?" He answered with another question.

"Oh, that's easy," the professor said, rocking from side to side, "for the money and status."

"He's honest," said Pickereill.

"The Archduke of Krakow sent me to the University because I was clever with figures. My father was a miller and I kept the books. . . ."

"His father went broke when he left."

"I was no more to the duke than a racehorse he'd bet on."

"Indeed, you're not blooded," said the hollow-chested Pickereill.

Skarra listened to the insults the other professors paid their colleague and he was glad to know that if there were cliques to divide them, there were the natural hostilities to keep each other in check.

"I'm honest, with no illusions about myself. I used my wits to change my station."

"I suppose we all try," Skarra said.

"Money was what I wanted, but they don't pay enough to marry so I have to whore for relief."

"You could get a peasant girl and marry," said Pickereill, "but he's a damned snob."

He glanced up, showing much white in his eyes. "Are you a wencher, Scotsman?" He was ugly with his long jaw.

"Never," Skarra said.

"You do not care for women?"

"Hoot, man, there is a hope in Scotland to have men and women learn together, with the notion that they must one day live together."

"Women in a university?!"

"I don't believe it," said Piippo.

"We wouldn't have to prong whores," said Pickereill.

"We could prong our students."

"And our classmates!" a student shouted.

"Hurrah, women!"

"A toast, gentlemen, I give you a toast," said the gaunt Pickereill, rising with his wine goblet before him. "A degenerate faculty leading a sodden and copulating student body while all Europe burns with religious certainty!"

"Wisdom, true wisdom," said Dodderhoff standing at his side, and Skarra realized they were a pair of outrageous support. "Wine, and the Moorish poppy!"

Skarra heard the table of men slurp and spill their lager and wine, exhaling and grunting as they stood and stretched and shuffled back down on their haunches.

"You've smoked poppy?" Skarra asked.

"Oh, yes. Wine and poppy are meat for the soul."

"I've heard of the Moorish poppy."

"It's better than wine. No hangover."

"I've heard of the mad dreams."

"You must try it. Dodderhoff is our smoking Turk," said Pickereill.

"If the Sultan only knew what loyal Turk he has in me," Dodderhoff said.

"And Veblen?" Skarra said.

"Oh, he hates Papists," Dodderhoff said.

"That's his poppy," said the slender Pickereill.

Skarra walked home after supper in the Commons. Piippo and some other new friends accompanied him. The winter night was magnificent. The snow squirked under his boots in small sounds of crushed ice. The Northern Lights hung across the black night, and dragged tentacles of shifting fire.

"A good sign," Piippo said.

"Yes. They're grand."

"You've seen them before?"

"Scotland."

"I didn't know you could see them there. We have them in Finland."

"Eerie," one boy said, watching streams of colored lights shading from green to orange to red, and breaking into chains which ran along in the heavens.

"Like the stars beyond, it's such a relief to know they are there," Skarra said.

"But some stars shoot in fire."

"Yes, but all by laws that never change."

To look into the clear night sky brought everything into bearable perspective on earth. "Lord, it's cold," Skarra said. He felt an exhilaration in being out on the town, as if he had come back into the company of life. He found his mind turning to Geness, to her smooth white skin, to a desire for her.

"My lord," said a boy, pressing closer to him from the group they walked in, "the purpose, my lord, what is the purpose of life?"

Skarra saw a bright face wreathed in a fur, and he realized he was being pressed into teaching. He could think of a hundred clichés to explain life. None were more than hollow rote to embalm outrageous misfortune, to make people endure the unspeakable. "There is no plausible reason for your life except the miracle of being," he said. "To that you are obliged, nothing else, and obliged to all life as a part of you."

The boy smiled.

"Fools and charlatans should make you glad you can choose to be a man." Skarra clapped his arms about his body and blew great puffs of chilled white air out ahead of them, feeling buoyant in his chest from the cold.

They all went up the wide steps of the Inn together, stomping off the snow on their boots. The great door opened and orange firelight came out and cast a yellow slant down the steps and over the snow.

"Keeper, innkeep!" bawled the quiet youth, over the heads of soldiers in hunting brown, woodsmen in animal skins, tradespeople, other students, and a tableful of Russian troika drivers whom Skarra recognized by their skirted coats and long hair and beards, and their smoking samovar. Earthy smells, laughter, and cheerful curses burdened the air of the great hall.

"One schooner," Piippo said.

"Only one for me," Skarra said.

"Maybe two."

"No, one. I want to go to my quarters," Skarra said.

The large steins came with foam down the sides. Skarra lifted his in toast as the young men locked arms at the elbows and swayed from side to side, singing the songs of boyish sentiment of the Teutonic people. He consented to a second stein, to celebrate his first day as their don. And he joined them in the ritualistic urination among young men, by standing in a long line of them to urinate against a snow bank, while laughing and comfortably breaking wind in a community of masculine good fellowship.

"Now, I must go," he said, tying up his fly flap.

He had seen Geness serving food and drink at the railinged dais where officers and people of rank sat in wood chairs, a bit away from the broad "pit of commoners." Passing through this area, he intercepted her with a tray of steins.

"Come up."

"Now?"

"Yes."

"I can't. The Royal Courier is here for the night."

"Give him his beer and come."

"They're having a party for him."

"What is that to us?"

"The King is coming."

"I want to talk to you."

She lost the professional mask from her face and ran her tongue over her lips, and swallowed. He felt a dry tingle over the inside of his mouth. "Come," Skarra said, and mounted the stairs to his quarters.

Skarra shook the grates in the stove, bringing fire shadows to life on the walls, and took off his outer clothing and wrapped himself in a quilted robe. She came into his room.

"After a day of cheerful banality I am reminded of the beauty that you are," Skarra said.

"Now you want me."

"The shouting and carousing at the university—whatever—it made me remember what I am."

She crossed by him to the fire, shifting wooden chairs close to it. He watched her fine hair cast forward in front of her shoulders, shading against the flesh of her neck. "I see, and now you love me?"

"*That* life is so hollow. I had forgotten."

"Forgotten?"

"You are life."

She did not look up as she puffed the cushions to sit upon. "I wondered if you'd love me."

"You have been reading my Latin books." Skarra was quieted at her composure.

"Yes?"

"You are more educated than my students."

"Perhaps."

"You did not tell me."

"That I read Latin?" She looked at him. "Why shouldn't I read Latin?"

"And speak it?" He wanted to touch her with his hands. "Oh, Geney, it's not the reading, it's knowing a man's world."

She laughed gently, pushing the chair so he could sit. He swallowed, seeing the clear unguarded face, the eyes open into her soul. "I'm an ignorant wench to our patrons—oh, pretty, they would all like to prong me for it. But men're furious with a woman who knows more than they, and mocking me eases their stupidity."

"Aren't you furious?" He sat down and she lay her hand on his arm.

"Angry at life?"

"How old are you?"

"Eighteen."

"When did you lose your chastity?"

"Roglan broke me in for gentlemen at fifteen, only for gold this past year."

"God, I would hate them all, if I were a woman."

"Oh, no, the gentlemen were usually drunk and so degenerate they couldn't get a bone up. I would sleep with them and they would paw me, and in the morning I would ask for a little money to keep my tongue with their secret, and we'd laugh and they would pay."

He shook his head.

"But I was torn once."

He listened to her, watching the embers glow and fall into each other.

"You have to be raped only once to know how to squirm your way up the bed to keep from being hurt. I was a very poor whore because I remember my people, my real people."

"Who taught you to read?"

"Our pastor. My father."

"Voltoff told me."

"Dear Voltoff." She nodded.

"Was he Lutheran?"

"Yes."

"What have you read?"

"Every book I could find."

He took her hand and drew her into his lap. "Your father was a sensitive man."

"He was a priest who had become a Lutheran pastor. He tried to find the Old Faith in the new faith."

Skarra felt her very still in his lap, listening to his breath and heartbeat, which she pressed her spine against, for his reaction. "What happened to him?"

"He went insane and they killed him."

"Who killed him?"

"I don't know."

"Do you know why he went insane?"

"I don't know."

"Did your mother say?"

"Yes, she said he thought he'd destroyed God."

"Poor man," Skarra said.

"Yes, he is happier."

"Dead?"

"He couldn't satisfy either side."

He closed his eyes and listened.

"Mother was a lay-sister and she was afraid to give up the Faith, and ran away with a soldier when my father was killed."

"Do you remember them?"

"Very much."

"Did you love them?"

"Yes. That is why I'm not insane. I can love."

"And you're not angry?"

"I hate the wicked and the hypocrisy and cruelty, but I can love. I waited."

"I see," he said.

"And Rogland took me in. He is my benefactor."

"Benefactor, that man!?"

"He pays my expenses."

"He doesn't own you."

"Bruce, you're so naive."

"Ravished you?"

"No, he likes to pinch me, that's all."

"Does he know who you are?"

"Oh, yes, we are distant cousins."

"Rogland and you?"

"My family was important in our village, so naturally it's something of a sport for him to have me degraded."

"You never yielded?"

"People like to see pretty things broken, every woman knows this."

"Lord, such a burden."

"Bruce, my father was a good man. I never did anything wrong I didn't have to do."

"I don't want to hear any more," Skarra said, feeling her warm buttocks atop his thighs.

"Now you're talking like that decent Scotsman."

He realized she was at ease when she tilted her head and looked at him. "If I love, there can be nothing more for me, because that is life to a woman," she said.

"God, Geney, I don't know." He hugged her slender waist into his belly and felt her diaphragm rise and fall over his forearm, and her heartbeat thump inside the palm of his hand. He had a masculine feeling from it, of power over her frail body, and he was very protective of her.

"I want you very much."

"Now?"

"I think I always have."

She nodded her head, not looking at him. "But I can't undress for you."

"Do you want to? Shall I do it for you?"

"Do, undress me."

He caught his breath.

"Do. God, to be ravished by a man you love . . ."

"Love, Geney?"

"Lord, let's try."

He had his hand wrapped in her light hair, drawing her head back to kiss her slender throat, knowing he had wanted her since he first saw her.

"Put your head forward," he said, untying the top lace of her bodice, and opening the bow ties under her bosom. It seemed that she came apart in his arms and hands, her body expanding as cotton and ribbon and skin unfolded out of layers of flimsy cloth, until she was standing naked before him, between his arms that had run all over her body to free her clear flesh.

"You are lovely—God, you are so lovely." It was with difficulty that he breathed. He stood and drew her into his chest, turning her fragile mouth up to kiss; she filled his mouth with her quick tongue and enraged a fever in him to draw all the taste from her, and yet to seek at the same moment to plunge his own flesh and breath into her, through her sweet mouth. He was gasping for air, yet he could not stop kissing her.

He was vaguely aware of tearing off his undergarments as he carried her to the large bed, where she seemed to coil in love before him, sliding her clear white flesh under his rough hand and in his forearm, that had gone to iron in his great desire for her. She was up against his body, which sought to press against and to penetrate her, with an urgency that he could feel burn over his skin in an overwhelming passion.

Her breasts were pure against his mouth. He could feel them swell under his breath, heaving in and out of his mouth where his desire raged for her body. She was faired beauty, perfect in symmetry of limb to leg to body, the wide hips cradling the navel he put his mouth to, the lovely belly his mouth tasted, the hips in his hands to raise the flesh he sought to kiss and devour with love, his throat wet and afire as it sought to say he could love her, to love all that lived.

He felt her clasp his life force and his body in her arms and legs, and the driven hope that whipped his passion against her wet lips and into her loins to sow life in her seized him. It was the dawn of the universe he felt—of sunrise and all the starlit nights that ever were, of every clean breath a man could draw in pure delight—whirl up the vortex from his spine and spill over him an ecstasy that pumped his life into her until he felt the backs of his hands flutter in spasms against the feather mattress, where spending trembles drew past his knees. Sleep swept against his skull, and he drifted off in contentment.

4

He turned away from the restorative heat of the stove, and walked to the casements to stare out the ice-crusted windows. The town seemed to huddle into the snow, cringing before the low clouds. The chill of it turned him back to the massive bed where Geness' hair lay tousled at a single place in the vast rumple they had slept in.

"Everybody was such a fool when I was a child, and I never wanted to join what I considered misfortune." Skarra wrapped a wool blanket about his naked body. "I tried, but I failed."

He saw a bare hand come up out of the bedclothes and gesture to him on a supple wrist. "You were too bright."

"No. I never thought I was."

"Bruce, you would be the Lord of Skarra with fewer brains." He heard her laugh in the bed, though he could not see her. "Come to bed." The hand patted the covers.

"No, let me think." He turned back to the window. "My older brother is a thief. He disappeared into the Highlands to lead the Highlanders against the greed of the Lowlands. All he will get them is desolation of their impoverished glens and banishment to America. They're already slaughtering the Highland cattle and deer to graze sheep for wool. And my father robbed the Church of its corruption, and now he hates the Church out of his guilt, and he wants me as the laird, but he cannot bear me because I find nothing to religion."

"What we have is right."

"Yes." He spoke absently.

"Skarra. I would love to see Skarra."

"It is an old stone house surrounded with rhododendron and fuchsia."

"Will I be the mistress of Skarra?"

"If I marry you."

"Will you marry me?"

"No need."

"Never?"

"We have the bliss of love."

"Would the love be bliss if I were pregnant?"

The words came like a strange message out of reality, of an urgency that had to be served.

"You can't be."

"Yes." She smiled at him, the fragile chin set atop the slender back of her hand that rested on the covers over her knees.

In the pregnancy of her there was the velvet crush of a fresh life pressing at him borne out of the spiritual void, the lost years he had lived. Set against it was the outrage of another life snatching him from his masculine luxury, to fling him headlong into commitment at the side of a woman, to break trail for a helpless infant. He was jarred by the thought of a child in his image; and yet delighted that something of him would live outside of himself.

Skarra refused to marry her under the aegis of a divine, nor in the hall of any church, being very Scottish in what he wanted to do. Skarra, himself, would marry them, reading from the new Bible of the Scottish King.

He held her hand in his, the somber Bible before them, and faced the ice-radiating window panes convoluted in lights from a faint sun.

"It is important to you, isn't it?" Geness said.

"Yes."

"Do you mind?" She looked down at her nightclothes, to her bare feet, which were fragile and a soft continuation of her skin and hair. "I'm not dressed."

"It doesn't matter."

"But you." She gestured at his boots and strews and Highland tunic and gorget at his throat and white jabot. "You look so formal."

"I have to dress."

"I could borrow a silk gown from one of the girls. . . ."

"No. A woman needs only to be herself at her wedding. The aspect of womanhood, decorated or in her bare skin, composes the essence of marriage."

"I'm glad you know what to do."

"Now, let me read the Bible."

"I think the children will look like you."

"If they get here with all their faculties, I'll be grateful."

She nodded her head.

"We shall take what comes."

"Bruce, my lord." She pressed her mouth into his upper arm.

He heard his own voice admonish them to cleave the flesh into itself, so the man and the woman, though separate, would become one, and the child would be each, though alone to itself, as their flesh had once been.

He stared out the window in silence while she held her bosom against his arm.

"I'm glad it's done."

She nodded.

"Sentiment is never right for love nor children, and God knows what wrongs are done from it."

"Our child," she said.

"The mirror of ourselves, that we dared to live."

"I want to please you."

"You have."

"Are we married now?"

"Yes."

"Will I go to Skarra, someday?" She looked up to him, her eyes searching his for the ultimate truth.

"You will go to Skarra."

"With you."

"We are together forever, beyond death or time."

She put her face into his chest and he felt her shudder in waves as she cried, until he felt the tears wet against his skin. He took her quietly into his arms.

Skarra found his students a refuge and, in their decency, a consolation in the world outside his personal quarters with Geness. His cheerful apartment was more than he had known in Edinburgh; in fact, not since his nursery years at Skarra on the coast of Scotland had he ever loved life so much as he now did with the girl. Surely humanity was true, and mankind a credit to the miracle of life, and to live, the delight of being. He loved the girl.

The hall he taught in was cold as a tomb, and some of the boys brought flagons of wine to stir the blood, and Skarra found vodka a source of heat as he spoke. His lectures were famous, not for his love of whiskey nor for his bold insights into the condition of humanity, but because Skarra liked his students and he loved the truth. This happy rapport filled his classes. The students often sat in the aisles and about the podium entranced with his images of the Classical world which interpreted the current world. Often the discussions were convoluted, as the time Piippo raised his hand and said, "If there is no certainty, how can there be knowledge?"

"If one is certain, then one needs no further knowledge, and so one is ignorant," Skarra said.

"And how?" There was a hush in the lecture hall.

"Wisdom is the acceptance of ignorance, while knowledge creates absolutes that please us."

The students stared at him from the rounded hall, wrapped in wool mufflers and shawls and fur mantles. He had obviously lost them, and he felt a rash of heat run over his shoulders in his annoyance with himself.

"I mean," he said, "that wisdom accepts love as the final criterion, while knowledge sets the intellect ahead of all."

"Bravo! Bravo!"

"Magnificent! Master. . . ."

He saw the lecture hall come to life before him, the hooded youths rising and applauding, and some upending flagons. They thronged forward.

Skarra was glad to go in a group to the Inn. The party-going impulses of his students were a keen delight to him. Though the students were armed with knives and cavalry pistols, fights were unheard of, and common among them was their sense of optimism. Finding fault was considered bad taste, and to be a boon friend of humanity the goal of most. Considering the religious wars in Europe and the closed ecclesiastical minds who guided the public, Skarra found his students a refreshing voice for hope. With Geness he seemed to be living in borrowed space, a sequestered retreat, warmed by the plain wood beams and walls, and Skarra wondered how long this tender life could go on in the face of human disquietude.

He and Voltoff had searched the countryside for a cottage with more privacy, and away from the usual routes of the King's visit.

"Damn this mud," Skarra said, listening to the suction of wet earth his horses' hooves lifted against.

"In time it'll go, my lord."

"They said winter was springtime."

"Ah, yes."

"I wish we had the troika."

"The snowbird of the winter, my lord."

"Keep the horses stabled."

"Since you bought them, they are now ours."

"Ours?"

"I go with the horses. You bought our bread." Voltoff was assured.

"I didn't buy you."

"Must the idiot and I starve, my lord?"

"You can appeal to Providence, same as any other man," Skarra said, feeling the chill of the damp forest across his shoulders.

"I have, my lord," Voltoff said.

"I'm a Scotsman, not one of your Russian nobles, and I don't keep slaves."

"You bought our lives, my lord."

"I have no money!" Skarra reined up, angry with Voltoff.

"My lord, every man must belong to someone, living or dead, or he is lost."

Skarra did not look back. Voltoff was part of an alien world where slavery was cherished as a form of love, which he could never understand.

Gustavus Adolphus rode through Dorpat on a large bay horse, imperious with his gold beard and commanding size. About him rode handsome officers of his staff, ahead of the King's standards and the blue and gold Crosses of Sweden. Skarra and Geness watched from their windows, free of ice scarcely a fortnight. The horses plunged in caracoles and made their plumes wind in the air.

"Is that the King?" Geness pointed to Gustavus.

"Yes."

"He's the biggest man in the army."

"That's just his retinue."

"How handsome they are."

"Aye, it's the fancy crowd from the palace."

They watched the cuirasses of the riders, burnished against the oiled coats of the horses and glinting in the fading sun.

"When I see soldiers, I want to join the army," Geness said.

"We must leave. It bodes no good."

Skarra was glad he had brought the formal dress of Scotland for the ball, and would not appear as a London fop dripping lace over a leg, nor as a Highland ruffian in the kilt which he truly favored, but rather in the Gaelic trousers that caught under his short boot. His strews. He faced the copper mirror adjusting his short jabot which was as formal as his silver buttons at his cuffs and the small epaulets of his Highland jacket.

"Every woman there will fall in love with you," Geness said, watching the reflection of the short curly hair above the angular face of the tall, blue-eyed young man.

"I'll not know it," he said.

"No eye for beautiful women?"

"I have one, and I don't need two." He felt her tickle his flank. He was uneasy because he would not let anyone mention Geness, and since his cousins, Captain Dumaine and Colonel Monro, had accompanied the King, they were sure to ask him to explain himself. Since she had had a public name, and he was part of the established class, there was no way their love could be reconciled in the public mind.

"Try to enjoy yourself," Geness said, noticing the corners of his frowning mouth as he hooked his cloak at his throat and tilted his braided bonnet forward over one eye.

"As a Scot I dinna' like 't."

"My lord, you will never be taken for anything but a Scotsman mad with his dreams."

He turned back at the door, hearing the mirth in her voice. "Ah, little tit, come to me." He swept her into his chest. "I'll make them accept you one day."

"No, love, don't. If you keep your own counsel our silence will be our invincible weapon. But if you talk, we are lost." She shivered and he felt her soft belly and quick breasts against his hard body. "We have eternity already."

Voltoff had brushed the fur on his wool hat, and the light carriage was immaculate. Polonitz, the retarded boy, rode on a step behind him, giving them considerable style, which was not lost even with the boy's bare feet which seemed red in the flares lighting Dorpat for the celebration. Skarra watched the spokes of the near wheel rotate into sight and vanish in shadows as they rolled toward the Kremlin. The Governor's Palace seemed to perch in a bath of fire which swathed the night in gold from the rows of fire knots along the terraces.

Flunkies in black satin trimmed with silver at the knee took his cloak and feathered bonnet. Officers glanced surreptitiously at his six-foot-four height and a group of three ladies stared boldly. One of the women had milk-white skin, especially about her bare breasts. A virgin, in the English fashion. He moved among them, fingering the lace at his cuffs, and glad he had something to occupy his hands.

He was at the double doors of the ballroom and engulfed by men and women. Elegant officers seemed to ring the vast room, stretching their stockinged legs and showing their clothes like preening birds, while beautiful women swirled their feet and gowns to the minuet.

Skarra looked for a familiar face toward whom he could move and not feel out of place.

"Lord Skarra," said a lady coming up from behind.

"Yes, my lady?" The woman was short and wore her white gown up to her throat.

"Helen Bofors, the Governor's wife." She put out her hand, which was fat and flushed red, as if from the heat of cooking.

"Most honored." He took her hand.

"Bofors said I was not to miss you."

"Ah, I am a bit adrift."

"You men are all alike."

"Thank you, my lady." Lady Bofors had an earthy force about her, like a fresh-tilled field, which her silken finery did not hide.

"Oh, there he is, the Scotsman."

"Indeed," said a goateed man who set the lorgnette to his eyes in the French manner.

Skarra turned to see a middle-aged woman, whose face was rigid with make-up, peering over her fan. The older man glared at Skarra. "Indeed."

Skarra nodded, knowing he had been insulted but pleased the insult was ineffectual.

"The Lady Helga," Lady Bofors whispered to him. "Her set she fancies to be the most fashionable in Dorpat."

"Dorpat? Society?"

"Dear boy, people form social strata even in Hell, the Governor says."

"I had never thought of it."

"You are just like the Count," she said, striking his forearm with an ivory fan, as though Skarra had made a witty remark.

"Truly, I see no purpose in these doings."

"Nobody does, but we can't do without them."

"We?"

"Come, Lord Skarra, you are indulging your youth. The ball is to let people nourish their illusions of friendship while preserving their enmity."

"Not if you are in love," Skarra said bluntly.

"Quite, but anger is more common." The woman spoke while looking out over the dancers. "Ah, the Princess Lydia Merkalov."

"Lady Bofors," said a dark-skinned girl, curtseying before them. Her blue eyes were startling set against the smooth olive tan, and she had full lips, which she licked twice.

"Lord Skarra of Scotland." Lady Bofors gestured to him.

"Bruce McTaggart," he said, bowing to the Russian girl.

"Do you like your time in Dorpat?" Lydia said.

"Very much."

"Words no one believes." She smiled, looking across the ballroom toward the dais, where Gustavus Adolphus stood in a group of officers and gowned ladies.

"Princess Merkalov is a close friend of the King," Lady Bofors said. "One of the Russian refugees from the civil war."

"We are grateful for our lives, my lady."

Skarra raised his eyebrows.

"We have nothing but the clothes on our backs and our titles," the girl said, her eyes showing defiance. Skarra saw the heavy weight of dark hair piled atop her head.

"It is sad to leave one's home," Skarra said.

"It is a living ache." The girl looked into his eyes, and for a second, before it vanished, he caught the universal sight of humanity, of the sweet wish to go home.

"Come, you and the Princess must dance," Lady Bofors said, hearing the solemnity come into their voices.

Holding her fingers through her silk gloves, he moved his body in the stylized walk of the minuet, dragging his heels and tapping his toes as he reversed himself, then pirouetted and shifted her hand as he did. The Princess Lydia Merkalov was a beautiful woman, though her nose was too short, yet it was refined about its bridge, and the nostrils were as delicate as parchment in proportion to her small jaw. The mouth was large and she displayed her anxiety when she licked her lips. Her eyes never left him, pressing his eyes for an understanding.

"You hate dancing, don't you?"

"I had other things to do," he said.

"You pound your feet and your body is stiff. No supple grace."

"If I don't fall the dance is a success."

"Never change." He heard her laugh.

He was swept with an intoxication of warmth, that he had pleased a pretty woman on a ballroom floor in competition with men who made the ballroom another arena of strife. And he was swept with a pang of guilt, for he felt his pleasure betrayed his love for Geness.

"This is our bread and butter. Only the brave can dance with their conquerors."

"Why do you tell me?"

"I can talk to you because you're the stranger whom nobody would believe." She watched his eyes.

"I am not your conqueror."

"We've thrown in with Sweden because we are prisoners if we don't."

"That sounds wise."

"We have no choice."

She went into the hand of an elderly man in a water-blue silk waistcoat and a wig so thick his temples were sweating. Skarra danced with a succession of women who seemed intent to know him better, for all knew his name, but he pretended he did not speak their language.

When Lydia came back into his hand she spoke offhandedly. "If I loved the ball, I would pray that every man would covet my naked shoulders, but now I am ashamed of my life, and I cry at home with my father and we pine for Russia."

"The bonds of family are never broken without grief," Skarra said.

"Beautiful trophies and tame Russians." She smiled brilliantly, letting her fine teeth reflect in the hall by candlelight, and he saw she kept her face toward the dais where Gustavus Adolphus and Prince Merkalov and the authorities of Sweden had gathered. "We are alive."

"Hope in that," he said.

"They say you are living with the pastor's daughter at the Inn."

"I beg your pardon?" Skarra said.

"Count Bofors' cousin, Geness, the whole town knows you're in bed with her."

"Really," he said.

"Really. Now you know two women who've swallowed their pride." She was gone into the hands of a man whose face was patted white with powder.

Skarra was glad to find himself in the tow of Helen Bofors, who guided him toward the dais. He caught sight of Lydia at the punch table talking to a man who was admiring his outthrust thigh.

"The Princess Merkalov said the Governor and the girl at the Inn are cousins."

"Oh, that."

"Are they?"

"Dear boy, everybody in a small village is related. Of course they are cousins." She stopped and faced him. "The girl is pretty enough, but marriage should advance one's station, otherwise it is fatal."

Skarra was annoyed with the invasion of his privacy. "Madam, I shall be obliged if you will not express your opinion at my expense."

"You arrive in town with seventeen dead Cossacks and crawl in bed with a homeless ingenue and refuse to come out for a month while you read Latin. What else do you think Dorpat has to talk about?"

"Don't they have their own lives?"

"Dear boy, Sweden needs good men, and your cousins are here with His Majesty."

They were at the dais and among the staff and entourage of Gustavus Adolphus, mingling with those in power of Dorpat. He saw Veblen in his academic robes, pursing his lips and looking artfully wise by adjusting his massive neck on his collar.

"Bruce, you little devil!" A bluff hand seized his upper arm and swung him about while another man pommeled him in the ribs. "You little bastard!"

It was the Scots, Colonel Monro and Captain Dumaine, his cousins.

"Kinfolk!" Skarra laughed and swept his arms about the two officers.

"Scotland forever," Dumaine said, his face wrinkling in delight. "Said they were Cossacks."

"They didn't kill me," Skarra said.

"Nice university student like this," Monro said.

"I told your father Edinburgh University was no place for a man compared to a Highland regiment."

When they were free of strangers for a moment they brought Skarra the news that his brother had been killed in a raid against Lowland sheepherders and that his father was beside himself with grief, but was too stubborn to ask Skarra to return and too healthy to fear death and yield in penance from it. And that his mother sent her prayers. Then Monro lowered his voice and leaned close, his dark eyes looking off behind Skarra's head as he spoke.

"What's all this we hear of ye keeping company with a wee Swedish tit?"

"Yes, I am."

"D'ye love her, boy?"

"Yes."

"Alas, that's bad."

"Man's in trouble when he loves," Dumaine said, shaking his head.

"They say she's a strumpet."

"She was."

"Hoot, a strumpet's part of every woman, no worse there." Monro shook his head. "The love is the raw thing, it softens a man. It's not a fitting spirit to get a man in shape for war."

"I was lonely."

"That's the way love comes, when a man's heart is aching with hollow thoughts, and a girl's the only cure for it."

"Aye, that's how it came," Skarra said.

Skarra saw the King differently than he had seen him in Stockholm. Then Skarra was a footloose university wit, whose insolence assured his independence. Now alone in the snow country, and in love with a girl, he felt himself more a man able to see another man for what he was.

"The passage was clear," he heard the King say. "Water like glass."

"A placid lake, this Baltic," said a gentleman in a lace collar.

"If it is not the weather it is the mud, Your Majesty," said a lady just behind his shoulder.

"Aye, life's bits of trivia without which we should go mad." The King was sipping from a silver cup. He was a large man, whose hair was cut short in contrast to the age. His eyes were searching as he looked about him under their oriental eyelids. The full mouth was framed by a wide cavalry mustache and a fine goatee, yet the King was the plainest-dressed man in the ballroom. He wore simple butternut, relieved only by his white collar and his sash of authority across his chest.

Though he was supposedly nearsighted, the King caught sight of Skarra before the others about him. "That young Scot, bring him, Monro."

"Your Majesty," Skarra said, bowing.

"Up, boy, men were not made to bow."

Ripples of polite laughter traveled around them, but the King did not smile.

"All I've heard is your martial exploits."

"Would to God I had come in peace," Skarra said.

"It takes two to have peace, and the choice lies with one."

"It is gross to be at such caprice, my lord," Skarra said.

"Yes, and the same caprice rules a King, so you have no call to suck an old wound."

Skarra looked into the light northern eyes that seemed to penetrate from a mist of gray, so that it was hard to discern what Gustavus meant.

"I understand, my lord."

"What is this you're not for the army?"

"Just that, your Majesty."

"No knighthood in a Scot?"

"Chivalry is dead, if it ever existed."

"So you don't believe?" The King's eyes were harsh.

"No, my lord."

"The dangers of a King—thought." He turned on his pumps, remarkably elegant for so large a man. "We build universities and religions to control thought and we always fail."

A flunkey set another goblet in the King's hand, then turned to the other gentlemen and ladies and served them briskly.

"It was America or Sweden, Your Majesty," Skarra said.

"And why Sweden?"

"I wasn't that angry, my lord. If it were America, I would never come home."

"So Europe won you."

"The divines and philosophers in Scotland are all for a Republic in America. It's to be a rebirth of mankind in an unspoiled paradise, and—"

"Young Scot, all Europe is afire with grand ideas of Greek and Hebrew republics in America, the Greek democracies renascent in a pure wilderness, they call it."

"Yes," Skarra said, pleased the King had turned his attention to the subject.

"Scotsman, no nation ever lived from knowledge."

"The minuet, my lord," said a lady with brilliant eyes and an aging face. "Is not the minuet lovely?"

"Thank you, my lady," Gustavus said, touching the lady on her forearm.

The people on the dais waited to see which way the King would go. Gustavus faced Skarra, and Colonel Monro and Captain Dumaine.

"The power is the gall that wrenches all these notions, and men need thoughts to mask the power. Rub a fellow and you'll find he slavers for power, and none will admit it, save the kings." The court listened gravely to the King. "Hate is the fatal heel of democracy, and if one is to flourish in America, it will vanish as did the ancients."

"We are having war now, my lord," Skarra said.

"War makes men kings, so men fancy," Gustavus said, "but the King is the pawn, not the commoner."

"I am a teacher." Skarra was pleased the conversation had got easier.

"And when we taught people how to read, they read the word of God but without divine humility."

"Humility, my lord?"

"Yes, I have universities full of brilliant tyrants."

"America is to be mankind's last best hope," Skarra said. "A land of equality with work and freedom for all."

"Oh, everybody wants to level down his betters. It is the dream of mankind since Cain killed his brother. But nobody wants to *level up.* America won't change human nature."

"Your wisdom is well known, my lord."

"Oh, no wisdom in that." Gustavus Adolphus smiled easily in the magic hall of candlelight, the gowned women moving as a white fairyland of grace among dancing men.

"But only the commoner sees God in his own image and talks to God out of this illusion," Skarra said.

"Indeed, Wallenstein is the better general, but I have God in the hearts of my men. I'll commit the final blasphemy by using God and our armies will fight to the death, in the name of God, which I will lead."

"My students should hear you, sire."

"Young man, we came out of Eden to find adversity so we could know to live." He clapped Skarra on the shoulder with an open hand.

Skarra could hear the strains of music from the hall where he collected his cape and bonnet. The few people about him were yellowish from fatigue and the emotional exhaustion of displaying themselves for half of the night. The coatroom flunkey had backed away when he heard light footsteps.

"Bruce, wait!"

"Of course." Lydia had her skirts pulled up as she ran.

"I didn't finish talking."

"Too many fine gentlemen in French perfume." He grinned happily.

"Bruce?"

"Yes." He wondered what she wanted.

"You may call." She searched his eyes, to see the effect of opening herself to him. "At my apartments on Shabatsky Street."

"I am honored," Skarra said.

"Oh, I see."

They looked at each other for a moment. "Why me, of a sudden?"

"You were kind."

"Kind people are everywhere," he said.

"Why won't you call?"

"Certainly it is not personal."

"It was an insane thought."

"What was an insane thought?"

"That you could take us out of Dorpat. You have power, while we are impoverished émigrés."

"Lord, impoverishment is a great inspiration."

"I could have your children, you will need children, every man does." She set her hand under her heart.

"Hush, don't say it." He closed his eyes.

"You want them, don't you?"

"Yes, dear Lydia, but why here?"

"Bruce, we must get out of Dorpat. Someday Russia will return and any Russians they find will be killed as traitors."

"Please," Skarra said.

"We know the terror of Russia."

"I am in love."

Her face drained of color, so that the two blue eyes faded. "Love?"

He nodded.

"I'm too late?"

"Nothing is ever late, if it's true," he said.

"The Swedish girl?"

"Yes, I married her."

She searched his face. "You love her?"

"Yes, very much."

"There was no ceremony."

"I read the service myself."

"Oh. I didn't know." She licked her paling lips as the color drained once more.

"I suppose I made a fool of myself. A fleeting hope went past me, of a real man and not a fop with perfumed hair. I saw the terror lift, and oh, I could have loved you and had the children you will need. . . ."

"I'm sorry," Skarra said, drawing her into his chest as much to silence her as to console her with warmth.

"I made a fool of myself."

"No." The flunkey turned away in embarrassment.

"I don't know what possessed me."

"Don't explain." He saw the moisture smear her cheeks.

"I have never done antyhing like that before." She laughed to herself, as though coming out of a seizure.

"You are very much a woman."

"Thank you. You fell in love."

"Yes."

"I said we were two women who had swallowed their pride." She composed herself.

"Perhaps we can be friends."

"I would like that."

"We're having a child."

"Truly?"

"Yes."

"That is how it should be. Now I must go."

She pulled out of his arms and he watched her go down the hall, seeming to float in purpose as though nothing had occurred.

The night sky passed over his face and he breathed deeply of the air to clear the ball out of his body.

"My lord did not care for the ball?" Voltoff said, from the front of the carriage.

Skarra grunted and felt the wheels jolt on the rutted path.

"It is for women, not for men."

"I met the Princess Lydia Merkalov."

"I was her grandfather's serf." His form seemed to draw down in a bob.

"Yes, I met her."

"Ululululula," the Russian crooned to the horses in a voice of sorrow and brute strain.

Skarra felt the stove warm his bare flanks as he undressed and shucked his inner garments. He crawled into the vast bed and heard Geness mumble and push her buttocks into him to be held, which he embraced as it droused him.

With the dawn he was up, having breakfast of tea and oatmeal.

"How was the ball?" Geness said.

"Oh, it was the usual, everybody advancing his own cause."

"Even the King?"

"He was rallying the people to more war."

"Immediately?"

"Thirty years of war, I think they are calling it. No end in sight."

"He wanted you for the army, yes?"

"Yes."

"And you told him."

"Yes. That I'm not a soldier."

She nodded her head, making her hair sway. "There's something you're not telling me."

He looked into her face, and felt himself stricken with guilt, for Lydia's protestation, for the offer of another woman, who, even if he did not take her, still, he could have, and under other circumstances would have, so it left him guilty of betrayal just the same as if he had.

"Lydia, the Russian refugee."

"What did she say to you?"

"Nothing important."

"She offered herself? Her body?"

"Ultimately, yes."

"So she is a woman."

"What else does a woman have besides her body?" His voice was pensive.

"It starts with her body and ends with her soul."

"She wants to leave Dorpat."

"I sympathize with her."

"Dammit, is there nobody contented in this squalid town?"

"She touched you then?"

"In her simplicity. She offered to have my children."

"Could you live with two women?"

"It would depend upon the women."

"If the women could arrange it?"

"No, I would never impose such an arrangement on women. It would mock their love."

"You told her I was pregnant?"

"Aye, she begged my forgiveness and began to cry."

"She is a lady too."

5

Geness did not show her pregnancy under her full skirt, but she tired more easily. Their quarters at the Inn were vulnerable to the King's officers, who roistered and wenched all night.

"I drove out with Voltoff. We found a cottage on the creek," Skarra said.

"You bought it!" She clasped her hands together.

"No, but if you want it, I will."

"I'd love a cottage."

Voltoff and Skarra and Polonitz carried out their things, making several trips to the cottage with the carriage piled high. They had the hand-rubbed timbers of the big bed on the stairs when Roglan met them.

"What are you doing?" His eyes were bloodshot.

"Moving," Skarra said.

"You're stealing my bed."

"No, I'm buying it from you."

"With what? Professors aren't paid."

Skarra eased the headboard to the floor, while Voltoff held up his end.

"You can't go. Married! My rump," Roglan snorted.

"She's a free woman." Skarra wiped the sweat from his forehead.

"Hell, I bought and paid for that damned strumpet two, three times."

"Let's go, Voltoff," Skarra said, picking up the headboard once more, hoping to bluff their way out.

"I'll not give that wench a thing save a chop in the musk," Roglan said.

"Send down the blond cunt!" Three officers were at a table by the stairs.

"Ayeayeayeaye," the retarded boy said.

"My father was ordained," Geness said.

"Gurd fancies a spiced tit."

"Bofors slut!" Skarra watched her flung loosely down the stairs and plop in the sawdust at the foot of the officers.

"Divvy her up, gentlemen!" Roglan said.

"He's broken a man's back, my lord!" Voltoff croaked.

Skarra was aware of the angry mouth and bare teeth and the fists coming up. His own fist surprised him as it covered the image, setting the teeth inward. He saw the head go away from him, leading the body outward into the air, and he was startled when it looked as though Roglan might land on Geness. He seemed to float out and fall into the table of officers, where his body made a breaking noise of timber. The officers struggled to get free of the heap of broken wood and stumbled around Geness.

"By Jove, look at those teeth," said an officer, picking up something of white from Roglan's face, which shone in blood.

"It's the Scot Bofors wants."

Skarra ignored the officers and went to Geness, lifting her, and saw his hand was bleeding and showed uneven roots of a tooth stuck in the sinews. "My God," he said, "are you all right?"

"Oh, I'm fine," Geness said. "The sawdust is soft."

"Eight to five it'll take two buckets of water to stir him," said an officer, peering at Roglan's inert body.

"Arrogant bastards," Skarra said.

"Only in work and love is there any life, my lord."

"Oh, Voltoff," Skarra said, as Geness poured whiskey into his wound, "and I crave a dram."

Their cottage was the typical small abode of the Baltic and Scandinavia with the curled eaves of White Russia. The adzed logs were faced with moss packed between planking under the wide galleries in front and back. There was one window of glass, protected by thick folding shutters, and a massive front door barred with iron slots.

"Strong enough to hold out against raiders," the owner had explained.

"It's so warm, like it grew from the forest," Geness said.

That first summer Skarra found it easy to work until exhausted, absolutely possessed by planting, building garden pickets and stringing vines to grow the arbors and the wisteria, and putting in hollyhock and sunflower seeds, as well as the vegetables. The two large rooms were just right for Geness and himself. The bed was more an altar on which they lay, somehow assured from each other's resting body that if life was in the touch, perhaps this was God.

Skarra found little pleasure in intellectual strife, and spent his time at work around the cottage when not actually teaching. The university students came often to help him dig and tie stakes and hang gates, drawn by a vicarious longing to housekeep with a girl.

"The midsummer days will stretch these vines," Piippo said, winding the melon vines along the gallery to mix its leaves with the wisteria. "What if we could cross them?"

"Cross what?" Skarra spoke with his eyes closed from where he rested.

"The melon with the wisteria. We would have melons among the flowers on the roof."

"Oh, God." He heard Geness and the boy break into laughter.

The summer daylight hung on the horizon until the dark began to crowd with the chill of autumn. Geness was unwieldy with the child, and Skarra built the crib himself.

One day Skarra saw Lydia coming at a distance. He was surprised he recognized the wide hips and olive skin.

"Geness, I think it's Lydia Merkalov."

He heard her roll heavily from their bed.

"So lovely to see you," Geness said, as Lydia came through the gate.

"I put off all summer to come, waiting for these flowers to bloom, to bring the baby good fortune." She came toward them uncertainly, holding out the flowers. "A child is a flower."

"How kind that you should see my child as a flower."

"It's lovely out here," Lydia said. "The whole town seems to cluster in the vines and gardens of summer, such a relief from winter."

"Short as it is," Skarra said, placing roughhewn chairs for the three of them.

"So sturdy, Lord Skarra." Lydia ran a hand over the arm of one.

"I should die if it got hotter." Geness sat in the unbalanced discomfort of a pregnant woman.

"When is your due date?"

"November."

"Alas, the snow again."

They all three felt the self-conscious occlusion of people who know more about each other than they wish and were silent.

"I think we've seen each other in town several times," Geness said.

"It is a woman's nature to know every other beautiful woman," Skarra said. The two women laughed unguardedly.

"And so are you beautiful," Geness said, looking at Lydia.

"With child, you are a fragrant chalice of life."

"How gentle of you to say so."

Skarra saw them turn to look into each other's faces, in surprise at the unintended candor. They sat that way staring quietly off into the ceilinged distance where the stratus clouds measured the sky. When it seemed they would not speak again, Skarra stirred his body and said, "You haven't seen our new horses."

"Trotters, he's getting as bad as Voltoff." Geness touched his arm.

"Tireless, go all day."

"Bruce, the two of you might walk the grounds to the stable. To be pregnant means one cannot walk and I do miss it."

They stood and Geness stepped deliberately back into the cottage. "If I didn't want life so much, I'd hate to be pregnant."

"Her hips are narrow," Lydia said.

"Yes. Too narrow." The act of childbirth was too much raw truth for him to entertain.

"I've never really known what to expect."

"We cry for what is and pray to change it," Lydia said.

"Oh, bother," he said, shouting "Voltoff!" and walking ahead. "In Scotland we fight what is and pray for more strength."

She walked quietly at his side for a few moments, and he heard her say, "Do you ever win?"

"Get out the horses!" he bellowed at the Russian.

"My lord," Voltoff said and bowed, holding his tea glass in both hands.

Skarra and Lydia sat on a bench in the shade of the stables while the horses were brought out and harnessed.

"If a woman loves a man, she is not going to fail, hips wide or narrow."

The horses were trotted before them singly and hitched to the wheeled troika, yet the responsibility of the impending childbirth weighed heavy on his mind and the horses were no real pleasure.

"Perhaps Lady Lydia would like a drive?" He turned to her.

"No, thank you. He can put them away."

"He can drive you back to Shabatsky Street."

"No, I'd rather walk."

He nodded his head to Voltoff. "Put them away."

He sat back on the bench at Lydia's side. "This cottage with our love does seem reasonable when I feel no affiliation with anything else, not even the university."

"And success?"

"It's small and it's mine, and in it I can say I've succeeded."

"To hide?" She looked at him. There was no taunt.

"With a pregnant wife, what else?"

She stared over the hedge of stilting hollyhock pods. "Yes, love is too fragile to live in the mind."

He saw her away from the woven pickets and down the lane which led into Dorpat.

6

Skarra's days were a succession of university students moving behind a bland mask of innocence. His concern was Geness. She was slender and the child seemed vast within her, pulling vertical ribbons of discolored flesh over her belly. That her love for him could evoke this was unfair. Her strength had ebbed until she could not turn in the bed; he would wake to shift her weight, being careful not to catch his hands in her hair nor her frail limbs beneath her.

"Oh, Bruce, will the baby never come?"

"Yes, be easy, love."

"Oh, I think we've been forgotten."

Their voices came out of the dark, seemingly strange when they lay so close. The winter chill sweeping the land made their chimney suck and the fire move in spasms of light. He knew childbirth would bring them to the edge of death, and he was terrified from it, yet he knew he would have to stand firm. The snows came in late October, quieting the garden and filling the lane with gentle drifts.

"Bruce?"

He thought he heard her voice rousing his being into mind, amidst the soft linen of their bed.

"What, love?"

"The child, I felt something."

He felt a shock of reality, of life chucking him from the bed, and into the open glare of their cottage where a naked girl would have a child. In a flicker the lover's joy was gone and the bliss a hollow mirage.

"Aye, we shall have it," he said, sliding sideways out of the bed so he wouldn't throw a cold draft against her body. He pulled on his wool shirt and knee socks and went to the fireplace, where he heaved up the ashes, watching them glow and then catch flame as he put on fresh logs.

"It was just a feeling."

"They say women know." He heard her move in the rumpled mound of bedding and he pulled on his leather breeches, and slid his feet into his buckled shoes.

"Wonder where's the dawn?" He took his linen shirt from the bedpost.

"Kiss me, Bruce." He put his mouth carefully to hers, and felt the swollen lips and got the taste of her parched breath in his mouth. The childbirth seemed to drain away the life and sweetness of her mouth and nostrils to her womb.

"Bruce, don't leave me." Her eyes shone in the dark.

"Never."

"Like my mother. We're alone." She touched his cheek.

"No matter, I'll see it through."

"I wonder where I was born. I mean the house. Who was there? What was it like?"

"Most people just suppose they came—their birth such a joy, the difficulties naught." He touched her temple.

"Bruce, what if I hurt?"

"You'll hurt a bit."

"What if I scream?"

"Just scream."

"I mean truly."

"And I said 'scream,' exactly that." He nuzzled his face into her hair. "We'll have the child. Life is the hope of God."

She nodded and sank back into the bed.

He recalled what he could of childbirth from his friends in the medical school of the University of Edinburgh. If there were no complications, it seemed fairly simple. Yet by instinct Skarra knew civilization brought pestilence to mankind, and that animals cooped up in paddocks or stalls did poorly, while those in natural state were healthy.

"Voltoff!" He called to the stable, where his voice carried on the snow. A muffled shape appeared.

"Come when you've eaten."

Voltoff seemed to fill the kitchen of the cottage. "I want the fires kept up at all times and the kettles on to steam."

"My lord." Voltoff mumbled.

"The steam will warm her naked body."

The head bobbed.

"I want you to go to the midwife, she lives three houses down from the University. . . ." He waited to see if the words evoked the correct image.

"Yes, my lord. I'll get her."

"And stop at the University and tell Piippo to bring me a keg of vodka."

"Vodka, my lord?"

"Yes, vodka."

He could hear the sleigh bells of the troika as Voltoff swept around the cottage and down the lane to Dorpat, and he noted with satisfaction their rooms seemed balmy in the steam vapors.

"How do you feel?"

She looked at him, then glanced away.

"The pain?"

"It comes regularly."

"How often?"

"I don't know."

"Could you tell me?"

"Yes."

She seemed to be withdrawing into that place where women go to be alone, to do what only they can at childbirth. He watched her pale skin against the white sheets, her eyelashes the only color to her closed eyelids. She was little more than another rumple among the bedcovers.

"How do the pains come, my lord?" Voltoff had come in.

"It's a long way off." The wait of hours seemed like moments.

"Some of our students were glad to know my lady is near childbirth."

"Piippo?"

"Yes, my lord."

She seemed to know Piippo was there. She opened her eyes and smiled briefly at him, then looked over his head, and he saw a veil close off her soul to him.

"Can I bring you anything?" he said.

"Your voice is so loud that it hurts even when you whisper, and I'm terrified to be touched."

"I'm sorry, love."

"It's like fire all through my belly, that wants to be torn open to pour it out. Lord, I hurt."

"Oh," he said softly.

He watched the childbirth pains draw her away, almost as though she had gone into a sunny woods, to where he could see her in a nest of leaves among the slanting sun shafts breaking through the limbs overhead, to where she lay down and turned into herself to have the child, and to where no man could go to help her.

He walked to the fireplace and stirred up the coals, and set some oatmeal to boiling for porridge, being careful not to clink the poker on the andirons. He followed her contractions by the flinching in her sides and the tension which drew up her knees.

"I'm hot," she said.

He lifted a layer of quilts, and adjusted a throw over her bosom.

"The pain, I hurt."

It was so useless to say anything to a woman laboring in childbirth. "Would you like a little water?"

She nodded her head.

He brought her the water and held her head and shoulders forward so she could drink. She moistened her lips and licked her mouth. "Thank you"—and stretched back into the bed.

"Ohhh," she said, and he saw her flanks sweep in a dip under her rib cage and move in a wave down the thin flesh on either side to her loins.

She dug white crescents in the flesh of her palms with her fingernails.

"Voltoff, get the midwife."

He was at her side when he felt a cold draft and heard Piippo come in.

"God, she's trapped on her back," Piippo said.

"She's sweating. I don't want her to chill."

He saw her recognize them and crinkle up the corners of her mouth. "Bruce, my feet are cold."

"Your feet?" He leaned close.

"I'm hot, but my feet are cold."

He strode to their rawhide trunk and brought out a long pair of woolen socks and leaned over the bed and took a foot into his hand and slipped the sock onto it, sliding it up over her knees to her thigh. When he had her legs covered it seemed to him indecent to have a woman prostrate and defenseless with her secrets bare, yet, who in her composure found only that men could serve her with trifles, while she ignored them and moved her body in command to nothing short of life itself.

"Do you think she's all right?" Piippo said.

"Yes. So far."

They heard the sleigh bells in the yard, and heard Voltoff usher in the midwife. Skarra saw a lean woman with heavy bones enter the room.

"It's the Roglan tart, is it?"

Skarra looked at the woman, amazed at her social insolence.

"Madam, the lady is my wife. You will be paid for your professional knowledge, not your company."

"Oh, I hadn't heard."

"I'd never have occasion to tell you, madam." He went back to Geness. "She's been in labor for seven hours."

The midwife stared at Geness, her sinewed neck turning the heavy jaw and craggy nose, which had random hairs poked out the nostrils.

"She's thick."

"Yes. Quite obviously."

"She's square—twins."

He heard Piippo breathe and saw him look closely at the vast ribboned belly.

"Twins. The belly's square."

"Rubbish."

"I'll feel them." She set her hands about the taut skin. "Upper head, yes, an upper head. Too big for one. Moves. Other head down here." She put her hand into the sparse hair at the base of the huge swelling. "One down, one up, like this they lay." She set her balled fists over her forearms, folding them across her bosom.

"I see."

"Bottom one head first, upper one feet first."

Skarra nodded his head.

"Let's see her lips."

Skarra stared at the large knuckled hand which moved its fingers between the legs through the ivory hair he had loved to touch, manipulating the swollen folds.

"Wait," he said, grabbing the arm and lifting it. "You didn't wash."

"My lord?"

"Your hands're unclean."

She held them up. "I washed them this morning."

"Voltoff! Have her scrub her hands, then rinse off with vodka in boiled water." Voltoff came into the room, gesturing to the midwife.

Skarra had avoided looking at the private parts until the midwife had outraged him with her casual professionalism. Only he could see the beauty of it. Of the lips gorged with blood as they colored deeper with life like a flower opening, the fragile layers of petals stretching to release the fruit inside.

"Get me a boiled washcloth," he said to Piippo.

"You scared hell out of that midwife." He handed the cloth to Skarra.

"Only the Hebrews and Egyptians knew anything about medicine. And it was always 'Purify.' " He washed the swollen lips. "That harridan, how dare she touch Geness."

"But you did send for her."

"To look. I'll tell her when to touch."

"Bruce?" The eyes looked out at him from a vast distance.

"Yes, love."

"I have to wet."

"I have linen under you."

"No. The pot."

"All right. Piippo!"

"Hello, Piippo," she said. They raised her out of the bed and held her heaving body over the white chamber jar, each with his hand under a buttock, and letting her legs dangle. She was frail in her nude form and he heard the water tinkle as it leaked in the uncertain spray of a child.

"I didn't know you were here." She looked at Piippo.

"You couldn't keep me away."

"Thank you." She sank back into the bed and was lost to them as she slipped into her world of labor and pain.

It was not going well. Skarra thought he would go mad with grief if he fought, yielding inch by inch before death, and lost. She was in hard labor. The screams came almost as a blessed signal that she lived, felt pain, and yet wanted life.

He and Piippo stayed in the bedroom. He called the midwife a goddam bitch and ordered her to the kitchen when she said Geness would die, but he was afraid to dismiss her because she might know something.

Her hips were too narrow. There was the Caesarian birth of Classic Rome, but it always left the mother to bleed to death. They justified it on one life saved instead of two lost. No. He would not yield her—what was life to any of them without the mother?

It was darkening outside, and he heard sleigh bells circling the cottage. People were in the kitchen. The screams came continuously and he watched the flanks heave, falling in at the pelvic bone.

"Lord Skarra, we've got to start a child."

"Yes," he said. It was the governor's wife, Helen Bofors. "Oh, I didn't know you'd come."

"Lydia is in the kitchen."

He glanced at the door and saw several people.

"Have you had children?"

"Nine. Seven lived."

"Thank God. I need someone to talk to."

"We've got to start a child."

"How do you start a child?"

"Twins usually lie head to feet, curled up facing each other. And it's so crowded one head's usually at the canal. If we can get that head started through, we'll win."

Skarra listened to the words as the woman spoke, her thick hand gesturing downward over the belly. She turned her flushed face to him, exuding a certain earthy confidence.

"Thank God! Anything!"

"We must get her up on a table. The bed's too soft."

"Piippo!"

"And get something in her mouth to bite."

Piippo slipped the flesh of his palm into her mouth, and Skarra saw the blood running over Geness' lips and down the sides of her jaw where she'd bit into the hand.

"Voltoff, hold her head, you people get her feet, and keep her legs open, and I've got her body." They put her on the kitchen table, which was brought in the bedroom to be close to the open fireplace, though the cottage was filled with boiling water and steam. The other men backed away as if by an instinctual fear of a woman in childbirth. Piippo's bloody hand was locked in Geness' jaws, where she seemed to share the pain.

"What have we here?" Skarra had heard the voice before.

"Who are you?" He recognized the doctor from the University.

"Having a little tussle, I see." The physician walked up and stroked his beard while he stared at the nude figure, then at Piippo.

"Goddammit, who sent for you?" Skarra said.

"His Excellency, the Royal Governor, Count Bofors." The physician did not look at Skarra. "Yes, narrow hips—Widow Olson said as much. We lose a lot of women that way. The vicissitudes of womanhood, particularly childbirth."

"You son of a bitch," Skarra said, feeling his eyes flame with blindness. "Out!"

The doctor stared at Skarra a moment, stroked his beard, and laughed a dry chuckle.

"Out!" Skarra seized the man and flung him into the kitchen, where he saw startled people stumble backward.

"My husband meant well," the Lady Bofors said.

"I feel better, anyway," Skarra said.

"We'll have to tie her down."

"Rope, Voltoff, and bring vodka and water! I touched that putrefied man!"

"My lord."

It appalled him to tie her to the table. All day he had fought for her, and still no surcease, no break of hope. He caught sight of his reflection in the winter-dark pane. The circles rimming his eyes were black over his cheekbones and his dry mouth rattled when he heaved for air, and he felt the terror slosh in his belly. Their love had turned into a nightmare.

"Tie down her feet at the edge of the table, with her knees up, and spread her legs so she can push and be open." Lady Bofors had one sinewed foot in her hand, looping a harness over it and down around a table leg.

Skarra tied the other foot, driven in the face of defeat.

"I've torn a sheet to bind her shoulders and armpits." It was Lydia who had bound her upper torso. Piippo had changed hands in Geness' mouth and was bathing her temple with a cloth which was bloodstained from his torn palm.

"It takes more courage to live with a woman than kill a man in war," Lady Bofors said matter-of-factly.

He looked up at her. "I could do with less courage."

"No, you would be unhappy."

"I'm terrified."

"We have a baby to get."

"God willing."

"Oh, she wouldn't be pregnant if there were no purpose."

He nodded his head, encouraged by the plump woman and her bare forearms and deft fingers. Her voice was the purest sound of hope he had heard in years, as though he had lived forever in one day, with the sorrows of a lifetime set aside on the breath of one good woman.

"The head has got to be over the canal."

"What if it's not?"

"Move it until it is."

He shook his head slowly.

"Bruce." He looked at her. "She doesn't have any other chance."

He nodded his head, feeling death again pressed onto his throat. "Voltoff, get me sand, I think you have it."

"My lord"—he heard the words from a hurrying form, shouting in Russian, and was aware of the crash of running boots and men slamming the outside door. The candles wavered.

Voltoff returned with sand, followed by another bearded face with a scoop, and he saw two of his students standing in the shadows with the midwife.

"Put it on the boards." He gestured at his feet. "I've got to grind off my fingernails."

The room was deathly silent as he stripped off his shirt and peeled off his heavy woolen undervest, flinging them at the shadows, and crouched to the pile of sand. "Have the vodka and boiled water ready."

He thrust his fingertips into the sand and began to grind them in a circular abrasion. In moments the sand cut his nails down to the quick and he scrubbed them and held them for Voltoff to pour on the vodka.

"We've got to cut her, too." It was Lady Bofors.

He was numb, even to his bleeding fingertips.

"She's small."

"Voltoff, my knife, and stick the blade into the Scotch."

He was between her legs, and it was as though he were in a dream, but her screams kept coming at him. The sweat ran in wet trickles along his naked flanks and his eyes burned where the salt washed in when he blinked. He seemed to be in a pit of vapors, where images went out of focus on faint light, and beyond appeared the solemn faces of students and girls, one of whom screamed, while an immense beard hung over felt boots and looked reproachful. "My God, a nightmare."

"Cut, Lord Skarra," said Helen Bofors, noticing his dismay.

"Yes." He nodded his head.

Between her legs he saw the lips turning out in swollen folds.

"Not over half a inch!"

The steel blade shrank to a flat point.

"Just start it, and on a slight bias."

"I hear!" His voice seemed to clear his mind.

"I don't want her to tear straight back to her vent."

He lay his forehead on his arm.

"And you've got to get your arm in."

"Please, you're distracting me."

Her flesh was fine, as though her body filtered into one place at which she labored, the tapered legs and small hands he could hear beat the table, and the gossamer hair which lay as a fairy mantle before him. He put the knife point into the bottom corner of the fold of gorged flesh and moved it downward, parting the lips in a trail of fresh blood. "One half inch," he said aloud, watching the blood run into the crevices that seemed now to be splitting her body in two halves.

"Wet your arm," Lady Bofors said.

He dipped his hand into the saucer of vodka then plunged his arm into the tub of water.

"Ease in your hand, Bruce."

He crouched over her lips, seeing her innocent knees bent in front of his face, and pressed his hand into the folds, parting them as he did, and felt the wet tissues slide in warm velvet against his knuckles and grip his wrist.

"Where is it?" he said.

"Go on up slowly, to the canal."

He felt a soft warmth against his knuckles, and his arm was bathed in a flood that poured out of her.

"God," he said.

"Oh, the water—it broke!"

"Lord, I thought I'd hurt her."

"No, feel for the canal."

He eased his hand forward. "I feel it."

"Yes?" The russet eyes fixed themselves onto his face. "Yes?"

"It's small."

"It's got to do," the woman said. "Feel inside."

He cramped his fingers and eased them upward.

"Anything except a round head is wrong."

"I've got something." He felt something like a bit of gristle. "A limb, I think."

"Hand or foot?"

"I don't know."

"Fold it back inside, anyway it wants to go."

He nodded his head, aware of the total silence in the cottage, where the people scarcely seemed to breathe. "It's back," he said, starting to withdraw his arm.

"See if you can ease a round head over the canal."

"I don't know." He shook his head. "I can't tell."

"Feel!" Lady Bofors pressed her hand down the slope of the belly and Geness screamed. "Feel for a head!"

"God, you're hurting her." He flinched.

"Hold your hand in and feel."

He held his hand inside her until he felt the only thing within the womb that had form. Surprisingly, it had been there all the time.

"I felt it!"

"Get it over the canal!" Lady Bofors' face was ashen.

"I've got it. There!"

He was conscious of the woman's muscular arm and bare shoulder as she drove her palm into the indentation in the swollen belly. "Fight, girl!" she shouted.

Skarra heard the muffled groan break overtop the scream as Geness pushed, her spine coming up off the table and her hips rising on her doubled legs, against her bound feet, her whole being strained to turn itself inside out, to fling the new life into their midst, where they watched in desperation. Her body flopped back onto the table.

"Try, love," he said. "Try once more."

They waited until they saw the contraction sweep down her flanks. "Push!" Lady Bofors shouted.

"God," he said. Her legs seemed to tremble and open, and the swollen lips stretched outward, tearing at the cut, and he saw a bud of flesh appear, unfolding a head smeared with blood and wax. He took the protruding life into his hands.

"Suck out its mouth," Lydia said.

"What?" he said.

"Suck out its mouth and nose." She was at his side, her mouth over the crowded features of the small face. He saw the small shoulders alternate as they slipped into view. Lydia spat and he heard the naked child cry.

"Lay it on her belly," Lydia said. "Let her feel it."

He saw Geness' head come up.

"Show it to her," Lydia said.

He raised it.

"Oh," she said, her head falling back. "He's so beautiful."

"One more?" he said, looking to Lady Bofors.

"Yes." She nodded.

Lydia carried the baby to the crib. "I want the wax left on it," Skarra said, when it was being tied.

"The poisons of the womb, my lord," the midwife said.

"There are no poisons in the womb," Skarra said.

"You'll have to take both feet and draw them through the canal, and I'll push."

He breathed so he could hear his own lungs, again fear-struck. His eyes were bloodshot from sweat. "Voltoff, water." He turned again to the organs which hung in disarray before him, ruined by childbirth, where love had disfigured all that he adored.

"For lovers we've paid dearly."

"Find the baby's feet."

His face was cold as steel as he touched the folded sticks of tissue. "Feet, I think," he whispered.

"Ease them downward."

"Oh," he said, feeling the small legs slip out of his fingers and wiggle free like a tadpole skittering into shallow water to escape. "It doesn't want to come out."

"No wonder, but go get him," Lady Bofors said.

He had the feet in his hand and drew downward as they came out, slippery in his fingers.

"Hold tight!"

He had the small mass of red flesh hanging upside-down, strewn to the torn lips by the living cord, and Lydia sucked out the mucus from the nose and throat.

"Praise God!" The Lady Bofors put her forehead down onto the back of her forearm. "You'll have a future." She wobbled her head from side to side. "I didn't know if we'd beat death, but oh, God, we did it."

"A girl!" Piippo said. "A boy and a girl."

Skarra held the child up so Geness could see.

"Put it on her belly," Lydia said.

"Oh, Bruce, two of them."

He walked to the head of the table and kissed her. "Thank you, love." Her lips were blood-caked and her eyes shone in triumph.

"They're beautiful," Lydia said.

He pressed her back onto the table and went to the crib and stared at the two small bundles of linen and a tuft of flesh color. Life was improbable, even implausible, out of the sterile firmament the globe spun through, and yet her womb under her heart was more than all the knowledge on earth would ever encompass.

"One stitch, only," Lady Bofors said, looking over his shoulder where he knelt between the blood-smeared legs.

"One stitch it is," he said, glad Geness was now numb to pain. "Does it end here?"

"No, life never ends."

"Lord, I need a drink."

Voltoff brought skins and made a pallet for him by the fire and Lydia arranged a pallet at the foot of the bed. Subdued laughter filled the kitchen as his friends relieved the tension and bid each other good-bye. The brush with death had made them stout company. Skarra kissed Lady Bofors and watched her go off in her troika to vanish in the snowstorm.

At the fireplace he put the jug to his lips and drank until he felt a huge fire rage inside his chest. Taking it down, he wiped his mouth with the back of his hand and said, "Piippo, a life without friends is death."

Piippo shrugged his shoulders and grinned in the firelight.

"Even lovers, if they're friends the tour's worth it," Skarra said.

7

After the birth of the children Skarra found lonely memories of his own childhood recurring. It was easy to stare at the children as they slept against the breast of his wife, the milk smeared on the small face which had fallen back, and recall the humble fright that began all life. It was as if the children had lived forever, even at two weeks old.

Yet it was also true that his cottage life had isolated him from what he was in his public life as a professor. The professors were absurd as they argued abstractions measured by death and power. "I'm so tired of men who wrangle all day with their mouths," Skarra said.

"Voltoff, have you ever been on a wolf hunt?" He heard Piippo.

"A wolf hunt, my young master?" Voltoff sounded guarded.

"Yes, a wolf hunt. The sport of Russia."

"The sport of Russia?"

"Everybody hunts wolves in Russia."

"I am a peasant, my lord," Voltoff said.

"Bravo! We need peasants to scare the wolves."

"My master, Lord Skarra, will determine if I am to hunt a wolf. . . ."

"Bruce, we need Voltoff!" The voice crashed into the bedroom. "To hunt wolves."

"Who needs to hunt wolves?" Skarra said.

"All of us."

"What on earth would I do with a wolf?"

"They just catch it," Piippo said.

"Then what?" Skarra said.

"We tame the wolf."

"No! There'll be no wolf chained up in the barnyard."

"Of course not. I'll take the wolf to college with me."

They laughed and one of the infants opened a small hand which pressed the breast it was suckling.

"Voltoff?" Skarra asked.

"My old master was insane about coursing wolves, my lord."

"The gallop might be fun," Skarra said, "particularly if the wolf escapes."

"Excellent, one wolf hunt is all we want."

Voltoff returned to the kitchen, talking to himself and to the other troika driver who was having afternoon tea with him.

Word spread about the University and through town that the Scotsman was organizing a wolf hunt, and that he was going Russian, in the company of Lydia, who spent many of her days at the cottage, until Skarra called it "the damned wolf hunt."

"And now the whole town wants to go," Lady Bofors told him.

"Lord, it was just a gallop on the snow."

"And my husband wants to go."

"He's as crazy as a hare."

"Yes." She commenced to laugh, apparently delighted.

On the morning of the wolf hunt the cottage was like a command post at a battlefield with troikas and mounted men and officers crowding down the road from Dorpat. Booted men stomped their legs on the gallery, booming the cottage with noise. Geness had changed her mind and did not want to leave Charles and Fanny. "Never, I won't go!"

"Geney, the whole town is waiting."

"I have changed my mind." She held a child.

"That's not the point."

"What *is* the point?" She clutched the baby to her.

"Out that door the whole town is waiting to go wolf hunting with the Russians because you did not stop it."

She started to cry.

"Oh, God, don't." He saw Lydia and Voltoff and Helen Bofors in the kitchen.

"Oh, Lady Bofors, tell him they're all fools. You said they were."

"I'll stay with the children," Lady Bofors said, embosoming Geness and the baby, and gesturing to the wet nurse to take the child who began to cry.

"You will?" Skarra said.

"Charles, it's little Charles," the wet nurse said.

"Fanny," Geness whispered, placing her cheek to feel the warmth in the skin over the soft skull of the other baby, where it lay in its crib.

"Let's go," Skarra said, as Lady Bofors took the second child away from Geness.

"Dorpat is ready for wolf hunting," Piippo said from the door.

Geness turned to the armoire and took out a cloak lined with marten and wolf skin.

"What's the delay?" It was Bofors striding into their midst in a welter of salutes.

"Geness changed her mind," Helen Bofors said.

"Oh." Bofors tilted his head and looked speculative.

"Geness is going and I'm staying."

"Fortunately, something has been settled."

"Yes." Helen Bofors seemed to ignore her husband, drawing the wet nurse to her as if by divination, and each moved her body to quiet the child she held, oblivious to all turmoil.

"Who have we here?" It was Prince Sergei Merkalov, Lydia's father. The old prince was brittle like parchment, and shrunken in his neck sinews. His elegant furs were powdered so that he seemed a ghost, yet about his eyes were the dash and curiosity of youth. "My friends, our brave wolves will not wait!"

"My lord." Voltoff bowed deeply as the old prince entered.

"They're two months old," Lady Bofors said.

"Nine weeks and four days," Geness said, gathering her cloak at her throat.

"Ah, the young mother, Lydia has talked of nothing else." Prince Merkalov spun on his heel, and swept his arm low over a slender boot.

"I lied about the wolves. I only wanted to enter your abode of purity to meet a lady, and to see for myself God's living edifice from the earth, motherhood." He bowed again before Geness, as if only out of the decadence of the aristocracy was there an awareness of the grace of simple decency.

The trotter under the high bow in the middle flew over the snow, while the two gallopers drove ahead in graceful springs that set their manes flying.

"The troika is like living forever in an instant," Geness said to Skarra. The sleigh swept over the snow on silent wings.

"Ground fog." Skarra could see the random trees in clutches on the misty plain. Behind were the following troikas moving abreast in a frontal passage. Horsemen were everywhere. They saw Lydia pass them at a canter. Compared to the troikas the horsemen seemed to be slovenly on the snow.

He tugged at Voltoff's furs. "Why are the horsemen floundering?"

Voltoff looked, then nodded. "Our horses have no weight to their backs. Nothing in Russia can catch a troika."

Skarra watched Lydia. He saw her horse lunge forward and collect its legs. Lydia rose clear of the saddle, her mouth open to scream, and the horse leaped clear of the ditch and stumbled in a plume as it landed.

"Aha!" Voltoff had seen it.

They watched the officers ride their horses into a mass of scrambling hooves and cursing men who went down out of sight at the same ditch.

"I hate her." Geness pushed her lower body into him.

"Lydia was a friend in need."

"Perhaps that's why I can't forgive her. I needed her, and besides she wants you."

"My lord, the wolves den up not far from here." Skarra saw Voltoff's beard was bright with splinters of ice. "Whoa, whoa, my lovelies, whoa!" The sleigh came to a stop, while the horses pranced.

"My lord, I have your horse with Ralawitz's troika."

"I want no horse," Skarra said.

"My lord, you must ride to the capture."

"What do you mean?"

"The other men will measure you as a horseman."

"To hell with them. I like the sleigh."

"It is not a horse, my lord." The heavy head shook from side to side.

"Bruce, at least gallop in the field," Piippo said. "Let them see you."

"Ride, I'll follow," Geness said.

"You mean even at play I must humor folly?"

"It's a trifle, Bruce," Geness said.

"Aye, but I'd hoped to be a happy observer."

He saw a copse of evergreens wisping through the ground fog. Horsemen were cantering and gesturing. He could see men on foot coming into sight on the verges of the forest leading hounds that ran with their noses close to the snow and he heard them baying into the cold air.

"They're flushing the wolf." Piippo drew up his chestnut gelding.

"Easy, girl," Skarra said, enjoying his dainty-footed mare. The hounds began to chop and he saw their ears flapping ahead of their paws.

"The wolf!" Piippo shouted.

"Where?"

"Still in the forest, but he's coming out!" The horses threw up showers of dry snow.

"Borzois! Look, borzois!" Piippo's face was ecstatic.

Two large dogs, folding their slender quarters beneath their deep chests, burst over the snow in a stream of light brindle feathers.

"Wolfhounds!"

Piippo tore off his hat. "Russian wolfhounds! They're off!"

Skarra heard the thunder of hooves, and felt his mare spring forward in the wave of horses and cheering riders.

"Where's the wolf?" Skarra shouted.

Piippo pointed ahead. The horses tore loose a blaze of white chips while the riders urged on their mounts in desperate competition. Skarra was glad the mare was carrying him out ahead of the field.

"Halloo! The wolf! *Voilà*!"

Prince Merkalov gestured over his booted knee as he passed them.

The old man was easy in his saddle, the thin gray hair gently astrew.

"The wolf!" He heard the shout and saw the wolf in a detached gallop. The hounds were fleeting the distance but the wolf maintained a steady gait.

"There's the wolf!"

"Bruce, how wonderful!" It was Lydia. She veered her horse away from him and stood in her stirrups and waved at the field of horsemen who followed. He could hear her laugh a shrill note of dismay. "Fools!" The hunt was more a military charge.

Skarra could feel the chill on his face as the horses raced along. He kept his eye on the old prince and the handful of Russian keepers at his side. He could hear them shout.

"Beauties of air, run!"

"Jigaro! Jigaro!"

Piippo nodded to his left. They caught sight of their troika. The horses' necks were stretched out like graceful birds as it skimmed the snow, racing into and out of view on the mist. Geness stood in the back seat and waved.

The shouting drew his attention to where riders raced down the edges of a grove of aspen and dark fir trees with snow caught in their branches. The wolf was still ahead of the hounds.

"Watch out!" Piippo shouted. He could see a frozen creek marked by the limbs of willows trailing through the snow. He saw Lydia ride into the creek. "Lydia," he said. She flogged her horse while gathering the reins. They went into the jump in a beat of snow showers. He saw the horse spring forward and clear the mist, over the willows, unfold its legs and sweep ahead, and he heard her laugh.

Skarra found a low spot in the snow field and guided the little mare toward it. He saw Piippo grin and shout and beat his gelding, while he pressed the mare with his knees and gave her her head. "Dainty, little girl, step dainty." She picked her hooves gingerly on the ice and was across.

"Bokaloom!" Piippo's horse was down, the bobbed tail cartwheeling over the head. Piippo went out of sight under a mass of legs and long horsehair. When the horse stopped sliding Skarra saw Piippo sitting in the snow. "Up!" he shouted.

"That damned horse." The chestnut scrambled onto his legs and Piippo vaulted into the saddle.

"It's a great jump if you live," Skarra said.

"My wolf!" Piippo shouted.

The wolf turned to fight showing his teeth, but the wolfhounds fastened their jaws onto either side of his neck behind his ears. The wolf lunged forward over the snow in spasmodic bounds, dragging the wolfhounds, and collapsed.

"Jigaro! Jigaro!" The Russians cheered.

The keepers rolled off their horses and thrust the hardwood stakes between the wolf's jaws, which Skarra could hear snap together. In a moment a keeper had the muzzle over the wolf's head.

"Let's go see him," Piippo said.

Skarra led his mare. Behind them it was chaos all the way to the creek, where he saw more men and horses on the ground than on their legs.

"Why, it looks like a battle." Piippo began to laugh.

Riderless horses were cantering up through the confusion, inept with their empty saddles. Skarra and Piippo watched the last riders of the field pitch headlong into the creek.

"Lord, those men are killing themselves," Piippo said.

"Piippo, the army is not our concern." Skarra walked up to the wolf, whose paws were bound. Prince Merkalov had dismounted and was among the keepers.

"His Grace would deign to view the wolf?" said a Russian huntsman with an unshaven jaw and rotting teeth.

"Magnifique," said the Prince, ignoring the commen men, who stepped back. "Ah, such bravery in an animal." He glanced at the Russian huntsman. "Too bad the human species lacks his breeding." He ran his fingers through the thick fur and felt the sworls running over the wolf's body. "What clean teeth, tut tut."

A keeper handed the reins to the Prince; he mounted his horse and collected the reins and nodded to Skarra and Piippo and Lydia, who had joined them, along with Geness' troika.

"Look at the hairy brute," said an officer, dismounting.

"Let's skin him."

People were talking on all sides of Skarra.

"A big Saxon broke his neck," another officer said.

"Kill him?" someone asked.

"Another turd in the ground, ho, ho."

"Hold that wolf right there." It was the assured voice of the Royal Courier, Captain Gurd Halvorsen, who had appeared in the throng. Halvorsen put his boot onto the wolf's rib cage and drove the wolf into the snow, until they heard cartilage yielding in small tearing crunches as the bones broke.

"What're you doing?!" Piippo threw aside the officer while the wolf stared calmly at his murderer through his amber eyes.

"Killing the wolf."

"He's my wolf!" Piippo's voice broke into a falsetto.

Halvorsen laughed with some of the others at the immature sound. "You press down over the heart until it stops beating. No mess, and one superb wolf skin." He settled his weight again.

"It's the boy's wolf," Skarra said. The other officers stepped away from the prostrate body of the animal.

"His Grace bestowed the brave wolf," said a Russian huntsman, honoring the Slavic tradition that the wildlife belonged to the nobility and the Tsar.

"Where's Prince Merkalov?" Piippo said.

"Him?" Halvorsen said. "Why, he's no prince." He put his boot onto the wolf again.

"In Russia the wolf belongs to the nobleman," said the huntsman, looking up to the Prince. Skarra saw a perplexed look of public humiliation sweep the eyes of the Prince.

"I don't want that damned wolf," Skarra said, "but I don't want him dead either. Now take your foot off the wolf."

Halvorsen faced him. His cuirass was swathed in mink and in his cavalry jackboots he was splendid in his martial power.

"Scotsman, if I don't choose to lift it?" The coarse nose bristled with hair.

Skarra saw the contempt, and he raised his long leg and set it against the steel breastplate and shoved. Halvorsen went over backward into the snow, where he lay and worked his arms and legs like an armored beetle turned onto its back. The hush of consternation broke into waves of guffawing.

Halvorsen cursed for his sword until Count Bofors rode into their midst and ordered him to his horse. "Someday, Scotsman, someday," he said.

"If I want to know a man, I take him hunting," said the old prince to Bofors while gathering his reins. "He'll lie about the number he kills, and his wish to kill is open."

8

When Skarra walked home through the snow from the University in the twilight sun, he found his mind racing ahead to Geness and the children. Voltoff would be waiting for him in the woodshed with the cross-cut saw held on end. First he would go in to change his clothes and have tea with Geness.

"Was it a pleasant day?" Her fingers were at the samovar, from which a gust of steam spluttered amid a wash of water.

"Oh, dull."

"Dodderhoff and Pickereill?"

"Witty with pointless knowledge." He hobbled in a loose gaiter.

"I missed you." She handed him the glass.

"And the certain thought I had a home got me through the day." He sat on the bed.

"I'm so proud of you that you can talk pretense with men and still be jolly at home."

He set the glass down on the hearth and picked her up. "Not many men on this globe can hold their soul in their hands, and lift her down to kiss."

"The children brought it to life."

"Aye, that is why I'm happy to sip tea in a cottage and split wood with old Voltoff, and stay blind to folly."

She shrank her length into his form. "Bruce, oh Bruce, I missed you."

"Yes, I know. At night I reach for you in bed to feel, not from lust."

He could feel a crisp cheer come into his legs as soon as he stepped out onto the snow of the stable yard. He bent and took the handle of the cross-cut saw into his hands, without a word to the old man, and heaved backward on the saw and felt the satisfaction tremble in his arms and body as the teeth rushed toward him in a blaze of flying chips. "Ahaa," he said. Voltoff nodded and rolled his massive shoulders away from him, exhaling in a whistle that made a steam cloud. He settled his legs in a wide stance and exchanged the blade through the log.

"She drops, master." The log dropped in a run of dust and white flakes.

They brought the log into position for sawing again, and Skarra spat into the palms of his hands.

"Master loves to work," Voltoff said, huddling his mass against the saw.

"Work to fertilize the mind."

They sawed up five logs. Voltoff had the pace, and he was delighted to see the pile grow. There was a special pleasure in picking up the newly sawn log end and heaving it to the pile of wood.

"My maul and wedges."

He set the block of wood on end and balanced the wedge atop it. Voltoff looked uncertainly at him. "Go to the cottage. I can manage."

Voltoff picked up his hat of wolf fur and walked into the cold twilight.

"Whooof!" Skarra shouted as he leaned his whole body forward to the block and felt the sledge pull backward. The wedge came down across his vision in a blur and he saw the wood explode. One part went up, and another flew into the stable yard.

He saw Polonitz race after the stake and pick it up and come toward him.

"Hello, Polonitz!"

"I saw it fly down from the sky."

"That's good," Skarra said.

"I knew if I waited, something good would come." The blue eyes fairly burst with joy.

"If you'll hope, you'll win." Skarra reached over and shook the boy by his shoulder.

He spun the double bits of the axe as he felt the power grip his arms when the wood rent again. "Such a delight to chop wood," he said, more to himself than to the boy.

"I saw it come down from my wheel in the sky."

"Where do you keep the wheel?"

"Oh, it's right up there." He pointed into the darkening twilight. "Can you see it now?"

Polonitz turned and stared into the sky. "Oh, yes, the dark does help."

Skarra leaned the axe handle against his hip.

"When you're up on the big wheel you can see all the way to Poland and even to Stockholm, out across the waters. And when I'm up on my big wheel I can see the trees along the skin of the earth, just like brown hair and green moss, only it's the forest. . . ."

Skarra was entranced with the flood of imagery from the boy's mind. There was a purity after the duplicity of the backbiting university professors that made the retarded boy an absolute pleasure. "I'd love to climb on that big wheel some day."

"I'll let you know."

"Good."

"And when I'm on the wheel I can see Voltoff and the horses pull it round and round in circles in the sky, but they don't make a sound, like trotting in the new snow." He threw back his head and laughed.

He had stooped and split again when he heard a voice behind. "You are a very kind man." It was Geness.

"You heard us?" He was glad to hear her voice.

"Yes."

"For some mad reason I like to talk to him."

"Innocence."

"Am I that lost?"

"Not if you have your innocence."

"Two creatures on the verges of nowhere." He took her hand.

"We can live forever if we're innocent," she said.

"I would like to live forever."

He heard her breath catch in her throat when she realized he had seen into her heart. "Ah, Geney, only a fool wants more than simple love."

"The universe, and it's ours."

"My eyes and ears become my soul's limbs to love when I cannot."

"Hopeless, we are."

That winter Skarra's only annoyance was the wet nurse, a peasant woman named Penelope. She was an affable, rawboned woman who nursed the children at huge breasts which seemed to be everywhere when she had one swinging out with a child tuggling in moist pleasure. When she was not eating herself, she was feeding a child.

Penelope had never lived with people other than crude peasants, men who beat their women, and at first she was cowed by the grace and endless quiet of their lives at the cottage. When she grew to be at ease in Skarra's presence, she smiled endlessly at him.

"It's that bland stupor of incredulity," he said to Geness.

"She is in love with you," Geness said.

"Bosh."

"Why wouldn't she be?" Geness stroked the weight of her hair.

"And you don't mind?"

"Fault her as a woman? May as well fault myself."

When he dressed in the morning Penelope was always moving through the room with a child. She seemed to take delight in staring at his chest and hairy legs and arms. The scars from his wounds evoked the same words. "It's a merciful God that protects thee."

"Privacy should follow godliness, a man could hope," he said.

Skarra often worked at his desk, which was set across the broad window of their bedroom, and at night the desk was lit by a heavy Italian candelabra. As he studied he did not find the solace and human insight he had once found in the classics of Greece and Rome.

Often, as he was reading, he might see the hesitant movement of a small hand ahead of a crawling body on the floor. The small face was a marvel of balanced proportions and without the coarse lines of adulthood. As the baby crawled across the Persian rugs and wolf skins Skarra would pause, unable to tell if it were Fanny or Charles. They always looked the same to him, unless they were side by side, and he could never understand why women found his confusion unbelievable.

"But you are their father," they would say.

"Aye, yet I canna' tell one life apart."

The baby would raise its head, "turtling," as he called it, with the small hand in mid-air.

"Little one, here." He would lean forward at the waist.

Skarra would thrill in amazement that anything so small could fix and brighten its eyes on him, and surge in determination.

"Child, oh little one!"

He jumped up and stepped to the baby and lifted it, still crawling in the air as he held it. He hugged the baby to his chest and felt the small hands move about his neck and smelled the sweet odor of life that every baby seemed to have.

"Are you pleased, Bruce?" Geness asked.

"Aye, not so much with life since I rode my pony in the Highlands behind Skarra."

"You waited a long time."

"A lifetime."

She put her hands into his hair behind his ears.

"My father was a religious and political faddist, and he made Skarra a curse with his closed mind."

"And my father died of an open mind," she said quietly.

"I know." He was gripped in sorrow as he held the child either of those men would have given a lifetime to hold, and he felt like crying for his father.

"My father said only God could heal the nightmare between us and our parents." She slipped her arms around him and the child.

The baby's head wobbled as he sought to fix his eyes onto his parents. "Charles," Geness said.

"He adores us."

"Yes, we adore him."

"The children will take away our hate."

"Each life is a redemption, I must say."

"Oh, Bruce, are all Scotsmen like you?"

"No."

"I should hope not."

"I'm glad for my children. Only a fool would improve perfection."

She nestled into his chest. "The future always terrifies me."

"If we love them and not put our thoughts into their minds, they'll do well enough in their time, for they are us, if we love one another."

He walked to the bed with the child. "Penelope, bring in the other!" Geness climbed into the bed, holding her skirts up over her knees, and settled on the instep beneath her folded leg.

"Look, watch her crawl," she said.

They could hear the baby's fragile breath in its throat. "Fanny, dear little girl!"

The baby lost its coordination in the excitement of too many thoughts, and fell forward, onto its face.

"Brave girl!" Skarra shouted.

"Oh, you frightened her." It was Penelope, from the kitchen door. Fanny was crying in a nest of bedclothes.

"They take out the sorrow, don't they?"

"Oh, Geney, I adore you." He laughed easily and touched her.

9

Spring came with the gallantry of April, blowsing warmth against the earth, and the ground gave up the smell of musk and dormant life. They stood on the gallery and looked onto the fields showing blotches of earth in the rotting snow.

"We'll have a wonderful garden."

"Aye, we got settled a bit late last year," he said.

"And flowers."

"Lord, we'll have sunflowers and hollyhocks and marigolds, and anything you could want."

"Lydia called our children flowers." Her voice was pensive.

"Aye."

"And she breathed into their mouths, first."

"Aye, the breath of life she called it," he said.

"I'm grateful, yet I cannot help but hate her."

"Geney, this is springtime."

"I gave you your life back after I took it out of you, willing to die myself to do it."

"Let's get on with spring planting." She buried her face into his neck as he carried her to the fire and settled her.

For days they heard the light trickle of water slip away under the snow, until the creeks and rivulets rose and the wet oozed out of the forest. "The spring runoff," Voltoff called it. They were trapped at the cottage, for it strained the horses' legs to step in the mud which balled on the frog of the hoof.

"They are like caged lions, my lord," Voltoff said.

"Gallop them in the hallway of the stable."

"The hallway won't hold them."

"Gallop them one at a time."

"They pine for each other, my lord," Voltoff said, pressing Skarra.

"What does that mean?" he said, waiting to see which way the conversation would go.

"They like to run together."

"Obviously, but it is not possible in this mud."

"They will not be happy, especially Barbarossa—oh, such a stallion he is."

"It won't hurt him any."

"He'll go off his feed."

"He'll live."

"His disposition, my lord."

"To hell with his disposition."

Skarra realized Voltoff had pushed him, to reassure himself in his dependence on his master, in the compulsion to allay the fears of old age.

"If he gives you any trouble, I'll come out and thump hell out of him."

"Oh, my lord, he's a gentle stallion." Voltoff shook his head, making a pale shadow on the bark-lined wall of the stable quarters.

"Fact is, he can disport himself in the hallway before all his mares."

The old Russian's head drew down into his coat as he began to laugh without sound, too polite to show mirth, and Skarra walked back to the cottage, pleased with the company of the old man of whom he had grown so fond.

They had got the oxen into the rail-fenced garden as well as the Finnish driver, who carried a goad which quivered when he talked.

"They seem weak in their loins," Voltoff said, while they watched the span of oxen hump their backs when they sought to stand in the mud.

"The man is mad," said the Finn, who walked briskly, yet the balls of mud on his boots made him stagger as if he were about to fall onto his face.

"Dainty-footed, aren't they?" Voltoff said, tilting his head to look at the endless lifting of cloven hooves.

"Wait 'til you see them dig in, then call 'em dainty-footed." The Finn winked at a cohort who stood to the front of the span. They had weathered faces, and their sparse beards gave the look of a childhood masquerade.

"I think we've hired reindeer," Voltoff said.

"It was the cold winter, his brain is still frozen," the Finnish driver said.

Skarra listened to the two old men. Neither would look at the other as they paced about, trading insults. They were obviously having a very good time as old friends.

The oxen watched the men, following them with enormous eyes as gentle as their lack of sex and their acceptance of a life of travail. Never before had Skarra seen such hulk of curried flesh which rippled in tones of muscle.

"High-oh!"

He heard the goad crack as the Finns cried out.

"Slosh oop!" He turned to see the near ox fall, in a wide fan of dark water and liquid mud. The men were drenched. There was a convulsion in the bog, and he saw the far ox dragged head down into the hole out of which the fallen ox thrashed. Then he saw the buff hindquarters of the far ox rise vertically into sight, the massive bull's haunches without testicles seeking to counterbalance the yoke his fellow pulled him into the mud with.

"Good God!" Skarra said. He saw the upside-down ox crash down atop his span-mate, who continued to thrash.

"Moooaaaooo!" he heard one of them low in the most disconcerting manner, almost as though the oxen themselves were casual bystanders at their own chaos. In the mud the two huge beasts, down off their short legs and their necks yoked, had an insane quality.

"Moooaaaooo."

"I can't believe it," Skarra said.

"By my saint's day, they can't even stand up."

The Finns broke into the great oaths of the lumberjacks of the north country. The old man threw down his goad.

"What are you doing?" Skarra said.

"They are my life."

"Magnificent in their effort," Voltoff said.

"How do you get them out?" Skarra said.

"Easy, the goad." The Finnish driver hopped in squooshy sounds.

"Does it work?" Skarra said.

"Oh, yes, watch them leap to!" He cracked the goad. The oxen did not so much as bat an eye. Obviously they had never been goaded nor beaten.

"I don't think they're afraid of you," Skarra said.

"Oh, they are very well behaved, they are," the Finnish driver said.

"Lot of damn foolishness," Skarra said. "Putting these beasts into a garden with water standing in the ditches."

"I had hoped we might tone them up," said the Finnish driver uncertainly.

"Tone them up! For what, pray God?"

"For spring ploughing, my lord," said the Finn.

Skarra walked to the edge of the garden, losing a boot in the mud.

"It was a great show," Geness said, coming out of the cottage.

"You liked it."

"A diving cow, Penelope called it."

"He's a friend of Voltoff's."

"They seem placid."

"They are." He shook his head wryly. "More aurochs than cattle."

He pulled off his other boot and dragged off his leather breeches. "I can't walk with clothes on."

"You look like you're wearing mud trousers."

"Give me that goad!" he said, as he turned back to the men and advanced on the oxen and watched the four eyes, which showed some white of apprehension.

"Shout when I beat them!"

"Oh yes, my lord," said the Finnish driver.

Skarra took one horn in his hand and bellowed, "Up! Up, you lazy bastards, up!" He brought the goad down, "wheeaack," lacing the muddy backs with thatching.

"High-oh, high-ee, high-oh!"

"High-ee!"

"Sloosh oop!" It was as if the mud had ruptured into a new life of awkward convulsions. He tried to jump away but his bare legs were caught in suction, and the wall of wet earth and hair came down on him.

"The master . . . !"

"My God, oh, my God!"

He heard the men and Geness screaming. His head was caught against the muddy hair, and he could not turn it to look. He was pinned.

"Voltoff?"

"Oh, my lord." The voice trembled.

"Leave them yoked. One holds the other."

"Geness?"

"Yes, Bruce?" He could not see but felt her hair against his face.

"Run to the University and get the students."

He heard her turn away.

"Run, love."

"I'll cut their throats if they move." It was the Finn.

"No need in that."

"I love my beauties, but you love the strumpet," the old Finn said. "They're not even bulls, alas."

Skarra closed his eyes, feeling his legs grow numb under the oxen, and grateful the mud yielded. He could have cried in the terror that he would leave the children orphans to be exploited.

"Fools, oxen in this weather!" He heard Lydia.

"Go get the students," he said.

"These peasants! They are fools!" She knelt at his shoulders.

"Get the students."

"My Arabian can run in this mud." She ran in wet strides, with her cries going off toward town.

It seemed like hours after he heard the tolling of the Kremlin bell that he heard bright voices.

"There he is!"

In moments the students were all around the oxen.

"Piippo?"

"Yes?" The face was against his eye.

"You have one try, or they will kill me thrashing about. Am I clear?"

"Absolutely."

"Do it, then."

The students were stirring on all sides of him, big hands had his biceps. "Get the bastards by the tails and twist—No! Not now! When I tell you!" Piippo was in authority.

"By God's grace," Voltoff said, moving among the students. "I never saw such oxen."

"Whack!"

"High—oh!"

"Twist, men, twist!"

The students broke into shouts and twisted the oxen tails.

"Moooaaaooo!" He felt himself chucked suddenly from a mound of earth, the suction rippling his wet legs, and he saw the oxen running in awkward strides and butting impotently, while the students laughed.

"Oh, Bruce!" Geness lay her head atop his chest.

He ran his fingers along her back. "I should have known those two neutered monsters could kill a man."

"It was awful."

"Weren't the students magnificent?" Lydia knelt at his other side and held his other hand.

"Such brave young men," Geness said.

"Good for something," Skarra said, wiping his mouth.

"Oh, here." Lydia reached to help.

"Lydia, you are always here." Geness' voice was chilled, causing Lydia to shrink.

"Perhaps I helped save his life."

"No, I can save his life, and I don't need any help."

"I'm sorry, I intruded."

"Yes, you did."

"I won't again."

"You may come, but only if I am here."

"Of course." Lydia sloshed through the garden.

"Let her come, Geney, to share our family," Skarra said.

"I hate her." Geness trembled.

Eventually the mud hardened into earth rich to crumble under the plough, and the clear days of spring came. The evergreen forests lost their winter darkness, and Skarra could strike the garden furrows with the blade of the hoe and spray earth over his feet.

"Let me till, and you seed," he said.

"The master's eye makes the beast grow fat," Skarra said.

"When I follow you, I have a warm excited feeling inside my stomach," Geness said. A strand of hair stuck on the sweat of her forehead, and her dress was caught up, leaving the white legs as dirt-streaked as his.

"And I crave you when I see you so true," he said.

Voltoff often came to join them, carrying a shovel to set the irrigation ditches, always in his boots and baggy trousers.

Skarra noticed Voltoff looking up when he heard the quick hoofbeat of Lydia's Arabian. "She runs from sorrow, my lord."

Skarra waited while Lydia walked across the garden, stripping her gloves and lifting her veil. "Adam and Eve in paradise."

"Brave words." Skarra leaned on his hoe.

"My father says the truth must be laughed at 'else we would cry."

"Aye, what's laughter without sorrow?"

"But I'm not the serpent." She smiled uncertainly at Geness, who was getting up from her knees.

"Ah, dear Lydia, I have loved and hated you—but . . ." Geness said, wiping streaks of mud from her arm.

"Love can never be harmed," Lydia said.

"Work will cure you, Lydia. Doff your finery and onto your knees," Skarra said.

"May I, Geney?"

"Only if you know he's mine."

"I swear it."

"You lie."

"No, your children. I would never try."

"Damn you, Lydia." Her lips quivered in a light froth.

"Envy, yes, but treachery never."

"Good!" Skarra walked between them. "If we are to live as men and women we must accept the right of the weakness of us to live as well as the strength. We cannot keep company as people, otherwise."

"Oh, Bruce, how else can we put it?" Lydia said.

"Oh, come any time and as often as you like," Geness said. "How could any three people ever have more exposed their sorrows and their secrets, and still face each other truly."

Lydia took her hands into hers. "Thank you for being who you are."

"Oh, Lord, I may hate you, but I owe you my life."

Skarra leaned on his hoe and watched them dissolve into a bundle of common hair and clothing as they embraced.

10

That second year, in 1631, word came from Scotland that his father had died, and that now he had inherited the title and estate and was Lord Skarra of Skarra. The news haunted Skarra, for it would mean the loss of his cottage life and the assumption of power as a Scottish chief at a time when England, Ireland, and Scotland seethed with discord. In the cottage with Geney he could do anything with his hands, from prime a musket to bathe a child. He flung himself into his cottage days, as though each were his last. "It's time for haying," he said to Voltoff.

"The scythes will be here at sunup," Voltoff said.

"How many?"

"Twenty, men and women."

"Some are women?"

"They'll outlast the men, they will, my lord. No man can endure like a woman, not in the heat and flies and summer sun."

"I suppose," Skarra said.

Before dawn he heard the muffled voices and bare feet shifting on the kitchen floor.

"My lord," Penelope said, appearing with a glass of tea.

"Thank you." He took it without seeing her and looked for the white chamber pot. Drinking the tea he felt the heat swirl into his chest and lungs and strength flood his loins and belly. "Thank you," he said, handing the glass to the woman, "and empty the pot before the children knock it over."

"Yes, my lord."

He dragged his rough canvas breeches onto his legs and pulled on a loose work shirt and ate a bowl of porridge. Voltoff came to him and said, "The peasants are in the meadow."

He nodded and walked along the cottage gallery.

"Will the master mow?"

"Yes."

"I have your scythe, my lord."

"Good."

"It is very sharp. The peasants have never seen a nobleman in the hay field."

He walked ahead of Voltoff, his boots soft from the dew. The sun diffused yellow light from the east, then heated the night fog which lay in a tissue web through the bottom lands and hung in the evergreen copses.

The peasants had the smooth faces of the Livonian peoples, and some were bearded in the Russian manner. They watched him while listening to Voltoff. "We'll rest at midmorning, and when I signal."

Skarra set the pace with his scythe, and moved deliberately across the meadow in swathes of wet grass, followed by the peasants, who mowed in unison to him. At the midmorning rest Skarra sat in the edge of the woods a little apart from them. He could hear their laughter and jolly talk.

"Five months along she is, and she takes to the meadow," a man said.

"A girl—a boy would drain her," said a woman.

"He'll be a boy," said a girl's voice, obviously the expectant mother's.

"The first-born's always got to be a boy, then they don't care," said another man.

Skarra listened to the peasants talk. It was the mystery of life they seemed drawn to.

"To please his father."

"Who is the father?" There was scattered laughter.

"I knew she was too pretty to stay a virgin," said a man.

"And when you're through with us, we're neither pretty nor virgin," said a woman.

When he took to the meadow again, Skarra felt the sun pinned like a weight across his shoulders. He sweated along his temples and his eyes smarted when he looked back at the windrows of hay in lines where they had crossed the meadow. At the woods he noticed that someone had dropped back from the line of mowers, and saw it was the pregnant girl. "Voltoff, who's the girl?"

"Sanya, my lord." Voltoff wiped his eyebrow with his thumb.

"Send for her."

"Come here, Sanya."

A woman took the scythe handle from her and she walked quickly to them. She had soft features and a rich flush on her lips.

"Are you expecting a child?"

She looked quizzically at Skarra, then back to her people.

"She is, my lord," said a woman.

"Tell her to rest in the shade."

"Do as his lordship says," said the peasant woman.

"Keep the pregnant women out of the field," Skarra said to Voltoff.

"My lord."

"I know it's hard to ascertain, but try."

"I've told them no pregnant women, but the men will bring them anyway."

"I don't want it."

"It's the silver, my lord."

Skarra did not answer. It annoyed him to see them without their innocence.

At noon he walked to the cottage, taking off his shirt and wiping his torso. He had perspired until his body had lost its rank scent.

"Dadda! *Voilà, Papa*!" a small voice called in piping tones. It was Charles, the delicate face alive in joy and the small body seeming to flutter over the grounds as he ran forward.

"Charles!" He lifted the little body high over head. "Where's Fanfan?" He heard an even finer treble along the gallery. "Dadda, Dadda!"

"Oh, Bruce," said Geness, coming out the door, "you didn't bathe, nor did you chew a willow twig."

"Too busy." He picked up both children.

"I'll have to rise at dawn if you won't wash your face and clean your teeth."

"Yes, my lady."

"You shame me." She kissed him.

After lunch he mowed until midafternoon, when he came back to the stable to watch the hay being stowed.

"Too dry, for we cut it late." Voltoff broke a handful of new-mown hay.

"We'll shock what's to be cured and scatter the other in the loft."

He heard the two-wheeled carts squeaking in the still summer light, and he watched the vaulting pile of hay come into sight around a curve in the lane. Each cart had a sedate motion as it brushed the shaded corridor of trees.

In the fall Skarra liked to take the children up astride the "English ambler" with him and go off in the afternoon to fish at the forest lakes. The children loved the tick-tack beat of the ride, as well as scampering in the evergreen needles and examining the occasional fish he caught. The salt air off the Baltic and the tang of the hemlocks eased his mind to think of his next obligation.

He found Lydia waiting to join them at his favorite spot. She had the hamper spread and was half smiling as he handed down the children.

"I must say you're persistent."

"I just happened by." She led the children to the handsome white tablecloth spread on the grass.

"I'd say men are the better liars by sex," Skarra said, tying the horse.

"Don't you get tired of lecturing?"

He enjoyed the picnic and basked in the last days of warm sun. That he caught no fish made the day more jolly. Lydia watched the children while he stretched out and dozed.

"Bruce, could I be your mistress?"

"No," he said, hearing the warmth in her voice.

"Are you that pure?"

"No, I'm not pure."

"Why, then? Other men have found me attractive."

"You are most beautiful, far more than one share."

"Then why?"

"Because when I love my wife I love all women. If I seduce Geney, I seduce you and every other woman who lives, and if a woman seduces a man, she seduces all men."

"Oh, Bruce, how can a woman argue with that?"

"It was a lovely picnic." He laughed contentedly.

When the snow came Skarra realized he had delayed until the Baltic was frozen, and they would have to remain in the cottage until spring. Gustavus Adolphus had launched his invasion of Germany, cutting a swath of turmoil that blocked any thought of overland travel to Scotland through Europe by sleigh.

"I suppose I just could not bring myself to leave the cottage," he said to Geney.

Gustavus, the Snow Lion, had pitted himself against Emperor Ferdinand of Austria. Ferdinand could not fight, but would oppose the thirteen thousand Swedes with Johann Tzerclaes, Count of Tilly, an old man of seventy; the Count zu Pappenheim, a dashing soldier; and in desperation, there was the most hated man in Vienna, Albrecht von Wallenstein, Duke of Friedland, who was considered invincible on the battlefield, a brilliant farmer, physician, lover of astrology, and patron of Christianity, and contemptuous of all men, including the Emperor. All Europe waited for the outcome of the grand adventure of Gustavus Adolphus and Wallenstein, one a king and the other a viceroy, who would match their armies and decide the fate of Europe in a day.

"I think we should go out into society," Geness said, "so I'll know what to do at Skarra."

"Aye, we can pass the winter that way."

Even though Dorpat was a frontier town, it was riddled by concentric and tangential circles of society groupings. The women at the top had wealthy husbands who held powerful positions of government, and the circles often fell into competition with each other, each forming a coterie of followers to support itself.

"All it takes is iron cheek," Skarra said, "and never ask a personal view nor be positive." He had a man's traditional opinion of society.

"Do you really think I can do it?" She touched her breast.

"You should know those old bats who rule Edinburgh."

First was the Royal Governor's Mansion in the Kremlin, then the routs held for all commoners of wealth at the Inn. Skarra enjoyed society more than he had realized he could. In the company of other women Geness was particularly beautiful in an ethereal way, almost too fine for gross life. She would walk ahead of him, causing people to stare at the heavy weight of her hair balanced against her elegant mouth and lips, on her slender neck, with her eyes shining in certain dignity.

One night Skarra had helped Geness from the sleigh and they had entered a large country home that rested on the snow of the garden as a contented pod of golden lights. He followed cheerfully behind Geney, a tidbit in one hand and wine in the other, surrounded by the faces of society where the scenes and costumes varied while the men and women all spoke the same words. Skarra was amazed at Lady Biba's lips, which were raised in a changeless grimace, and noticed the colonel whose lean shanks were exposed by his floppy stockings, and he saw the surgeon who had a florid smile settle his belly against his waistcoat.

"Lord Bruce," said Lydia's father, who was dressed in a Tsarist caftan which swept the floor.

Skarra shook the old man's hand and watched Geney, who was chatting amiably with a couple who had large, sweet eyes.

"Winter affords us a wonderful season," Geness said, touching her fan to the back of her wrist, and for an instant seeing the image of her childhood crib flash through her mind. She heard her father walking in the snow toward their snug house at Bofors. She ran to greet him and he swung her off her feet and embosomed her to his chest, and she was thrilled to smell her father—the smell had never gone.

"You must come call on us," Geness said to the couple, and her mind raced away to her childhood nursery. She could hear the deep, sure voice of her father answering her mother, and the admiring love which warmed their words. She saw the unsteady shadows from the fireplace come through the darkened nursery from her parents' room. She heard Skarra's voice behind her. She turned suddenly and whispered, "Bruce, I love you."

He followed her, contentedly nibbling a sugared plum, while she felt herself expand to the edge of self-assurance and social poise. Geness realized she did not truly like the soirees, but she felt a great sense of achievement in attending them that erased the degradation she had had to endure, and she knew her love with Bruce and their children had repaid her parents for the life and love they had given her as a child.

"The town seems so jolly at night with the windowpanes shining on the snow," Geness said to a young officer whose eyes glittered. She felt a warmth under her throat when she thought of her mother, and how proud her mother would have been to see her move through society as its equal. Bruce had done it for her. The more she loved him, the more she loved her children and her parents' memory. The evening was a triumph.

"Play, princess!" The fogged voice rolled across them from the harpsichord by the corner window where Lydia played in the midst of a group of laughing young men. Skarra saw Lydia swoop her bare shoulders out of reach of one of the officers, and come toward them.

"Bruce, let's go," Geness said.

"Already? Fine." He saw a handsome profile wreathed in eyebrows and sideburns. "Oh, that bastard." It was Halvorsen. "Iron nerve and cheek, love." He touched her elbow.

"Bare flesh everywhere and they think they're hiding," Halvorsen said.

"Lady Geness of Skarra," Lydia said, dipping before Halvorsen.

"More untapped women in this place." Halvorsen's glance moved onto Geness' long neck and nubile breasts. He looked to Skarra, "You, she married you?"

"Lord and Lady Skarra," Lydia said.

"Say, I know you."

Skarra saw Geness' throat swallow but her eyes were assured, though he saw all color had drained from her face.

"Yes, how was it? The daughter of the parson, oh, children of Israel, weep for your lost virtue."

"You address Lady Geness of Skarra." Lydia's voice was a croaking sound.

"Halvorsen, you're showing your breeding," Skarra said.

"Carl, come here, Carl!" The officer guestured to a friend.

"What's up, old man?"

"An old friend."

"Ah, a blond nymph."

"More, old man, more. She shudders like a child when you stick it in."

"Tonight?"

"Alas, she married a nobleman." They laughed together.

Skarra felt the rage blind him and make him clumsy.

"Shall we eat?" Lydia turned Geness' arm and they walked together toward a table of cold meats and savories.

"I should not have come to the ball," Geness said.

"A squalid man," Lydia said.

"God, I could kill," Skarra said. He drained his glass of vodka.

"Regardless, I think we should eat," Lydia said, leading them to a small table with chairs. Skarra gnawed the leg of a goose and raged in silence with the raw whiskey burning throughout his chest.

"Professor, we were up at the University this morning."

Skarra got to his feet. Halvorsen had come up with another officer. His face was grave. "Recruiting for the King."

"None of my students will fight in your damned war." Skarra felt better.

"No. We were flimmed by the dons."

"Good for the dons," Skarra said.

"Sweden needs soldiers."

"Captain, you are dismissed." Skarra dropped his plate on the floor in front of Halvorsen, instinctively reverting to his Highland tradition of warriors. "Dismissed, soldier!"

The two officers glowered and their jaws were hard-muscled. They backed away.

Skarra was steering Geness and Lydia through the cloakroom,

where they were saying good-byes to the hostess. In the hall he could hear loud voices as the soiree broke up.

"We're joining the King in Saxony. Going overland by Russian sleigh."

"Capital adventure." It was old Prince Sergei Merkalov.

"We have the finest horses in all Russia!"

"Wrong, young bloods," said a portly businessman. "I sold the finest horses in Russia to Lady Skarra."

"Out the door," Skarra said ushering them forward.

"The King's service commands the finest horses." Halvorsen's voice was clear.

"I didn't sell you the fastest horses in Russia. I said the Baltic." He laughed.

"Damn you!"

The hall was swept in a quick silence at the eruption of anger.

"Lord Skarra, I want your horses!"

"Over my dead body." Skarra faced him.

"In the name of the King."

"The King's a fool—no one nation can conquer Europe."

The people near them recoiled as if touched by a sober ray of light.

"I demand those horses."

"Touch them if you dare."

The burly face of hair and bone confronted him. Skarra felt his heart thump with his lust to kill and was satisfied Halvorsen shared the murderous wish.

"I'll race him for the horses," Geness said, stepping in front of Skarra. "Your troika against mine, and in public." Geness' face iced with contempt. "If you want my horses, take them fair." She tugged her gloves. "Come, Bruce, he's filth."

"Hurrah, a horse race! Troikas!"

"Capital solution!"

Skarra followed Geness and Lydia under the flare held by the servant.

"Forgive me?" Geness said.

"What's done is done."
"If you'd killed him they'd kill you."
"God, it's madness."

II

Skarra woke early the morning of the race with a deep sense of foreboding. He lay abed and watched the winter night fade in the east. The fire shadows played across the room from the hearth.

"Bruce, we could still give him the horses." Geness spoke.

"I don't know whether he'd accept them."

"If I could crawl as a woman, I know you can't as a man."

"I can swallow my pride to save my life," Skarra said. "You sure it's not your pride?"

"Pride? After what I had to do?"

"Love, a woman can't compete with a man in a man's world."

"I'm not. He slept with me and he mocked me for it, and now I'm a mother."

"Oh, God, a woman is above a man as long as she remains a woman, no matter what she does."

"No, I do not want my children to crawl."

"Oh, it's all madness—insanity."

"Please, let me drive with Voltoff."

"I still think it's pride."

"No, every woman is seduced the same way, and we all must feel the same. He mocked my privacy in public."

"But you're measuring your life by his, and he's nothing."

"And if I don't race him, he makes you crawl. . . ."

"Hell, I'll kill him."

"No, he might kill you. Besides, I was aggrieved."

"Very well, but Voltoff drives."

"I could see death in his eyes." She started to cry. "We have to fight."

The race was to be run before the town on the fresh snow which lay over the ice of the river. Voltoff was to lose rather than race dangerously, and he had been in communication with the other driver, Ralawitz. "My lord, in our arms rests peace," Voltoff said. They drove slowly down the lane from the cottage and past the homes nestled in snow. When the troika came over the bluff and looked down on the frozen river, Voltoff reined in, saying, "Look, my lord."

They could see swarms of people along the river bluffs and moving amid fires built of the driftwood out on the ice. Troikas galloped here and there, and they could see the skaters leaning forward as they flung their legs. They saw the tent set up at the start and finish line flying the Royal Governor's standard.

Skarra sank into the furs and wanted to be sick except he had had no breakfast. Piippo stood in the sleigh, and sat down. "The whole countryside's here, Bruce."

"I'll beat him for my children." Geness avoided their eyes.

"We didn't say good-bye to the children," Skarra said.

"I watched them sleep, their curly heads swaddled in their cribs. If I'd woke them, I'd have cried."

"I'm going to end this nonsense," Skarra said, sitting up. "Voltoff! Turn around!"

"My lord!" He stood and sawed the reins, whistling up the horses.

"Bruce, I beg of you." She clasped him about the waist. "It's victory or I'm a public whore forever, and I'd rather be dead."

"Voltoff, turn back to the race." He closed his eyes and listened to the troika turned again. About him were thousands of normal people cheering them on to a nightmare beyond their control. He wanted to scream he was a college professor who lived in a cottage and loved his wife and children.

Voltoff drove them down the bluff road. Skarra could see Barbarossa casting his head from side to side before the other horses, and the wing horses went into a comfortable gallop.

"The Master! Halloo!" It was a group of students frolicking on skates and lifting flagons of drink.

"The King gets you if you lose."

"To hell with the King," Piippo said.

Rough men in patched skins shouted at them. "Married a lord, did she?"

"I put a year's pay on her, and I didn't get to see her."

Prince Merkalov cantered beside their troika. "Lady Geness, you have captured the soul of the Baltic." He reined his chestnut gelding aside, and they saw the quandary on his face under the heavy Tartar hat.

"You should stop her," Piippo said.

"My God, it's the smell of blood."

They were at the boxes for the nobles, around which milled people and sleighs. Skarra saw the Royal Finnish Ski Patrol under Captain Lund. The track led directly up the river on the compact snow. Lydia waved her white muff from a box.

"Why the public spectacle?" Skarra said to the Governor as their sleighs came abreast.

"Sports have always pacified the common folk."

"There's Halvorsen." Piippo gestured at a troika drawn by three cream-colored horses. Skarra saw the wide insolent face. The driver had his mouth open as if in horror at their sleigh.

"Roast grouse! Roast grouse on race day!" It was a hawker pushing a steaming sleigh through the carnival crowd.

"Five times around the course, drivers!" called out Prince Merkalov, "and keep to the right of the beacon troikas."

Piippo kissed Geness on the lips and jumped out.

"Let 'em run!" It was a roar from the crowd.

"Let Voltoff drive," Skarra said, kissing her temple.

Her eyes were bright with a fever. "Bruce, when I was dead you made me live and our children. Now let me honor what you did." She clutched at her muff.

He kissed her mouth and stepped down.

"Follow me, drivers!" Prince Merkalov called out, "at a trot, keeping abreast." He cantered the gelding ahead of the troikas, which slipped away from him, Geness' face showing her fear as she swallowed and said, "Good-bye, Bruce."

"They're off!" A roar went up from the river and echoed against the trees. "Whoom!" It was a cannon fired from the river bluff.

Skarra was standing in the Governor's sleigh. He could see the sleighs were side by side, skimming down a long avenue. His troika dwindled in sight, and he saw the people wave on the far bluff.

"They'll be back in a few minutes," Bofors said.

"Oh, I see them!" Piippo shouted.

He could see the sleighs speeding through a mass of heads, the two drivers like hunched dolls behind the horses' manes.

Skarra put his head down and listened to the cheers, and the boasts in the crowd around the tent.

"A light horse beats a dark horse!"

He opened his eyes to see the two troikas coming into view. His horses were on the outside, with Barbarossa in a long trot that sent him off the snow in poised floats. The horses' eyes rose and fell ahead of a white mist.

"Hell, he hasn't opened up yet." Piippo gripped Skarra's forearm.

The cream-colored horses of Halvorsen were chopping at the snow in desperation.

"We're ahead!" Piippo shouted. People pounded each other on the back and fell down and scrambled on all fours as if in an ocean storm as the troikas passed.

Skarra's wing horses galloped ahead of a cloud that foamed off the ice.

"Geney." He saw her face searching for him.

"Go, Voltoff! Go!" Piippo and Count Bofors were shouting. Voltoff was about half a length ahead of Halvorsen's sleigh.

"One songbird doesn't end the winter," Skarra said.

The second time the troikas came past, Voltoff's was a whole length ahead.

"Catch that sleigh!"

"You've ruined us, Gurd!"

Skarra heard the shouts from the group of officers, who had now been joined by a sizable crowd of well-dressed people, all of whom seemed to curse his troika.

The third time around, Skarra saw Halvorsen was on the driver's seat, lashing his horses, his sleigh a good two hundred yards behind Voltoff. Geness was composed, her veil tied into her fur hat.

"We've won!" Piippo shouted.

Skarra watched the cream-colored trotter under the bow break stride and reach out into a gallop. The cheering rose across the course from Skarra's party as the sleigh began to close.

"Disqualified! Captain Halvorsen's disqualified!" Prince Merkalov raised his crop.

"The hell he is!"

"Now we'll have a horse race!"

Skarra saw a figure topple off the driver's seat of Halvorsen's troika and bounce out over the ice when it was hit by a sled runner.

"Somebody's fallen off his sleigh," Piippo said.

There was a pause in the endless roar of voices, digesting the excitement. "He's thrown out the driver," Bofors said.

"He's driving himself."

"He can't do that," Count Bofors said.

A rough figure shouldered his way toward them, running blood down his beard, which was freezing.

"My lord, he threw me out."

"He's bleeding," Lady Bofors said, getting out of the sleigh.

Skarra watched the sleighs come around the bend. Halvorsen was lashing his horses and shouting. He saw of an instant that the troikas were rushing through a cloud of snow and a mass of people who crowded onto the track.

"Clear the track!" Merkalov yelled at Captain Lund, whose men began shoving back the people with their flintlocks.

Skarra could see Geness was shouting at Voltoff, who was hunched into his crouch, the reins running from his arms to the horses' mouths. He heard her scream as the other troika pulled ahead. "Barbarossa! Let him run!" She hit Voltoff with her muff. "Run! Or we're done for!"

Voltoff came upright off the seat and bellowed a sound. The sleigh fishtailed on its runners, pluming a skiff of ice. The crowd went wild, throwing things into the air. Along the backstretch the rolling cheers followed the two troikas.

"She'll be all right, Bruce." Helen Bofors touched his hand.

"That son of a bitch," Piippo said.

"Stop the race," Bofors said. The crowd wavered as the two troikas shot into view. Voltoff was too wide and sloughing off a fringe of people who fell on the ice trying to get away. Skarra could see the horses had their necks outstretched, like great birds racing over the snow. The troika strewed a line of fallen and limping figures in its path who seemed to shed clothing on the ice.

"It's a runaway!" Merkalov gathered his reins. "Stop them!" He stood in the stirrups and waved his crop.

"Whip up the horses!" Bofors shouted at their driver. The sleigh began to jerk as the horses pranced to be off.

Skarra watched the two sleighs come by. Voltoff was way ahead, but the three horses were racing each other with their mouths open to suck the wind and passing in a sound of hoofbeats.

"Look, Voltoff's bloody!"

He saw Geness hanging to the back of Voltoff's seat, her fur hat gone and her hair loose in the cold mist whipped up behind the sleigh.

"We won!" Piippo shouted.

"Whooomm!" It was the cannon from the river bluff.

The troika leaped into a group of people, who spun down the sides of the sleigh in screams and curses and drunken laughter. Voltoff was standing in his seat, wrapping the reins up his arms, and Skarra saw Geness' white face looking back. Horsemen and troikas raced toward the bank to turn them.

"After them!" Merkalov shouted, galloping in the midst of the troikas.

Skarra could see Voltoff turn the troika as it scooted sideways on its runners in fans of spray-ice. The people on the bank had grown still when they realized the troika was heading toward them. Heavy tree trunks caught in the ice protruded at angles from the river onto the bank. Skarra held his breath and watched his life speed crazily away from him.

The wing horse dragged Barbarossa into a turn. Voltoff was bound in reins, up his arms and about his body, to get a shorter purchase. The sleigh was stretched out in profile. It had turned.

He saw the sleigh erupt in frail pieces of wood behind the horses, who seemed to leap ahead, carrying Voltoff into the air. He could see her light body flung into sight among the pieces of wood. They came down slowly onto the ice. Her body slipped into the logs that wrecked them.

"Mmmooaamm"—he heard the concerted moan from the stillness of the spectators.

"Catch them!" Prince Merkalov was waving his crop at the three horses now dragging the bound figure of Voltoff across the ice like a dark chip of wood.

He jumped from the sleigh and slid on his knees to where she lay. A sled runner was under her foot.

"Geney?" Her head lay in the snow.

"Bruce, the children. I'm dying."

"No."

"Something broke inside. I feel it."

"You're not hurt." Her head was like a spent leaf.

"We beat him, but, oh, God, I wish I hadn't." Her eyes were flooded. "I want my children."

He slipped his arms under her and raised her off the ice. "I'll hold you."

"Take me home. I want to see my children."

Skarra put his ear to her bosom and felt the slight breath. Shouts were about him for troikas, and beyond, the common people watched in silence.

"Oh, Lord, forgive me. I put my vanity ahead of my life."

"No, you did no such thing," Skarra said, carrying her toward a troika.

"I can still repent—oh, Bruce, I repent. I won't die insane. I want my children."

Helen Bofors and the Governor were at the sleigh with Lydia. "Bruce, how is she?"

"I'm numb under my breast."

"Geney, you'll live," Lydia said.

"I'm so glad you came. You must take the children. I was such a fool."

"No, Geney, please."

"I don't have time." Skarra held her as her eyes searched Lydia's. "You've loved my husband and you wanted my children."

Lydia burst into tears and hid her face in her hands.

"My nightmare is your dream come true. . . ."

"Oh, forgive me, Geney."

"No, I don't mean to be cruel. I betrayed my dream to my vanity. Lord, God, Lydia, don't betray your dream."

"I'll make your dream come true." Both women were crying.

"Thank God I didn't die insane." She moved her eyes to Skarra. "Take us home."

Halvorsen's troika came through the crowd and hauled up before them.

"Scotsman, can you hear me?"

Skarra nodded in the deathly silence which settled over the people.

"Scotsman, your taste in horses is better than your taste in women. Next time try a true whore and not the pastor's bastard child."

Skarra was aware of the stunned look in people's eyes as they avoided his face.

"Bruce," she whispered, "promise you will not fight him."

He nodded to her in his confusion, unable to grasp the enormity of the nightmare of her death.

Her breathing was labored if he lay her out in bed, as though her lungs were filling with fluid, so Skarra swaddled her body in the down puffs from their bed and crouched on the edge of the bricks of their bedroom hearth to hold her. She rested the back of her head into the palm of his hand, and he listened to her diaphragm pull against the ribs, slowly increasing its contractions as she died.

"*Maman,*" said the little girl, staring into her mother's face, frightened by the toil in her father's eyes.

"So lovely," Geness whispered.

He heard Penelope rush from the room to sob in the kitchen, where he could see and hear people stirring. "Lady Bofors," Skarra said.

"Yes, Bruce."

"Have the servants leave the house if they cry."

Charles looked from one to the other of them, and moved close to his sister, seeking some familiar sign of joy and welcome in his parents.

"Let me touch you, Charles." Geness' outstretched hand waited to caress him.

"Put your head in her hand." Skarra spoke softly.

"Ah, so lovely." She smiled.

"*Maman,* we missed you today," Fanny said, hearing the familiar joy.

"Your father and I adore you." She opened her mouth and he saw the blanched lips. "We love you."

"They are so beautiful." He saw her eyes flood with tears.

"Kiss your mother."

The children stepped close and kissed her. "I just love you, *Maman,*" said Fanny.

"We adore you," Geness whispered. Charles touched her hand.

"Take them to Skarra."

"We're all going home, love."

"No." Her eyes turned to him. "Take my children. I'll never see Skarra." She tried to smile.

"No, you'll live."

"Bruce, please."

He put his head down and suffocated in his sorrow.

"I always wanted my mother and my father and to love my children." Her shoulders moved in his arms. "I wanted to go home. Now I will die in their arms, in your arms."

He raised his head and felt himself choke.

"Bruce, you have been my mother and my father, and I will die in their arms—oh, God, I don't want to die—hold me, love, my mind is swaying in the light."

He held her as her lungs quickened and lost their strength. She watched the children, who had kissed her uncertainly, until Lady Bofors took them away.

"I swear to God they'll live."

She stirred in his arms. "Bruce, I love you." He saw the light fade from her eyes, as though drawn out by invisible webs.

"Geney." He heard her breath fail and saw her eyelids flutter against his cheek, and he knew he had lost her.

12

He lost count of time and of himself, not daring to move as he held her, just as she was when she died in his arms. He knew she was dead, he could feel the water run out of her body, wetting his knee. Her arm that was outstretched toward the children gradually set in the rigid muscles of death, and her head no longer weighted his hand that held it, but was tense on the neck. She had stopped breathing long ago, but he could not stop holding her, and listening for the heartbeat and human quiver that would never come. It was hours.

There was someone in the room. "Bruce, I think she's gone," Lady Bofors said.

"Yes, I know."

"Would you think we should prepare her?"

"Yes, we should."

"Would you like me to?"

"Thank you, I'll do it."

"Dear boy." He felt the elderly woman stroke his crown.

"I was afraid to look because I didn't want to see her dead, then I'd know she was dead." His voice sounded like a stranger's to him. "If I held her, maybe, like I used to do, I thought she might come back, and she wouldn't be dead."

"I've rearranged the whole cottage."

"The children?"

"In Penelope's arms with Lydia."

Skarra placed Geness on the table in their bedroom. Her body was slight in the image of a child. Her mouth was open and the eyes blank, which chilled him. He undressed her, slipping her silk dress off each shoulder and sliding down the undergarments until she was nude. Lady Bofors took the clothing but did not touch her.

"Set silver on her eyelids." She put the coins on the table.

He closed each eye and set a piece of silver on it.

"When the muscles release, bind up her jaw."

He nodded. "This was the same table the twins were born on."

He bathed her body, working from the face and head down. The flesh was cold and not resilient to follow his fingers. He washed her, feeling the breasts he had loved to kiss, where his children had suckled, now standing slack over the frail ribs. All gone in death. Her face had lost its tension and her features slipped into their ease, and she looked like a pretty naked woman. The teeth crowded the lips, which gave her the trace of a smile, and in the bowed mouth he could see the resemblance between her and the two children. "Three children," he said to himself, "and I lost one."

He washed her pubic region, where she had had their children, and felt the life gone from where he had dared to pull her children out of her. Washing and tending to her dead body seemed to ease his soul, and bring him to confrontation with death, and from it, a hallowed love of her memory that was burnt in his heart and a sign in his breast as long as he should live. The death of her body was so complete, the frail ivory hair now barren to touch, that her life when with him now stood out as if she had been a goddess, and he knew that if a man and woman ever find love, they are then immortal in that love, and can never die, even if death comes. He ran his hand down her naked flank and belly to her thighs and leaned and kissed the stretch marks.

"I'll shake up the fire for you," Lady Bofors said and flung a log into the fireplace which showered up in a spray of small lights.

"I'll rest by and by. First I'll read my Bible."

"The carpenter will come in the morning."

He picked up the Bible.

"The Protestant service?"

"It doesn't matter. I don't think God's as particular about religion as man."

"Sleep if you can."

"When a man's wife dies it leaves a hole in his heart any sorrow can slip through unfelt."

The Classics could only tell him life was this way, but there was no solace. Skarra wanted solace. He was aware of the shadows playing along Geness' body, paling the dip in her flank over her hip bone. "Surely death confronts man with God," he said to himself, "yet if life leads to death, then the improbable must reverse itself, and death lead to life." He could not accept it, but the children proved it. "Geney believed it, why can't I believe it?"

The Book of Ruth fell open and he was pleased to know Geney had set her life to his. In the Book of Job was the sorrow he could grasp. His eye drifted through the Testaments until he found the metaphysical admonition to live despite the feet of clay, because Redemption was for all and hope in sorrow, and nothing could ever live unless it had already been. He breathed deeply and nodded with the acceptance of exhaustion.

The dawn light was about him in their bedroom. A gossamer haze played off the curtains she had boxed and hung, giving the room a misty look of heaven each day he had woke with her. There were a thousand of those days.

He slept and saw Geness was alive and talking to him, and he was so relieved he woke with the certain delight that the sorrow of death was only a dream, and that he had reversed the waking world with a dream world. When he stood he was shocked to see Geness lying dead. The nightmare was reality and the dream a wish.

He picked her up and placed her in their bed, where they had found life and had been blessed from it. He settled her as though asleep.

When the children were brought that morning he spoke to Penelope. "I want you to continue to nurse them as long as they will suck."

"Yes, my lord." She seemed relieved.

He held the boy and the girl in his arms and walked up to the bed with them.

"*Maman, Maman* still sleep," said Charles, pitching toward the bed and his mother.

"Oh, little one," Skarra said, catching him in his hand across the child's breast. "*Maman* still neepy neepy."

"*Maman* neepy neepy?" Fanny searched him for an explanation.

"Later, *Maman* wake."

"Oh, later." Fanny looked to her brother and said, "*Maman* neepy neepy, but other time *Maman* wake up."

"*Maman* wake, Dadda?" Charles said.

"*Maman* have ache," Fanny said.

"Oh," Charles nodded his head vigorously. "*Maman* little bit sick."

"When *Maman* feel better?"

He hugged the children into his chest, distraught with the questions he could only divert, but never answer. He kissed the flesh of their smooth cheeks and was moved by the small mouths so full of life, and their eyes bright with eagerness to trust him. He closed his eyes and felt the silent tears flood his vision.

"Penelope, come," he whispered. He felt her take the children. "The sorrow has weakened me."

"Oh, yes, my lord."

He was grateful to have Lydia keep the children, but he charged Penelope, the peasant woman, directly. "They are not to be out of your sight day or night."

"I put up the rails around the porcelain stove," Lydia said.

He nodded, avoiding Lydia's eyes. In the children Skarra saw Geness in every sound and motion, even as her body lay out in the bedroom. But Lydia aroused in him a sense of outrage that she should be alive, while his wife lay dead.

"I'm sorry," Lydia said and took each child by the hand.

"I'm ashamed, but I'm furious that everything else is alive."

"I can understand that."

"I want to kill something." He would not look at her—to hide the anger. "Only the children make me feel better."

He could hear the carpenter shaping and pegging the coffin and he carried Geness to the table for Lady Bofors to dress in a silk gown. The longer he worked to prepare her body, the more remote she became to him. It seemed that she gradually withdrew into the world of the dead, her body taking on a repose that accepted death, and he felt a terrible isolation. To see their dream broken in her stiff body, complete and detached and now a law to itself, sent a chill into him, and a sense of death into his own body. His arms and legs felt immensely vibrant, the hair on his calves and forearms sensitive to draft and cold, but the saliva of his mouth had the taste of gall and brass.

"My tartan," he said, taking the heavy McTaggart tartan he had wrapped about him to sleep in the fields as a boy, and over his shoulder as a university student at Edinburgh. "Wrap her in it."

When Helen Bofors had swaddled the body he handed her a heavy silver brooch. "Pin it over her breast. My mother's." It had the word "Skarra" inscribed under a rampant phoenix.

"Now put up Lydia's candles and let in Voltoff's priests."

"The Governor wishes to bury her by the church wall in the Kremlin."

Skarra nodded.

"The town wants to come."

"It was a public shame," Skarra said. "And I was most to blame."

Lady Bofors said nothing.

"Men are their dreams and women reality, and when they make life, it's about as close to God as a man can ever go."

"I'm so sorry, Bruce."

"God, the ache, and I did it myself."

Her bier was in their bedroom and he stood or sat in one corner of the room, talking softly to Piippo or Lydia or to Lady Bofors while his students walked in to pay their respects. The Chaplain of the college had come to offer him the right to place her bier in the University chapel. "Thank you, but we found God in here," he said.

In the evening Voltoff brought "his people," the Orthodox Russian priests and other friends.

"How are your wounds?" Skarra said.

"They are nothing." The old man was crying.

"Here"—Skarra pulled a linen handkerchief from his sporran, and handed it to Voltoff.

"My lord, it is too fine for me."

"Nonsense."

"She was a flower that bloomed despite sorrow." Voltoff touched his cheek and handed the linen back to him. "My lord is dressed differently?"

Skarra glanced at his heavy kilt and socks, the Scottish dress he had never worn as a university professor. "I'm taking the children home, to Scotland."

"Will I go there, my lord?"

"Only if you like. It is different from Russia."

About the candlelit bier the priests were swinging fragrant censers on chains and bowing, while chanting the liturgy and holding long candelabras in their hands.

"You are not our conqueror," Voltoff said.

Skarra nodded. In the twilight of the garden he was aware of people and he heard them sing. Never before had he heard such human suffering in the throats of men as in the voices fusing onto the evening.

"They have known much grief." He walked outside with Lydia and Piippo.

"I think all we've ever known is grief and conquest, until that's what we are."

"Aye." The peasants seemed to blend into a mass of huddling skins and shawls and mouths which held notes of pathos and exquisite beauty. "God has blessed them, regardless."

"They know it."

"Thank them for me."

"No need to," Lydia said. She walked into their midst. The men bowed and the women genuflected before her as she touched their faces with her bare hands.

In the morning, alone, he lifted her from the table and laid her in the coffin. She was cold and filled with death in his hands, though in her face he saw the quandary of a child, the mouth crowded with teeth and the smile of having slipped away to the quiet of death, and the closed eyes he felt crying as she looked at her children and died. Nobody would ever touch her again. He leaned into the coffin and kissed the lips, dying in his belly when he tasted the lack of life in them. He put his fingers into the pile of fine hair at her temple.

"Bring the top," he said to Piippo, and he lay it over her and drove the wedges, sealing her into his thoughts at each blow, and himself from his old life with her. If she was dead in her coffin, she could never die again as long as he lived.

He and Piippo and Lydia and some of his students were with him behind the troika as they left the cottage and walked in the snow, down the lane and toward the old Russian church. His students were very subdued before him, he noticed. He was in his felted Highland jacket with its brass-buttoned cuffs and heavy studded epaulets, the feathered bonnet and kilt, and the long claymore which swung on a slant below his hip from his baldric. At his waist was a pistol, and a short knife dangled by his sporran and a dirk thrust out at his bare knee. They had been used to him in an academic gown and soft capuche flung across his back and a Latin book under his arm. He reeked of war, when they had been so used to a kind professor, willing to admit a thousand variants to a single truth.

The bell was tolling as they entered the gates of the walled citadel. "Look," Piippo said in a whisper. People were everywhere.

"He has to appease the public," Skarra said when he saw the Governor at the church steps. They passed the guards in silence, not acknowledging the salute of the officers' swords. Voltoff drew up the troika at the church, which seemed to float between the snow and the low clouds on its graceful onions now painted with bright cheer.

"Is there anything to appeal to besides God?" Lydia said while they watched the students carry the coffin inside.

He watched the coffin, which was raised before the altar, where prayers were being read among the organ notes. The coffin seemed to want to be off on its journey. He felt an impulse to shout it was all a mistake, and to stop the insanity and go get Geness out of the coffin.

"I don't understand," he said to Lydia.

Lydia looked as stunned as his students and the university professors who stared at his weapons and haggard eyes. The children were at his side, but he did not touch them out of a wish to spare them the intense sorrow of death.

"Geney was alive two days ago." He glanced at Piippo, who looked away to follow the coffin out of the church, where it tilted going down the steps. He caught sight of the open grave, which glazed with ice crystals. Fluffy snow fell into the raw hole. Reality came to him. Geney was going into that hole. He would bury her forever in the ice of a distant land and take her children to where she had wanted to go.

"Gently," Piippo said to the students who placed the coffin over the grave. They stepped back into the waiting throng of peasants, merchants, and soldiers.

Skarra unslung the claymore and put the bell of the sword into Lydia's hands and walked to the coffin with the Book of Common Prayer. He read the words of harmony and misfortune and faith that life on earth was akin to the Creator. He looked to Lydia and Piippo and said, "I am the resurrection and the life. . . . Earth to earth, ashes to ashes, dust to dust. . . ." His voice collapsed to a whisper. "Piippo, help me do it."

He straddled the head of the coffin with Piippo at the other end, while the students slipped out the scantlings. They eased the coffin down and he felt the chill earth crowd the shoulders of Geney, until it lay beneath him, forever caught in its earth nest.

He stood upright and he saw the look of horror on his students' faces. "The shovels, Piippo."

He drove a shovel into the pile of frozen earth, and lifted it and turned it and heard the rain of clods rattle on the top of her coffin, and felt something tear in his loins that carried a tart bile into his throat. Piippo paced him, shovelful by shovelful, filling her grave while the elegant people in furs stood behind them and the ordinary townfolk stared from red eyes.

When they had filled the grave he took the claymore from Lydia. "I'll leave for Scotland within a week."

"Do you need help?" Piippo said.

"Will you come?"

"Yes."

Skarra nodded.

"Will you kill *him?*"

"No, I'm keeping Geney's promise."

13

Skarra sent to the University for Dodderhoff and Pickereill to come to the cottage to get his books.

"Surely, Bruce, you'll need them," Dodderhoff said, his round face pulled in lines.

"The use of books is endless," Skarra said.

"Yes, what is a professor without his library?" Pickereill said.

"Keep them to remember me."

"We'll ship them to you after the war."

He shook his head. "When you're a boy, you dream of Utopia out of naiveté. Then you know wisdom comes from sorrow turned to innocence instead of anger."

"Scotsman, you love beauty. Look at your cottage."

He saw the two children staring out the bedroom window into the winter twilight, which diffused about their heads. They held each other's hands. "You play *Maman,*" one of them said. Skarra heard a dry oath rasp in his throat and went to his children.

The stonemason came in the morning, a gaunt man whose callouses scraped in Skarra's hand.

"Do you read?"

"No, my lord."

"But you chisel any flourish?"

"It is my gift, my lord."

"Good. Then chisel this into the tombstone." He handed the man a parchment, the top of which bore a cross. "This is the top," he said when he saw the stonemason turning the parchment.

"What does it say, my lord?"

001 Skarra read very slowly, tracing with his finger the words:

Lady Geness of Skarra
beloved wife of
Bruce McTaggart
of Skarra
Mother of
Lord Charles and Lady Frances
of Skarra
1611—1632

A Good Woman Is The Divine Masterwork

xxxxxxxxxx

"Just like that?" the stonemason said.

"Yes."

He looked at the parchment. "I'll have it here tomorrow."

When Voltoff brought the man who made sleighs for Dorpat, Skarra said, "I don't want a heavy closed thing to be hauled through drifts, like a log, but rather a light skimming sort of sleigh to hitch behind running horses."

"It will be cold, my lord," the man said.

"I'll nest it with furs and warm it with hot bricks."

"I understand, my lord."

The snows were crisp into March, and he could skim over the ice and maneuver through field and copse to escape pursuit.

"A thousand Cossacks loose in Kurland," Skarra said, looking at the unemptied child's pot at the foot of his bed. "The fastest horses in Russia?"

"The fastest, my lord," Voltoff said.

"The fleetest sleighs I've ever built." The man smiled at the image of the adventure he could help prepare.

As his days at the cottage drew to a close, Skarra was filled with a great lassitude. He found his eyes drawn to the door-jamb, to the imperfections in the windowpanes, the heavy posters of their bed where he had slept at the side of Geney's body, the ten thousand moments when she had turned a shoulder, the quiet breast loose against his arm, her foot against his calf, a form touching his skin—the bed was them. He walked the grounds and the winter-crusted garden where they had worked on hands and knees, and pined for her life and groaned under his own.

The cottage of our love where she touched every lintel and her voice soothed us. She was the only God he had ever known. The fear of death is so absurd, he thought, once you have loved, but I would give my life to have her back a day, then we would both die. No, I owe her the children.

The sleighs were short-coupled and stood high on their runners. Skarra and Voltoff stretched reindeer skins over the hoops with the hair side out. They lined the seats with furs so that it was like a Lapland hut.

"They are like two ships with hair sails, my lord," Voltoff said. "Perhaps the Cossacks will fear them."

"For their sake, I hope you are right."

Voltoff glanced at him.

"I'm in no mood to *parlez* with any man between here and Scotland."

Skarra decided on spare horses tied at lead and hay banked on the tailgate as a firing platform for the blunderbuss Piippo was to serve.

"My God, it's a cannon," Piippo said after it splattered stumps and tore out ice clods.

"It's the element of total surprise and devastation. It's reality."

Piippo stroked the belled snout of the blunderbuss. "I've never understood how a college professor can understand so much about war."

"It's the only thing that can get a man's attention and change his mind."

Three days before they left, Count Bofors came to the cottage to explain the misfortune of the Swedish invasion of Europe. Gustavus was not doing so well as they had hoped. He had joined forces with John George of Saxony and had fought a brilliant victory over the Count of Tilly at Breitenfeld near Leipzig, in September of last fall, putting the Imperial army into rout, and had thence threatened Vienna while John George split off with the Saxons to occupy Bohemia. All that was in the fall of 1631. Now Wallenstein was in the field with an entirely new army, and John George was threatening to make a separate peace, betraying Gustavus.

"I am Scottish," Skarra said. "I want no part of Europe."

"May my wife accompany you?"

"Of course, send her, but spare me all this talk on politics."

The next day while Voltoff was resetting the shoes on the horses, Lydia and Prince Merkalov arrived.

"Ah, young Scot," Merkalov said, taking his hand, "an old man craves a boon, and a young woman her life."

"He means we're dead if we stay here," Lydia said.

"But you are Russian and this is your home."

"We have a price on our heads, young Scot."

"It's out of the question."

"Please, young man, our lives." The old prince looked at his daughter. "Her life. Mine's not much left to go."

"It's terrible that gentlefolk should have to bargain for their lives. Shall we have tea?" Lydia turned to the cottage.

They had tea. Skarra heard himself agreeing to take them, while listening to the old man assure him he could fight his way through Cossacks thick as blowflies on a dead Tartar's belly. Skarra could not look into Lydia's face, for his resentment that she was alive, while Geney was dead, but he could not bear the thought of leaving her.

The two loaded sleighs waited down the lane from the cottage. He walked through the rooms once more to taste for a last time the insane craving to be where she was, to see what she had put her hand to. He looked through the deep windows across the snow-white garden, and he walked along the low galleries, hearing his hollow boot heels. He felt a panic at being so close to her yet not being able to evoke her. He turned in at the kitchen, and looked at the table and at the stove where she had worked a thousand days. It was seldom that a man knew exactly when a time and place of joy had come, and had gone, and he knew it. He walked deliberately toward the sleighs gripped in a trance.

They passed through town and Voltoff drew up at the gates of the Kremlin, and Skarra vaulted out. He crossed the snow to her grave and saw the new tombstone set in the disturbed earth. He put his hand on it, stared at the outlines of the grave, but he could not weep. "I'll take the children home," he said, and stumbled away.

The Governor was at the sleighs when he got back, taking leave of Lady Bofors.

"All Europe's in ashes," Bofors said. "Beware of the Cossacks."

"I'll have a care."

"You're a rare breed, Scotsman!" He seized Skarra about the shoulders. "God be with you."

"Set Geney's tombstone when her grave is dry." He swung up into the sleigh, his face hard as steel. "Voltoff!" The sleighs sped out of Dorpat.

Skirting the frozen Baltic, as a crow flies, Skarra had reckoned six hundred English miles to reach Swedish Pomerania. The horses could move fifty miles a day with ease, a hundred miles if pressed and if the daylight held. In something under twelve days they would be shipboard and bound for Scotland.

In his sleigh were the children, Penelope, and Helen Bofors, and the longbow and pistols. Above the muffled hoofbeats he could hear the troika carrying Piippo, Lydia, and Prince Merkalov. When they were into the taiga forests he climbed out of the back of the sleigh and joined Voltoff on the seat. Polonitz sat at their feet, wrapped in skins and bark.

"Many times I've driven to Riga, my lord."

"Drive on." Scotland lay ahead.

The flat evergreen forest had a bleak air to it, of brooding shadows closing off the tree trunks, until it walled the traveler with a chill. Skarra saw Voltoff watching as they swept along.

"We move too fast for ambuscade," Skarra said.

"I like the plains better."

At noon they stopped in a clearing by an abandoned woodsman's hut to have lunch and change the horses. The horses frisked past each other with their breaths snorting out in excited funnels. There was a brittle air to Prince Merkalov which Skarra and the others seemed to understand, of a man who had lived into another era, for which he was not born, and a pride among them that he had done it.

They melted snow to give the horses a drink and lunched on cold roast elk and black bread and drank two bottles of light wine. "More like a sleighing party," Piippo said.

The two sleighs rushed along in winter quiet until dusk fell. A small dog barked. Skarra saw they had passed a log hut, and the forest fell away. He saw several people stop to look at the two troikas as they entered the village. He jumped down at the inn and felt his legs bind in pain from sitting.

"Lodging for six adults and two children, and quarters for my three drivers," Skarra said to the bald innkeeper as he and Piippo pushed into the common room.

"So large a party, sire?"

"Lodging as I've said." The commons was full of rough men either sipping hot tea from samovars or drinking German lager.

"I am honored by gentlefolk." Porters appeared.

The lodging was one large room with beds set around a porcelain stove. Skarra and Piippo and Lydia went down to the common room to dine while supper was carried up for the others. They dined on the ham of a great bear. "It's fresh," Lydia said. Skarra was tired and ate in silence while sipping Scotch whiskey. After eating Lydia retired to prepare herself for bed in the privacy of the room.

"It's not right for a man to like the taste of whiskey," Skarra said as he and Piippo walked outside to urinate in the snow.

The revelers in the commons watched Skarra and Piippo in stillness as they passed through, Skarra armed with his pistols and knives and

Piippo carrying a Finnish axe in his belt and a small cutlass in a baldric. "We haven't been here long enough for them to mount an attack," said Piippo.

Their party was abed for the night, and Skarra's pistols clattered when he unbuckled his belt and eased it to the floor. "Shssh." Lydia spoke from a shadow against a pillow. He stripped down to his woolen undershirt and walked to the door. Satisfied it was drop-slotted, he tiptoed to the children's bed and put his ear down to the breathing that he and Geney had had to hear before they could sleep each night.

The party had eaten breakfast and were into the sleighs while it was still dark. Skarra watched the white shadow they followed through the trees by a waning moon. The horses moved fast and Skarra found himself dropping to sleep as the sun pushed into sight. At midmorning he told Voltoff to stop, though the horses were still frisky.

"Riga by sunset?"

"With fortune, my lord."

"Riga, yes, the Paris of the Baltic," Prince Merkalov said.

They boiled the samovar on the tailgate of Skarra's sleigh and ate smoked kippers and drank the Russian tea. Skarra noticed they were all at ease in the presence of each other and jolly conversation bolstered them. "I knew a young lady in Riga, once. . . ."

"The girl he did not marry," Lydia said.

"Not as pretty as your mother, my dear."

"Tell them, Papa."

"Not much to tell, beyond she was lovely."

"But you seduced her, Papa?"

"At the time yes, but in retrospect, I rather think it is the man who is seduced." He smiled laconically. "Success devours one's resources."

The children frolicked in the snow and Skarra hugged them and laughed as they blew against his iced furs.

"My lord!" Voltoff seized his arm and looked down the trace. "Someone comes." Their horses were heads up and looking backward.

"Shall we run?"

"No. It can't be soldiers." Skarra put the children into the sleigh.

"Brigands," Piippo said.

"Pull the sleighs into the woods, and we'll wait. It can't be more then one or two men. A company can't travel as fast as we do." Skarra calculated the odds. He had no desire to race his horses all the way to Riga.

He and Piippo crouched in the bank of snow. Piippo had a flintlock and sword, and he had his longbow. Two riders came into sight kicking at the jaded flanks of the horses, so tired they stumbled at every other step. The men were hunched down into their skins against the cold.

"Halt!" Skarra cried.

One horse jumped sideways in spasmodic leaps, rolling white into his eyeball. The man fell heavily into the snow. The other man's mouth opened and Skarra heard the free horse crashing through the trees in diminishing sound as it vanished.

"Who are you?"

"We have no patience," Piippo said.

"Two woodsmen, my lord," said the man getting to his feet.

"Where's your axe?" Piippo said.

Skarra had seen the knife scar carrying up into the split nostril of one of the men from the night before.

"Dismount and give us your girth and bridle." The man slid off and fumbled at the horse's flank. "Where's your camp?"

"Five miles ahead, my lord."

"To make an ambuscade with friends?" Skarra said.

"We are poor men, my lord."

"Not all poor men are thieves." Skarra walked onto the road.

"We would not have killed you."

"We did not let you. Now strip to your underwear and start running."

The men stared at him like furred statues, and Piippo began to laugh. "Strip, you bastards!" He unsheathed his sword. "You'll arrive at your camp in time for lunch."

Voltoff and Ralawitz, the other driver, gathered the pile of smelly clothes and tied the bundle to a sleigh runner after chasing off the single horse. The two woodsmen ran past their party on ruddy shanks and stringy white buttocks that scrabbled under their beards.

"Ah, the vagaries of Dame Fortune," Prince Merkalov said. "Those men had no idea plunder was to escape them."

"They meant to kill us, 'else they'd not have denied it," Lydia said. "We don't want their blood on us."

"Oh, Bruce," Lady Bofors said, holding a child.

It was dark when they came into Riga, and the horses were tired. They slowed at every movement of the reins. Lanterns flanked the stone buildings under mansard roofs and reflected in the snow of the streets. "Make sure the horses are restored to top strength," he said to Voltoff when he visited the stable. At the hotel, any venture into Kurland to the south was considered unthinkable. War had filled it with Cossacks, freebooters, and outlaws. Yet, as a frozen plain, Skarra thought he could get across it.

It was before dawn when they crossed the Dvina River and climbed onto the plateau leading south, and the lights of Riga went out of sight. After noon they passed peasant huts nestled in the snow and picketed round with small stakes marking gardens and bare fruit and shade trees. They saw no life.

"They don't come out," Skarra said.

"Strangers mean trouble, my lord."

"I suppose they're jaded with liberators at that."

They passed the ruins of a large estate. The chimneys rose as sentinels to show what had been, the charred joists and cellar beams thrust up awkwardly from the snow to mark the dimensions of the noble country house.

"Only the meek can live in peace, but they don't know it," Prince Merkalov said.

"We should stop before sunset," Skarra said to Voltoff.

They traveled another hour, watching the snowscape, and kept a fading sun to their right. Skarra saw Voltoff nod and followed his glance to a featherish stand of trees which led to a copse and hut. They turned the horses and drove to it. A peasant burst into sight and fled across the snow, Voltoff shouted, "Brother!" The man stopped and turned.

"Why did he stop?" Skarra said.

"He heard the peasant's sorrow of a brother."

"Ask where the Cossacks bivouac and how many."

They bedded down in the hay of the animal shed, not wanting to dispossess the man of his hut, and fed him at their fire. An emaciated little girl clung to her mother's skirt and watched them while the peasant and Voltoff talked. Skarra heard the word "Cossack" in every sentence.

"He says the Cossack patrols come every third day and they seek a tall foreigner who will be traveling with children."

"So they know."

"They say he will shoot arrows from a longbow, and they will pay five thousand kopecks for him."

"Quite a large sum," Skarra said.

"They're very angry, my lord."

"I suppose they are."

"Who could it have been?" Lydia said.

"God knows. We traveled faster than any horseman."

"What do we do?"

"Go on. No choice."

They slept late and started after dawn. The horses were striking their hooves in their desire to run, and pitching their heads and snorting. They moved across the white plain that was hemmed in by light fog and listened to the runners' crunch below them.

"Two hours to the woods of the Memel River," Voltoff said, "to their camp."

It was sometime around midmorning that he caught sight of a horseman moving in an extended gallop across a small hillock.

"A Cossack, my lord."

"Aye, let him arouse them." Skarra felt the hair on his legs rise. The party became very quiet as they came over the snow and he noticed the ears of the horses cocked forward. The shadowed diffusion of the trees on the river came into sight. He saw a scuffle of movement among the trunks and the forest seemed to ooze men and horses onto the snow. "By God," Skarra said, standing in the seat to get a better look.

"If I live to be a hundred," Piippo said, calling from the other sleigh, "I'll not forget this one."

"Let us hope we can live but a single year," said Merkalov.

"Drive on," Skarra said, "I want to suck them out on the plain."

"Bad odds, I'd say," the old prince said. He and Skarra and Piippo dropped the hair tenting so they could defend their sleighs.

"How many do you count, Piippo?"

"Hundred and fifty, two hundred, maybe."

"Slow to a walk." They walked ahead and watched the Cossacks form a long line of horsemen directly across their path. Their banners were on a front, snapping over the heads of their officers, and he heard their hunting horns dressing the line, which they advanced at a walk.

"Hold," Skarra said. Voltoff stopped his troika and Ralawitz did the same. The Cossack line was coming over the snow not a mile away. He had a wish to come face to face with their officers, to see if battle could be avoided.

He gestured to Piippo to walk with him ahead of the sleighs. They saw the line of horsemen prance in caracole, some going in circles as the line reined up, and he heard the notes of a French horn roll over them. Three officers and four Cossacks kept coming.

"Apparently he'll talk," Skarra said.

"Maybe we can parley, Bruce."

"No, they want revenge," Skarra said, hearing the military bugles.

"I count one hundred and eighty-seven," Piippo said.

"Kill the officers first. They'll have the fastest horses, and they'll be at the sleighs ahead of their men. You'll have two shots from the flintlocks, then you'll have to sword them down—"

"Or my axe."

"Yes, the axe will do." Skarra nodded. "But under no account fire the blunderbuss until you have a clutch of horsemen in a group and you hear me shout 'Fire!' "

Skarra saw the faint movement of Piippo's Adam's apple. "Without the officers the men will be insane with barbarism, and you'll have a good shot."

They waited a hundred steps ahead of the sleighs and watched the officers approach on magnificent animals. He recognized the Colonel by the gold embroidery on his karakul hat. His cheeks glowed in the cold and his blue eyes watered as he looked down at them from his tall dappled gelding.

"I come in peace!" Skarra shouted in Russian, holding up a hand.

The small cavalcade rode slowly forward until they heard the horses' hooves cutting in the packed snow.

"Who are you?" said the smallest officer in High German.

"Lord Skarra of Scotland, traveling with my family to Königsberg and Poland."

"We expected you," said the Colonel. He brushed his mustache with the back of his gloved hand, making a swooping motion on each half of his upper lip.

"We come in peace."

"I'm afraid that won't be possible. I have a warrant for your arrest, signed by the Archduke."

"What archduke?" Prince Merkalov said, joining them. He was dressed in the uniform of a Russian prince and carried a jeweled court sword.

"Does it matter?" The Colonel beamed. "All men come in peace."

"Don't I know you?"

"Possibly. Colonel Horst Wittenhauser, commanding, Fourth Regiment of the Don Cossacks."

"Wittenhauser, yes, I recommended you." Merkalov looked at Skarra. "Why, I got this man his commission. German he is. Good soldier. Adventurer." He looked up at the Colonel. "I'm your old commanding officer, Prince Sergei Merkalov. . . ."

"We have a warrant for your arrest."

"I command you to let us pass." The old man's voice cracked.

The three officers smiled and said nothing.

"What's a German doing leading Cossacks for the Russians?" Skarra said.

"My sword and honor do the bidding of whoever pays me." He snuffed his nose in a gesture of righteousness.

"Not much honor in that."

"Never cared for professional soldiers, but they do beat an armed rabble, I suppose," Prince Merkalov said.

"Who betrayed us?"

The Colonel broke into laughter, making his horse fret. "None other than the Captain of the Royal Swedish Couriers, a Captain Halvorsen, good officer."

"That bastard," Piippo said.

"Yes, it had to be him," Skarra said.

Prince Merkalov's face was unnaturally grave. "Such a shoddy life men make for each other, then they complain of the squalor of their own nature."

"I'm afraid the Tsar's prison is the only place you're going." The Colonel had a comfortable, assured air about him, of a man used to instant compliance with the law.

Stepping back a pace, Prince Merkalov unsheathed his sword and shouted, "Run, Scotsman! Save my child and I'll save yours!"

"What?" Skarra said.

"Filth, dogs, defilers of Mother Russia!" He leaped across the snow at the three officers.

"Halt!" The Cossack officer spurred forward, the three men drawing sabers.

"Save our children!" Merkalov screamed at Skarra, who saw the fight had started. Voltoff stood and the whip cracked like gunshot as the horses leaped forward. Skarra started to run toward them, hearing Lydia scream, "Save Papa!" "Papa!" "Oh, Papa!"

He drew his claymore and saw the horror in the old man's face. "Run, boy! Save our children!" Merkalov whirled against the side of a Cossack's horse under the saber swing and came out behind the horse. He hopped on his thin legs, against the Colonel's calf. "This time you die!" Skarra saw the Colonel stand in his stirrups, his eyes round with awareness he was in dire pain, and he made an awful sound: "Ahhahhahh!" He let go his reins and Skarra saw the old prince jerk back his hand, trailing a slender blade running blood. The Colonel flopped over his pommel and rolled off the horse, one booted leg thrusting into the air as he fell.

"A reason to live and a purpose to die!" It was the old man's voice.

Skarra saw the remaining horsemen swinging at the light figure on the snow who scampered among them shrieking his anger.

"Papa, run!"

"Tsarist dogs!"

Skarra saw a Cossack being dragged over the snow by his boot and another man on the snow before he saw a saber flash and the old man drop on the snow.

"My lord, they come!" It was Voltoff's voice.

"Hang on to Lydia!" Skarra swung onto the back of his troika as it skidded past him. "Voltoff, turn north, and not too fast!"

"Bruce! My father!"

He looked to Lydia in the next sleigh, her hair strewing from her head, the eyes seeking his for the impossible.

"His last words were to save you!" He flung his hand out to her. "Lydia, help Piippo with the weapons." She was crying but she nodded her head.

"They come, my lord!"

He looked back to the cavalry. He could see them gaining on him, but still in a dressed line of the traditional charge. Their banners were brave above their flashing sabers and he saw a company of lancers with guidon pennants.

"Lancers!" he shouted to Piippo, who nodded. He looked to Voltoff. "Ease the horses just enough to tire the Cossacks and keep them behind us at all times."

"I understand." Voltoff stood and scanned the cavalry.

He could see the cloud of snow mist rolling behind the massed horsemen, following them as they swept over the white field. The faster horses were moving ahead, and he saw the flanks begin to close in. He looked at his own horses skim the earth in front of their sleigh.

"Slip the tethered string!" He freed the trailing animals who ran ahead of them.

"They're bunching up!" He took his bow and flexed it to limber the wood, watching the Cossack charge begin to string out. He saw a clump of perhaps thirty horsemen running behind a good fifteen horsemen with sabers and lances. "That's the gang to blunderbuss!" he shouted to Piippo, who grinned.

"Hell, we're going to win!"

"Piippo, these bastards'll kill you!" Turning to Voltoff, he shouted, "I want one Cossack at a time on the back of this sleigh!"

"My lord, I swear by my saint!" At Voltoff's knees he saw the innocent blue eyes of Polonitz, staring calmly into the gathering cavalry charge.

He found a strange exhilaration in his body as he tensed himself to fight. His legs and arms were light as wind and still hard as iron. There was a great fury in him. At his legs he could feel his children showing confusion at the shouts and fear in the adults, and a gorge seeped against his throat.

He watched an officer gallop against their wash of white snow scud, until he was two lengths away. The face was hard, and the cold eyes on him. The officer pointed forward with his sword. His horse was at loose rein, the nostrils distended.

Skarra drew the bow string and drove the arrow into the man's chest, and the man flipped backward out of the saddle instantly. He notched another arrow and drew and sent the arrow into the face of a Cossack whose dark eyes stared at the fletching bobbing in front of him as he tumbled out of sight. The horse shied at the rolling body.

He looked at Piippo's sleigh racing beside him to see Lydia had one of the flintlocks in her hands, loading it, and saw Piippo shoot a squirt of flame at a string of six horsemen. Nobody fell. He aimed his bow at the officer behind Piippo's sleigh. The arrow hit the man under his armpit, sticking out as he galloped forward. He saw the man turn his face to him and stare, in surprise, then begin to cough blood in sprays. He fell into the snow spume.

He shot three other men out of their saddles. They could not seem to realize he had motion on his side, and if his horses were faster than theirs, then all they could do was ride into their deaths. It was the military mind at its worst, but he had no choice. Killing children was as old as mankind. "Not my children!" he heard himself shouting.

He saw a lancer ride into Piippo and was amazed to see Piippo grab the lance and draw the man in, hand over hand, until he thought Piippo had gone mad. He saw the circular motion of the axe as Piippo buried it into the top of the skull, exploding it in pieces of bone and a mist of blood and brain.

"Kill him!" Lydia screamed.

"Good God." At his feet he could hear Penelope crying. "Hold the children to your bosom," he shouted to her.

He was busy emptying the saddles of the horsemen chasing Piippo's sleigh when he heard Lady Bofors. "Bruce, a Cossack!" He flexed back, avoiding the swing of the saber that split the back seat of their sleigh. He snapped up the claymore as the man galloped almost at his knees.

"You bastard," he said involuntarily, looking into the dark eyes of a total stranger. The man hesitated, gathering his strength in his shoulder and clinging with his thighs to the saddle. The saber rose, the mouth was open, and Skarra could hear him gasping for air along with the horse, who strained to keep up with the sleigh. Such ungodly effort for such waste, he thought. He saw the look of death in the Cossack's eyes, of glint and cold passion.

"Hahhh!" Skarra heard the breath exhaled as the blade cut at his bare thigh. "Wrong!" He caught the blade on the brass and uncoiled his arm and body in riposte. His claymore cut across the man's face and he was surprised to see the beard opening in a raw slash that peeled hair and blood. The man went out of sight and he heard Penelope scream.

"Bruce!" It was Lady Bofors.

A Cossack had come in from the other side. The man was in the sleigh on top of the women and children. Skarra raised the claymore, seeking a clear place to strike among the flopping bodies.

"Bastard!" he shouted, drawing his dirk, when he saw the Cossack's legs move in spasms that meant death. He was face-down. Skarra pulled him upright, seeing Penelope's vast breasts swing out into sight between the crying children, and a slick mass of blood and intestines on her lap and knees.

"Damn you!" He felt the man go slack and saw the light fade under his eyes. Penelope's hand held a curved knife and her arm was wet with blood and fecal matter up to her elbow. She had disemboweled the Cossack, "For God's sake, don't cry," he said. "Throw him out."

They threw out the Cossack's body and watched the coil of intestines ravel over the back of the sleigh, showering them with blood. The man rolled on the snow, the intestines winding around the fur-clad body in a bizarre exchange of place.

"Piippo, the gun!" Riderless horses were all around them.

He saw Piippo drop to his knees behind the blunderbuss. The hard core of men determined to carry through the charge were pressed knee to knee before him.

"Aim high to shower them."

He watched the great ball of smoke roll out of a streak of fire. The rain of lead splattered into the clump of horsemen. He saw it fall, the horses tumbling, men flung into the bodies and shrieks of pain mingling with the death agonies of maimed horses, all skidding out of sight in the cloud of snow.

They were alone in a moment, hearing their own hoofbeats. They raced along and he watched the survivors reining up at the carnage where he had fired the blunderbuss.

"Slow them!" he shouted to Voltoff. The melancholia of his triumph stifled him, and he opened his mouth to breathe.

He galloped the troikas another five miles until they were hid behind a low ridge, where he pulled up to change and walk the horses. Penelope and Lady Bofors brushed at the frozen blood on their furs. "You did well," Lady Bofors said to the nurse. Voltoff and Ralawitz scampered in the snow collecting the free horses that had galloped with the troikas to stay with their stallion, Barbarossa.

Skarra saw to their arms and then he held Lydia to his chest, inside his furs, while she poured out the tears of a person who has lost the final blood-tie to family and now confronts life as a refugee.

"Aye, he was so gallant, and he died for life," Skarra said, feeling the waves of sorrow pass through her, until she was exhausted. She was beautiful, yet even her beauty brought its melancholia, for all he could see was destruction. The soldiers would have killed them all.

In the dark he ordered the troikas toward the woods and river. They came down the battlefield, passing the dark shapes of dead horses. They saw shadows vanish over the snow. "Wolves," Voltoff said. "They have taken our prince." They searched for his body but found no officers in the scuffled tracks.

"My lord killed many," Voltoff said.

Skarra looked over the scattered shadows. "These people were insane with anger, so that only death would suit them."

The Cossack fires were sprinkled across the occluded light of the woods, casting an orange glow up into the gaunt trees. "Climb in, and let's go!"

The sleighs swept into the forest. "Whoom!" Piippo fired the blunderbuss and Skarra saw men and horses crashing through the underbrush, amidst curses for salvation as they ran through the fires and glowing embers.

They crossed the frozen river, climbed the hill and moved onto the plain, and drove the rest of the night. Skarra hunched down into his furs and felt he had departed from his body, and escaped into a gloom where he was not proud of what he had learned about the human race in the thirty years he had lived on earth. Even Geney slipped off into a memory that was unreal. He sat that way all night.

At Königsberg Skarra took long walks on the frozen sea wall where the ice shoved against the rocks, knowing the ocean was their refuge, yet there was no way to be on it. Sometimes Lydia joined him and he was glad to have another person to keep him company. After the death of her father Lydia seemed to find solace in his dour silence and followed him like a child, yet he was haunted by guilt that he could see anything beautiful and did not look at her.

Königsberg was full of tales of desolation among the German states as Gustavus Adolphus and Wallenstein sparred with each other for the mastery of Europe. Skarra had a keen grasp of what happens when armies swing around each other, each cut off from its base and living from the land. The situation creates concentric swaths of rapine and plunder, with the collapse of all ordinary human commerce. Virtue is swept aside like a feather while death is the handmaiden to every exertion. "We must find the Scottish Highlanders," Skarra said.

He and his party left Königsberg in late winter, and were diverted south into Poland. The spring floods along the Vistula passed them through Posen, and into Frankfort, where he sold the sleighs to a band of gypsies, camped for the winter on the banks of the Oder. He wanted one of their covered caravans, a topheavy wagon they could travel in. They had been moving through Europe for over a month, and they had grown tattered. His beard itched. Lydia's elegant habit dragged about her legs, and she had shed layers of underclothes. The tops of her kid boots were cut off, giving her legs the effect of dirty feet thrust into clogs.

"Lord, I never felt freer," she said, noticing him staring at her. "Look at my fingernails." They were grimed in dirt.

"Remember when I first met you?"

"Yes, at the Royal Ball. The King, Papa. Now I'm a homeless peasant."

"It's the meek who endure," he said.

They moved slowly through Saxony, aware that the King had gone into winter court at Frankfort on the Main, receiving the homage of Europe after defeating the Imperial armies at Breitenfeld. John George, Elector of Saxony, had his army just to the south, in Bohemia, while Wallenstein was waiting on his estates in Moravia for a desperate Emperor to call him into action, and Count Isolani, leading the Imperial Light Horse, harried anything not defended by fortifications.

The German states were buried under their weed-grown fields and empty villages. Their sorrow was strewn in unburied corpses and underclothes for miles, while desolate-eyed cows wandered in the ditches.

"Nobody left but the dead and the cows," Piippo said as they walked through the moist spring day.

They had breakfasted early on a goose which Piippo saw duck his head into the high grass a split second late. All morning they had walked in the sunlight under the fresh limbs of the poplars and linden trees.

"This place is a paradise," Skarra said, remembering the rank gorse and mists of Scotland.

They came into the village before they realized it. He saw the usual cobbled paving wet with offal piled at the doorways and the shapes of unburied animals. They had a shrunken look. "Old corpses," he said, meaning the war had swept by last year and it was safe.

"Halt!" a man in a tunic said, stepping from a water-stained building.

"Friends," Skarra said, putting up his hand to stop Voltoff, who was driving.

"Who's the woman?" The man looked at Lydia and put his fingers into his beard.

"Mine."

"Looks gypsy."

"Mine."

Other men appeared in light maroon tunics with frogging across the breast. Skarra heard horses' hoofs.

"Let's get the hanging over with," one of the men said.

"You like a hanging, eh?"

"Who are you?" an officer said.

Skarra spoke to Voltoff in Russian. Then he said to the officer, "Polish. We were driven out."

The men laughed. "Did you see that little gypsy dish?"

"Belongs to him. Let's hang the prisoners."

Skarra waited while two men were brought into sight and shoved across the square in front of the small moss-covered church. Their hair was disheveled and one had a bruised lip.

"What are you about?" Skarra said to a soldier.

"Hanging prisoners."

"For what reason?"

"To hang them." He stared at Skarra, seeking to understand the miscomprehension. "Would you like to see it?"

"I can see well enough."

The men began to cry when they saw the makeshift gallows, a pole resting across wine barrels.

"Who are they?" Skarra said.

"Who gives a damn. They're not with us, so they got to be against us."

"We told you everything," the blond one said. "You said you'd spare us if we talked, and we told all."

The soldiers smiled among themselves, as though any entreaty by the men was insane in the face of their certain fate. "If you'll tell on others you'll tell on us."

"Hang them," the leader said, annoyed at confronting his lie in the mouths of the condemned men.

The soldiers lifted the men into the air and slipped their heads into the nooses, and a soldier jumped onto the back of each man, clinging around his arms and wrapping his legs about his loins while the figures began to contort wildly. The legs rose and scissored, then huddled upward under the chin, the body breaking wind. There was excited laughter. The figures straightened out, each executioner peering like a grimacing fool over the shoulder, gritting his teeth to hang onto the dying man.

"Look at his codpiece!" one of the men shouted. "A cock that can't crow!" The confused body died in an act of decadence.

They walked out of the village and Skarra noticed they were silent the rest of the afternoon. Finally he said, "This offense of men against God through murder is human reason carried to the extreme." He shook his head slowly. "Reality is a nightmare if the dream comes true; now we're for Scotland."

"Let's get on to Scotland," Lydia said.

"Bruce, I've walked so far, I don't believe there is such a place," Piippo said, "and before I'm through, you'll say I've got to swim."

It was a lovely walk through Franconia and across the foothills of the Alps, which they could see shrouded in mists beyond the near clouds. They forded many small streams, where they always stopped to bathe. After the cold winter and their long walk in rags a dashing creek could not be ignored. "By God, another bath would do us good," Skarra would say, and he and Piippo and Lydia would shuck their soiled wrappings and wade naked into the water. Skarra laughed for the first time since before Geney died, at the delight of sitting in water up to his neck and sloshing Lydia and Piippo, who shouted and splashed. Once he noticed Lydia was lovely in her nude body, with the sheen of water on her flesh across the wide hips and loins and her black hair wet atop her breasts.

"Lydia, you are lovely," he said, embarrassed that she had seen him staring.

"It does no good." She flushed.

"I can't indulge myself with pleasure."

"If you could cry, Bruce, you could live."

"If I ever let myself cry I would never stop."

She waded to the bank where the older people waited with their garments, and Skarra could hear her crying as he followed. Hurting her made him withdraw again, where he avoided her eyes, though they lived as a family of forgiving intimacy and mutual respect, still bathing at the streams, but never touching.

14

The sound came insensibly on his mind, a fading then a rising of skirls, and he stopped.

"What is it?" Lydia said.

The faint rhythm came once more, a ghostly shrill of distant pipes.

"My God, I think they're pipes."

"Pipes?"

"Yes, the war pipes of Scotland."

They stopped in the evergreen forest, hearing a raven break into their minds with his sharp protest. "Yes, it's different," Lydia said, cocking her head to hear.

"Bagpipes." He turned to them. "Those are Scotsmen!" He seized them in his arms and hugged them. The pipes were clear as the skirling sound echoed against the mountainside. He held up the children so they could hear. "Bagpipes! We're going home to Scotland."

They lashed their way through the woods, seeking to catch up with the pipes and rolling snare drums of a Highland regiment. He could hear the men singing in Gaelic and in English, and he felt the hair rise on his legs and he gasped for his breath. "My countrymen!" he shouted to Lydia, who ran barefoot at his side, shying glances behind her to keep clear of the clawing hooves of the horses he led. The caravan was crashing over roots and dragging into limbs, and he could hear the children crying. They broke into sight at a clearing, and he saw the skirmishers wheel into a scattered line on the flank as a squad of cavalry cantered toward them.

"Scotland forever!" he yelled, throwing his torn bonnet over his head and filling the air with his old war cry. "Ahhee-EE-aaa!" The regiment faltered and began to dissolve toward them.

"It's Brucie of Skarra!" The laughter was all about him, of childhood friends and distant kin, "And Robbie McNaughton, part Campbell and part McDonald, and hated by both clans." It was an insane moment of childhood memories seizing the hopes of grown men, and friendship rising as an ecstasy among children to banish adult sorrow forever. They laughed and shouted and pounded each other on the back.

"He walked from Russia!"

"And the girl, did ye see her?"

"I want to go to Russia!"

"Does she have a sister, Bruce?"

Half the regiment was clustered about Skarra and the caravan, until Colonel Murray swung up into his saddle and bellowed for files on order and gestured down the road. With much laughter the Scots heaved the caravan onto the road, and it began to move sedately through the German countryside in a long line of kilted Highlanders.

All week it was a delightful procession of friends who wanted to see him in person.

"I never saw so many tall men calling each other 'little bastards' in my life," Lydia said to him while they lunched. "I didn't know it meant 'friend.' "

"It does in a way."

" 'Bastard,' you have to be a nice friend to use it." She tilted her head and smiled at him.

"Yes. The best. Old friends of my childhood and my family."

"I'm so glad for you." She touched his hand. "That you have such friends."

He avoided her eyes and ate his lamb stew. Nothing was more helpless than a good woman without family, or friends, and he had heired her as she stood, all but naked in her rags. Still, he would not look at her.

Skarra's friends assumed he had come to claim his command of a Highland regiment. There were six Scottish generals, thirty colonels, fifty-one lieutenant colonels commanding, or coming to command, and already five thousand Scotsmen in Gustavus' army of eighteen thousand men, with another five thousand on their way from Scotland, marching south from Pomerania. If Skarra could "kill Cossacks with mad abandon," as they said, it just didn't make good sense to not lead a regiment.

"No, I'm on my way home with my two children, to Scotland."

One tall officer looked at him and saw the truth of it, and wept openly as he shook Skarra's hand. Lady Bofors had included the details of 'why' to the King, who sent word back to Skarra, welcoming him to his protection, with the message "A fighting cock has to see a fight before he fights."

"I've never been a strutting rooster, God knows," he said.

The Imperial army, shattered at Rain—its general, Johann Tzerclaes, Count of Tilly, killed in April—was now led by Wallenstein, Duke of Friedland, who had rallied forty thousand men to its banners. "Solely by his martial skill," Skarra's friends explained to him. Worse, it had moved between the Swedes and Scots and their base in Pomerania. They were on their way north, and at Nuremberg the Allied army dug in. "The King is an earth-digging fool," they said, and Skarra never saw such a feverish scrabbling in the ground as the Allied army throwing up fortifications. Skarra rode out each dawn with friends and watched Wallenstein's army come up to within three miles of their defenses, where it also dug in. But he would not attack. "Neither general has ever been whipped. All of Europe rides on the battle."

The two armies besieged each other all summer. Skarra did not feel safe away from the Scottish brigades. "They won't run, and I don't think the Imperial army can kill all of them," he explained to Lydia, though Piippo was all for making a break for the coast. Gustavus apparently felt time running against him, and made a desperate sortie against the redoubt, Alte Feste, in which the Swedes were repulsed. It was obvious to Skarra that Wallenstein was playing for time against the Allied army, using famine to weaken them. The reinforcements had come, but still Gustavus had only twenty-five thousand men to Wallenstein's forty thousand.

Around Skarra's tent and caravan the Highlanders went quietly about their business, the war pipes never silent, playing the great laments of love and causes lost that never died. "I thought I'd go mad when I first heard the bagpipes," Lydia said. "But if I couldn't now, I'm sure I'd lose all my nerve. Besides, the children love them."

The Allied army moved out of its entrenchments in late October, striking north. At Erfurt, Gustavus bade farewell to his queen, Maria Eleonora, and sought the Imperial army, which had moved to cut him off from the Baltic, at Leipzig. Skarra made sure the caravan moved in the middle of the Scottish train, surrounded by ten thousand Scotsmen; however, he personally reconnoitered the endless cavalry harassment by Count zu Pappenheim and Count Isolani of the Imperial Light Horse. "We shattered the jolly Pappenheim at Breitenfeld," the Scots told him, "and he's a mite gun-shy." Skarra did notice the cavalry never charged the Highlanders who marched to the skirling notes he could hear for miles, their flintlocks always bayoneted for hand-to-hand grappling. "Piippo, I told you this is our only safety."

"You are proud of them."

"Very."

"But you won't fight."

"No. I swore to Geney I'd not."

"Not even to kill *him?*"

Skarra spurred up. Halvorsen was present in the King's entourage, and he avoided the Swedes because of it. It was in late October, with the fog resting on the wet fields, that Skarra heard a cavalcade come by their party. "The King!" someone shouted, and Skarra saw the large monarch, wearing no armor but a gold beard fluttering to the middle of his chest, and astride a seventeen-hand horse.

"Your Majesty," Skarra said, swinging into the saddle of his mare.

"Lord Bruce, you still say 'no' to me?"

"Not to Your Majesty. Never."

"No. Lady Bofors told us of your trek through Russia." He put up his hand. "You're not a weak man."

Skarra listened.

"The odds are against us." He shook his head. "Most men would rather say 'no' than 'yes.' It is more rewarding to punish than to please, for weak men. But you are not weak, so truth is in you. And you will fight." He laughed, a rumble in his chest, and spurred his horse.

It was a cold night in the middle of November. He rested in the caravan, drifting off to sleep when he could, his boots off but in his kilt and tweeds, rolled in his tartan. The women stepped over him barefoot and the small faces of the children peeped from the upper shadows of their tiered bunks. "Wake me at the gunfire," he had said, seeing a bare ankle pass his face as he lay on the floor.

"Bruce, sleep if you can." Lady Bofors had refused to remain with the Queen at Erfurt.

"Voltoff is watching the enemy campfires," Lydia said, kneeling at his head.

"Shsh, the children," Lady Bofors said.

"Is Piippo asleep?" he said.

"For hours. Wrapped in furs, under the tailgate."

"Have you slept, Lydia?"

"God, no, not with sixty thousand men ready to kill each other."

"You should."

"Shsh," whispered Lady Bofors.

"I don't need sleep." Lydia touched his eyelids.

The touch seemed to quiet him, and he drifted into a pale sleep, where he could feel himself on the brink of expectation, and was astonished to wake well after dawn with Lady Bofors' hand on his shoulder. He sat up, surprised to hear the children laughing in play at the tailgate with Penelope. He saw Lydia at his feet, face down, her body crumpled and her hair disheveled, and sound asleep.

"The battle?"

"Fog. They cannot see each other to fight."

"They're all blind, Bruce!" Piippo's voice swept over him, and he smiled at the keen face.

"Maybe they won't fight," he said.

"When they can see each other, they will kill each other." Lady Bofors spoke matter-of-factly and roused Lydia. "I have tea for you." She brushed the loose strands of Lydia's hair away from her eyes.

"Oh, I must have slept."

"Finally, yes."

"I shouldn't have."

"Why shouldn't you sleep?" Lady Bofors stood and went out the door, her dress swaying as she walked in a determined earth-rooted way. Piippo ducked back and greeted her respectfully.

Skarra was into his boots and had burnt the roof of his mouth with his tea he was so eager. Voltoff had his black mare saddled, and for Piippo, the Russian *donnets* horse. "Stay at the caravan," he said to Voltoff. The horses were tied in a rope corral at the side of the vehicle, under reindeer skins as tenting, and quite warm with the hay. "Lord, the Gordons and the Campbells and the McPhersons, they've formed up by now."

"Nobody can see," Piippo said.

Highlanders moved into and out of the mist, the kilts swaying around the sturdy bound legs and claymores, and each man with the Swedish flintlock. It was exhilarating to hear the gentle Highland airs of the pipers.

The Gordons formed for battle not a hundred yards from the caravan. The men were at ease, the regiments overlapping at the ends, and the colonels—Hepburn, Ramsay, and Leslie—were having tea at a small fire that glared in the fog.

"If it's too strong, ye can have a dram," Colonel Hepburn said to Skarra when he came up.

"The tea'll do, John."

"We'll want a dram before the day's out," Leslie said.

"Has anyone spotted them?"

"Aye. English sappers, and our pickets say the whole Imperial army's drawn up seven hundred yards away."

"It's not a day to be counting noses," Hepburn said, and the officers grinned as though they had lost all care for life if they could have but a single moment of passion with death.

Skarra saw a lightening of the fog, and he was surprised to see his caravan loom among the Black Watch who were drawn up to his left, and further on he saw the Swedish infantry in brown tunics and white stockings. The battle line seemed to bristle like a spiked hedge of bayonets, lances, and swords.

He heard a great yell roll up from the men down the hill and saw the green fields and patterned hedgerows, and the white banners of the Imperial army, fluttering in the movement of men formed up in "battalias," or squares, who sprawled into position. Horsemen in burnished cuirasses galloped before the squares, which shifted like clots of animation that spilled across the fields. His mind came back to the Scots. They were cheering in joy and fury with the enemy in sight, and he heard the war pipes rise to a pitch that seemed to howl for battle.

"Keep your dress at all times!" General McMurray shouted, and he galloped off, the Cross of Saint Andrews seeming to chase behind, a red flag with a blue cross. The flags of Scotland were everywhere.

The fog settled again briefly, isolating the men to their own being once more, seeming to disappoint them. Just before noon the fields cleared and Skarra saw the Imperial army packed ominously across their front and enveloping either flank.

"Whoom!" "Whoom, whoom!" "Whoom!" He heard the Swedish artillery fire. The cheering rose along the regimental front. He saw the Imperial artillery counterfire, coughing great balls of white smoke under the low clouds.

"Look!" he said to Piippo. They could see the Swedes firing faster than the Imperialists, and watched the shot laying furrows through the massed squares like grooves, in which the men up the center line seemed to dissolve while those on either side fell away from the gash. Then the mass would seem to shuffle among itself, and fill in the gap sliced through it by the cannonball.

"My lord! Oh, my lord!" Voltoff seized him by the arm. "Polonitz!"

"What?"

"He's run off! Oh, my lord!"

Skarra dropped the reins and ran for the caravan. "Where?"

"Oh, Bruce, the cannons! He's terrified!" Lydia ran toward him.

"Which way?!?" He was running and his claymore banged against his heels. He saw a small deformed figure running on bare feet and careening through the massed horsemen and companies of shouting men under arms until it went out of sight.

Skarra stopped chasing him and turned back to the caravan. Voltoff lay on the ground and wept, his marred eyebags puddling with tears that ran over the hair on his face.

"At least an idiot knows the truth," Skarra said.

He stayed at the caravan and watched the brigades dress their lines, when he saw the King gallop out ahead of the army, followed by a retinue of flag bearers and bodyguards. Gustavus reined up, and the trumpeter continued to gallop toward the Imperial army, a man in a knight's plumage astride a horse draped in silk brocades, with long white feathers pompomed atop its bridle. Skarra could hear the notes of challenge floating over the field between the two armies. He saw the Imperial trumpeter gallop out to accept the challenge to battle.

"By God, it's still called an honor," Skarra said, using Lydia's spyglass to see the details.

He could see Gustavus stand in his stirrups and point his sword at the Imperial front, and he stepped back at hearing the roar in the combined throats of both the armies, rolling from up and down the lines. The war pipes rose to a fury so loud he could scarcely think, and he saw masses of handsome men on horseback racing through the green meadows and over the fields between the armies. In seconds it was all confusion.

The Scottish brigades advanced against an immense square of men who pulled up, as though to receive them, their banners seeming to fold down when the square stopped. Skarra could see the men in front firing in a ragged chain of smoke and red spurts, yet nobody fell. Then he saw the quiet bodies of men on the grass, left behind as the Scottish brigades advanced.

"Too far for a blunderbuss," Piippo said, and Lydia joined him. They climbed atop the caravan to watch the battle.

The Scottish line seemed to hesitate, the front rank kneeling, and Skarra saw fire crash out in long needles at the mass who shrank in on itself and withered along the edges. "Dead men," Skarra said.

"Where?" Lydia said.

"Along the edge of the square, where the fusillade hit."

"God, they can't miss," Piippo said.

Skarra caught sight of a wave of shining horsemen who were circling the square. "Cuirassiers!" he said. They galloped across the flank of the Scottish line under their lances, which swayed over them like a sterile forest. He could hear the Highland bugles blowing and the piercing cries of the officers who were wheeling the Scottish line to face the lancers. The cavalry came at a walk.

"Listen to the ground tremble," Lydia said.

"Do you think they will hold?"

"It's Count zu Pappenheim, himself."

The horses picked up to a trot, and Skarra saw the red and yellow and black banner of the Count. A general quiet settled along the whole right flank of the battle, with all eyes on the massed horsemen.

"Here they come—oh, Bruce!" Lydia grabbed his arm.

They could feel the ground shake the caravan as the cavalry broke into their charge. He saw the upright wave of lances fold down ahead of the horses and the cuirassiers lean close over the pommels to present only their creased helmets and armored shoulders.

"Fire!" The command came.

The Scottish line fired, and he saw the second line scamper through the kneeling men and drop to their knees and heard the crash of regimental fire under clouds of smoke. Then he saw the first line of horsemen had fallen, though many desperate animals floundered to rise and held their long necks up as they sought to escape the men who struggled to drag them to their feet. The field writhed in confusion.

"Charge!" It was the Scottish general in Stuart markings. The Highland regiments leaped to their feet and rushed into the mass of unhorsed cuirassiers, and they watched the flintlocks swung as clubs to brain the men who scrabbled in their armor.

"We've killed Pappenheim!" the men shouted.

"They held," Skarra said when Lady Bofors joined them to watch the battle. She said nothing.

Twice the cuirassiers charged the Scottish regiments, and left a front that was lined with dying horses which heaved their bodies over broken legs and the forms of armored men who had been bayoneted or shot or clubbed to death.

Cheering drew the observers' attention and Skarra saw the Swedish infantry had advanced into the center of the Imperial army. He could see the swaying banners of the Archduke, Maximilian, and of Wallenstein. Men surged in a narrow edge which was the division between the Allied and Imperial armies. Pieces of clothing, naked buttocks which were naive on the plain, heads on twisted necks, and swords and flags and upthrust lances and muskets lay over every square foot of the land.

"I've seen other battles," Lady Bofors said. "They try to undress to ease their wounds, and they die naked." She got down off the tongue of the caravan and went to where the children fretted.

Skarra heard the cheering throughout the Imperial army, which began to seep slowly toward them, against the frantic smoke lines of Swedish infantry, spread out over the battlefield. He saw the Swedes running, their white stockings and brown tunics scurrying in many starts and stops. The soldiers would group and run at the advancing enemy, then turn compulsively to scatter. Officers galloped over the battlefield and waved their swords at the confused Swedish infantry, trying to rally it to hold. Men began to come past the caravan, their eyes unable to fix themselves, roving and bloodshot in their fear. They had lost their flintlocks and were breathing heavily, as much from panic as from exhaustion.

"God, look!" Piippo said.

They could see the Imperial cuirassiers swarming across the battlefield, skewering the infantry. One rider had a man on the end of his lance who ran in giant strides and screamed. The cheering rose like thunder.

"Hitch up the horses!" Skarra said.

Voltoff and Ralawitz had Barbarossa already in the harness. "In, you lovely devil!" Ralawitz drove his shoulder into the smooth haunch, spotting the horse beside the tongue of the wagon.

"Bruce, the King!"

"His Majesty!" Lydia was jumping up and down, clapping her hands. "The King will save us!"

Skarra heard the trumpets and saw the Swedish cavalry swirling into a massive chain behind the gold and blue crosses at its head. He could see the great bay horse and the King. Gustavus was in brown and smiling as he waited for the Swedish nobles to ride into position behind him. Trumpeters galloped up and down the line under their bobbing plumage.

Skarra saw the worried look in Piippo's eyes. "Hell, he's going to attack forty thousand men."

"If he doesn't his men won't fight," Skarra said.

"They'll kill him."

"He knows it." Skarra nodded toward the Swedish cavalry. They watched it move forward behind the King, whose arm was up. In a moment his beard was flying over his shoulder.

"There they go!" Lydia was jumping up and down. "Lady Bofors, come, quick! It's the Tsar!"

Skarra could see the Imperial army shrink in on itself and grow silent as they saw the royal banners of Sweden racing down the small swale, through the field of dying men, leading the massed cavalry who were armed with horse pistols.

He saw the King's horse come up against the edge of men under a pale line of smoke. He could hear the crackling noise of pistol fire as the point of the charge drove over the mass of infantry.

"Good God!" he said. He could see the King's horse seem to float into the midst of the army, carving it open with the wedge of cavalry, the horsemen standing in their stirrups in a line of flailing swords. He saw the men running away in falling motions on each side. He heard the cheering on all sides of him where the Allied army watched Gustavus Adolphus.

"The cuirassiers," Piippo said, nodding.

"Damn, always the unforeseen," Skarra said.

The Imperial cavalry swirled up and down the flanks of the Swedish cavalry, disjointing it into fragments which turned to fight. He looked back over the mass of infantry, who seemed to have paused, and saw the white and gold banners of the Emperor and of Wallenstein moving over the heads of the footmen to where he could still see Gustavus. The horsemen about the King were leaning into the footmen above swords which rose and fell in cold air.

Skarra could see the horses disappear one by one, down off their frail legs, their bodies enveloped by the infantry who killed them and their riders.

"The Swedish flags," Skarra said. They seemed to fold and sag into the excited movement, and he could see the Imperial banners swooping and dipping like colored birds of prey. Skarra and the others watched in stunned silence. They could see the cuirassiers level their lances and bend low. The King went down under the lancers, who stormed over the pile of dead men Gustavus fell among. They watched the King's broken body stabbed and shot by many men.

"You break the pitcher when you carry it to the well," Lady Bofors said. "Bruce, the children?"

Skarra brushed past Lydia and Piippo. "My mare!"

"Bruce!" Lydia began to cry. "No, no!"

To his dying day he would never know what thought rushed into his mind out of his soul—the lust for fight, the sense of outrage at the King's death, or his certain knowledge escape lay only in victory, for they would kill his children and rape and murder his women if he lost.

"Piippo, stay here!" He wheeled the little black mare and galloped to the Scottish line. "Save the children!" he shouted at Colonel Hepburn and the Scottish officers, and seized the flag of Scotland.

"Bruce of Skarra! Scotland forever!" The officers shouted.

He felt his small mare plunge uncertainly as she placed her hooves to avoid the corpses and scattered arms. He rode down the broken front of the Allied army, ignoring the wounded who rose on elbow or kicked about to watch him. He wanted the common people in whose heart every virtue lived and all vice was possible.

"Northmen!" he shouted, standing in his stirrups, "Northmen, rally to the body of the dead King!" He towered above the mare's back and raced the flag before the men.

He saw the Swedish line hesitate, the coarse faces shadowed with a day's fury and their eyes glazed, looking up to see the tall officer in the feathered bonnet.

"A Scotsman!" A surge of men curled into sight. It was the Finns with their axes and shields who ran to keep him in view.

"Dare to live once more!" He gestured toward the enemy with the flag.

Behind him he heard the Scottish brigades shriek in joy at death and strife—"Ahhee-EE-aaa!"—and the war pipes raised the hair on his neck. He saw the Highlanders move out in a forest of bayonets that shone in the cold light. The Swedish line burst into a gross roar of outrage and the whole army moved slowly toward him.

"Northmen, face the edge of death as freemen!" He waved his claymore at the Imperial banners and the silent infantry who waited under their pikes.

"Into the gap of sorrow for the sacred body of the King!" His voice was swept away in the thunderous roars for battle which made his mare hump her buttocks and run toward the enemy.

The short-legged men surprised him as they swept in on his left, shying the mare. It was the Finns, their axes held at the head as they raced across the sodden grass where naked dead turned their limbs in odd gestures.

Cantering diagonally back to the Scottish regiments, he saw the banners of Bernhard, Duke of Saxe-Weimar, race out ahead of the Allied army.

"Bruce! Wait!" He saw Piippo running alone across the battlefield, his shield on his forearm and carrying his axe.

"The children and the women!" He reined up the mare.

"There'll be no women and children if we don't chop our way free." Piippo's eyes were still guileless.

"Lord, it's a sorrow to live." He slid off the mare. In a second he had slipped her girth and dropped her bridle, and they watched her race across the field between the armies, searching a way back to the caravan and her stallion.

"My Lord Skarra," said a Highlander, taking the Scottish flag. Colonel Ramsay came by on his horse, shouting, "Keep your dress! Fire four volleys, then rush them with the bayonet!" His face was blanched in contrast to his deep voice. "Cold steel, and they'll run! Cold steel!"

Skarra stood aside with Piippo as the Highland regiments fired their salvos in a precise step, almost like dancers changing places in a kneeling minuet. He lost sight of the enemy line, but heard great screams and rolling curses to his left. He knew the Finns and the Swedes had reached the Imperial army.

"Ahhee-EE-aaa!" He heard the war cry he had known a lifetime, and he raced ahead of the Scottish line which was rushing the massed enemy.

In seconds he had jumped the thrashing layers of wounded and dying men peeling from the edges, and was facing tired men. Blond or dark, they raised their swords and stabbed unsteadily with bayonets and cumbersome pikes. He struck and parried and struck again, always at the blade then into the drawn face that bled in the white groove or tilted on its neck and wept or cried as he thrust the point into the body. He stood on bellies that slipped underfoot like sacks of water and on chests which had a springy bounce, and on thighs and buttocks which yielded in slack ripples, the men's lives gone. The cries and dark faces were a live sea on all sides, and he heard the terrible crunching sound of Piippo's axe, and felt his ear stung where a sliver of bone flew out from Piippo's blows.

"Oh, my lord," said a Highlander, sliding to his knees. He had caught his bayonet in a man but could not pull it free, and the dark-haired fellow had driven a sword into his belly. Skarra recoiled as Piippo drove his axe into the fellow's breastbone. He dropped dead on his back and Skarra stared a moment. The handsome face drained white in seconds, and the mouth and lips were beautiful as they eased into a purity, bowing like a woman's.

"My God," he said, turning with the claymore, the dirk parrying in his left hand against a halfhearted thrust of a bayonet. The man dropped his musket and ran. They were running.

"Look! Oh, Lord, they run!" He saw the whole mass of men dropping their weapons and running from the fight. "Oh, thank God, they run! Oh, thank God!"

In seconds he saw a scurrying horde of men, rushing over and into each other, leaving a trail of weapons and limping creatures who fell behind or lay on the trampled earth and cried for mercy. They were killing the wounded on all sides of him and kneeling to strip the dead. It was the bubbly sound of death, and he turned back toward the caravan looming on the skyline.

Piippo spoke. "It's the King."

"Lord, that poor man."

"They're bringing in the King's body."

He pulled up as the cortege of men, bound in rags where they had bled, stopped before him. They carried the body of Gustavus Adolphus of Sweden. The swords and lances and bullets had cut and riddled it until only the beard was human, and it dripped blood at the base of a head that glistened in caked gore. "Lord have mercy," Piippo said.

"He never killed prisoners," Skarra said. "And men hated him for it."

"He was so handsome," Piippo said, a quandary in his throat. "Why, Bruce? Don't say there's no place for a good man on earth."

"Love's unforgivable. Let's go see the children."

Lydia ran down the low hill, as they walked up it. "Oh, Bruce!" Her hair was loose and shifting in motion. He pushed the hilt of the claymore aside as she rushed into him. "Oh, it was awful, but, oh, God, we won."

They looked across the battlefield and into the distance, where he saw the village of Lütgens set in a cluster of white shapes. The moving passage of men seemed to shrink to enter, then expand on the other side, over the evening-dark fields and out of sight.

"The melancholia of victory," he said. "Lord, the sorrow. Only the children will ease it."

She took his hand. "They're just perfect. I had Penelope keep them in her bosom, when I looked for you."

They were boiling tea billies and samovars at the caravan and Voltoff was cheerful once more. Skarra held the children to his chest, and searched their faces. In Fanny he saw Geness clearly, in the tilt of her eyebrow and the set of her nose and line of her mouth. "The lips move over her teeth exactly the same," he said. After caressing the children and sipping tea and eating a bowl of porridge, he said, "I broke my oath to Geney."

The party grew still where they had been eating and lounging. "Will you kill him?" Piippo said.

"Aye, I've killed a dozen good men this afternoon, who did me no wrong."

"Can you live with yourself if you kill him?" Lady Bofors said.

"I've killed too many to not kill him as well."

"Would you measure yourself by what is wrong?"

"I've broke my oath and I've waded in gore, now let me avenge Geney."

"Oh, Bruce." Helen Bofors stood the claymore at his hip to be buckled, and Lydia set her hand at his dirk.

Skarra and Piippo walked through the campfires of the bivouacked army. Men spoke quietly, on mellow voices in the moist air, and carried the bodies of the dead to the burial ground. Skarra could sense the personal shame of the victory and the regret shared by the men. He found the officers' tents and lifted a flap. "Halvorsen, I'm looking for Captain Halvorsen."

"Over there, one tent down," said an officer who spoke without looking up from his writing table.

"Halvorsen!" Skarra called before a tent. Even the word set a taste of bile in his teeth.

"Who wants Halvorsen?" It was a voice beyond a campfire.

"The Scotsman."

He heard a rush of talk, and Halvorsen spoke as a group of officers came into sight out of the mist.

"What do you want?"

"You." Skarra saw the well-set man emerge into the light with the fire playing on the mass of lateral hair girdling his face.

"Me?"

"Your carcass, to be exact."

"The King forbade dueling."

"Not today and not for us." Skarra walked into the firelight.

"The Scottish officer who rallied the army . . . to the dead King . . . !" He heard the voices of the men who came out of the tents to see and whom Piippo turned to watch.

"Yes, arm him," Skarra said, seeing Halvorsen strap a cavalry saber about his waist and take a dagger into his hand from an officer.

"Ye mocked a woman in public for what she does in private," Skarra said. "Ye riled me."

"Afire, over a common bawd."

"The time has come to measure your tongue with your life."

"Fool!" Halvorsen searched Skarra with strong eyes that seemed to show the cruel satisfaction of having hurt another man, of having broke life irrevocably. *"En garde!"*

Skarra stepped around the fire as the body expanded toward him when the saber lashed out of its scabbard. He drew the claymore and felt it calm him with a sense of absolute peace. The blade shifted in quick reflections.

He slipped his dirk into his hand, determined to stab Halvorsen to death. He saw the dark features circling him as he played with the claymore cocked up to entice the saber. The spectators revolved around and around behind the heavy figure shining in the cuirass in front of Skarra as the points of the swords played about each other like serpents.

"Haah!" Skarra caught the saber on the down-pass, seeing sparks trail the blades. He jumped clear as the heavy dagger slashed at his forearm. He was surprised when he felt blood dripping from his elbow. The claymore was trim as a goose quill and as light and he spat with excitement.

He pressed the blade, and shouted, striking aside the saber, and circled backward. He saw the wave of doubt in Halvorsen's eyes, of a man glimpsing the unexpected but blindly driven by his insolence and its consequences.

He stepped into the saber-arc and let the sword blades lick each other in raining sparks, then parted with a sliding clatter that glinted in the firelight between them. Again he took the blows over his head, and along his body, the blades following each other up and down, steel on steel, and not yet able to cut flesh. Skarra fought with a strange joy he felt rise within his person, running from his breath to the nerve endings of his wrists, a joy of peace rising out of rancorous fury. He knew he would kill him.

He feinted, seeing the man's teeth grind and the saber drop, the arm straightening as the body lunged and the muscular legs drove forward. He passed the blade down his left side and yelled, jumping forward with the dirk. He had the short blade into the pommel notch of the corselet, knowing it when he felt the lower intestines packed against his knuckles. He saw the appalled finality darken the eyes.

Halvorsen stiffened and rose on his legs to climb off the dirk, but he raised it into his belly, and watched the mouth open and blow out. The terrified eyes searched his, knowing it was too late.

"That's the dirk I used to open Geney's womb to make new life," he said. He jerked out the dirk as Halvorsen clasped both his hands to his bleeding crotch. "The sword of the Lord is two-edged, and ye reap what ye sow."

The large man blanched and folded down over his knees, and flopped onto his face and kicked his legs, and moaned. His muscular buttocks were pathetic as he churned on his belly.

"You've killed him," said one of the officers.

"He killed himself," Skarra said, wiping the dirk on a handful of grass.

"Can you kill a man so easy, Scotsman?" one of the officers said.

"Look out on that field and blame me for your insanity." Skarra sheathed the claymore and the dirk.

" 'Tis murder."

"Aye, and murder takes all forms. At least we fought as equals."

On the way back to the caravan, they stumbled upon the open pit into which the Swedes were carrying their dead. Each shrouded body was stiff between the two men who shuffled awkwardly through the open grave. The men were careful not to step on the corpses lying in the fresh dirt and veiled in the fog. It struck Skarra as a nursery of dead children in the gawkish poses of childhood sleep, until he saw the open mouths and gared eyeballs frozen in protest as they had died. The dirt showered them as the burial parties followed the line of dead.

He heard a man crying behind. Piippo had his hands up to his face as he sought to stifle his sobs.

"Piippo?" Skarra said.

"Bruce, is this it?" Piippo managed to gasp. "Is this all there is?"

"No." Skarra held him closely into his chest.

"Halvorsen, that poor man, he'll take hours to die."

" 'Tis a sorry doing."

"Bruce, there's got to be more."

"Aye, but Geney drowned in her own lungs, crying for her children."

"Oh, Bruce, I don't know if I want to live."

"Piippo, dear God, men can be so much, yet they choose to be so little, that's the amazement of life, for a man's a universe." He listened to Piippo struggle to control his tears, and saw their shadow across the grave from the fires behind them.

"It's got to be more."

"Only the Lord is more than his image, and we are but an image." He hugged Piippo hard, and spoke softly. "Life itself should be gift enough, this thing was madness."

He felt Piippo compose himself, and he wiped his nose with the back of his hand. "I always wanted to fight in a battle, but I never thought of what the dead would look like."

"A damned sorry day it was. Let's go to the children and Lydia."

It was easy to book passage from the Continent to Stockholm. The French had allied themselves to the Swedes, and what had originally been a religious war became a general war, and he was anxious to go home. They found a captain willing to build a stable in his well-deck, where they loaded the horses.

He stood at the taffrail wrapped in his tartan and he heard the rigging snap under full sails which drove the bows into a sea that rushed out in white spray.

"Home," Skarra said. "Soon we'll be home."

"Bruce?"

He saw Lydia's quandary. The fine nostrils betrayed her anxiety as they opened with her breath, and she swept the tip of her tongue into view when she talked. He knew what Lydia wanted, and he would never deny her; yet, what she wanted was a land and a home foreign to her childhood, and once she chose it, she would have to stay all her life among foreigners, with no chance to ever return. It was a terrible decision.

"Yes?"

"You know what it is."

"No, not completely."

"May I come?"

He could see the spindrift clouding the wave tops. "You're asking to accompany a man in his grief."

"And his children."

"Yes."

"I breathed into them."

"You made it most clear." He shifted his stance. "Scotland's a cold, dour land, with a sentiment to equal the gravity of eeking the victuals from the earth." He looked at her. "Lydia, you were born a princess in a heathen land."

"Bruce"—she took his hand in hers—"callouses, feel them?"

"You've worked, aye."

"I'd have the children and Penelope and Voltoff."

"Will he come?"

"With me, yes. . . . Now he declares I'm all he's got left."

"I don't know."

"You said all nations were savage."

"On occasion."

He felt her watch him, and looked across the ocean to avoid her. "Who do you have?" she said.

"Me? A clan of Scots."

"Yes, but who is to live in your soul?"

"Memories."

"Memories live out of love."

"They do."

"But you must nourish the old love with new love."

He was silent.

"You lived in a cottage in a foreign land, teaching at a university, out of love."

"It was what I wanted."

"The love did it." She moved around to face him, and he felt the taffrail caught against his back. "You cannot rule your estate without love, and with it, I could live in Scotland, same as you in Russia."

"Scotland is now Protestant, as am I."

"I'll give up my faith."

"Never say that again." He stiffened.

"I don't care. With love, all that's yours is mine, forever, to death, and beyond."

"Oh, God, all this talk! Come, I don't care!" He wheeled and brushed past her, then stopped. "Lydia, I can't love you now, and I don't know when, for I hurt all down inside me, but stay with me. And bring your faith, for the less would not be you."

It was the first week in December when Skarra arrived in Stockholm. The port bustled in a forest of varnished ships' masts docked close against the Royal Palace, now ruled by Queen Christina, only child of Gustavus Adolphus. "If Christina reigns over the palace, Count Axel Oxenstierna rules the nation," the Swedes explained to Skarra when he was summoned from their hotel. Piippo accompanied him to the Stockholm Palace, which was a huge stone and wood building now stiff under icicles and as phlegmatic as the frozen countryside. Soldiers and officials seemed to expect him. He was saluted on all sides.

Count Axel Oxenstierna, Prime Minister of Sweden, was waiting for him in a small chamber, warmed by a tiled stove. "Come in, Bruce," the large man said and walked toward them. "Helen and I are cousins."

"Helen?"

"Lady Bofors."

"A rare friend," Skarra said, taking the hand, "and this is Piippo."

"Yes. Impossible feat of arms."

"The Countess was a friend in need when the whole town turned its back."

"Ach, the squalor of provincials—will you take a command, young man?" The heavy eyelids seemed to envelop him.

"An army, my lord?"

"Whatever size you might wish."

"No, Your Grace, I've never seen the purpose to war beyond vanity."

"You know better. You killed to save your children, but go home." He chuckled to himself. "Wisdom is so rare I dare not tamper with it."

"I'm sorry, sire, for I have a profound respect for the Swedes and Finns."

"War is man's final betrayal to knowledge, and they call it a primitive instinct."

"It's the bare ass of a sick ape," Skarra said.

"Let's not blame an innocent monkey."

"I want to go home, sire."

"Go, and take the Russian girl, beautiful creature they tell me. The Russians would only kill her. Each Ivan is more terrible than the last, and they all prey on the royal family of Russia." He breathed.

"Thank you, Your Grace."

"It is not often that I find a man." He clasped Skarra to his heavy robed body and brushed him loose immediately, and spoke to a secretary who waited at a wide desk. "Put Lord Skarra and his children and party—yes, and his horses—on our first ship to Scotland." He looked out the frosted windowpane at the harbor. "It's the least Sweden can do for a soldier."

They had shared four frantic days getting the horses aboard another ship and shopping in Stockholm. Gnawing at Skarra's soul was the parting with Piippo, which he postponed until they had to go out on the tide. He wanted to say what a professor should say when he says good-bye. He hugged Piippo, then said, "Piippo, I only taught you what you already knew, but did not know you knew it. To love life is to be true, and beyond this it is useless."

Piippo began to cry. "Yes, we were always in your cottage to see if you really believed what you said."

"Aye, so I noticed."

"I could go to Scotland."

"No, you must be free to find a pretty girl who wants to make a life, and start, one step at a time, and you'll take a trip to the end of your life."

"Oh, Bruce, I'll never forget."

Skarra hugged him hard—"Go, to your own life"—and turned to the ship.

"Bruce." Lady Bofors took his hand.

"Tend Geney's grave," he said, and burst into tears.

"Every day, but keep her children with care."

He nodded, unable to see her in the glaze of tears.

"Let Lydia come to you in time."

He could not speak when Helen Bofors embraced him.

"God keep you." She walked through the gangway, and he quieted, as though from the older woman's touch.

It was an easy passage down the Baltic and through the Skagerrak. They were eight days out of Stockholm, under a light canvas, when Skarra smelled the Scottish gorse on the leeward mist.

"Land-Ho!" The words rolled onto the moist deck, where he waited with the Swedish captain and listened to the water slap their strakes as the man-of-war sought the headlands of Skarra.

"Where away?!"

The Swedish sailors scampered up the rigging and into the fog and the wheel creaked behind him to ware away the ship from the rocks. "Whoom!" came the cannon in the forecastle, and he listened for the return echo. The Captain smiled. "Ah, two miles, deep water."

The ship moved onto a green sea and he saw the old Watch Tower of Skarra on the headland, just as he had seen it a lifetime ago.

"Skarra," he said, "we're home." Lydia and Penelope and the children clustered around him. "Wrap their throats at all times." The boy and girl watched the murky land and held onto his fingers. The land grew massive as the ship rounded the spit and eased into the firth.

"What ship is that?" The words were more vast than a human voice, yet they saw but a single horseman watching them from the shore.

"Her Majesty's *Northern Sovereign,* eight days out of Stockholm!"

"Are you in distress?"

"Bound for Skarra!"

The ship was close to land, which had apparently excited the Highlanders, for he saw cotters moving in the hills.

He vaulted into the chains, where his voice would not be clouded by sail, and bellowed, "Bruce of Skarra! Tell my mother I'm home!"

He saw the men talk to each other, and one ran to the edge of the cliff. "Is that you, Bruce?!?"

"Aye, go tell my mother!"

In moments the ship had wared about the shoal. In the distance he saw Skarra.

"Is that it?" Lydia said.

"Home." The hedge of fuchsia went up the hill from the quay to the yew trees that stood about the grounds. The rhododendron was nestled in a dark mass along the Italian piazza his mother had added to soften the stone walls of the old Scottish manor house.

"Bruce, it's so fog-bound."

"Fires on the quay!" the lookouts shouted when they saw the range beacons.

"Bruce, I'm afraid."

"No need. They're part of me."

"Bruce, the house looks so dark, and it's all stone."

He saw the profound quandary in her eyes as she searched his. "Give it time. 'Tis Scotland."

They watched the ship warped to the quay by a hundred men while the park and drives of the manor house filled with people. He saw his mother with Sarah, his old nurse. Both women were tall and in black. "My mother," he said.

"The people are so quiet." He felt her shiver.

" 'Tis a dour land of much privation, yet they'll love you."

"I'm terrified."

"Do what I do."

He led them over the gangway to the dock and walked to his mother, who had rubbed her hands as she waited in her anxiety to touch him.

"Mother," he said, and kissed her temple. The touch brought her to life and he felt her gnarled hands dig at his ribs and heard her throat catch in a gargled sound. He held her gently and was surprised she was so frail in her body, and she was now old, without the fullness he had remembered in his childhood. And at the University he was too busy ever to hug her.

"Mother, I'm home."

"So I've prayed."

"The children are behind me."

"Their mother is dead, so Dumaine sent word."

"Aye."

"Ye loved her?"

"More than life."

"Children of love, then." He heard her sigh.

"Her father was killed over religion."

"Aye, men've made God a curse."

She came out of his arms and bent to touch the children's heads. "Little ones," she said, her crooked fingers in their hair. The children shrank back and looked to him for understanding. "This is Dadda's mother." The children snuggled into his chest for refuge when he knelt.

"Time we had love in this house." She patted the top of his head aimlessly and began to cry. He took his mother into his arms, knowing it was the furious convictions of his father they wept at, and the sorrow they shared knowing he would never see his grandchildren. "Rejoice that ye loved and knew the grief of it," she said. "Now greet your kin."

"Thank you, Mother, and this is Lydia."

Lydia stepped back into a deep curtsey, and bowed her head as the crowd of several hundred Scots seemed to inhale their breath, staring in a hush at her long neck and thick weight of hair, which bent toward the cobbled paving.

"Child, don't!" His mother reached unevenly for her. "Tell her never to humble herself again." She looked at Skarra.

He raised her by her hand and she smiled uncertainly to regain her composure. "She's Russian, Mother."

"Whatever my son favors needs no other advocate." She patted Lydia's hand. "Greet your kin, and let's go inside." She led them toward the manor house.

Skarra enjoyed a round of shouting and grabbing and cheerful oaths as when he had greeted the Highland regiments. He drank from the jug and passed it to the other men. "These are my children and the others are my close friends," he said, and the Highlanders smiled but did not try to speak.

They walked to the house, and he heard the pipes playing light airs as they entered. The great hall was warmed by tapestries, with the clan armaments locked in cases by the side of the fire. Lydia looked at the heavy fretted woodwork and raised her eyes to the regimental banners along the beams. "Bruce, it's like a fort."

"We'll go to our apartment," Skarra said, leading the way to his father's room and following his mother. They walked up the broad staircase, and paused on the landing to look out at the North Sea. His mother stood at the side of the door. "Your father's room."

"Bigger than our cottage," he said, leading them in. He walked to the curtained Jacobean bed and set his hand on a carved chest at its foot. "Put a pallet here for the Lady Lydia." The servants followed him. "Never let the fire go down, and hang steam kettles night and day." Stopping in the light of a broad window, he said, "The children's beds go here, with a pallet at their foot for the wet nurse. And a pallet in the hall for Voltoff, should he wish to be close to his mistress. And quarters for him in the stable."

"Jump!" His old nurse clapped her hands together. "Ye heard Lord Bruce!" He watched the white-capped girls and gillies stumble to carry out his orders.

His mother came slowly into the room. "Come, Mother, as you wish."

"No, ye're the laird."

"To all save you."

"Bruce, they say ye killed men enough to shame the Lord."

"Yes, I killed them till I was ashamed, but I couldn't get them to stop their anger."

"You dinna hate?"

"No, no hate."

"I should not ask, for I raised you to honor men and praise the Lord."

"Aye, you did and I do."

"And respect life as a most unique mystery."

"I do, Mother."

"I wanted to hear ye tell me."

"There was no pleasure in it."

"Do ye love the girl?" She gestured at Lydia, who had taken off her outer wraps and was warming herself by the fire with the children.

"A dear friend, Mother, but I'm hollow inside for my wife."

"The keenest sorrow comes out of love. Be grateful."

He shook his head and looked into the fire, where bright wisps of light played against the sooted stone.

"One love binds all women," she said. "Ye'll find the love ye once loved, if ye can love another."

"I do not know, Mother."

"Love never dies." She left the room, and he was alone as they had been in Dorpat, even hearing the samovar whistling in the hall.

"Shall I make tea?" Lydia said.

"Lord, yes." He slipped off his weapons and kicked off his buckled shoes. He took her by the hand and walked to the large window that looked across the firth at the rolling hills of Scotland, where he could see a yard of deer against the dark bracken. "We have no secrets."

"None," she said.

"You're fair enough to love a lifetime."

She nodded her head.

"Someday, maybe."

"Let me wait."

He nodded.

"I'm a woman."

"We'll live the days as they come."

She touched his wrist and put her head down. "If we're true the life will come."

BOOK II

Lydia

1

The sweet mass of dark hair lay disarrayed on the pillow at his side overlapping the eiderdown puff which covered her, and he felt a contented delight that his wife was there, nude at his side, in the dawn light coming in on them.

"Love?" he whispered, but the woman did not stir, and Bruce McTaggart of Skarra smiled to himself at the moment of quiet bliss.

It was 1650, and Skarra was amazed at the long procession of small delights life had shown him and Lydia in their middle age, which in gratitude they had taken, knowing these were brief moments to be savored. The pleasure men sought often became their despair, and seeking happiness often brought boredom and insolence, followed by sorrow, yet joy burst in upon him at every crook, in unexpected guises. With the passage of years Skarra had found it this way, and he loved his life with growing awe for this reason.

The dawn light refracted off the sea fog lying on the water and expanded along the hills of the Scottish firth, and bathed his grand bedroom with a white radiance. He was glad the manor house of Skarra was set above the fog line, away from the dank, and he felt Lydia move somewhere at his side in the postered bed. In the dawn his mind turned back to his beloved Geney, the love he had buried on the Baltic, to the fragile memory that ached forever.

He had married Lydia, for the only reason a man could and expect contentment with a woman, because he loved her. That he could forever love one woman, and have her die and bury her with his own hands, and still go on to love and marry the second woman who was the cherished friend and rival to his dead love, was beyond his understanding as a man. He had not been able to divine the conflict which divided them as women, but still saw them together as one woman, each continuing and fulfilling the other, and was woven into his soul as one grand love, with each woman separate and yet the same.

The blond children, Charles and Fanny, showing the slender grace of Geney and of Sweden, were the oldest of a succession of children, the six dark children with the olive skin of Russia and the blue eyes of Lydia; they ran together in a continuous dream of eight delightful lives whose rushing existence filled his days with pleasure.

It was the only real pleasure he had, besides Lydia, he realized, as he lay abed in the dawn. The whole British Isles were swept with awful civil wars and endless rebellion, Scotland inflamed in treachery, England mad with greed and power, a brave and foolish king, and a brilliant and deadly Parliament. And the stories out of Ireland held the pure horror of Dante's *Inferno.* Truly, it was a marvel to be alive while all men changed sides at will.

He felt the sole of Lydia's bare foot run up his calf, the warm padded flesh of her instep and toes caressing his muscles as she pulled the hair on his leg.

"Your feet," he said.

"Yes?" Her voice was lost in covers.

"I think I love you for your feet."

"Nothing else?"

"I have to get up."

"Tell me, what else?"

He thrust his hand through the rustling weight of bedding until he felt the rich mass of her black hair, and wrapped his fingers into it, and drew her through the bed to his mouth while she cried, "Bruce!"

He crowded the wide mouth with his face and tasted the salt of sleep on her lips washing out with the gush of wet passion from her throat.

"Bruce!" He heard her gurgle as she pulled free of him and was engulfed in covers. "You hurt me."

"Not likely."

"Don't get up. The household is still asleep."

"I cannot sleep. Not now."

"Afraid?" He felt her hand slip into his.

"Nothing is resolved. You are Catholic, and I Protestant, and all who envy us are thereby armed."

"Bruce, it is only your own stubbornness that keeps me a Catholic." She sat up and shook back a thick mop of black hair.

"No, I will not let you give up your faith any more than I would give up mine."

"Bruce, our lives, I'll do it."

"No, not yet. Surely mankind cannot remain insane forever. Faith in God is beyond any man's judgment. You will not give up your faith."

Bruce dressed slowly in the dim light of his bedchamber, sipping a cup of English tea which the tall Scottish woman held in a saucer when he was drawing on his long drawers and peeling out of his nightgown that laced up under his chin. He took the wet cloth and swamped off his naked torso before a dim mirror, and handed the washcloth to another woman and took the towel and dried, absently pulling on and buttoning up the long linen trousers he favored over the Highland kilt.

"Ian McGregor is in the kitchen, Lord Bruce," said the woman, holding the cup and saucer to him.

"Up already." He savored the urgent scent of the tea in his nostrils as he sipped.

"Aye, across the firth and back, my lord, and now he eats like a glutton."

"I suppose he would have to eat from all that activity. The tea is a warm ecstasy, truly." He smacked his lips and handed the saucer to the woman.

"From London," Lydia said, swaddled in the midst of the big bed, watching him dress with the assistance of the maidservants. "From Ceylon, near India, they say."

"An addiction, tea, but a harmless addiction I should say, if a man must have an addiction."

"And your wife is no addiction?"

"Aye, but not a harmless fault."

"A fault I am?"

"Every woman is a fault to some man." He kissed her quickly and went to his office. "Send up McGregor!" he called to the maids.

He was in the fourth-floor office of Skarra, a bright room with high Palladian windows and warmed by an open hearth fire. Ian McGregor, his bailiff, was a stocky man who wore kilts. "The Galloway cattle are doing well, my lord." The thick sandy finger pointed at the heart-girth measurements recorded in the estate accounts.

"Aye, they flourish. I think cattle will support more cotters than sheep."

"The wool makes the gold, my lord." The short dour man spoke without emotion.

Bruce nodded idly at his chair before the table. "The sheep drive off the people for the gold, yet the gold brings naught but sorrow."

"Ahhee-EE-aaa!" The call floated down from the ridge behind Skarra, causing Bruce and McGregor to look up.

"An alarum, my lord."

"Alarum, there should be none. The Highlands are at peace." He rose and walked to the Palladian window and saw the figure running down the mountain behind the manor house.

" 'Tis Duff, Lord Bruce."

It was a limping scarecrow of a figure who filled the air with Gaelic cries of alarm.

"I had not realized Duff could run so fast." Bruce watched the figure lurch in awkward leaps, festooning a soiled tartan. He was past the yews and brushing through the rhododendron. Duff had a stone cottage overlooking the approaches to Skarra as well as the firth.

"Something has afeared him."

"McDougels!" The cry rose from the garden.

"Traitors," the bailiff said.

"Aye, but we are at peace." Bruce spoke laconically.

"Earl of Connok, Lord at Drimlar, English titles on a Scot."

"If we have peace, we have life."

They watched Duff hurtle into sight in the midst of the formal gardens of Skarra, dashing past a handful of maidservants and a boy who seemed especially fresh in their clean linen by comparison to the tall hair-wrapped image. "My lord! Strangers!"

"Seems a trifle riled," Bruce said. "Come!"

Bruce circled quickly down the broad stairwell of Skarra, his boot heels clattering from landing to landing and passing old Voltoff, who lay on a pallet at the side of the hall fireplace, now a white-haired ghost in white robes, always praying before the icon of a doe-eyed Russian saint and waiting for his tea samovar to boil. Bruce saw him seek to bow as he passed but he moved too quickly for the old man. It was no good to tell Voltoff to stop the heritage of a lifetime.

"Papa!" He heard Charles, noticing the two graceful blond teen-agers, amidst a scurry of dark heads who turned or trundled along the table edge and on the Turkish rugs.

"Lydia!" he called, ignoring his family, and wanting only that his wife go to their bedroom and bring him his sidearms.

He met Duff coming through the kitchen. "Lord Bruce, horsemen with hounds, and all armed. They come at a gallop and they be at the break."

"Bar the windows and the doors," Bruce said as Lydia came flying down the stairs with a baldric and pistol in each hand, passing servants who were running into and out of sight along the hall as they barred the old country home. "Did ye count them?"

"Aye, half a hundred at a glance." Duff had lost an eye, and the face was twisted into a leer where the knife had cut the muscle in that long-ago fight. The lone eye gleamed out as a singular beacon of life in a gaunt hawkish face at the side of a broken nose.

"The Highlands are at peace," Bruce said, seeing McGregor had not only buckled on his English pistols but had slung his claymore. He looked for his son and saw the immature slender grace of Sweden in the boy's lips. Oh, Geney, he thought. "You are to stay on the landing at your mother's side, the small children upstairs, and you are not to leave."

"Yes, Father."

"And you are to cock and prime eight Swedish rifles, which you are to fire in succession, from rest." He caught the boy's eye, seeing the excitement turn to waves of doubt and fear. Charles nodded his head.

"And you are to aim low to kill, and squeeze slowly."

"I will, Father."

"But only if McGregor and I fight."

"I understand, Father."

"The war is in England and the Lowlands and on the border. The Highlands are at peace."

"I could see their weapons, my lord," Duff said, his shaggy unwashed tartan and kilt reeking of a rough outdoor life in their midst, the wool bonnet seeming to have grown to be a part of the gray hair it set atop. "McDougels!"

"They be our kin," Bruce said, turning to the front doors, and yet disturbed. An armed band of men sent outriders ahead to quiet the countryside as they passed, if they came in peace.

"You said a man's enemies are the kinsmen in his own home," Lydia said.

"So I did," Bruce said, smiling wryly at her and turning to join McGregor at the front door of Skarra. He felt secure, yet still annoyed at the crass intrusion into their peace.

He watched the horsemen come into sight. He could tell at a glance by their blooded mounts and the lumpy movement of the riders' bodies that they had been drinking, that they were rich men of power, and he also knew he could rout them if he had to, by killing one out of five, the leaders, and save his home and family, even if they were to be invaded of a sudden by an armed company.

He stood on the broad piazza at Skarra overlooking the firth and watched the horsemen clatter up the cobbled drive.

"My Lord Skarra!" McDougel called to him, raising a gloved hand and crop.

Bruce nodded and waited for the cavalcade to come to a stop in a slowing motion of reining and stomping horses and laughing men. "Angus," he said, wanting to ignore the mask of titles.

"We want to hunt your deer."

"Why not hunt *your* deer?"

"You have the finest parks of deer in the Highlands." McDougel smiled and leaned forward over his pommel. "We've come to hunt with our kinfolk."

"I'm kin to all of Scotland and half of England," Bruce said. "Where are your own deer?"

McDougel searched his face, from atop his stallion, and Bruce heard the men wait for the outcome of the talk about the chase they all craved.

"Our deer are gone."

"You harried and slew them."

"Wool, we had no time for creatures that brought no profit."

"Yet you still want my deer?" Bruce stared evenly into the raw face, which flushed with a wave of anger, then smiled.

"Bruce, you have a tart tongue."

"No, Angus, you have come to my estate to hunt my deer for your sport because you killed your own deer out of your greed, so you can graze sheep."

"If you like," McDougel said, knowing Bruce would still have to accept the hunting party or risk open conflict.

"I don't usually entertain so large a body of armed men."

"We're peaceful."

"You betrayed Wallace and Melrose."

"Traitors! Traitors to Scotland. . . ." McDougel sat upright.

"English gold and Cromwell's law betrayed Scotland to her own greed. Gold will prove any man a traitor."

The retainers of the McDougels were silent and some glowered at Bruce, not expecting to have their unsavory deeds so openly discussed.

Bruce looked at McGregor and shook his head slowly. "They slew their native red deer to make room to graze sheep for the profit in wool, and they betrayed their kinsmen to strangers, for profit, and now they come claiming kin to me and wanting to kill my deer for sport."

"Not a happy prospect, my lord," McGregor said, his blunt sandy red face never leaving the gathered eyes of the horsemen, his hands resting on his English pistols.

"Yet we will entertain them, lest we betray the kindness of the Highlands."

"You have nothing to fear, Brucie!" McDougel leaned forward, his fur-trimmed cloak showing a rich brocade as he moved.

"McGregor is a *proscribed* name, my lord," McGregor said.

"Not in the Highlands, and we are at peace."

"We seek no Catholics nor McGregors, Brucie, just deer." The long jaw slipped open to show a double row of mottled teeth as McDougel smiled.

The manor house echoed with masculine sound as the McDougels filled Skarra with affable companionship. Fourteen of the men—Angus McDougel; his son, Mar; those with titles and knighthoods; and gentlemen with their retainers—were bedded in Skarra. The houndsmen, grooms, and those of lesser rank were put up with the cotters around the manor. There was a continual throbbing of boots passing up and down the stairs from the great hall of Skarra, where tables and boards were spread and fires laid, to the sleeping quarters on the third floor.

"I want every door kept locked," Bruce said to McGregor, who kept the keys to Skarra. Only the key to his vast bedroom was not on McGregor's ring. Lydia kept that key, and in his bedroom were stacked the Swedish muskets and pistols and his claymore. Beyond their bedroom was the small door in the stone wall leading to Charles' bedroom and to Fanny's room, adjoining, and the secret passage which led into the kitchen, hidden behind the posters of his daughter's bed. Iron drop-bars lay across all the doors so they could not be forced, and if they were battered down, Bruce had sequestered his firearms to have them where he could slay whoever came through the wreckage.

"You still keep that heathen devil, eh, Skarra?" Angus McDougel said to him as they lounged before supping; behind them were the tables where servants were laying haunches of venison and setting great clay tureens of lamb stew and the haggis, the dish Bruce hated but ate because it was the national dish of Scotland: To relish the stuffed intestines of a sheep was out of the question.

"What devil, Angus?"

"That Russian."

"Old Voltoff?"

"Aye, a strange devil, not human, I'd say."

"Angus, how do ye qualify to know what is human?" Bruce enjoyed insulting the gross man because he was so blatant in his self-assurance.

"Catholic, did ye say?" McDougel felt the insult and struck back.

"You said you were hunting deer."

"The English have beheaded a Catholic queen and a Catholic king." The small blue eyes flickered in slants of anger as he threatened Bruce.

"Voltoff is a peasant, Angus. Apparently you have a taste for a peasant's head." He stared evenly into McDougel's eyes, seeing the grave threat, for all Scotland knew Lydia was Catholic. "At least the English had the taste for royal blood which you seem to lack."

"You would jest?"

"Aye, that or kill you." Skarra sipped his drambuie, knowing he had to be as hard as the man and his threat if he were to keep his respect, for weakness would surely invite assault.

"Ah, Brucie, we've come to hunt, not to jaw." McDougel clapped him on the back and turned up a mug of ale which covered his face and swallowed noisily. The dinner table was alive with people who supped off pewter plates, and drank from sterling goblets, creating an air of gusto which ignored the splendor of the crystal and silver and the grand candelabras. Bruce had placed McGregor to his left, and lounged easily in his chair at the head of the table, pleased at the grand scene and the meat and stews he could provide at Skarra, knowing a man with a full belly is too content to be hateful. "We'll cross the north burn and enter the moor at dawn," he said to McGregor.

"Aye."

"A good massacre of deer atop a fine victualing ought to return them to Connok."

McGregor glanced into his face, the sandy freckled eyes showing the latent suspicion of a survivor of a Scottish clan which had been proscribed and exterminated to the utmost by its enemies. He nodded.

"Leave the finest archers and axemen at Skarra," Bruce said, sipping his goblet of claret.

McGregor nodded. "As my lord has instructed."

"The young men can chase the deer. Only the old men know of treachery, and will fight to the death for home."

McGregor nodded, a flicker of light crossing his eyes as he understood Bruce, who spoke casually, sipping his claret and enjoying his household and their boisterous guests. The whiskey had clouded them with shouts and noise.

"You will stay with the Lady Lydia."

"Not with my lord?"

"Stay with Lord Charles and Lady Fanny, I'll go alone with Duff and two archers to stay at my stirrups. Lord John Bollingale is on the moor."

"Aye, Ruff and Jamie at your stirrups." McGregor did not repeat the name of Bollingale, the English nobleman who had found refuge at Skarra.

He looked past the weighted silver candelabras and enjoyed the sight of Lydia. She seemed to burst in life from the French gown that bared all but the tips of her breasts, whose gentle swells lay beneath the single pendant of diamonds set in a fleur-de-lis at her throat. Her eyes fairly glistened as she spoke first to Angus McDougel on one side of her, then to Lord Sidlaw, and obviously pleasing herself as well as the men, for she had their absolute attention.

"Brucie," McDougel said, calling down the long table, "Lady Skarra says they hunt in Russia!"

Bruce nodded amiably but did not attempt to answer.

"Says they use hounds."

Bruce lifted his goblet in understanding and said to himself, "Lady Skarra is a brilliant rider."

"Apparently the Russian nobility is fabled, my lord." McGregor spoke.

"Rides better than those soused oafs."

McGregor nodded.

Bruce enjoyed the sweet mint and the Spanish oranges which were served as dessert, and noticed with satisfaction that he had used his fork and knife with the ease of an Italian while his guests seemed to still favor their fingers.

When Lydia rose, the table came apart into individuals who struggled contentedly to their feet, some belching discreetly behind closed fingers according to the French etiquette and others stretching cramped thighs and buttocks in conviviality, all seeming to arrange their gorged stomachs and intestines into comfortable containment within their bellies.

"Would you deny my lady's company at the hunt?" McDougel said, coming up to where he stood.

"The Lady Lydia's company is demanded at home," Bruce said, handing his goblet to a maid.

"And not entertaining her guests?"

"Not when her duty is to her children."

"Brucie, you are a dour Scot."

"Aye, a dour Scot." Bruce looked into McDougel's eyes, seeking to understand why he wanted Lydia. It was Scottish tradition to take prisoner the person and body of the nobles, including the kings and princes and queens, and to hold them kidnapped for ransom. To stir up a Highland rising from so bold a scheme did not seem reasonable. But he could fathom nothing in the white-flecked blue eyes. McDougel was too used to deception to tip his hand, Bruce realized.

He walked idly through the great hall under the regimental flags of his clan and its close relatives, passing suits of armor taken from slain English knights at Bannockburn.

"Lord Connok, you must bring the ladies of Drimlar, if you wish me to go riding," Lydia said.

"My lady, the ladies of Drimlar Hall are sparrows to a pea fowl by comparison to you," McDougel said.

"My lord should not be so plain," Lydia said, leading them to the fireplace, where a lutist played Elizabethan airs and a kilted Highlander waited to be bidden to play the warpipes.

"Drimlar is full of Scottish beasts," McDougel said, contentedly insulting his own women.

Bruce smiled and looked away, where he saw McGregor's frown.

"Lord Connok, your speech is shameful indeed," Lydia said.

"The truth, my lady. I have no Catholic lady to grace my court."

"What has religion to do with grace?"

"No French queen, no Russian princess—Skarra, you are a lucky dog."

"McDougel, you're drunk—play, piper!"

The hall burst into the swirling skirl of the bagpipe, all but drowning their conversation.

"Brucie, it's indecent that a man should have such beauty in a woman to lay his hands upon!" McDougel said, shouting above the sound of the pipes.

Bruce turned away, shaking his head, noticing Lydia pretended not to hear, and McGregor scowled.

"The English Puritans would pay to purify her beauty, I'd say."

"My lord!" McGregor said.

"Aye, the Puritans hate the flesh," McDougel said, touching his jaw with his fingertips.

"Angus, I don't want to kill a guest in my own house," Bruce said, speaking quietly, "but you are talking about a man's wife."

"Oh, I have no fear, Bruce." McDougel stared evenly into his face. "Lady Lydia is Catholic, foreign, and worse, a Russian. And Cromwell buys Catholics."

"Stay with our guests," Bruce said to McGregor, "and report to me when all are abed."

He walked up the broad stairs to their apartment, pausing to glance at Voltoff. The old man was in wide white Russian breeches, a Ukrainian shirt and jacket, and a long white Circassian coat. His pallet and icons, composing a small altar with candles, were set up across the corridor from the door to their quarters. Bruce touched the old man on the shoulder as he walked to his door, saying, "Another ten years, Old-Timer, that's all I want from you."

He had peeled off his Gaelic strews, the leg-clinging trousers he favored, with their Stuart plaid, and was in his long wool nightshirt and quilted satin dressing gown when he heard his guests ascending the stairs, a convivial troop of drunks.

"By God's teeth, what an outlander!" Bruce recognized Mar's voice, the Scottish burr not erased by his years at Christminster College, among the English at Cambridge. Bruce seized the massive silver candelabras, and went to the door, knowing his guests had encountered Voltoff in their cups.

"He belongs to me," Bruce heard Lydia say, and saw her gesture at the old man to settle himself once more on the pallet by the hall fire.

"Slavery, there is a bad one for a Christian."

"Rooshian, that's Rooshia."

"Or Virginia. The Americans have slaves."

"Gentlemen," Bruce said, drawing their attention away from Voltoff and a maid who was making the pallet comfortable.

"Brucie, if you walk with the halt, you limp," McDougel said.

"Nobody is halt, unless I shoot him," Bruce said, holding the candelabras high over his head, the flushed affable faces of his guests grinning at his remark.

"Slavery?"

"Voltoff is no slave," Bruce said.

"He *is* my slave," Lydia said, her face arranged in the fixed smile of a triumphant hostess. "Voltoff is a slave, he is a serf, and he's mine."

Bruce saw her anger and the defiance of those she had entertained. "Lord Connok, it is better to be loved as a slave than hated as a freeman."

The nobles and gentlemen laughed and shifted among themselves at Lydia's remark.

"My lady, there is no slavery in Britain," Bruce said, understanding his wife and yet not wanting to admit anything so obviously absurd before his potential enemies.

"The poor are slaves to want, and want is everywhere."

"But we are free," McDougel said with as much emphasis as a man could after an evening of whiskey.

"Aye, the nobles are free because the poor are enslaved with contempt."

"My lady!" Bruce shouted.

"My lord." Lydia floated down into her taffeta gown and bowed her head.

"Come, love," Bruce said, taking her hand and leading her into their quarters as the crowd in the hall trooped happily upward to their bedroom on the third floor.

"The English and the Scots are so smug about their superior freedom," Lydia said as she undressed with the aid of Penelope and a Highland girl with a reddish nose.

"This is not the time to reform them, love."

"So moral."

"Aye, and so are the Chinese."

"We don't live in China." Lydia spoke testily, brushing her long black hair over the white flesh of her bare shoulder.

"Yes, my love."

"Clannish, ill-bred clods, all of them."

"Yes, my love."

"Calling Voltoff an outlander."

"They were drunk."

"Poor old man."

"They'll be on the moor at dawn."

"In Russia when we get drunk we kiss, but in Scotland they fight when they are drunk."

"Oh, love, let's not quarrel." Bruce smiled slowly, running his fingers across the white scar of flesh over his left eye. "You mean, love, those Cossacks would have kissed me if they had been drunk?"

"Oh, Bruce, forgive me!" She flung herself into his arms.

2

Bruce had slipped quietly out of his massive Jacobean bed, yet Lydia crawled through the covers after him, clutching the hem of her loose nightgown in her hand, and he saw the smooth round shape of her folded knees as she came.

"You don't have to rise."

"I have no intention of sleeping," she said, shoving a fine bare leg out of the bed, reaching for the bearskin rug with her open toes, and stepping before him. He watched her shuffle her shoulders and body, throwing back her hair in the assured movement of a woman certain of her man and her love, and content to confront him with her half-nude figure to please him.

"Boots and britches and pistols?"

"And the Orloff-Norfolk cross, I told McGregor. My finest horse."

"Bellsinger," she said.

He saw the blond head of Charles, and heard logs being thrown on the fire, and realized the large bedroom seemed to be alive with his children and their nurses, who had slipped in through the small wall-door.

"Lord, it's the dark of night yet, why are the children up?" He turned to Lydia.

"They know you are not hunting with friends."

"Tush. Affable drunks, all." Penelope and a Highland woman were helping him thrust his stockinged legs down into massive cavalier boots. One woman held the britch and tugged on the loose over-knee bell while the other straddled the leg and heel and shoved upward. "Damn, kilts are the only clothes fit for a man."

He stomped about the room on the Turkish and Persian rugs, seeking to settle his legs down into the boots. "Charles, you are to stay with McGregor, and he will take his directions from your mother."

"Yes, Father."

"I expect our guests to be entertained by the kill, yet, you are to keep doors and windows iron-slotted and six cotters are to be kept in the kitchen, armed with the bill, the axe, and . . ."

"Yes, Father?" The boy's large blue eyes searched him from out of the pale smooth skin of adolescence.

"And the claymore. *You* are to fire the Swedish flintlocks."

"Yes, sire."

"Your men are never to fight in the open where they can be ridden down. Only on the terraces and from behind balustrades and in doors."

"Yes, Father."

"McGregor has been instructed."

Bruce was conscious of the clear silence in the large bedroom, where his women and children listened carefully.

"Further, you are not to let yourself be captured or killed, and do not worry for me. I'll have the best horse in the field and Ruff and Jamie."

"I promise, sire."

He grabbed the boy into his hands and dragged his frail-seeming body into his arms, feeling the slender rib-cage and limbs, and laughed deeply to feel his son. "Ah, Charles, Charles." He hugged the boy.

He swung up into his flat saddle, gathering the reins into his fingers, his eyes on the brace of Swedish pistols slung on either side of the pommel, and reined his stallion into a rearing turn to clear the cavalcade. "Up, Bellsinger! Up!"

In the light of the torches held by servants on the piazza of Skarra, he saw Lydia and Charles and Fanny and McGregor and Sarah, his old nurse, beyond the massed heads of the huntsmen and riders. He raised his gloved hand as he saw his groom duck out of sight and felt Ruff and Jamie tug at his stirrup leathers, where they would run at all times when he was afield with possible enemies, as his bodyguards. As his stallion cantered down the paved drive, Skarra heard the McDougels and their kin strung out in shouts and yells as the footmen and horsemen collided in the dark to follow him.

"Cling tight, men," Bruce said, feeling the rough hands caught in the leather under his knees. "We'll be over the burn and on the moor by sunup."

"Hold up, Brucie!" He heard Angus McDougel's Norfolk stallion clatter in close to him.

"That's a handsome horse you ride, Brucie!" McDougel shouted. "Sleep well?"

"Well enough."

"If you slept like you drank, you should be fresh." He watched McDougel shake his head.

"What will ye take for that beast?"

"I bred him on Skarra, and he is not for sale."

"You own Skarra."

"No, Skarra owns me."

McDougel shook his head and grinned maliciously. "You professors, you be all alike. Talk in riddles to honest questions."

"Angus, all any man owns is his life, and the rest he borrows and puts back."

"I own Drimlar Hall and Connok Castle," McDougel said.

"Who owned them before you?"

"Well . . ."

"That is your answer, and my horse is not for sale." He guided Bellsinger down into a slight path forking from the road, and heard McDougel curse and say he was a dour Scot and an ungenerous host. "Hang tight, men!" Skarra said. He saw the tips of the bows slung over his runners' shoulders and the quivers of arrows. As the great stallion plunged down into the shallow burn and clattered across it, he felt his sword and other weapons joggling on his saddle, and Ruff's and Jamie's shoulders bump against his knees.

He felt the exultation fill his lungs with each breath he drew of the moist air, almost tasting the tart green of the heather and the rhododendron he rode through. It was in his nose and wet his tongue and filled him with life.

It was easy to lay out of his mind the preparations he had made for the hunt. He had sent ahead his runners and drivers, and gillies had gone out with Highland ponies, packing his elegant French tent, the present the ambassador of France had given him, seeking to have him help lead an uprising of Highlanders against Edinburgh and England, and the Lowlands. Of course he had refused, but accepted the tent. He knew Cromwell was no king but a man of money and could not last, and he had had too much of Scottish treachery to lead any Scot into war against another Scot.

They rode over the wet moor in silence. He listened to Bellsinger's hoofs squish and could see the burnished chestnut shoulder muscle yield and gather to lift the foreleg. The mist lay capped in strung-out wisps of white from the green rolling mountains he rode through.

"They's fierce beasts," he heard Ruff say, obviously speaking to Jamie at his other knee, for they could hear dogs snarling.

"McDougel breeds the meanest hounds I have ever seen," Bruce said, still searching ahead on the moor for his tent and menservants.

"Neck-breaking, the McDougels calls them," Jamie said.

"Big brindle staghounds, biggest as I've ever laid eyes on, my lord."

"Aye, don't let one of them bite you," Bruce said, still sweeping the gorse and discoloration of the bracken for his fine tent and servants.

"They be on the Blue Elbow of the Deveron," Jamie said to him.

"Aye, but should not we be there?"

"Not yet, my lord."

"I should be able to see that gold and red and green French tent."

He saw the soft fold of silver widen into the River Deveron as they rode through a gap and came out on the shoulder of Ben Lawkar.

"Ahhee-EE-aaa!" It was the war cry of Scotland that rose from a yell into a curdling scream and seemed to echo from mountain to mountain along the Deveron. "Those are my men," Skarra said, more to himself.

"Aye, beyond the dip, my lord."

He saw his camp. The elegant Continental tent was perched amidst a coarse mat of rough gorse, the bright colors seeming to shrink into themselves to avoid the cold Scottish mountains, making them even more striking and foreign.

The smaller tents of the McDougels were drab, rather huddled into the greenery. He was pleased to see the colors of Skarra atop his tent, a rampant phoenix with heather and a quiver of arrows in its claws, gold against a white and green banner. He took the English tea as he dismounted, a groom taking Bellsinger as his bodyguards followed him into his tent, carrying his pistols.

"The Deveron is beautiful," he said to his cook.

"The McDougels have mocked our tent," said the cook, a rough man with hairy forearms. "They say we are soft."

"I don't care," Bruce said. "The River Deveron eases my soul."

"Aye, my lord."

"My lord," said a slender man, following him.

"Ah, Bollingale?"

"The beaters and drivers are formed into a crescent between the Don and the Deveron."

"My God, what butchery," Bruce said, knocking his feathered bonnet against his thigh and listening to Lord John Bollingale, refugee from England and now almost a prisoner as much as a guest of Skarra.

"Aye, my lord, those were your instructions." Bollingale searched him with the pale unfocusing English eyes, and from his narrow, almost effeminate face they gave a feeling of the horror in the delicate man's soul.

"So I instructed. If it's a yard of a thousand deer, they will likely go mad with greed and kill only a handful, while if only a few, they will kill them all."

"My lord," said the Englishman, bowing and speaking in the cultured accent of an Oxford graduate and university don.

"Come, let us have tea, before McDougel brings his jug." He clapped Bollingale on the shoulder, knowing he was a survivor from the Royalist army of Charles I, the beheaded king. With a price on his head, John Bollingale was to be trusted next to McGregor. "Let us sup and we will retire." He walked to his pallet of cushions as his bodyguards settled into their tartans at the door of the tent.

His gillies and huntsmen were close about him. He could hear the stomp of their Highland ponies' hoofs in the moist heather, and could see an occasional gray shape loom past him as he sat astride Bellsinger. The dawn fog and wet air chilled his face and he shrank down into his tartan while he waited in the dell. The McDougels had been posted just under a long curving ridge that lay across a broad valley, turning onto the Deveron, and down which the red deer would be driven. It was still too early to see his guests, who were posted in the "military position" of the ambuscade. He had decided against joining the slaughter, but would stay astride and ride over the ridge to watch the killing once the great yell was raised and the huntsmen sprang forth.

"Harken!" Ruff said.

Bruce kept his chin tucked down into the Stuart tartan, not pleased by the faint sound of hunting horns which came on muffled notes in the fog. He heard the drivers' cries, the hooting yells. The deer would be in front. He could discern his men all about him, and along the ridge he saw the clan McDougel.

"They come!" Angus McDougel shouted to him, gesturing with his arm.

Bruce shook his head imperceptibly and sat immobile. The horns were clear. The drive was just over the hill. He saw the McDougels shifting to slip the leashes on their staghounds, which he could hear slavering and snapping at each other and their handlers in their excitement to chase down the deer.

"Whook-a-laa!"

"Ahhee-EE-aaa!"

The cry ran up and down the ridge, and he saw the men leap to their feet and aim flintlocks and the archers draw back elbows, while the line surged ahead. Smoke and wild yells and gunshots seemed to cloud his eyes and mind as he watched the kill launched through the mist in a line of running legs.

"Move up," he said, nudging Bellsinger with his boot heels.

"The sounds of Hell," Bollingale said. They could hear the bleating of the deer mingling with the ecstatic shouts and snarling of those who were killing them.

"Move up, men!" Bruce waved his arm forward and saw his servants turn their attention to crossing over the ridge to join the McDougels.

"Sounds like the Puritans swording and praying as they killed the Catholic whores at Naseby," Bollingale said.

"Aye, a virtuous ecstasy," Bruce nodded. "Move up, men!"

His line of retainers, kinsmen, and servants were rising at the crest, watching the occasional head and rack of antlers coming in and out of view, when three deer broke over the ridge into his men.

"Zounds!" Bollingale shouted.

Bruce saw the large staghound running off the near haunch of the lead buck, and he saw the arrow thrust out its brown belly. They came through the wisping fog, straight at his men, and he heard them shout and a musket-shot clap the air.

"Big bastard," Bruce said, watching the hound, a wire-haired reddish-coated dog, lunge against the shoulders of the buck, grabbing for its windpipe.

The buck shied away, and the dog came down out of balance and caught its head and open jaws in the heather, turning them under the muscular body. "Pawp!" Bruce could not believe it.

"He's snapped his spine!" Bollingale shouted, spurring forward. "Bruce! Look!"

"By God, so he has!" Bruce reined up Bellsinger, who was pounding his hoofs in a rhythmical beat, trying to gallop.

"My lord, the brute is dead!"

They watched the massive staghound's body quiver in chucking ripples as the muscles obeyed the chaos of a broken spinal cord. The head was twisted under a shoulder, and a single amber eyeball glared fiercely at a shard of heather not six inches away.

He heard the rapid beat of running hooves, and turned to see the buck speeding toward his line once more, followed by a small pack of staghounds. Shots were echoing in the glens, and rolling against the mountain. He was surprised to see deer running in all directions, flinging themselves against their pursuers in sudden bursts of speed but losing heart and cutting back at the last moment.

"Good Lord," Bruce said, more to himself. It seemed the deer would dash from line to corner, back from where they came, in a frantic desperation, while the hounds chased them in packs, slavering from their open mouths and lolling pink tongues as they panted.

"John?" Bruce said.

"My lord?" Bollingale spoke at his side.

"It's an apparition."

"What is that, my lord?"

The fog and sweet heather smells mixed with the clouds of tart gunsmoke, the panting hounds, and the screams of the men swept his mind with an unreal effect, which the wounded deer that struggled in death, down in the wet moor, seemed to dispel. The final grace of dying gave a lie to the insane need to kill, it seemed.

"Cut his throat!" Bollingale spoke to a kilted Highlander who was wrestling down a deer which struggled to rise and pumped blood from a neck wound in two-foot spurts with its terrified heartbeats. "Quick about it!"

"John, these were my deer," Bruce said.

"We raised them on Skarra, my lord," Bollingale said.

"I thought I adored to hunt."

"Bruce, you crave the chase, not the kill."

He stared out on the field of struggling forms and men who bent over them, stepping back and wiping bare forearms, seeing knives that lay easily in rough hands, and tried to ignore the drip of blood from the steel edges.

"Did any deer escape?" he said.

"Two thirds, at least," Bollingale said. "Left at the Don."

"How was that?" He looked into the faded light-blue eyes of the Englishman. "I thought I instructed the whole yard to be herded down."

"Aye, you did, my lord." The eyes focused into infinity. "Bruce, they would slaughter every deer on Skarra if they could. I convinced your Highlanders of this, and they disobeyed you."

"I see." He nodded his head. "You did right." The Englishman saw it in practicality, while he saw the affair as a Scotsman, whose insights were marred by hope and sentiment. He looked down at Ruff. "Was I alone not informed?"

"Aye, my lord."

Bruce was glad to be away from the McDougels and the hunt, and in his tent. He was more angry with himself than he was over the slaughter of his deer, and he was furious about that. He had played the royal fool to men of a common death lust, offering up all his deer to honor men of no honor. And his gillies, his cotters, his kin, and even the Englishman had known the McDougels for what they were, and had saved his deer, lying to him and disobeying him to cope with his appalling folly and deluded sense of honor.

"Whiskey!" he shouted at a gilly.

The young man held up a bottle of French wine, raising his eyebrows in perplexity.

"Bring me whiskey and help me get my boots off!"

He was pleased to be inside his tent. He could hear the rain falling in a sodden flow, darkening the gold and green over his head. Perched on the Scottish moor, overlooking the Deveron, the tent was an absurd protest that man was civilized.

"Where's Bollingale?" he said, sipping a pewter tankard of straight Scotch, and working his legs against the tugging of four young men who were pulling off his boots. The whiskey eased his folly.

"With the horses, Lord Bruce," said an older man who was the cook.

"I want him now." The horses were stabled in a lean-to of bracken, open but out of the rain. The Highland ponies ran free, unaffected by storm and cold. "I was a fool."

"Nay, my lord. Ye've been too much educated in England." The cook looked carefully into his eyes, placid in his righteous opinion.

"Bosh! Bring food when John comes."

"Lord Bollingale?"

"God, yes, who else?"

"I like my instructions straight, my lord."

"Go, don't badger me!" He waved his tankard of whiskey, sloshing some on a cushion, yet secretly delighted with the bucolic pride and wisdom of his clan.

The whiskey warmed his chest with peace, and he settled back to await John Bollingale. At the entrance to his tent he saw the two gray wiry heads of Ruff and Jamie. They were settled into folds of skins and tartans, sipping straight whiskey from a ram's horn which they shared, and he could hear the guttural slurring as they spoke Gaelic to each other.

Their faces were masked in wrinkles and grooves, with tufts of graying hair clustered in their nostrils and out their ear holes. Their pale blue eyes passed onto him every other moment, he noticed, as though to assure themselves he was well—then back to their inscrutable talk, which, as their laird, was denied him.

Bruce felt isolated, even among his own kin, with their suffocating wish to protect him, or to betray him, and he longed for Bollingale.

When Bollingale brushed into the tent, shaking water from his hat and cloak, Bruce stood and thrust a tankard into his hand. "Slosh it down, John."

"Aye, to cook the victuals."

"Supper!"

They sat across from each other on their low pallets eating lamb stew from wooden bowls and washing it down with whiskey.

"What do you think of McDougel?"

"The usual." Bollingale spoke without looking up.

"And how's that?"

"Oh, show him kindness, and he'll want your life."

"Lord of Connok and Drimlar Hall?"

"Aye, greed springs from riches, my lord." He looked up and Bruce saw the engaging smile of a frightened man suddenly at ease.

"The Cambridge philosopher."

"It's universal."

"Not too much optimism there."

"Would you care to tell me how you killed those seventeen Cossacks they talk of?"

"You win, John."

The Englishman studied a succulent morsel on his fork. "In flight from Cromwell and the Puritans I have but one worry."

"The Highlands are secure," Bruce said, setting down his tankard.

"To be hanged or eat mutton until the Restoration is the question, my lord."

"Ah, John!" Bruce laughed and wiped his lips with his broad French napkin.

"McDougel knows I'm proscribed by Cromwell."

"Not from our clan," Bruce said, knowing John Bollingale had killed enough Puritans to have earned the enmity of a nation.

"Every man on the moor has a burr so thick you can cleave it with an axe, save you and I, and you are no Englishman."

"That is no surety you are a wanted man."

"Five thousand pounds' sterling on my head? In Scotland they can smell it."

Bruce munched slowly on a light oatmeal cake, feeling the crumbs fall from his lips to his midriff. "Nay, not so. The Highlands are Stuart, forever."

"The murderous poet of Cambridge, they called me. I am particularly hated because they know I understand the rights of Protestantism, for I studied under John Milton when I wooed his daughters, and yet I reject it."

"Certainly either way is folly," Bruce said, studying the leg of a grouse.

"Old John Milton thought I was another maiden among his flock of maids."

"That fair look of Ariel," Bruce said.

"Aye, when they took Cambridge I pretended to welcome them, and it was easy to kill them. Only after you know a man can you hate him, and I grew to hate the Puritans when I realized how much they hated each other. Lord, they were such a hateful, ugly folk, full of judicious contention and hanging each other for treason. Say they are off to build a paradise in America, they do. Some paradise, that." The narrow effeminate face searched Skarra's, the eyes focusing as though Lord John Bollingale could only see when he recalled his past. Bruce nodded and stopped eating to hear out his friend.

"The Catholics made me Protestant and the Puritans converted me to Hell." He shook his head slightly, as though in dismay. "I truly relished killing them."

"Who?"

"They did a lot of praying, and I knew they knew I had fought at Marston Moor and at Naseby and I knew they were constantly ferreting out sinners, even using children to betray their parents, so I knew my time was running out. But I wanted to kill veterans, men who had fought, Roundheads, the regiments who had fought with a perverted god on their lips. . . ."

"John, you took that affair pretty much to heart."

"Aye, we lost at Naseby because we did not believe any cause was worth killing your brother over. But, I learned. Killing Puritans became my religion. I wrapped my left arm in a cloak, with enough hanging free to shield me, and I used an Italian dirk, and I entered evening services when the flares were down and a great spring rain was blowing in to wet their muskets. I entered the church and quietly shoved the dirk under the breastbone of the man who prayed at my side. I eased him to the flags, and stepped into the next man, whose eyes flared when he looked at me and realized I was murdering him. He had a big bald round head and he said, 'Bollingale, Lord Bollingale,' and I caught his weight as I stuck the next Puritan. It was easy to do. They did not know I was killing them until I put the stiletto into them." He looked at Skarra and then down into his tankard of whiskey. "Bruce, I like to kill. The ecstasy of seducing a woman is equaled only by thrusting a knife into a man's belly or heart and hearing him gasp in outrage that he has been robbed of life in an act of passion."

"By God, John, I wager those Puritans do hate you."

"Oh, yes. I was blood all over, and fact is the flags of the church were thick with an oil skim of blood, and when they realized I was killing them and raised a cry to capture me, they all slipped into a clutch of men who scrabbled on the floor and screamed religious oaths, and knifed each other, not knowing who it was that was guilty. And I threw down my dirk and cloak and ran out into the night storm, to where I had hid my horse in the shadowed lea of a great oak, and I mounted and rode north all night, sleeping by day, until I had reached the Highlands, until . . ."

"Until you were captured by my Highlanders."

Bollingale's eyes focused past him, into the coals of the brazier. "They were grown men in armored breastplates, and I could hear the women screaming as they sabered them at Naseby."

"And so you became the instrument of the Lord?" Bruce searched the pale features and fine bowed mouth.

"It did seem just."

Bruce nodded. "You must stay at Fendrath. It's too dangerous at Skarra."

"Thank you, Bruce."

"Next to pestilence, religion has been man's greatest curse." He sipped his tankard. "We will have Angus over shortly."

"I never thought I could kill a man."

"Nor I. It deranges a man, but so can life."

"Aye, life itself sometimes seems a disease. Pestilence and religion."

"I can understand how the Puritans hated Oxford and Cambridge," Bruce said, pointing to a bottle of drambuie standing on a folding credenza and which a gilly turned to. "Contemplation desolates absolutes."

3

The tent was alive with the chaos of hungry men more interested in drink than food, as they shared the exaggerated camaraderie engendered by the hunt. His guests had insisted on roasting enough deer carcasses to continue the revelry another day. Bruce did not mind, for it kept the McDougels occupied in the field, away from the sanctity of Skarra, and he enjoyed looking down into the haze of light that lay on the placid Deveron, seeming to soothe the gorse-covered mountains it lay between.

He was glad the weather had been clear. He had grown to hate camping in the rain, though he did instruct his gillies to roll up all his bedding and wool throws and to lay down matted bracken. "The finery will only make them angry with envy," he told his servants.

"Brucie, you keep the homeliest folk I have ever seen," McDougel said, licking a deer's shank with his tongue while looking at the cook.

"They grow coarse, out of the bracken."

"Aye, and I have noticed all your household is not Scottish."

"I am not particular."

"A man is known by his company."

"Aye, and a man can get killed by platitudes."

"If we weren't kin by the same blood, a man could take offense."

"Yes, a man could. And if Abel had taken offense, Cain might not have killed him."

McDougel smiled and shook his head. "Bruce, you are the only man I have ever known who could jest with the holy word of God."

"Perhaps I do not jest."

McDougel searched his eyes, and Bruce saw the man glimpse his somber determination to live and triumph in simplicity. A wave of anger passed through the white-flecked eyes, of having understood and been thwarted. "Lord Skarra, it is a grave annoyance to find a man who says what he means."

"True, McDougel, and it is a grief to find a man who does not say what he means."

"We who have campaigned together . . ."

"I raised these deer to chase after, not to kill."

"Come, let us not quarrel." He clapped Bruce on the shoulder. "I have a taste for a Highland tit."

"You have to bring your own tit to Skarra," Bruce said, calmly eyeing the noblemen and gentlemen who passed in and out of his tent and up and down the spitted carcasses which lined the mall in the gorse. "Every tit on Skarra is spoken for."

"Come now, man. All of Scotland knows of your taste for women."

"Then all of Scotland is wrong. I love only one woman, Lady Skarra."

"Come, we are men, Brucie!"

"That is why I love my wife."

"God damn, that double tongue!"

A silence gripped the tent at the angry words. Bruce saw McDougel's jaw quiver, the muscles tautened.

"Come to your senses, Angus. I am a family man, and I am near fifty years old."

"A man needs a tit, by God. I am tired of stale flesh."

"My Lord of Connok," Bruce said, handing his tankard to a gilly, "it is easier to build a marble bridge to the moon than reach the naked body which lies abed beside you, as man or wife. But if you do, Heaven is a disappointment and death is of no consequence."

"I want a tit, not talk."

"Go find your own tit!" Bruce turned and walked out from the tent, gesturing for his groom to saddle up Bellsinger. He was deeply angry. He did have a loose name as a lover, and it was not fair. He had loved the women he had seduced, yet on the common tongue it sounded squalid.

He felt the muscled body of the stallion move light as a feather beneath him. He had a sense of infinite power to be astride the animal. He let the reins fall idly through his fingers and gave Bellsinger his head to choose his way among the deer paths that wound through the thick gorse of Ben Lawkar. Bruce loved the mist-fogged mountain, and enjoyed looking for the quiet Deveron, hearing the hooves move softly on the wet sod. Behind him he could hear the hoofbeats of the Highland ponies Ruff and Jamie were riding, and somewhere trailing was John Bollingale.

"Hark, Lord Bruce!" He heard the guttural call of Ruff, but could not see him in the fog. "Brucie!"

"Here?" he said, and saw the shapes of two horsemen emerge.

"A maiden crying, my lord."

"What did you say?" He spurred Bellsinger forward and noticed one of the ponies flatten its ears at the stallion's approach.

"A maiden, my lord," said Jamie, staring in bucolic tranquility. Both the Highlanders were bundled in tartans atop the gray ponies, with only their blue eyes to give life from their leathered faces.

Skarra listened for a second and heard only John Bollingale's horse floundering over some gorse, obviously lost.

"There, my lord," said Jamie, and Ruff nodded imperceptibly.

"A woman?"

"Aye, by her voice a young'un."

"Screaming?"

"Distressed, my lord."

"Where are you, Bruce?" It was the cultured Oxonian voice of Bollingale. "I cannot hear your horse."

"Here! We've pulled up." In the silent moment of the mist he heard the faintest wisp of a treble cry which seemed to pierce the fog, then float out of earshot.

"I heard it," he said.

"What?" Bollingale rode out of the wet white mantle about them.

"A woman crying," said Ruff.

"Aye, but where?" Bruce stood in his stirrups to get a better height by which to hear.

"A false echo, my lord," Jamie said, reining his pony to the right. "Up the mountain."

They rode up the faint trails of the Highland deer and the wild shaggy cattle which Bruce still kept on his estates, following the two elderly Highlanders, who were mounted and leading the way since Skarra was alone on the moor, safe from enemies.

They came onto the crest of a knoll from which the mist had drifted clear, and he could see the distant river below them and a series of green bluffs divided by dark escarpments. He saw Jamie gesture across a dell to indicate he saw some movement. "The young woman," said the Highlander.

"By God," Bollingale said.

Bruce reached into his pommel pouch and pulled out his Italian spyglass and raised it to his eye, aiming it over the ears of the stallion, which was head up, searching the scurrying forms in the gorse.

At first he saw only the lopsided movement of foliage and brambles as he moved the glass, everything unnaturally expanded. Then he saw a man in trousers, trying to keep his balance as he shied from side to side at a clump of gorse. His white hands were in the shrubs.

"I see a man," Bruce said, as they heard another scream.

"There be a woman and three men, my lord," Ruff said. "And they be chasing the woman."

"A lass, she be, by her full head of hair." Jamie spoke matter-of-factly.

"Damn this glass," Bruce said.

"I can see them, Bruce!" Bollingale said.

He got the glass focused again, saying, "What in hell are they doing?"

"Rape, by the looks of it."

The figures came clear. He saw the girl scrambling in a frantic way, sometimes thrashing into the clumps of gorse and then falling clear and crawling on all fours. He could see her bare legs up to the fold behind her knees, and he saw the man closest to her was laughing and waving an article of her clothing. Then he saw two men were in close pursuit, while a third cut up the knoll to head her off as she dodged to get away.

"She is not yet stripped." Bollingale was at his side, watching the four scampering figures.

Bruce could see her bare arms and shoulders, yet she was still in her camisole. Her flesh was fresh and pink-hued against the green foliage she struggled through. He saw her burst out into a clearing where she ran frantically but in the labored movement of a woman with wide hips and a nubile body and legs. The men had her surrounded in a moment and he saw them tear small articles of clothing from her until she was bare. He heard her scream, twisting her arms as they held her hands. "By God," he said, not really believing they would rape her, and transfixed by the spectacle he knew was true but could not accept. Her long auburn hair fell past her narrow waist to her buttocks.

"Is she one of my women?" Bruce said, feeling his spine crinkle in outrage. He thumped Bellsinger with his boots, and the stallion leaped into the gorse.

"Aye, my lord, one of our crofters," Ruff said, as the two grizzled Highlanders lashed up their ponies and ducked through the wet limbs.

"The men?" Skarra shouted, as the stallion took the bit in his teeth.

"Lowlanders, my lord."

"Aye. No kilts."

"Obviously, our guests," Bollingale shouted from the rear.

The girl was pulled forward over her knees, a man dragging her arms until she lay stretched out on her belly, the nude flesh gleaming. He watched the other two men reach under her hips and thrust their forearms through her crotch to pry her onto her back. Skarra could see her struggling. She was onto her feet once, scrambling to get her balance. In her awful moment there was a heroic grace to the girl, to the beauty of her full buttocks, to the rich white breasts quivering behind the tangle of her hair—all seemed to cry out in innocent dignity as she was brought to earth and ravished.

"By God," Bruce said, hearing his own voice quiver.

"They may kill her," said Ruff.

Skarra saw the girl brought down off her feet as she was swung by the hair of her head. He watched the three men pounce on her as she rolled, one man stretching her arms over her head, while another held her bare feet and spread legs about the waist of the third man, who was into her crotch, his trousers hanging down over the back of his gaunt thighs and scrawny buttocks.

"Shall we kill them, my lord?" Jamie called out.

"Aye, but I am the laird."

"This way, Brucie!" Ruff shouted.

The small gray ponies were swirling into and out of sight, leaning into the shrubbery as they ran along the game trails, the two old Highlanders standing in their stirrups to look over the gorse and unwrapping their tartans from about their bodies so they could fight. Bollingale had disappeared somewhere behind. Despite the massive bounds of Bellsinger Skarra found Ruff and Jamie rushing along at his side as they charged down the knoll and burst into the clearing.

"Bastards!" he shouted, unable to control himself, and he reached instinctively for his claymore while gathering the reins in his left hand to collect Bellsinger.

The men did not look up. They were obviously taking turns using the girl. Two of the men had their trousers down and the one stretching her hands over her head had his feet on her shoulders and was laughing while the man kneeling in her crotch was slapping the girl's mouth, which she would fling from side to side to avoid the full blow into her lips and teeth. Her face was a maze of blood and welted flesh, from which she sobbed "Please, I beg of you! I beg of you!"

"Bastards!" Bruce was cursing and trying not to overrun the men with Bellsinger.

In what seemed to be one fluid motion he saw Ruff drop from the saddle and rush the men while the pony dashed on. "Ruff!" He saw the dirk in the old Highlander's hand.

"Ruff, I am the laird!" He had slowed Bellsinger and turned him slightly when he tried to dismount to stop Ruff. His right foot touched the ground as he felt the stallion leap ahead, the bit still in his teeth. The ground seemed to grab his foot and he felt his head slammed into the earth as his eyes sought the blue sky that swooped and went into small lights which floated past him. The claymore was in his right hand, and he suddenly felt very old. "John!" he shouted for the

Englishman. "Stop them!" He crawled over onto his hands and knees. "Ruff! No!"

He crawled toward the men and the girl, his eyes out of focus and bleeding from his nose from his fall. He saw Ruff kneeling by the man who had held the girl's hands, and he saw the astonishing vision of death in the man's startled eyes. The dirk was buried into his belly, and Ruff was pushing his hands aside as he reached for the handle, something like small children patting hands, it seemed.

"No, Ruff!" His head was swooping as he got to his knees. "No more!"

A wiry hand was under his arm lifting him, and he saw the cavalry pistol John Bollingale had leveled at the two remaining men, who had come free of the girl and were facing them. "I have got to try them."

"Try them for what, my lord?"

"By law." He clapped a handkerchief to his bleeding nose.

"They have debauched the girl."

"Aye, much mischief." He saw Ruff ease the man onto his back and pull the dirk out of his bowels. "Ruff, only by law."

"Aye, my lord," said the grizzled man, wiping the blade in heather and standing.

Skarra knelt by the naked girl, who stared up at them from terrified eyes which roved from man to man, unable to stop. Her mouth was a dark hole of torn flesh easing blood from the corners of the lips and oozing color onto the tongue and into the gullet so that he was unable to discover the exact nature of her wounds.

"The laird," Jamie said, kneeling beside him.

Bruce nodded and set his hands to her jaw to see if it was broken. "Did you know them?" The girl looked back, and blinked. He found that her jaw worked well when he felt her close and open it against his fingers. Then he saw her teeth. "Fellow loosened your teeth."

"Angry a bugger as I have ever seen," Bollingale said.

"Tie them, John." He slipped his fingers between her cheeks and teeth and aligned the teeth, easing them gently forward, opening and closing her jaw to check his work. It did not seem possible that he could set things so right, since the teeth were loose pieces of ivory sticking out of swollen chunks of bleeding flesh.

"We will send a man for snow from the mountaintop so she can suck it. The ice will set the teeth." He stepped back, looking at the captured men for the first time.

"Whose men are you?" They were young, handsome with muscular torsos and full legs and shoulders.

"The Earl of Connok's." The young man's bowed mouth crinkled up at the corners in a smile of insolence.

"Manners, boy!" Jamie's gauntlet and fist smashed across the young man's lips. He ducked with the blow, and came upright sucking blood. "This be Lord Skarra."

"Aye, we saw him at the hunt."

Bruce took the cavalry pistol from Bollingale, who was gathering up pieces of torn clothing to dress the girl. "Why did you rape this woman?"

The young men looked down, away from each other, then glanced back at him, almost shyly. "She was pretty," one of them said.

"You have used her beauty poorly." He turned away, shaking his head, ill at ease at the barbarism he had encountered in such young, attractive, and even courtly young men. "I cannot understand it."

"My lord," the darker of the two said, stepping forward. Bruce turned back in time to see Jamie clout him on the ear, felling him to his knees.

"Easy, Jamie."

"Aye, Lord Bruce."

"We did not mean to hurt her."

"Yet you did."

"It was just a game, a showoff sport."

"Love reduced to a sexual display of privy parts? God damn!" Bruce's voice rolled over the knoll like a single clap of thunder.

"I am sorry, my lord." He bowed his head.

"What any woman will give you," Bruce said, regaining his composure, "you have forced from her against her will."

"She resisted, my lord." The voice had an incredulous, uncertain note to it. "All three of us."

"Aye, that you would demean her, denying her grace to yield."

"She resisted the inevitable, my lord."

"No, you scarred her body, not her soul. The body heals, but not the soul, and she can live without disgrace. She did not yield. You forced her."

He waited long enough at the crofter's hut to see that the Highlanders accepted his directions for snow and his commands that the girl be treated as if she were not damaged. Since he was the laird, he was able to persuade the girl's father and brothers that "trial by combat," which was Scottish and certain, was not to be resorted to. He believed in his heart that one death was payment enough, and three deaths might throw the Highlands into open warfare. And, for the girl's sake, if she were ever to make a life, her chastity could not be the cause of sorrow. He realized he had a classic Roman view of a Presbyterian matter, but he knew he was right. Again he felt isolated among his own people. Only Bollingale, the Englishman, and Lydia, who was Russian, would understand him, and his mother would have, Lady Flora Duncan. "Surely, not just my own people are insane," he said to himself, for in his isolation he felt his folly press upon him. "Any solution simply accommodates barbarism."

He rode into their camp followed by his men and their two prisoners and the dead man, who was strapped across the back of a pony, his head and arms dangling down one side and his legs down the other, with his buttocks in the air. His bowels had moved in death, staining his trousers and further humiliating the image of the man, and Bruce wondered whether men might be more cautious about being killed if they knew how pathetic they looked when dead.

In a moment he was riding through McDougels, Stuarts, Duncans, Duffs, and McLaughlins, and he sensed the inevitable lull, with the excited expectation a death would bring.

"Shed blood, did ye?"

"Whose hand bears the blood?"

He ignored the comments and rode to his tent, dismounting and calling for Angus McDougel, Earl of Connok and Lord of Drimlar.

"So ye have had a bit of sport with my man, Brucie?" McDougel said, brushing into his tent. His eyes were fiery red.

"No. I caught them ravishing one of my crofters."

"They said she was a strumpet."

"They lie. She was a lass, spoken for."

"They said not." His teeth were clenched.

"You should have let the crofters kill them, and we would have no lies," Bollingale said.

"Lord Bollingale, there is a way to silence you. Hanging by Cromwell."

"You drank my whiskey, you insulted my wife, you slew my deer," Bruce said, feeling coldly detached from the rising crisis he could see confronting them, "and you raped my women. And if I had not stopped it, my men would have set upon those fellows and killed all three. And now you say I lied by taking the word of common felons."

"You it was who spilled blood."

"Aye, and you threaten my friends and servants with hanging, for no offense."

"Who killed my man? Just tell me who." He looked back and forth between Bruce and Bollingale. "An eye for an eye and a tooth for a tooth, the good book says."

"Your man was killed against my orders, by a Highlander."

McDougel turned and looked at Ruff and Jamie. The two grizzled Highlanders stared back evenly, their blue eyes cold slits among the wrinkles of their leathered faces.

"They are my bodyguards, and I am responsible for them," Bruce said.

"By God's teeth," McDougel said, his face livid in rage and his mouth open to a noisy hole, "a Catholic whore, a Russian Catholic, an English murderer, and you a Presbyterian! Protecting this human trash!" The dirk came out and Bruce caught the wrist as he drew it.

"McDougel, you fool!" He twisted the wrist until the dirk fell to the matted bracken. John Bollingale picked it up, but Bruce clung to the wrist, both because it impaired McDougel's effort to arm himself and because he commanded McDougel's attention by twisting it.

"Your men raped a woman, who by happenstance was one of my women. Not you nor any other man can rape a woman, not against her will." He heard himself gasp for breath because his heart had begun to beat fast and he was angry that he had to confront a grave problem with a gross man. "A man can do anything to a woman he wants to, anything, but he must have her consent, for a woman lives in her desire for slavery to a man, her need to be subjugated by a man and to risk her life, her body made a wreck, by the man, if she is any kind of woman; and you can do all these things to a woman—risking her life and even killing her—but, by the Holy God in Heaven, you have to have her consent!" He was heaving for breath, and he was shaking McDougel by his shoulders, making the head wobble as he bellowed, "A woman is how life gets here, and I will kill any man who denies it!" He flung McDougel back into a pile of stacked pallets. "Your men raped my woman and mocked the holy bond that ties a man and woman into eternal love."

He turned to his servants. "Strike the tents and pack the horses. Send runners to Skarra! We are for home!"

4

Lydia felt secure in Skarra, even though Bruce had been on Ben Lawkar on the banks of the River Deveron with the hunting party for two nights and three days now. She had compulsively gone up and down the stairs and through the halls and galleries of Skarra to check the windows and doors, setting her hand against the iron bars and slots, touching the chains, to reassure herself the old stone manor house was closed against sudden assault.

"My lady misses my lord," said the maid who followed her, carrying the small portable loom and shuttle with her tatting.

"A weakness of our sex," Lydia said, as much to herself as to the maid as she raised her face to see the upper bars dropped and bolted. "Each sex lives in the weakness and dread of the other, Bea." She looked at the Scottish woman with the red sandy complexion and red-rimmed nostrils.

"I do not understand, my lady."

"Only a man or a woman can ease the dread the other finds in life."

The maid looked puzzled.

"Oh, Bea, I'm sorry, I confused you." Lydia put her hand on the sleeve of the young woman, whom she genuinely liked for her candor, but she was always amazed at the naiveté.

"I dread nothing, my lady, least of all a man." The blue eyes searched for a deeper meaning.

"Alas, I did not mean we dread men, but rather, both men and women have a deep fear in living, and only if you can find a man or woman whom you can love is there any way to ease this dread of life."

The woman searched her face, from eye to eye, then broke slowly into an attractive smile, the lips as soft as the eyes' understanding. "Lady Lydia, dear dear woman, never ye fear, why, Lord Bruce is fearless and our house is safe as God and our axemen can make it—Lord, have mercy on any who would trifle with Skarra. . . ."

"Yes, Bea, I know that." She pressed the woman's forearm to interrupt her, for Lydia was terrified of Scotland and the savage passions of the Scottish with their insane enthusiasm to fight, not only each other but the English as well. Lydia was baffled by Europe and Britain, though she was much sought after socially, to grace the formal galas at Edinburgh Castle, Sterling, and St. James' Palace and about London. Her grace as a Russian princess seemed a marvel to her hosts, all of whom looked on Russia as a land of extreme barbarism and on the Tsars, to whom it was known she was blood-related, as monsters of terror; yet Lydia knew of nothing in Russia that could match the English king who had beheaded or divorced four queens out of whim, nor had Russia ever burned its greatest poets alive in public for writing books the nation worshipped; nor had Russia imitated a Scotland which refused to save its king, "Charlie Stuart and his noble airs," because English gold had bought the Scottish army. And if Siberia were a terror, Lydia could never grasp a nation that depopulated whole shires and counties, driving the impoverished cotters into slaveships where they were shipped in bondage to Canada and the Americas, in order to make room for sheep, which grew wool. "Profit, not life, that is Europe and the West," she had said to Bruce many times, "and yet your kin malign Holy Russia."

But she loved Bruce, and if terrified of Scotland, the Highlanders had heard her scream in childbirth, and this awful act of private travail had become the cherished image of the common people, and the Highland Scots outdid themselves to honor, to humor, and to embosom her and her children.

"Thank you, Bea," Lydia said, turning to go down the long gallery lined with Turkish rugs. "Having lived with the Scots, I can love them."

"I beg your pardon, my lady?"

"I love the Highlanders."

"We know that, my lady, even if you are a foreigner."

Lydia did not look back, but smiled to herself, knowing the unmentionable had been left unsaid. Her religion. When she crossed the flagged hall into the private dining room she felt a surge of joy rise in her heart as her children came into sight. Sergei saw her first, turning a mouth still munching a crumpet, and Lydia could see the marmalade glisten on his pink cheeks. It pleased her to notice they were more interested in eating than in recognizing her, for she did not want to sentimentalize her role as mother, making the children dependent on her to feed her vanity, and she had never done so.

"*Maman,* the tea is delectable," said slender blond Fanny, leaning over the polished boards to pour her mother a cup of tea.

"My indulgence, English tea." Lydia swept into the room in her farthingale to where Fanny was pushing aside the half-filled cups and mugs and half-eaten breakfasts to make room for her. She sat down at the girl's side.

"Rattling the chains and slots, for the thousandth time?" The girl smiled, showing the crowded Swedish look about her sensuous mouth, of teeth and pale gums from her mother, that made her terribly attractive.

"My weakness, fear." Lydia smiled and touched her bosom, taking up the teacup to her lips and looking into the blue eyes of the girl who had breathed her first life from Lydia's own lungs, yet who had come from another woman's womb. "But mine, I swore, and I made her so, before God," she thought.

"Oh, Mother, the kitchen is full of Highlanders."

"Your father's axemen, God forbid." She sipped her tea.

"Poor Charles is afraid, I fear."

"No wonder, but your father should be home soon."

Lydia took three cups of tea, almost in succession. "How is Voltoff?"

"Fine, Mother."

"Just fine?"

"He prays to the icons and sips tea."

"No, my child, he prays to God whose image the icons bear, because he is a simple man, pure of heart, and cannot imagine God without an image."

The girl bowed her head, knowing she had made the same insensitive remark so often heard in Scotland.

"Your father finds God in the forest glades and in the wet glens where the red deer run, and in the quiet mists rising off the River Deveron, or in the salmon that come home to die so their lives may continue in spawning."

"I know, Mother."

"I know you do."

"I'm sorry, Mother."

"Kiss me, Fanny. When you kiss me, daughter, I know God exists. Kiss me."

Fanny rose and leaned down to kiss her mother, her long blond hair strewing the face of Lydia as their mouths touched and their arms clasped each other until their breasts were pressed together, most affectionately, as mother and child unabashedly embracing.

"To know life is to know God," Lydia said, patting Fanny's arm as they came apart, "and my children are my life."

Lydia felt her whole being flow into repose, easing the muscles of her arms and legs and quieting her body, from the presence of her swirling roomful of happy, eating children and the kiss of her daughter. She let her eye travel along the massive Italian credenza, bearing the samovar which hissed, impervious to all human strife, like a steaming Buddha in silver and brass. She smiled. The gilt mirrors from Paris, the leaded windows looking down onto the mist-strewn firth across rich bracken. She was at ease.

But it was her children who sustained her, she realized. She could forever look atop their tousled heads, smell their sweet earth-scented breaths, see their clear pure eyes search hers, and hear their clustering voices as they shouted and chased each other in the delight of an innocent childhood that made her know her life was not in vain, that eternity was not oblivion, for life sprang forth out of nothing to refute it. God was in her children, and all life shared this implausible divinity.

Lydia sighed and sat back in the massive oak chair, knowing that in marrying the Scotsman she had defied the awful odds against love's thriving when divergent ways of life combine, had won the man's heart when it was broken, and had put it back together, despite the suspicion of a family inherently hostile to strangers. And she felt the sweet bitter ache of knowing her husband kept a quiet room deep within his heart where he preserved the memory of Geney, a love which seemed to permeate his being with an enduring patience and clouded his sight when he looked at her and saw two women instead of one, never her alone. Yet Lydia knew she had to take him as he was, for he was not such a man as to ever divest himself of what he had once loved, without killing him; and also, if Bruce could ever slough off love, he would not be the great man she adored, so she expected him to love forever whatever he had loved; and she was surprised to find herself smiling as she realized she kept it all alive, out of her love, a love from one woman for all the aches and sorrows of a household of adults and children.

And she knew she had the strength of all humanity under her heartbeat and in her womb. She had made her dream come true, as she had promised her husband, following him to be his, and make his all hers, out of love alone.

After breakfast Lydia climbed the stairs to the offices of Skarra on the third floor, where she knew McGregor, the bailiff, waited. She crossed herself at the icons and fireplace where Voltoff stayed, from right to left in the Russian Orthodox genuflection.

"My princess," the old man said, leaning forward.

"No," she said, settling her hand on his shoulder to stay the movement of his body and noting the fragile sense of bones just under the Ukrainian peasant shirt, and putting the back of her other hand to the bristling white hair about the shrunken lips of the old man, to be kissed. "Do you feel well this morning, Father?"

The old head bobbed uncertainly and an incoherent sound followed.

"Good, rap on my door if anything does not please you, Father." She withdrew her hands and swept on up the stairs, followed by Bea and a scattering of children, all of whom crossed themselves at the shrine of icons and greeted Voltoff as "Father."

McGregor was his usual dour self, even more taciturn, it seemed, being left alone on the estate. His sandy-flecked eyes were searching hers in his native restlessness. She saw the English pistols slung over the back of a chair in the cavalry pommel pouches, but she said nothing.

"I have never followed the accounts," she said as she came up to the table before the open ledger, "though Lord Bruce tells me verbally of his profit and loss." She did not say "our profit or loss," for she had to be careful not to intrude by laying claim to Skarra or the estates if she were ever to win the Scots, which she knew she had to do for the sake of her children.

"Wool is always sky-high, my lady." McGregor set his fingers against the page at a particularly high figure.

"Lord Bruce is always amazed."

The man nodded and eased the chair up behind her. "A great source of wealth."

"Yes. All the noblemen of Scotland and England have slain their wildlife and filled their parks and peasants' commons with sheep."

" 'Tis a pity, my lady."

"Alas, the poor are always with us," Lydia said, noticing the introduction of Galloway cattle to the West Burn of Skarra.

"So the good book says, my lady."

"Indeed, yet one wonders if mankind was as impoverished before the Bible was written as now."

McGregor stepped back, and aside, to stare down at Lydia, as though assailed by a malevolent thought, and astounded by its apparent emanation from his mistress.

"Oh, Ian, did I shock you?" Lydia said, seeing the disbelief. The eyes were large and glazed.

"Surely, my lady jests."

"Do I, Ian?"

"Oh, my lady, nothing was ever before the Holy Word of God. Nothing existed."

"How do you know, Ian?"

"Why, we have the Bible."

"Must we blame our iniquity on the Lord?" Lydia searched the sandy freckled eyes, which eased, and she saw she had circled the subject that millions had perished to resolve.

"No, certainly not, my lady."

"Vengeance is not ours," Lydia said, pushing from the table as McGregor slid back the chair for her. "Skarra is armed, of course?"

"My lady, only the space needed to swing an axe limits the number of axemen and archers within these walls."

"My husband's orders." She turned away, followed by Bea, who was snuffling her nose and daubing at the nostrils with a damp handkerchief.

"Lord Bruce's orders, my lady." McGregor bowed awkwardly as she left the Palladian loft of Skarra, passing the bright fire in the vast hearth, where she noted four very grizzled Highlanders she had not seen when she entered. They stared at her but did not get to their feet, about which lay a harvest of axes, knives, and swords. As Lydia circled down the broad stairs to the kitchen wing of Skarra, she was struck by the implausible and irreconcilable conflicts dividing the human soul, even among friends. "Thank God, I have the children to think of," she thought, "and not the discord."

Lydia carried her hands extended on the hoops of her farthingale, swirling the wide-hipped extensions from side to side as she descended, and it occurred to her how truly absurd were fashion and swank. "Vanity, I must remove these awful French creations," she said.

Bea closed up behind her to hear what she had said.

"Nothing, I was talking to myself."

The Scottish woman looked sympathetic and fell back a step as she followed. Lydia loved Bea, just as she loved Penelope, the Livonian peasant woman who had wet-nursed Charles and Fanny, whom they had brought from Russia, and who now slept on a pallet within their great bedroom and seldom left those quarters except to watch for Bruce's return from riding the estates of Skarra or to chase a child and scold the Highland nurse in very coarse Finnish oaths.

Lydia entered the kitchen wing of Skarra, which was the base of the "T" shape that formed the manor house. The kitchen was solid stone, as was the rest of the manor, except it was one and a half stories in height, with a flagstone floor over its cellar. Around the sides were half-balconies on which were stored crocks containing preserved meats and ciders, and where servants spread their pallets at night. Lydia found the kitchen cheerful because of the open hearths and ovens which were always burning, being only banked at night, and stirred afresh at dawn. It was a vast stone hall reeking of rich food odors and steaming soups and stews, alive with brawny Highland women and men, sleeveless to their armpits, and very much a woman's domain.

Lydia saw the heads popping into and out of view in the kitchen as she came through the center hall of Skarra. She knew she would never be able to come upon her servants unawares. "They have eyes in the backs of their heads," her father used to say of Russian servants, and Scotland was no different.

"Rosalee," Lydia said, acknowledging her chief cook, a gray harridan of a woman, gaunt of face with sagging breasts. She was absolutely loyal to the family—"Worth her weight in gold," Bruce had said, "considering the English gold in Scotland is enough to poison any Highlander or Lowlander."

"My lady doth fear without the lord," Rosalee said, wiping her swollen red knuckles on her apron.

"Aye, Rosalee, the woman dominates the lady in me."

"Truly, my lady, that is what makes a woman a great lady," said the Highland woman, complimenting Lydia.

Lydia smiled and nodded and passed among the Scottish women who without exception turned toward her. They were gaunt women of sandy complexion and gravelly skin—as were all their middle-aged counterparts, it seemed—whereas the girls were exquisite of limb and with skin pure as thick milk. Around their blue eyes were the lines of sorrow of the rough Highland life, of the grief of burying the beautiful blue-eyed children with the curly blond heads.

"All is well, I would suppose," Lydia said.

"Aye, my lady, nothing wants," Rosalee said, following Lydia as she moved into the quiet hall of servants.

"By the Almighty, let them come!" A low door clattered back against the stone wall, and a rough voice filled the hall, drawing everyone's attention.

"Who are they?" Lydia said, looking at the group of Highlanders shoving into the kitchen.

"Lord of Hosts, we will raise the clans." It was the loud voice of men.

"Make the English fight on our terms. Oh, Bannockburn, oh blessed Bannockburn!" It was a small man who shouldered his way through the four men who had caught sight of Lydia and had stopped talking.

"What is the meaning of this?" Lydia said, looking up at the half-balconies lining two sides of the kitchen. Armed Highlanders in kilts stared quietly back at her. "Ian! Ian McGregor, Charles!" She turned, feeling her stomach sink and twist as though she wanted to vomit, and her knees tremble. "Rosalee!" She put out her hand to the cook. "No!"

The cook came forward and Bea took her hand as the other servants withdrew from her toward the armed Highlanders.

"McGregor!" she screamed in the silence of the hall.

"My lady," said the Scotsman, stepping forward, unnerving her because she had not seen him though he had been right behind her all the time.

"My husband, Lord Bruce of Skarra, has forbidden the clan to rise!" Her voice was chilled and controlled, and she was grateful it did not betray her by trembling.

McGregor stared at her through his sandy eyes, then looked up at the balconies lined with coarse Highland men who lounged on claymores and axes and bows, with an occasional flintlock among them.

"Lady Lydia, since the master went to the hunt with the McDougels, a clan mortal to Wallace and Scotland, we have had word English agents are in the Highlands with five thousand pounds, sterling, seeking Lord John Bollingale." His eyes met hers for an instant. "I therefore armed Skarra, for I have no intention of seeing this hall carried by force."

"Pray tell, why was I not informed?"

"If you had the answer of how to defend your life, my lady, I'd have gladly told you."

"I see," Lydia said, gathering her composure. "Charles?"

"Yes, Mother," said the blond boy, whom she realized had been with her all the time.

"You knew?"

"Yes, Mother."

"I see. Then only Lord Bruce and myself, the master and the mistress, we alone are ignorant of these grave events, is that it?"

"My lady, often 'tis the parents who're last to know of trouble abrewing," McGregor said.

"And the talk of Bannockburn?"

"Loose Scotch whiskey, my lady," McGregor said.

"Lord Skarra's words," Lydia said, turning her face up to the crowded hall of Scots, "were to fight only in the halls and doorways and over the balustrades, for he said you would be cut down in the open like sheep in a fold, and God have mercy on us all, our enemies and our friends and our kin." She dropped her face and felt the tears flood her eyes as she put her hand up to hide her sorrow.

All night it seemed to Lydia that she turned her body and shifted her legs in the big bed. She raised her head and looked at the wide leaded window for any sign of dawn. None. No light, no Bruce, no dawn, just the terrors of the imagination. She finally swung her legs out of bed and drew a blanket about her shoulders and went to the small door leading into the children's rooms.

"My lady?" Penelope said, half rising from a pallet at the fireside.

"Go to sleep. I want Fanny." Lydia went straight to the girl's bed and leaned over the sleeping form. "Fanny," she said softly, taking the warm upturned palm of Fanny's hand on the pillow. She watched the rhythm of breathing change and the face shift sideways into the pillow.

"Fanny?"

"Yes, Mother."

"Come to bed with me. I cannot sleep."

"Oh, Mother, how could I have left you alone." Fanny swung back the bedcovers and slipped her fine white legs out of the bed in one movement, as Lydia smelt the delicious warmth of the girl's fecund body unfold in the rich odors of a nestling sleep.

"It seems I am haunted on this night. I have thought of Russia, of my childhood. . . ."

"Oh, Mother." The girl clasped her body to her mother's.

"Put your feet in fur slippers and wrap your shoulders."

"Poor Mother." Fanny swayed her shoulders in the half-light of a fireplace and searched her feet into slippers. "Would you like to pray?"

"Perhaps, I do not know." Lydia led the way back into the big room, where she let her daughter climb up and into the big bed ahead of her, and then followed. Under the covers, with the fresh life of her daughter at the quick touch of her whole body to reassure her, Lydia felt the insane terror of the dark night recede. "If I can hear you breathe and feel any part of your body, I know I am not alone and God is near."

"Oh, Mother, you should not let yourself think of the past."

"One cannot help the past, because our past is all we are."

"I'm sorry." The girl reached her hand into Lydia's.

"I think of my mother. She was a good woman, and now as I grow older I realize my mother lived a nightmare; whether it is in Russia or England, or Canada or the Americas, I have seen wisdom come only from grief, and yet happiness is possible from wisdom alone."

"Oh, Mother."

"I can see it in your father's eyes. When he was a young university professor he was so self-assured, and able to survive what no man should ever face, and triumph, but as he has aged, I have seen his face unsure that life has any solution. And it has turned me to my girlhood in Russia." Lydia spoke calmly, her eyes open and glinting occasionally in the half-light of the dying embers of the hearth.

"Russia is all a vast plain and easy to conquer, and so many nations and invaders conquered Russia that we gave our name of Slavs to slavery. And the Tsars came to free Russia in a terror more awful than our conquerors, and the Tsar had to call himself a god to justify the terror of his rule, but no mortal man can be a god, if he has cousins who know him as a part of their family."

"And so you could not stay in Russia."

"My father laughed at the Tsar and said he was a bad rider, which ought to be proof he was no god, even when Mother begged him to be silent in public, for as your own father says, a man's enemies are the men in his own household."

"Oh, Mother, it is just the awful night," Fanny said, squeezing Lydia's hand.

"When the Cossacks came to assassinate Father, they missed him but stabbed my brother to death, and then Mother, right in front of our home in our park of hemlock and frail linden trees. It was so beautiful in the spring morning and Mother was forever dead, her teeth showing in her open mouth as she screamed on my brother's chest."

Fanny held Lydia to her bosom.

"And now the awful feeling comes back to haunt me."

"Would you like to pray?"

"Yes."

"At the icons?"

"Yes, the shrine. I am willing to forever renounce Catholicism with my mouth, but in my secret heart, I shall always be Catholic."

They crossed out of the great bedroom and with the help of Penelope drew back the iron bolts barring the door to the hall. The small red votive candles came into sight immediately, casting uncertain shadows over the faces of the ethereal saints who stared in tranquil acceptance of all joy and sorrow as one and the same thing.

Lydia crossed herself at the shrine in the hallway and watched the candles. "When I was a child I used to imagine I could see my mother's face smiling at me when I looked at the candles, and I always had a happy feeling of hope. But now when I see the candles I think it is my mother's soul fluttering its wings in torment."

"Mother, I am sure my grandmother smiles," Fanny said.

"We can only live in the happy memories of childhood."

Fanny struck her breast in an attitude of devotion as they stood at the shrine in the Russian manner.

"I so loved my childhood, and it was lived in a nightmare for my parents. They gave me this, a love for life, which was being denied them at the time. A happy childhood gives the lie to the nightmare of adulthood. . . . Oh, I hope you have had a happy childhood, Fanny." Lydia began to cry.

"Mother, Mother, please, I have been happy." She grasped her mother to her bosom and felt herself break into salt tears as her body trembled against her weeping mother. Voltoff had risen and was at their side, a white specter of an old man, trailing shadows with a long white beard and hair to his waist, and Fanny heard the bare peasant feet of Penelope on the flags behind them.

"Father, I am so afraid," Lydia said, reaching to touch Voltoff.

"My princess, our Savior promised triumph over fear even at death, if we would but endure." He touched her hand.

"Thank you, Voltoff."

"Oh, my princess, I was a serf, then a troika driver, now I pray at my mistress' feet, in a loneliness so stark God will not take me, for it is pure, without evil." He eased down to his knees at Lydia's feet and kissed the back of her hand.

"Oh, Voltoff, dear dear Voltoff." She lay her hand atop the coarse white hair.

"And God let me live to see the life come from your womb, the new life in this heathen land."

She leaned and kissed the side of his face, clasping his head to her bosom.

"Our sorrow is our life."

"And our innocence is our strength," she whispered into the old man's ear.

"My sorrow in our exile became so great that it was my cross, and I lived to taste and know it, day by day, as a dear friend."

"I know," Lydia said, smoothing back the hair from Voltoff's temples. "I pined for the steppes of Russia until I could taste the heat and dust in my mouth, but always it was the mist and fog of Scotland, and the children came and I pretended, then I grew numb; and when they laughed, I heard my own laughter from my own land, but it was my children."

"Ah, my princess, it was only in the laughter of our children that we found the strength to live our torment."

"Children's laughter is the voice of God. It is innocent."

Voltoff dropped his head and wept the dry tears of the very old. "My princess and her serf . . ."

"My father, my Russia"—she hugged him to her—"parent and child in the eyes of God."

When Lydia had wept she felt a lightening in her bosom that enabled her to stand and once more bow before the icons and candles. "Eternal Father of all life, forgive us of our trespasses," she whispered, "and grant us the courage to live when death is easy. Eternal Father, let us hear Thy voice despite the insolence of our vanity, and let our eyes see Thy hand wherever we look on this globe, despite our tears of blindness."

They stood in silence at the shrine, then Lydia touched old Voltoff and turned to her bedchamber with Fanny at her side, the other women following.

5

Lydia knew she was still asleep when she heard the clatter of horses' hooves on the cobbled drive before Skarra, and as she woke she could feel the resilient shape of Fanny's body, the hard flat stomach and round firm legs pressed against her hipbone, amidst a sweet tangle of blond hair around her face. She was asleep with her near-grown daughter, yet she had definitely heard the horsemen.

"Outlanders, my lady," Bea whispered into Lydia's ear.

Lydia knew by divination it was true. There had been no Scottish cry of joy, the yell of exuberation to come floating down the firth by returning men. "The doors," she said, feeling the empty rise of fear drag onto every muscle of her body.

"Bolted and barred for Hell, my lady."

"The men?"

"Englishmen and traitors," said a tall dark woman who spoke in the broken man's voice of an ancient crone.

"Who?" Lydia rose on one elbow, trying to see who spoke.

"Your nurse, girl!"

"Oh, my nurse." Lydia let her head fall. "Yes, of course."

"Lord Bruce's nurse."

"Yes, Sarah, you frightened me."

"Rise, girl, the dawn is a quarter hour to come, and the house is surrounded."

"How many, Sarah?"

"Enough for mischief. We watched them ride through the moors all night. Their horses were like hounds in a bog as they lost their way and floundered."

"Dear God, where is Bruce?" Lydia clenched her fist and pounded it into the feather ticking, and Fanny sat upright. "Mother, what is it?"

"Get up, my lady," the old woman said, stripping back the bedcovers and exposing their semi-nude bodies and white limbs as the room began to bustle with women. "No tapers nor candles, and dress, Lady Lydia."

Lydia jumped from the bed as silent Highland servant women and girls scurried in the half-gloom of the dawn to dress her in the layers of camisoles, bodices, half-coats, hoops, and finally the farthingale, while her hair was brushed and set under a fashionable French headpiece of velvet.

"My lady," said the old woman after she was dressed, "the strangers have come across the moor at night, and they no doubt mean to take captive one of your children, or you yourself, to compel Lord Bruce to find that Englishman who is hid in the Highlands. The flesh and life of our children will be hostage to their success."

"Yes, Sarah," Lydia said, conscious of a frail note in her voice.

"Address them through the loop in the great door."

"Our men, Sarah, are our men armed?"

"Never mind about our men, girl. You play for time, until it is daylight."

"But are our men informed?"

The old woman cackled in the gloom, showing a single yellow eyetooth like a solitary fang in some strange species of animal, and Lydia swallowed and did not permit herself to shudder, not at the savage delight in the old woman but at what time had done to a once-beautiful child, who, in her ferocity, was struggling only to preserve her own children.

"My lady, you are Lady Skarra and a princess of a royal house. You must stall them until it is light enough inside the manor house so our men can see to fight."

"Oh, I understand, Sarah."

"Now go, my lady."

"Ian McGregor?"

"Our men are armed and waiting for the dawn."

"God have mercy on us."

Before Lydia left the big bedroom she gathered her children about her. "Sergei," she said, touching a half-grown boy's head, "and Nicholas, and Sasha—oh, where is Pierre and Alexei and Cassie?" The children were at her waist when she spoke, and bumped into each other and about as they sought to step closer. Their faces reflected the fear in their parents' purposeful talk and anxious silence. "Stay with Penelope and Bea." She ran her hands around the fresh skin of the children's necks and ruffled their hair. "*Maman* has to be busy downstairs."

The bolts slammed back and the door opened before her, and she saw Ian McGregor and two Highlanders she did not recognize. Then she saw Duff, his single eye aflame in the candlelight of the shrine. Voltoff was awake and on a small bench with a Highland girl standing at his side with a bowl of porridge, but the old man was watching his mistress. She crossed herself, whispered, and swept down the stairs with only McGregor following. Charles was behind the great door of Skarra with two axemen standing in the shadows on either side of the door.

"They have rapped, Mother." The boy looked especially pale.

"Have they spoken?"

"Yes. English, but not cultured."

"Not gentlemen, then."

"No, flat and rather nasal."

"Tradesmen."

"The officer wore red, in the Lord Protector's livery."

"Ironsides, Cromwell's own," McGregor whispered in a burr.

"Shssh, let me speak," Lydia said. Charles clattered the bolt on the loop of the great double doors of Skarra to attract the attention of the mounted troop they could see walking their horses in the crescent-shaped park before the Italian piazza.

"My lords, who honors us?" Lydia was surprised at her clear words and heard them carry across the men who she could now see wore breastplates and helmets.

"The Lady Skarra!" It was a man who appeared in red tunic and soiled white collar, and who lifted a varnished black hat.

"You come upon us unannounced, my lord."

"Ah, mischief has been done, my lady."

"No, my lord, all is peace in this abode."

The man smiled, showing the rows of dark teeth, rotted out in their crowns from the leached-out English counties. He was red-faced and very self-assured, smiling good-naturedly through the iron bars of the grill at Lydia. "Are you alone, my lady?"

"My children and I, Lord Charles and Lady Fanny and our wee ones, as the Scots say."

"Lord Skarra, hisself?"

"You cozen me, sir, for you would not be here if you knew Lord Skarra were home."

"Aye, my lady." The man chuckled to himself. "We have ways of knowing the whereabouts of all our Highland chiefs."

"Lord Skarra's title was an English honor," Lydia said, "recognized by the Lord Protector, Cromwell."

"Will you invite us in, my lady? We have not eht."

"Oh, you are hungry." Lydia chuckled to him, convivially. "Have you ridden far?"

"All night, Lady Skarra, and we have bellies that gnaw at our spines."

"You may tent in my park in front of the manor, and victual your men and horses right where you are."

The man's face clouded in lines which drew down between his eyes and nostrils to his compressed mouth. "Lady Skarra, you will do yourself a favor if you open these doors immediately, in the name of Oliver Cromwell, the Lord Protector of Great Britain!"

"Sir, I do not open my doors to any strange man."

The Englishman shook his head and smiled at the three other officers who had come up on the piazza to join him. "A thousand pardons, my Russian princess." He thrust out a clumsy boot and bowed awkwardly with his thick body. "I am Major George Atkinson, commanding, provisional brigade, Ironsides Regiment, and Independent Protestant."

"Not so many titles, Major," Charles said, pushing in front of his mother. "We can see your ill-breeding at a glance."

The officers' smiles chilled into clenched jaws as they stared through the grill at Charles.

"Ah, Lord Charles' comb is getting red," said Major Atkinson.

"What were you in trade, Major? A butcher?"

McGregor snatched Charles away from the door loop as Lydia smiled and licked her lips. "Lord Charles is not sympathetic to tradesmen."

"Charlie Stuart felt the same way, until we shortened his wit," said another of the officers, making his fellows laugh at the reference to the beheaded king.

"May we have breakfast, Lady Skarra?"

"Of course, but only the gentlemen, and I must rouse my servants."

"We are four English gentlemen." The officers laughed at their own joke and good-naturedly withdrew to the park, where they spoke to their ratings and troopers, obviously satisfied they would have their way at Skarra.

"From Lancashire and Lincoln, my lady," said Major Atkinson. "We are Puritans and Independents." He smiled pleasantly down the formal dining room table at Lydia.

"All four of you, are you each quite sure you are pure of thought?" Lydia said, presiding at the head of the table.

The officers laughed contentedly and exchanged quick glances. They were obviously at ease, though they had momentarily refused to enter the hall when they saw McGregor, who was armed with his pistols, though the Highlanders and axemen had been secreted in the library and great salon, across the hall from the dining room.

"As pure as any Scot, my lady."

"Scottish zealotry comes from their impurity, Lord Skarra says."

"Your husband, a wise Scot, him."

"Lord Skarra," Lydia said, smiling and correcting the Englishman.

"Aye, Lord Skarra."

"An English title to hold a Scottish chieftain," Lydia said.

"Noble airs come easy in a rough country, we Lancashiremen have noticed," said Major Atkinson.

"Aye, it makes a man balmy to have a title," said the short officer wearing a gorget.

"What should a man have," Charles said, "to remind him of his duty?"

"God."

"God?" Charles said.

"Aye, God will talk to him."

"And this is not a form of lunacy?"

The Englishmen exchanged quick glances.

"Charles accompanied his father to Westminster to see the divines debating the future under the Lord Protector, Cromwell," Lydia said. "We are to be a theocracy, I believe."

"It was a Persian fight of wild asses," Charles said, laughing outright.

"Your son has a tart tongue, my lady."

"Lord Charles?" Lydia said.

"Aye, Lord Charles." The talk grew still. "We have a warrant for his arrest."

"What? Arrest Lord Charles?" Lydia sat upright in feigned indignation. "Is that any way for English gentlemen to repay breakfast?"

"We are not gentlemen, Lady Skarra," said a gaunt officer with deep pocks on his slack lower lip. "We are commoners."

"Nay, we do not believe in an aristocracy. Republicans, where all men are equal."

"Then why not for America, where God and men have supposedly met on Massachusetts Bay?"

"We have work here, first."

"Like my arrest," Charles said.

Lydia glanced at him and saw the bravado of a frightened boy pushing him to the verges of his self-control. "Charles, whatever their politics and their religions, and even their station in life, these officers are our guests."

The four English officers glanced at Charles, then at McGregor, who ate in silence and never took his eyes off them, then back to Lydia, obviously impressed.

"His Majesty died with courage," said Major Atkinson. "If he had lived like he died, he would be king today, and Cromwell a carcass stinking in a hole."

The officers looked back to their plates, nodding. "If the aristocracy could do something well besides die, we would never part with them."

"A frightful way to win the admiration of your people," Lydia said, her voice calm and self-possessed.

"We are hard-working tradesmen and schoolteachers, and we truly believe if men and women will listen, God will speak." The short officer spoke earnestly.

"I am certain this is true," Lydia said. "And so will the devil speak. The question is, Which is Heaven and which Hell?"

"Oh, we always know the difference." The officers nodded vigorously with each other, obviously stimulated by the intellectual discourse.

"But the truth, gentlemen, cannot be known except through time, for the tree is known by its fruit, and one mind at one time, with one idea, cannot be judged of an instant as anything more than a passionate notion."

"Agreed, my lady." The officers were enthusiastic in looking up the table at her, laying aside their spoons to stare at her.

"But you are so certain, you have slain your monarch, would arrest my son, and have thrown all Britain into civil war."

The officers looked back to their plates, crestfallen, and commenced to dabble at their porridge and cakes. "A man is wise in his own conceit," Major Atkinson said.

"And is not the next man as wise?" Charles said.

"Where the aristocracy is educated, it foxes all us ordinary folk," said the gaunt officer.

"Truly, I would like to hear your views," Charles said, his facile lips moving intently, and a tremor of excitement alive in his throat, as he thrust himself into the frightening world of adults for the first time. "Unequal men strive to overthrow those men more gifted by nature than themselves, and are never content with the blessing of their lives until they desolate their gifted neighbor."

"God sanctions the overthrow of corruption, Lord Charles."

"No doubt Cain justified himself along those lines. Yet who, once he has bloodied his hands, will relinquish power to those beneath him?"

"None, my lord," said Major Atkinson.

"As I suspected. Then why should we relinquish to you?"

"Our weapons." The officer glanced to his pistols and saber hung over the back of his chair.

"So your morality is but a mask for your greed and lust for power—God is your drill sergeant, and little more, and this I have always suspected."

There was a silence about the table, the seven diners glancing at each other, as though suddenly uncovered in their naked selves.

"Aye, and we must take you into custody, in the name of the Protector, until such time as you be arraigned for treason, Lord Charles," Major Atkinson said, pushing back his chair.

"Wait, gentlemen, wait," Lydia said, standing, "I beg of you to wait. Lord Skarra commands the loyalty of the Highlanders, and blood will be shed if you precipitate this impetuous folly."

"It is folly to resist, my lady," said Atkinson, a white streak showing on the side of his lean jaw.

"Englishmen!" McGregor said, throwing back his chair so that it slid into the credenza, bringing down the samovar in a crash. "Walk out of this house and ride out of the Highlands!" The four officers stared at the Highlander, looking at his tweed tunic, his epaulets, and his kilt. "I have you surrounded and your death is all you will seize."

Atkinson breathed slowly and turned to Charles. "I arrest you in the name of the Lord Protector. All who interfere are enemies of the Commonwealth, and will be arrested and carried to Edinburgh in chains to stand trial for treason."

"Major, you don't know what you are doing," Charles said, his face ashen and his lips drained to a pale blue, his eyes light with terror as he faced the awful fight he could see coming.

"God have mercy on us," Lydia said, steadying herself with both hands on the table, her grace and elegant sophistry so obviously useless.

The English officers strode briskly through the room to the double doors into the flagged hall.

"Wait!" Lydia said, running after them. "Gentlemen, we are your own people! The aristocracy is the source of restraint and wisdom and assured tranquility in any realm, for we are your living heritage. Do not deny us, for you only deny yourselves, and you desolate your own souls in this rash contempt for your undying past! I beg of you!"

The four Englishmen watched her, their faces grave with the solemn wisdom of her grief. Atkinson's face drained white, his eyes kindled into a strange light, and his voice gargled. "Orders were imposed upon me. I must arrest Lord Charles." He turned toward the door to which the short officer ran forward, throwing open the loop as he threw up the iron-slotted bar.

"Ironsides and the Protector!" The cry filled the park as horsemen galloped wildly across the green, flinging up heavy divots of sod amidst Biblical cries of Old Testament fury.

Atkinson strode out the door which was flung open by the short officer, who turned back into the darkened hallway with a drawn pistol. Lydia could see the officers signaling with their arms from the Italian piazza and she heard the notes of a cavalry bugle as small masses of horsemen cantered across her view.

"Boom!" The hall roared with an explosion that filled the light with smoke, and Lydia could see the short officer double over his belly at his waist and fall onto his buttocks and flop onto his back, across the threshold of Skarra.

"Kick him through the door, lads!" It was the thundering voice of McGregor, who dashed through the smoke with a clutch of Highlanders, carrying a smoking pistol. The Scotsmen had the officer up off the threshold, held by arms and legs as his close-cropped head bobbed unnaturally, and flung his body onto the piazza, almost at the feet of Major Atkinson and the group of English troopers, who stared down at the body as it bounced like a sack of liquid and skidded to their boots.

"Take the bastard back to England!" McGregor shouted at the officers, who appeared dumbfounded at the precipitate death and the stalwart defense, their light eyes round in disbelief.

"Force the door!" Major Atkinson shouted as the door slammed shut and the iron bar dropped, clattering, into the slot.

Lydia had retreated up the stairs a few steps, watching the hall swarm with armed Highlanders who rushed back and forth, it seemed, clattering their axes and claymores, and some ran noiselessly up and down the stairs, heedless of her, their eyes to their chieftains and their minds to the defense of the old manor house.

She could hear the men huzzahing out on the piazza as the battering ram was flung against the front door, and she could see the thick wood boards shiver independently of each other, divided by cracks she had never noticed before.

"Wham!" "Wham!"

"Lift the bars!" It was the voice of McGregor in the hall before her, and she saw the double doors burst backward as a group of red-coated soldiers fell headlong across the threshold, and scrambled on arms and knees.

"Rush the door!"

"Into the manor, boys!"

Lydia shrank backward up the stairs as she heard the flat nasal voices of the Englishmen and saw the rush of armed men through the glaring daylight of the door, into the gloom where axeman and swordsmen waited. The Highland girl was at her side, her voice sobbing in terror as she watched the two sides come together in a death clutch. "My lady, old Voltoff wants you."

"Voltoff," Lydia said. "Oh, yes, Voltoff." Then she came to her senses. "Dear God, is he safe?"

"Yes, my lady, he wants you."

"Ahhee-EE-aaa!" The Scottish war cry filled the air amidst the measured cheering of the English troops.

"Hurrah!" "Hurrah!" "Hurrah!"

"I'm coming!" Lydia shouted as she saw the Highlander behind the door come down with his axe atop a helmeted soldier whose white eyeballs popped out over his cheeks as his head seemed to explode behind the eyes. Another Englishman's head was hewn apart, the live part still working with glared eyes and open mouth as the free part was lopped off in a hairy plate that bounced against the stone wall. The Highlanders went down out of sight under a forest of jabbing bayonets and swords.

"Ahhee-EE-aaa-EE!" The Scottish yell of fury and death filled her skull with a great din, and Lydia retreated up the steps, to the landing where Voltoff waited.

"Dear God, Voltoff, oh dear God." She clung to Voltoff and she heard the old man praying in Russian and she fell to her knees before the shrine, with Voltoff at her side, and prayed in the Russian of her childhood and trembled. The fight was everywhere up and down the hall. "Holy Mother of God, spare us from this barbarism," Lydia prayed, and heard Voltoff intone, "Mother of Russia, spare us from the Western savages, Holy Russia, spare us."

"Boom!"

Gunfire blasted before the shrine and Lydia was surprised to see Charles kneeling and looking carefully along the barrel of a flintlock which a Highlander had handed him. The cloud of smoke drifted down the stairs atop the clanging sweeps of what seemed a steady motion of sword blades, axe heads that rose and chopped, and armored breastplates and brimmed helmets moving against a cursing line of feathered bonnets and blood-matted Highlanders. And Lydia realized the Scots were without armor, and even if stout of defense, were at a clear disadvantage in a close-quarters fight, except for their chopping axes on long handles.

"Boom!"

"You hit him, my lord."

"Quick, I'm shooting them in the head," Charles said, licking his pale lips, and Lydia was stricken with an insight into the gentle child she had breathed into at birth and raised as a son.

"The Hand of Providence! Watch him fall!"

"Another head shot," Charles said, shaking back his long blond hair over his shoulders.

There was a pause along the hall as the soldiers looked up through the smoke, finally spotting them at the shrine, and where Charles was killing them with such precision.

"There's Lord Charles! On the stairs, men!" Lydia recognized Major Atkinson's voice and spotted him standing along the wall, sword in hand, urging on his troopers.

"Up the stairs, boys! A thousand pounds is on his head!"

The fight along the hall seemed to pause in the movement of upturning faces, seeking out Charles.

"There he is, a thousand pounds, boys!"

The mass surged in on itself and up the stairs, with Highlanders jumping to the bannister to head them off and being sworded back.

"No! Charles!" Lydia cried out, seizing the boy's arm.

"No, Mother," Charles said, aiming his last rifle into the advancing mass of English Roundheads, crowding up the stairs as an armored, clanking beetle waving sharp tentacles at him. He smiled grimly to himself when he saw the hard face of the leader, a rough grown man, who hesitated when he saw the flintlock pointed straight down the stairs at him.

"Boom!" The lead slug hit the man full in his chest, knocking a hole into the armor and driving the soldier backward with much force into his fellows, turning the advancing soldiers into a floundering clot of unbalanced cursing men, holding up a dead man whose arms and legs still flopped.

"After him!"

Charles drew his sword as the soldiers dropped their leader underfoot and swept forward once more. In a second he was engaging at least three blades, which were moved awkwardly by the soldiers as they dodged him, their faces behind their saber bells.

"After him, boys!"

Charles had no trouble lunging his sword into the exposed shoulders of two of the soldiers, which was not altogether an advantage, for it put two men out of the fight, leaving the third more room to feint and parry and riposte his blade.

"Ahaahaa!" Charles was appalled when he stabbed the third soldier in his throat and saw bubbles of blood flow out of the windpipe in a spew that clouded his lace jabot.

Charles was momentarily panic-stricken when he saw three more soldiers on the stairs, stepping over the fallen bodies of their comrades, slowly driving him back upon his mother and Voltoff and the shrine. He saw the hall was clear of English soldiers, except for the dead and dying, so that the Roundheads on the stairs were trapped between him and a mass of Highlanders on their heels.

"Lord Charles, give way!" It was a bellowing voice behind him. Duff. He glanced quickly over his shoulder and saw the single fiery white eye of the scarred Highland cotter, insane with fury and excitement. "Give way!" Duff gestured backward from the landing to him, and he caught sight of the stir of the great bedroom doors. He dashed backward, away from the soldiers, who pulled up when they saw the mad fury in the ancient one-eyed Highlander glaring down at them.

"Englishmen, whose greed shames Judas of Iscariot, surrender!" It was the shrill female voice of a crone.

"Are you wounded?" Lydia said, gripping Charles' arm.

"No, Mother, but listen to Sarah!" He nodded at the old woman who stood at the top of the landing, Duff to her left. "Englishmen, surrender in the name of Providence! Your greed will be your death. You are surrounded!"

The soldiers paused, looking down the stairs where Highlanders now thronged with muskets and axes and swords, then back at Sarah, the hairs fairly bristling on her chin and puckered cheeks as she closed her toothless gums, then to the savage single eye of Duff, the dead eye seeming inflamed from the long scar.

Charles watched the helmeted Roundheads pause, their red-rimmed eyes finally coming to rest on him, where he stood with Lydia and old Voltoff in a moment of exquisite silence, as though it were the last sane moment every living creature on earth would ever know. Voltoff's lips were praying and he held the gold Russian cross up before him and intoned the litany, chanting the Byzantine supplication.

"Idolatry, it's idolatry," said a soldier with a small boyish face. "And beside him stands a thousand quid!"

Charles watched the expression on the Roundheads' faces. The muscles tautened with ferocity at the invocation of religious anger and determination to gain the reward for his capture.

"Get him, boys!" They lunged up the last few steps as a single man when there must have been at least a dozen.

"Kill! Kill!" It was Sarah screaming insanely, and Charles was vaguely aware that the bedroom door was pouring out a solid mass of Highlanders as he was swept back before the English, dragging his mother who was screaming, "Voltoff, my slave! Voltoff!"

He was knocked off his feet by a gloved blow to his head and felt himself dragged aside by a group of Highland women who had been crouching in the upper hall, and he saw Duff clubbing a Roundhead with a two-handed claymore so that the brimmed helmet rained sparks as it was pounded into ridges, and Charles was amazed to see the Englishman refuse to fall. Then he saw the heavy cavalry jackboots flip toes-up over the bannister, and he knew the Roundhead had been brained.

"Kill! Kill the strangers!" It was Sarah urging on the Highland Scots.

"Mother," he whispered to Lydia, and he felt himself burst into tears. "Oh, Mother." He crawled to Lydia's bosom and felt her breasts trembling against his chest as she cried together with him.

"The Roundheads have Voltoff," she sobbed.

"No, he is harmless," he whispered, his nose running as he clung to her and wept. He kept his head down against the floor, beside his mother's, as they listened to the screaming of the dying and the wounded and the fury of the Scots, amidst the awful crunch of axes chewing up flesh and bone.

In moments there was silence. Lydia got to her feet with Charles and steadied herself on the bannister with her hand. "Voltoff?"

The Scottish women pulled back away from her, as though caught up with a sane thought coming in the silence after the awful fight.

"Duff, where is Voltoff?" Her voice had a plaintive note to it. The old Highlander who was at the short landing by the shrine turned his face to her, the single eye struck with the horror of hearing a human voice, for all down the long staircase lay the maimed bodies of dead and dying men, whose bowels had commenced to move in death, filling the air with a rich fecal odor that mingled with the pungent scent of the overturned Russian candles.

"Oh, my lady," the old man said, stepping to her.

She saw Voltoff lying on his back amid the scattered icons and against the silver cross. His eyes were searching for her. She rushed to him as the Scots shrank back. "Voltoff—dear, dear Voltoff. Oh, my father and mother." She seized his waxen hand, and saw it still held the Russian cross with its lower horizontal kicked aslant in the Savior's passion.

"Oh, Voltoff!" She buried her head into his beard and saw the three broad slits across his abdomen out which blood was oozing to stain the frail, white illusion of the man he had grown to be in his very old age, making him mortal when she had come to believe he was almost immortal, and not only the guardian of her chamber door but guardian of her soul.

"The English sworded him, my lady."

"Voltoff," she whispered, taking his spent bony shoulders into her arms and crushing him into her bosom, noticing the arms flap uncertainly, then fall away, too feeble to embrace her.

"Princess Merkalov," he whispered.

"Yes, Voltoff?"

"My princess." The voice was stricken and Lydia could hear the death rattle of blood within his chest.

"Speak, dear Father."

"Listen." He licked his lips; a pale tongue moved through the brush of white hair beneath the haunted eyes, which focused beyond the hall of silent people, who had killed in such fury, yet were apparently stricken to see their mistress down over her old guardian's body as he died.

"Yes, Father?"

"Our life . . ." He coughed and blood began to drain onto the white hair.

"Life is innocence . . ." He moved his lips again, the eyes searched down across the maze of bloodied and rough Scottish faces who watched, transfixed; then the eyes found Lydia's. ". . . and I am your slave, thank God." The eyes closed, and Lydia felt the body yield to death, the head tilted slowly backward, and the waxen fingers yielded up the Russian cross, which slid down a step against a dead Roundhead's bloody face and empty eyeballs.

Lydia stooped and picked up the cross, and stood. "Put Voltoff on my chest at the foot of my bed." She seemed to have a sudden insight into life, that horror was not an end in itself, but that having seen it, there was still more, even though incomprehensible. "McGregor!" she called.

The Scots in the lower hall turned their faces up to her and McGregor came briskly to the foot of the stairs, walking cheerfully atop the still, armored bodies of the English dead. "Yes, my lady?"

"Spare the English!"

"Quarter?"

"Quarter, McGregor!" Lydia's voice was chilled in its firmness.

"No quarter for the Scots!" Sarah's face was a mask of rising fury as she leaned over the bannister. "Our kin betrayed us and so did the English! No quarter for the Scots!"

"Quarter for all the wounded," Lydia said. "English or Scots." She picked her way down the stairs, avoiding the legs and arms, some of which still clutched spasmodically at the floor with fingers, or kicked boots into the air or along the boards.

Lydia walked out through the front door onto the piazza, where she found Major George Atkinson lying at the base of a Grecian urn containing heather; rhododendron leaves framed his blood-wet brow and matted hair. Highlanders were moving about everywhere. Atkinson did not move. Dead, she thought.

"Quarter," Lydia said, ignoring the Scots who deferred to her steps, not looking at her but keenly aware of her presence. "Quarter, McGregor, tell them quarter." She refused to look at the Highlander who followed her.

"Quarter! Quarter for all wounded!" He bellowed across the park and drive, and toward the wings of Skarra.

"All be wounded and the lucky ones be dead, Ian," said an aide, coming up to McGregor.

"Spare all lives."

"They be mad dogs, Ian!"

"Spare them—Her Ladyship."

"Her Grace is a lady, boys!" It was Atkinson, struggling to roll his body forward to gain his balance.

"Are you alive, Major?" Lydia said, coming up to him.

"By your grace, my lady." He looked up into her face, the lines of anger gone, and showed the lean Midlands cheek and gaunt jaw of a very ordinary man who has worked a lifetime.

"Don't rise, Major." She put her hand to his shoulder.

"My Gawd, those Highlanders." The thin mouth turned up in a soft grin, cracking the dried blood on his cheeks.

"I tried to warn you, Major. The English should not be in Scotland."

"Oh, my lady, I agree. It's not Scotland but France we fear."

"If you had only waited for Lord Skarra."

"The plan was to catch his home empty, my lady."

"And every Scot in the Highlands knew it, and escorted your troop through the moors."

"We did not see them."

"But they saw you, Major."

"Aye. Now I know it."

"Carry Major Atkinson to my chambers," Lydia said, rising. She saw the Scottish women pause and look to her. "Put Major Atkinson in my chambers. He is just a common man who did what he was ordered to by circumstance. McGregor!"

"Aye, my lady."

"But the Scots are to die." It was Sarah facing Lydia, the jaw outthrust in an unnatural lump under the closed gums, and particularly ugly from it.

"No more killing." Lydia stared into the turgid mass of each eye. "I will hold all accountable." And she walked into the manor and up to her chambers, feeling a numbness creep over her body and face, dimming her eyes with the sorrow she felt. It was a huge ache in her chest that would not leave her, and she wanted to double her body down into a small round shape to try not to feel the awful burden of it.

6

Bruce rode through the night air feeling the mist chill his cheek and wet his eyelashes, but he liked the cool of it against his eyes because it eased them from smarting. He could hear his men all about him, the hooves of the small Highland ponies sucking on the earth in a quick succession compared to the long striding gait of Bellsinger. It reassured him to hear so many Highlanders near him, first because he had parted the Stuarts and the Grahams from the McDougels, lessening an abrasive confrontation, but mostly because he had his Highland strength unimpaired by trial of combat. Within his heart, Bruce was soldier enough to know the Highlands could not stand against the English and the Lowlands forever, in open combat. Yet he also knew that if he could keep the loyalty of the Highlanders, who were Royalist and Stuart, and discipline them to fight in the mists of remote Scottish mountaintops, he could launch a will-o'-the-wisp campaign of savagery that might never be settled in peace, and he knew the English knew he knew this, and he also knew they had no stomach for such a war that could never be won.

Bruce also knew he had never betrayed the King, as had Alexander Leslie, Earl of Leven and Swedish Field Marshal, in taking the gold of the Westminster Parliament and then changing sides once more to oppose the Independents and Cromwell; and he also knew he had never betrayed the Cromwellian Protectorate, once he had declared for peace. Deep in his heart, Bruce also knew the Earl of Argyll of Scotland had wanted the English throne, and Scottish treachery was the keystone of English triumph. And with the collapse of this human iniquity, Bruce had preserved a clean name and had gained the respect of the English as well as the Scots.

Yet Bruce knew his true power lay in peace, and never coming into open combat, and thus, through bluff and delay, he could win his abiding passion, which was to have the Highland clans endure, even flourish, thus assuring national and racial survival in Scotland as well as, perhaps, in Canada and the Americas, where so many Scots had been banished. In his heart he knew the battle was never to the strong nor the race to the swift, and he was Classical scholar enough to avoid the insanity of religious certainty. And in his heart he felt the awful loneliness and sorrow a wise man discovers in the seat of wisdom.

The rhythmical stride of the horse carrying him through the quiet night brought a swaying motion into his mind which drowsed him, and he felt the delicious ecstasy of sleep droop his eyelids and he eased his head down into his muffler, utterly at peace as he was brushed into sleep.

He did not know how long he had slept when he felt his foot guides, who walked at the stallion's bridle, hold back the animal.

"Lord Bruce!" The whispered call came at his knee.

He raised his head and could see and hear nothing. His men had seemingly vanished. He shook his head and looked down at the two figures beside his horse. "What is it?"

"Strangers, my lord." Ruff raised his hands to help him down.

"When is dawn?"

"Not a half-hour off, my lord." Ruff gestured with his arms and Bruce slid down off the horse to conceal their silhouette against the skyline.

He followed his guides on foot as they skirted the main road leading through Buchan from Inverness to Stirling and Edinburgh to the south. Bruce had no trouble pacing his men, for he had been as abstemious in his eating as he was remote in his laughter, and his long legs carried his lank frame with ease. The gorse was wet and wiping across his face and shoulders at every step, and he noticed that the Highland tams and tartans wrapping his men turned back water in mottled spots and running beads, like unwashed sheep's wool. The game trail followed the road at a parallel but maintained its altitude above it, bending to the contours of the mountainside.

"Any scouts identified them?" he whispered.

"English, we think," Jamie said.

"How so?"

"Grand noise and loud talk."

"Unafraid, then," Bruce said.

"Aye, as if they owned all Scotland."

"When the dawn comes, I want a count."

The Highlander nodded his rough gray head without looking at Bruce, and behind them he could hear the horses and ponies being led single file through the heavy wet cover, which in the rising light of the dawn still was a deep, shadowed black.

They came out onto a promontory on the shoulder of the low mountain where they were actually well ahead of the High Road, and around which the strangers would have to pass. Bruce looked up into the lightening gray mist, then back to the road, where he could hear sabers rattling against leather. "Obviously English, and cavalry," he said involuntarily.

His men dispersed down into the yellow and green bracken so that he stood with only Jamie and Ruff and Albain, a subchief of the Grahams.

"No bloodshed." Bruce spoke quietly. "If too many, we let them pass, and if a few, we arrest them to seek their purpose."

"Aye, my lord." Albain dropped to one knee and spoke beneath the wet panoply of pleached limbs where the men had slipped into concealment. "No blood, and none dare to attack without bounden cry."

Bruce watched the small English troop of cavalry appear out of the rising mists of dawn. He could see the glistening breastplates of the troopers, ten, a dozen at most, following the clutch of officers, who wore fur-trimmed cloaks and wide-brimmed felt hats decorated with ribbon and plumes, clearly visible at such a distance. "By God, it looks as if the Cavaliers are leading the Roundheads," he said, more to himself than to his Highlanders, because he knew his rough Scots would never understand the fine differences between Englishmen. He regretted he did not have John Bollingale with him, but Bollingale would have to stay among the cairns and rude stone cottages of the Highland moors, hidden by the people, until such time as he could take ship to France or to the Americas.

"Looken! Lord Bruce!"

He was distracted by Ruff, who was gesturing to his left, up the road which turned before them. He saw two horsemen coming at a gallop, one in a breastplate and each bareheaded. He put his Italian spyglass on them and saw the cropped hair and the blood-smeared faces and one man carried his arm thrust into his tunic to support its wound, for the bone thrust out the elbow.

"Riding from Skarra, my lord."

"Aye." He turned and saw the two desperate riders would soon round the promontory and meet the larger force. "Capture them." Ruff nodded.

Ruff stepped into the high gorse, which was now a wet green canopy mantling the earth at the height of a man's head and hiding all beneath it.

Skarra watched the two riders jog out of phase on their mounts' backs, either because of their wounds or their lack of horsemanship, until he could see the blond hair and bright eyes which stared rigidly ahead up the road they sought to get down as quickly as possible, as though they each had some terrible fright they wanted to be away from.

"Soldiers, Roundheads, and they've been whipped," Bruce said, looking down at the wet crown of heather he stood upon. "They have thrown down their arms."

"Aye, Roundheads," Albain said noncommittally.

"What could have whipped them, and what are they doing in the Highlands?"

"Lord Bruce, ye were off hunting with our traitors." Albain glanced into Bruce's eyes.

Bruce nodded and put the glass to his eye to watch once more, listening to his Highland chief. "A wise man is, alas, played the fool by the knave, my lord, for the wise man is kind and the knave cruel, and if ye strive in equality, the wise man must lose, for the weapons are not equal."

"True, Albain," Bruce said, "but those look like two very tame knaves coming down that road."

He saw the lead horse shy off the narrow grass-covered road and spin its head into the bracken, the muzzle up and rolling white in its eye as the rider threw up his arm and fell out of sight. Highlanders were moving about the two horses and the men vanished into the high cover where the horses were led, leaving the road empty in a moment. Bruce exhaled his breath, pleased that no one was hurt, and looked back to the party of English cavalry, which was ignorant of the capture just around the bend from them. They were riding at a quiet walk, and he could hear an occasional gobbled sentence indicating officers of the educated classes. He was relieved that he would be dealing with gentlemen.

The two English troopers stood before him in the clearing, surrounded by wet gorse, their eyes roving in the fright of their morning's experiences. It was a jargon of words that fell from their lips as their eyes occasionally came to rest upon Bruce, who towered over them in his feathered bonnet and massive boots. The regiment is dead, we were ambushed in the hall, the axemen surprised us, nobody told us the manor house was armed, only a Catholic whore, the lady prayed at breakfast, all the officers are dead, we found horses down the road—it all came clear to Bruce.

"The manor house of Skarra?" Bruce said.

"Aye, that was it." The sergeant with the narrow temples and long jaw stared at him. "How did ye know, my lord?"

"I am Lord Skarra of Skarra."

The two soldiers seemed to come out of their trance of words, as the realization sank in that they were prisoners of the man whose house they had assaulted.

"My lord, we meant no harm."

"I am sure you do not now, particularly since recent events were so persuasive." Bruce spoke gently, but with candor. "Your names?"

"Sergeant Leadbetter," said the sergeant, "and this be trooper Jones. Jones has a bullet in his side, my lord."

"Aye, he is pale, and you have a nasty arm." Bruce gestured at the shaft of bone poking from his sleeve under his elbow.

"The axe."

"I am sorry, sergeant, but we will fight for your life." Bruce spoke quietly, almost tiredly, and looked back to the small cavalcade he could now see clearly, and he heard the English sergeant break into gargling sobs, apparently undone by the kind acceptance of his cruelty, which was to be repaid by kindness. They all knew the arm would have to come off.

Bruce watched the English cavalcade a moment and realized the nobility had taken service in the Commonwealth.

"Have you any idea who those people are?" he asked the two soldiers.

They stared, as though unable to recognize or to ascertain, or to evaluate a question—totally unable to answer.

"Put them in litters," Bruce said, turning into the gorse and sweeping his lank form from side to side as he strode down the mountainside. "I must capture whoever they are, before they raise a false alarum in Edinburgh."

His instructions were clear. He had posted his men, numbering seventy at least, in a noose on both sides of the road, and they were to close in as Bruce mounted Bellsinger and rode forward. He watched the English gentlemen ride slowly ahead, listening to a spirited conversation on whether it was sporting to put a fighting cock into the drag-pit for an ignoble fight to the death after it had fought nobly on the grit but had been unable to make a clean kill.

Bruce swung up into his saddle at this moment, raising his right arm and gauntleted hand, and bellowing "Halloo! my lords, halloo!" He was satisfied to see three of the troopers' horses whirl, throwing one man, and the two others dash madly back down the road, where he saw them shy again and go crashing off through the gorse, their riders standing in the stirrups and cursing as they dragged at the reins, whipped ragged by a hundred limbs slashing their faces.

He rode forward on Bellsinger, smiling and greeting the officers, who had reined up, too startled to do anything but stare in silence with sagging faces. "Welcome to Scotland, my lords! The Hand of Providence over all!"

"Lord Skarra?" said a large officer with long mustaches.

"Hailyham, Buckey Hailyham!" Bruce shouted, and rode quickly toward the officers.

"Hell, it's Skarra himself," said Hailyham to the elegant officer with the wet lace ribbons on his large-brimmed hat. His face was amazed, the eyebrows knitted, the voice uncertain, while the other officers looked first at each other than back to Bruce.

"The lord we have come to arrest?" said a very handsome young officer with a curling but wispy blond mustache and fair blue eyes.

"Silence," said the officer with the wet ribbons.

"Buckey, what are you doing on the moors?" Bruce crashed up onto the party. Highlanders were swarming out of the close cover and about the small band of Englishmen, taking the horses by their bridles and holding them as the riders stared in silence at this noiseless capture from ambuscade.

"Bruce! You bastard!" Hailyham shouted and commenced to laugh uproariously, his eyes running tears as his horse fretted and pranced sideways. "You have done it again!" The large man fairly bellowed with laughter. "You have taken us captive, when we were supposed to capture you!"

Bruce rode in close to him, and took the large florid hand of the red-faced Englishman. "You are not the first Englishman we have captured today."

"More troopers, I should hope." Hailyham grabbed Bruce by the hand and shook it again, as though relieved that his own capture had shed him of his guilt at coming to betray a university friend, an act of which he was able to see the insanity.

"I presume this is Lord Skarra," said the clipped voice of the officer with the ribboned hat.

"By Jove, I am sorry—His Grace, the Earl of Dorset," Hailyham said, outthrowing his upturned palm.

"Welcome to Scotland, my lord," Bruce said.

"Some welcome, here." Dorset nodded meaningfully at the mass of rough Highlanders on all sides of them.

"My lord, bloodshed breeds bloodshed, and I want none of it. You have been captured in peace."

"We come in peace," said Dorset, sitting erect and nodding his head in emphasis.

"I regret this is not true." Bruce looked at each of the five English officers. The two youths stared back at him in innocence, but the older officers looked down or away. "Last night, whilst I was away on a hunt, an armed band of Englishmen raided my home. . . ."

"Yes?" Hailyham said.

"They were hewn down in the hall and on the stairs of Skarra."

"Hewn down?"

"My servants fought to defend their home."

"Aye, what man would not?" Hailyham looked down and shook his head. "I told Westminster you would come to London on a posted summons."

"Agreed. I have had no stomach for treachery," Dorset said, putting his gloved hands atop the pommel and pounding them. "I have never understood Scottish politics."

"No gentleman does," said Hailyham. "Methinks the Lord Deputy in Edinburgh riles Scotland, not rules it." He nodded his head vigorously. "What Scotland needs is one good and true English gentleman."

"Aye!" Dorset nodded in assent.

"Scotland might disagree," Bruce said, turning Bellsinger. "Let us ride on to Skarra—and—Buckey?"

"Yes?"

"Please tell your men not to draw their weapons."

"Agreed! No weapons, men! Lead on, Bruce!"

Bruce rode at the head of a small cavalcade of Highlanders and the English officers, leaving the troopers to follow at a slower pace with the wounded. At his knees bobbed the tam-covered heads of Jamie and

Ruff, and he felt a great annoyance with the English for invading Skarra and threatening his family with terror. He kept his face a mask of formality before not only his own men but particularly the English. Yet deep in his heart he was immensely pleased to know the Highlanders had fought savagely, though he could not imagine McGregor and Duff killing forty Roundheads as the captured sergeant had insisted. Still, if the English came in stealth to slay and capture, there was a divine calm in the knowledge they had perished.

Somehow, he was not alarmed about the personal safety of Lydia and the children. If they had not been killed or captured in the first rush of combat, he knew the professional axemen and killers of the clan would have had them swept aside to safety so they could give battle in the insane, joyous Scottish way. Yes, the captured sergeant had called Lydia a Catholic whore, which meant his Puritan bile was not vented by her death. He smiled grimly, knowing his teeth were showing as the cool morning wind touched them through his parted lips as he breathed in rhythm to the slow canter of Bellsinger.

His mind turned to Lydia. Perhaps she was dead, yet he could not seem to feel the numbing horror he had felt for Geney's death twenty years before. He did not understand it, for he was still passionately attached to Lydia, in a physical manner he had thought a man would outgrow by the age of fifty years or close to eighteen thousand mornings of life. Still, he could not outgrow his passion for Lydia. It had half-shamed him, ten years before, that he could not just "settle down to middle-aged sobriety," as the English middle-class said—everything for them was "middle," and lukewarm and placid and uneventful and dull. He was still lustful about Lydia, had seduced and caressed and loved and conquered her so many times he was ashamed to think of it, and still she had triumphed, always willing to go further with him, to do more, until he had surrendered to her, dying and trembling in her arms so many times he could not imagine death in any way except in Lydia's arms, her breath on his face, and really, if so, then death had lost all fear for him. And he knew Lydia was far, far stronger than he, or all of them put together, and he suddenly understood why he was not concerned about her death. Lydia was impossible to destroy. She was life. And no forty Roundheads could kill her any more than the Russian Tsar. He felt a slow smile rise out of his bosom. He was going home to his love. He would see his wife within the hour. "This goddamned English treachery, serves them right."

"My lord?" Ruff said.

"Home, Ruff. Let's go see our kin."

The Highlander nodded his head and glided along beside Skarra's horse, the hand caught just under Bruce's knee, and the English officers could not seem to tear their eyes from the way a Scottish chieftain rode the moors and Highlands.

He felt his heart surge with delight when he galloped over the crest and saw Skarra strung out along the firth, impermeable and stone-rooted among the sentinel yew trees and awash in thick rhododendrons. Bellsinger bucked and switched his tail and Bruce had to gather his head with the reins as Ruff erupted into the Scottish war cry, and they heard it roll down the valley over the firth. In a moment he saw the figures appear on the grounds, especially the women, so he knew he faced no ambuscade. "Let me ride ahead," he said.

"Aye, my lord," Jamie said and dropped clear.

"Grab a pony!" Bruce set his heels to Bellsinger and felt the nimble stallion leap into the bit.

It was an exhilarating gallop down the cobbled road that ran along the banked hawthorns and rhododendron, and he exulted in feeling his horse lean his body into the curves, so that his face rushed pell-mell across a scene of leaves and gray limbs, just inches past his eyes.

"Halloo!" he shouted as he cantered up to his piazza, where his breath froze in his throat. "My God," he said, dismounting. It was a solid mass of armored but dead Roundheads. They were lying in neat rows down each side of his Italian balustrades.

His people were all around him as he walked up the steps from the park, everyone silent. Lydia came flying down the steps. "Bruce, thank God you're safe!" She clung against his chest as he stared over her head at the dead Englishmen. "They fought," she whispered.

"Aye. Treachery on all sides."

"No, not us!" She looked up at him, her eyes swimming but ablaze with indignation. "I begged them."

"I know. Whatever right we have lies only in our proof the strangers assaulted our home at dawn."

He walked past the dead trying to ignore them, but the dead have a peculiar self-assertive way of thrusting themselves onto the living, usually for the worst, and he saw it in the dead of the Ironsides Regiment. One strapping boy had spread his legs and raised a stark white bone for a thigh, where the thick red thigh muscles had drawn back, his only wound on a graceful body which had bled to death. The boy's mouth was closed, Bruce noticed, while beside him lay an older, bald man whose brain had slipped out onto the flags behind his head, so that he had a startled look to his exploding head, held in frieze. The image was ruined by the man's open mouth, where he showed his rotting teeth.

"Get them out of their armor when their joints loosen up," Bruce said, "or else we will never get them decently buried."

"How many?" he said, turning to McGregor.

"Thirty-two, my lord, including three dead officers."

Bruce looked into the sandy-flecked eyes of the stocky Scot. He saw the quiet satisfaction of a harassed and driven man who had finally faced his tormentors and had hewn them down in open and fair battle.

"Any living?"

"Aye, one officer and nine troopers."

"Thank God," Bruce said. "Witnesses. Thank God you spared the wounded."

"Nay, my lord, my Lady Lydia called for quarter." The Scot stared at him in defiant resolution.

"I regret I was not at your side, McGregor." He clapped his bailiff on the forearm with his hand. "Smooth words never hid a rancorous heart. You honored our fathers."

"Thank you, my lord."

"And thank God I have proof we did not start the fight." He turned to Lydia as the Scot seemed to release his breath and breathe afresh. "Oh, Lydia, your wisdom gave us witnesses."

"It was like killing children when they went after the wounded."

Bruce closed his eyes as though to shut out the words and the image and clasped Lydia's waist and walked forward into the house as she guided him. "Thank God for your mercy," he said, his voice failing as he began to cry.

He lay on his back on the tester bed in Charles's room with his eyes closed and worked his legs against the women who were pulling off his heavy boots. The sight of Voltoff's naked and bony white body stretched out on blankets as the Highland women washed and prepared it for burial was too much for him in his own bedroom, vast as it was. There was also the English Midlands schoolteacher, George Atkinson, Major Atkinson, with a sword thrust in the chest, and not too deep, he was glad to see, who touched his muddy boots and wept in gratitude for quarter. "I put him in our room to make sure they did not murder him," Lydia explained. They were moving all the wounded into the great hall of Skarra, under the banners of Saint Andrews and the rows of armor from English knights slain at Bannockburn, which had led Scottish arms to an excess of risk at Flodden Field.

"The Earl of Dorset and Colonel Buckey Hailyham and three other officers and ten troopers are on the way," he said to Lydia and McGregor, who stood at the bedside. "Some are old university friends. Take their horses but leave them their arms."

"Are they captives, my lord?"

"Yes, but only until I can write London. It's Argyll in Edinburgh who ruins Scotland." He paused. "The English cherish their ignorance about their neighbors and this is their gift to rule. They lack rancor, at least for their aristocracy."

"Not every Englishman is ennobled, Bruce."

"Aye, nobility is to be sweated for, and not many men will sweat for anything."

He said to McGregor, "Every horse on Skarra and on the moors is to be put under guard in the stone paddocks on the firth." McGregor clapped the bell of his claymore in assent.

He waited a moment, his eyes still closed, feeling the luxuriation of his calves and feet free of the massive boots. "Let me touch the children's heads. Their roundness always amazes me." He felt the smooth round life and thick hair of Sergei and Cassie, his arms stretched over the edge of the bed.

"Is that all, my lord?"

"Yes. Go see to the English."

He opened his eyes slightly to look at Lydia; she saw it and smiled, and took his hand, knowing he felt the confusion of a man of good will confronting a nation and a people split not only by civil war but by race and sex, and trying to bring some order into his own mind so he could accept and deal with the chaos of what should not be. "I think," he said, "that mankind has some grave resentment against God, and he hankers after death worse than he lusts for a woman, and women are just as bad. If it is a man's world, it is a woman who gives it purpose, and only in death of one's own kind is there any satisfaction of the blasphemy that if man cannot give life, like God, then he can negate God and kill life."

Lydia leaned over her folded thigh on the side of the bed and put her head down into his bosom. Her mass of hair on his chest, with the lighter weight of it on his lips and face, restored him.

"They have a warrant for Charles."

"I know. But we hold the moors."

"It's Bollingale they want."

"Aye, supposedly, but really it is the Earl of Argyll who wants to drive out the cotters and graze sheep all over Scotland. Bollingale is the cat's-paw."

Lydia did not speak, but lay her ear over his heartbeat, where she could hear the pounding of another urge of life to serve its own existence out of eternity, despite its inevitable death, and thereby authenticate the timeless God who let life come, then go, majestic in itself. She had never felt more Russian, and never closer to Scotland. It was her husband's heartbeat which was eternal under her ear, an inch away, that made her feel whole.

"Will Argyll win?"

"Eventually, yes, he will win."

She pressed her head against his breast.

"His dream will come true, and it will kill him. A man is doomed by his own triumphs, and time is on the side of endurance, not success."

"Not many would agree," she whispered.

"Time is on my side, and on the side of the Highlanders. I will win, not him."

"Oh, God willing, do be cautious."

"Never did a more cautious Scot walk the moor." He grinned slowly and kissed her lips gently, tasting the flesh and live grace of them. "I love to kiss you," he said.

"That I can please you." She smiled easily and searched the depths behind his eyes, and felt him ease in her presence within his being. He had never felt closer to another being in his life, and Lydia sensed it.

When he had refreshed himself with two cups of tea and had eaten a small oatmeal cake, and had bathed his face and neck and hands, he swung his legs over the side of the bed and put his feet into the Moorish slippers and put on the Scottish doublet decorated with silver buttons and bright cuffs and said, "Sarah, our own losses?"

"Five dead, Lord Bruce. The wounded will live."

"Old or young?"

"All old men, families grown or most grown."

"Good."

"The surgeon?"

"Riding from Fovern."

"Aye, damnable sawing or purging or bleeding."

"My lord?"

"Nothing, Sarah." He shook his head wryly. "And they call it healing."

"They died with joy, my lord."

"I am sure they did," Bruce said, knowing they had, in fact, died in utmost joy as only a Scot can die in a fight he knows is fair. He turned for the door, suddenly feeling the great cold wind of wisdom chill his heart. He looked for Lydia. "We must put things right." He took her hand. "I think anything truly great on this earth starts with a simple man and woman who are willing to try all over again."

He walked down the broad stone stairs past the servant girls who were still scrubbing the flagged hall and sloshing water through it. He tried not to imagine what had gone on in the minds of the Englishmen when they came up on the Italian piazza and saw the results of the battle. It would seem he had been ready and waiting for them, yet such was obviously not the case. He had not been at home, and his servants had fought alone. Still, any Star Chamber Court or Courts-Martial could prove anything and find any culprit guilty. England was no different from Russia, for that matter. All a court needs is "the national interest," and any fool on a jury would convict a man of anything.

The English officers were in the dining room eating noisily, Buckey Hailyham making a point with a half a broiled grouse. "I tell you, it's Louis who is England's enemy. My God, think what I could do to the French if I had a Scottish army!" He waved his two arms apart in a V, absolutely carried away with the prospect of such an idea. "God's teeth, we need these Scots in our army, instead of fighting them."

"Aye, the carnage was remarkable," Dorset said, nodding his head. "One does not expect to find so many fallen Roundheads, especially after losing to them."

"Lord Skarra," said the young officer with the wavy blond mustache. "Father." He nodded to Dorset.

"Ah, Skarra, your table is sumptuous." Dorset sat back in his chair. "They said you would join us."

"Aye, the grief was more than I had expected," Bruce said, taking the seat at the head of the table.

"Bad show, this treachery."

"Damned politicians in Westminster." Hailyham fairly growled.

"It seems that if I do not keep my hand on the exact pulse and reins of this moor and the Highlands, right at home, I am then forever taken by surprise." Bruce settled a napkin under his chin to protect his lace jabot in the French manner. "Would to Heaven I had not gone hunting."

"It wasn't your fault!" Hailyham said. "They wanted the manor empty so they could seize the boy."

"Charles, yes." Bruce nodded.

"And they were to hold him in Edinburgh until they got Bollingale."

"Yes," Bruce nodded. "And Argyll knows the Highlanders will never give up that Cambridge don, out of pure cussedness if nothing else, and he reckons if he takes my son I will be driven into leading a Highland rebellion, which England will put down, and he will then have a free hand to clear the Highlands and graze sheep."

The Englishmen watched him quietly as he buttered a small roll.

"Will you lead that rebellion?" Dorset's eyes searched his face.

"There will be no rebellion."

"My lord, will you rebel?"

"Did Cromwell rebel?" Bruce stared into the Englishman's face, then back to his roll.

"Aye, any Scot will rebel." The Englishman turned back to his grouse and plover's eggs.

"Any man will rebel," Bruce said. "My piazza is full of English rebels against their king, now cut down by Scots who rebelled against their dawn assault. Ask yourselves, gentlemen, Is not rebellion the purgative for tyranny?"

"Bruce, you have not changed since Cambridge," Hailyham said. "All this talk, when what I need is a Scottish army." He clapped his hand on the table for emphasis.

"Aye, you Scottish philosophers shame us English." Dorset smiled and continued to eat ravenously, which seemed surprising in so small-featured and delicate-limbed a man.

"My problem is to communicate with Westminster, avoiding Argyll in Edinburgh," Bruce said, "and we will have no rebellion or bloodshed, and I think you gentlemen can help me."

"Of course," Hailyham said. "Right, Dorset?"

"Yes, we stopped off in Edinburgh, but our commands originated with the highest authority in York and Westminster."

"Later, we will tend to it all," Bruce said. "We have the grief to honor with burial, and I have not had the pleasure of a formal presentation of the young officers." He looked at the two youths at the table, and glanced down to the Quartermaster, who had bulging eyes and had stared openly at Bruce, suggesting a more humble birth than the other officers. "I have a son and a daughter I would reckon to be their age."

"Yes, the warrant . . ." Hailyham said.

"You may deliver that warrant to me," Bruce said, "and consider your duty done, and my son will then be my prisoner."

The English raised their heads to look at him.

"I am the sworn Lord of Skarra, loyal to the Commonwealth and Britain. The warrant to arrest Charles was from Edinburgh, not Westminster, and Westminster is the capital of Britain." He looked into their faces, from one to the other. "You will deliver your warrant to me. Lord Charles is my prisoner."

"Checkmate!" Hailyham laughed. "A canny Scot, this Bruce, and bravo!" He pounded the table top with both his palms.

7

It seemed to Bruce that he had been to funerals all his life, and that of all the appalling facts mankind faced, the certain end of apparent life with the collapse of the blood into stink and the flesh into rot, as if a blatant mockery of the grace of what had been, was the final outrage of all existence. Somehow along the way he had relegated death to an inevitable event which prevented men from the irresponsible arrogance of a god gone mad, and necessary in holding vanity accountable to how life was spent. Yet, nothing on the earth could justify the death of the innocent, and though it was difficult to accept a soldier's death, he was stunned by the death of the young and the pure. The religious dialogues asserting life after death seemed to him the reincarnation of vanity, and repellent to any thoughtful man. But the burial of the thirty-two Roundheads had a ring of truth about it, of divine retribution, even if he pitied the men more in death than they were likely to have pitied themselves, had they lived, for life was pathetically simple to the simple. Again he felt lonely as he conducted their funeral. "Why must I always wonder," he thought, "when others willingly accept the outrage of loss and grief?"

He followed the long procession of Highland men bearing the bodies of the English dead, out along the crest of the green ridge that overlooked the Firth of Skarra to a fresh burial ground. Lydia and the children were with him, as were the English officers and troopers. His clan was already strung out along the way, and at the long graveside were the sweating men who had dug open the fresh earth and mounded it in a raw mouth, perhaps like a womb ready to once more receive an impregnation of new life, he thought.

"We could not stop them," Lydia said, her voice very low at his side.

"I know."

"It is so useless."

"What can anybody ever know?" He spoke to reassure her.

Lydia touched his hand lightly, and he saw the gaunt pallor of not only middle-age show under her skin, but the strain of being under assault by large and cruel forces able to wipe out their family and way of life.

He pressed her fingers and released them, for he wanted to show no emotion in public, particularly before the English officers, and he heard the Presbyterian minister commence to pray, which drew down all heads into common devotion.

The prayer drifted into and out of his conscious mind. "Our Heavenly Father who binds every wound and succors all sorrows"—a gallant effort by the gaunt Presbyterian professor, as the Scots called a minister, to assuage the unspoken anger of the more powerful English—"these courageous soldiers of God who so recently bore the cross of God before the Popish Anti-Christ of Rome and beat idolatry into Godly submission"—the face was narrow and the deep-set eyes searched the low wet clouds that joined into the mist about their breaths—"now have been gathered into the bosom of God, in the infinite mercy of Christ and beyond the understanding of man, for so great is the wisdom of our Heavenly Father. . . ." The voice droned on, the thirty-two sheeted bodies lying before the earthen mound, the silent Scots and the mist uniting them all.

" 'Idolatry' and 'a thousand pounds' sterling for Charles' were their last words as they lunged up the stairs," Lydia said, whispering but not moving her head.

"Dead soldiers are always heroes in death," Bruce said, speaking low.

"But it's all so false."

He nodded imperceptibly. "Aye, all a false mouthing of virtue now that they lie dead, all a damned lie."

She glanced into the side of his face and back to the funeral services.

"Nothing riles so much as an insult to top and gall a just retribution." Bruce spoke almost silently. "The Presbyterian knows his role well."

She nodded. "He spent hours with Voltoff sipping tea."

"Ah, alas."

He was relieved to see the long row of dead gathered up by the Highland men and handed down into the grave, each lying side by side. Along the row of the silent figures under sheets he saw an occasional knee thrust out, or a booted leg set awkwardly into the air in a motionless kick, and one rough hand was uncovered, the fingers clutching like a claw reaching back for life as the fellow twisted in his death throes. When he saw the angry face of a large man, his jaw set into an open bellow of outrage, Bruce looked to the Presbyterian and nodded for John Cramer's Common Prayer and lifted his feathered bonnet, pinned with the sterling phoenix of Skarra.

He closed his eyes and listened to the martyred poet's hymn to the ashes and the earth and all to dust and did not open them until he heard the scattered fall of earth upon the dead.

"Wait, here are the limbs the surgeon sent along!" someone called out.

Bruce felt Lydia look up, and heard the shovelers all pause and sensed the movement about him, but he could not look at what he knew had arrived from the hospital and operating arena under the tents on his piazza. He opened his eyes and lifted his bowed head, glad he could mask his revulsion for death under the guise of pious devotion, and saw all were watching him.

"Professor Graham," he said to the Presbyterian, and nodded at the two sacks and one basket suspended on poles slung between the shoulders of six Highlanders.

The Scotsmen moved briskly up to the edge of the grave, where they set down their burden and with gravity commenced to pull apart and separate the arms and legs and hand them down into the grave where others had jumped in once more.

"Parson, do I have to match the right leg to the right body?" a rough man called from the long pit.

"No, my brother, the Lord knows which leg belongs to which body, and will take care on that great getting-up day," the Presbyterian said.

"Praise God," came a voice from among the Highland women.

"Amen."

"Amen."

Bruce eased his eyes closed once more, hoping it would pass quickly, for the naked legs seemed so pathetic without bodies, and the white plump buttocks were like hams freshly de-haired and ready for curing.

"Good Lord, a brain!"

"Parson, it's a brain."

Again the awful pause while Bruce waited for someone to simply go ahead with the burial.

"I seen hit lying on the Eyetalian piza," said someone behind him.

"Throw it in the hole, he will never miss it!" came a thunderous voice to his side. Duff, he realized. "Throw it in, laddie, an Englishman will never miss his brain."

Bruce turned his face, trying to glare in rebuke, but saw the single eye of the savage Scot agleam as it stared at the Presbyterian and the massed mourners. Bruce shut his eyes, nodded, and bowed his head once more, feeling Lydia take his hand into hers as the bustle of filling the grave was resumed.

When the Roundheads were properly buried he led his family back along the green ridge and through the soft mist to their chapel, which stood in the lea of Skarra and often reflected in the chill waters of the firth. He had knelt in the chapel as a boy, when they still burned the votive lights before the carved wooden crosses, and the low belfrey had often wobbled in the water image as he came out and looked for the red deer across the firth, before his family had become so Presbyterian and his father, Lord Eric McTaggart, had been corrupted by Edinburgh in accepting Church lands. Now it was the sheep and wool which was corrupting them, and he had to bury old Voltoff, and he felt all weak in his stomach. He loved Voltoff.

"Light the tapers," he said to six elderly men, one of whose face and neck was covered by a dense mat of short white bristles which joined his white hair and the curling tuft at his breastbone.

He looked to Charles and saw his son's eye catch the depth of sorrow which bound his parents to another human being. Charles looked away, knowing his father was burying an old man who had known and loved his natural mother as well as Lydia, and a person so utterly different from Scotland and all that they lived and believed that the bond of love between his parents and old Voltoff was frightening to him, it was so great, and in respect he lowered his eyes to the foot of the staff bearing the cross.

Bruce looked up at the bier and nodded to the pallbearers, who seemed to hesitate in the small chapel, which was thronged with his clan and the five English officers and noblemen.

"All I can think of is him and the sleigh," Bruce said to Lydia at his side. "The awful race on the ice and the fight with the Cossacks, and him calling to the horses and his long grizzled beard flying as we ran for our lives against death . . ." He felt his voice falter and the tears flood his vision and run over his face.

He felt Lydia slip her arm about his waist and hold him in the heavy silence of the chapel, where he sensed his people waiting for him.

"I never knew how he could live in a strange land," he said, gathering his voice in a whisper to Lydia.

"It was the same for him as me."

He took the French handkerchief Lydia handed him and dried his eyes and face, stunned he could cry and yet at ease from the release of it.

He raised his eyes and looked at the bier and saw the old man stretched out in stiff repose—almost Byzantine, it seemed. Yet, the long white cassock and the polished wooden cross held in the wisping white fingers of bone and parchment, brushed by the long combed beard, gave an ethereal look to the image, as though Voltoff had, in fact, in life eventually transcended the flesh and earthly grief to actually mount up to the spiritual, simply by refusing to die and by praising God each day he could suffer afresh. Bruce kept looking at the utterly peaceful face of purged alabaster and long white hair, belonging to a very old man who was done with life.

He felt Lydia take his hand and he nodded. The pallbearers stepped up to the bier and Bruce saw the white specter seem to rise over their shoulders as the tapers and candles moved about them, and he heard the dirge of his pipers playing along the firth, taken up from the lament at the chapel steps.

He followed the coffin—open in the Russian manner—through the mist and up the graveled garden path to his family vault, watching the fine white hair strain droplets out of the drizzle until small beads gleamed on Voltoff's face. The body was accompanied by the large icons and tapestries bound in silk, borne on staffs by the aged servants who had known the Old Faith. Skarra followed Charles, who carried the cross, and ahead of them he heard the Presbyterian reading scripture from an open Bible and leading them to the grave. His mind was blank with the madness of "one more funeral," the lamenting pipers whose tunes echoed along the firth with unrelented grief.

Voltoff was perhaps the last true friend he would ever have, a friend who understood his virtue and could forgive it. "If I can bury this one more person whom I love, then I will be done," he thought. "After this I am oldest, and I shall die next, and then, thank God, I shall not know it, and I shall never bury another loved one—my family is all much younger than I, thank God."

"Bruce?"

"Yes?"

"We are in the crypt."

"Yes." He was surprised to find that they were in the small dank room lined with square rock slabs bearing the Latin names and titles of his parents and his ancestors. It seemed the room rose and fell upon his eyes as he searched the walls for a moment, above the masses of candles and tapers held by his servants and clansmen, with the glare of light never steady before the gloom.

"Bruce, they are waiting."

"Yes, Lydia?" He searched for her eyes and found them.

"Shall we bury Voltoff?"

"Yes."

He noticed Lydia nod to McGregor, who whispered to a grizzled man he did not recognize; and then he saw the lid set over the white image he stared at, and he realized Voltoff was gone forever. The pounding of the wooden pegs snapped his mind back to reality, and he heard the years fall away with an awful crash and felt the pegs driven into his heart at each blow of the maul when he had closed Geney's coffin twenty years before.

They stood before the open vault and watched the coffin lowered into a shallow rockbound rectangle in the floor, beside a long narrow flagstone which had been pulled up.

"He wanted us to stand on him," Lydia whispered, and she knelt, followed by the younger children.

Bruce nodded, hearing John Cramer's poem of mankind's tenuous domain between birth and his surrender to dust and earth, "earth to earth . . . dust to dust," and it surprised him to see the stonemasons lifting the granite slab over the rough oak coffin. He realized the Presbyterian was waiting for him, and he felt for Lydia's hand as she rose, and he took it, and followed her out into the mist and smell of wet heather.

The next day Bruce was compelled to face the stark event, without a burial to divert their minds, that his men and his home had been in open and successful rebellion against the Commonwealth. His only advantages were his remoteness in the Highlands, his proven loyalty, the endless Anglo-French wars, and his crafty aloofness to discord. If Cromwell could never quite trust Edinburgh, then perhaps Skarra could play this off with the assured tranquility of the Highlands north of Edinburgh. Killing thirty-two Roundheads in his hall did not enhance this image. And worse, Edinburgh now had a pretense to move against him, once the word had spread, which would be the case, for Scottish treachery would assure the betrayal. He had a week of time, he reckoned, at best a fortnight.

"I do not know what move to make first," he whispered to Lydia as he waited on the dawn, feeling the eiderdown against his face.

"Entertain the English."

"I beg your pardon?"

"They hate the Roundheads. You could see it."

"A party?"

"Yes, a dance."

"Lord, we had a funeral yesterday."

"Voltoff would not mind, and the rest were barbarians."

He nodded his head in the pillow.

"The young people need to dance and if we see them in jolly company we will be friends," Lydia said. "We need those English officers to intercede for us in London."

"Aye, they are powerful men."

"And they are our prisoners."

"Yes, I have their horses and Skarra is surrounded with Highland trackers."

"The nobles scorn the merchants," Lydia said. "It is us they like, not their own people."

"I went to University with them."

"Lord, the Roundhead officers were so sure and opinionated, all puffed up on demented religion, so pathetic in their ignorance."

"Aye, men invent religion in order to use it against each other."

"Let's have a glorious dance." She sat up, pulling the bedcovers off his bare shoulder.

He shoved his hand over and touched the fair skin of her back, feeling the knobbles of her spine.

The plans for the night of dancing went forward, to the appalled fascination of Sarah and Duff and their devout servants, who had a Puritan abhorrence of sensual pleasure, of which "prancing the naked duckies" epitomized a union of Popish idolatry and fleshly delight. Bruce did not care, and after the deadly fight he had noticed a profound change in his clansmen's attitude toward Lydia. For the first time since Lydia had come to Scotland he recognized a genuine respect for her, which he knew she shared. "That Russian capacity to understand, though never show it," he thought.

Lydia seemed to have slipped into an intense swirl of orders to maidservants and females carrying bright clothing and holding up petticoats and intimate flimsy things which caused endless small cries of admiration and approval. Sarah and Penelope, the two elderly, haggish women on whom they had so depended as a life-and-death staff, were forgotten, he noticed, and kept to the bedchambers, where they were occasionally seen, hunched, muttering, and seeming to wither, but refusing to die.

He came out of the master chamber, where McGregor waited for their morning ride over Skarra, and saw the frail lights of the votive candles.

"The shrine," he said, gesturing.

"My lady," said the bailiff.

"When?"

"Last night."

"Wait," Bruce said, turning back into his chamber to where Lydia was at her morning toilette.

"Love, when did you restore Voltoff's lights?"

"After you went to sleep." She did not look at him as she tied and circled her braided hair atop her head, a maid holding a French gilt mirror for her.

"Could not you have called me? He was my friend."

"He was my slave."

"He was my friend." Bruce spoke quietly.

"A slave is more than a friend," Lydia said. "A slave cannot withhold love, even when it is not deserved, while a friend is true only so long as equality is preserved."

He watched her arrange her heavy weight of dark hair, streaked with long strands of gray, her refined features avoiding his eyes, and he knew he had trespassed into that Oriental soul he could never understand as a Scotsman and a Presbyterian.

He looked down at his heavy square-booted toe, abashed he had been so insensitive with his wife, especially when he knew, or thought he knew all her secrets, and saw her hand reach out and take his fingers. Still she did not look at him.

"Bruce," she whispered, "a man and woman in love are slaves to the marriage that binds them into eternity, and men and women are equal only in love, and it is true for all here and no place else."

"Yes." He did not look at her face, though he knew she was looking at him.

"Our house is full of friends who serve our vanity or us theirs, while love serves life."

He was very still, almost waiting to be dismissed, keenly aware of the huge strength which had lain dormant in Lydia as a woman.

"Love serves God, and we serve our puffed-up intellects."

He nodded.

"Oh, Bruce, you taught me." She rose quickly and clasped him to her bosom.

"I had forgotten."

"Your dotage, you are in your dotage." Lydia laughed outright in the bedchamber, but he saw she was crying, the tears wetting her face. "Go, go ride the moor and the heather, go with the Scots—I have a party to prepare."

He kissed her very quietly and felt the solemnity in her soul restore him.

Bruce rode alone through the wet game trails which ran along the mountainside, and felt the mist ease the burning in his eyes as he searched for a remote place in order to think. The gorse lay like a green ground-hugging mantle, seeming to diffuse into the heavy clouds which brushed along the earth and wet his eyelashes. He caught a glimpse of movement a quarter-mile up the mountainside, and he knew Ruff and Jamie were riding their ponies on the high ground to him, keeping him always in sight.

"The Englishman!" He heard the mellow burr roll against his ear, and he knew John Bollingale was somewhere near.

In a moment he found the Scots at his side, nodding to a burn. "The stranger." Ruff spoke laconically.

He watched the fierce narrow face approach. Bollingale's frail body was tense astride the gaunt coupled English running horse they called a Thoroughbred.

"Halloo, John!"

"Ah, Bruce, a civilized man." The face smiled but the eyes seemed lost.

"Albain has you hid?"

"Too well. Sometimes under flat rocks."

"They have hid the Stuarts for generations."

"Aye, I have been crammed into mangers and dropped into wells and shoved into hot ovens."

"Penance for your sins," Bruce said, holding Bellsinger in check.

"I'm lonely, Bruce." The sensitive eyes caught his, and Bruce saw the quandary of an impetuous and sensitive man who had indulged his passion, and had gone too far to recover, and knew it.

"I'm sorry."

"The Scots say you had a fight."

"No, they attacked Skarra at dawn."

"Pity them," Bollingale said.

"Aye."

"Bruce, you did no more than me."

"So it would seem, John, but there is a difference. I am a Scot, and I truly bear no malice for any man, including Englishmen. But you are one of them, and in you they see the judgment of a brother who knows them, which is intolerable."

Bollingale searched his face, and Bruce saw each could understand without masks, in a moment of candor. "You know the truth, and this is unbearable."

"So now it is haggis and mutton." He looked across the wet mist atop the slack firth of Skarra below.

"Thank God you have a sense of humor."

"With laughter, insanity is even pleasant."

"No heroics. Get your rump underground whenever the Highlanders say."

"They have offered me girls," Bollingale said, looking back to him.

"They respect you as a man."

"Beautiful, exquisite, lush young creatures, but, my God, they cannot even speak English." The unfocusing blue eyes suddenly burned into Bruce's. "My God, I could not lay a woman I did not love!"

"Did you try?" Bruce said, staring levelly into the Englishman's face.

"Yes, but I was offended." He looked down, as the two grizzled Scots watched him.

"Offended? How? By grace and youth?"

"God, no, they yielded their bodies to please me, and they did not even know the beauty I saw in them, the poetry of their clear eyes and hot tongues that pressed into my mouth, and their breath, it was full of a rich musk scent, of life. . . ."

"Well?"

"I couldn't."

"Perhaps your quandary is why they yielded themselves to you."

"I couldn't."

"Most men could." Bruce was conscious of a tiredness in his voice as he ran his hand in the mane of the stallion.

"I wish I had some girl to talk to." He glanced toward Bruce. "It is easier to talk than to be so, so animal with a woman."

Bruce looked down at the back of his gloved hands, and spoke slowly. "John, there is an animal in a woman, and a man must appease it, even if it undoes him."

"I am lonely for talk and grand thoughts and elevating spirits."

They were silent for a few moments while the horses outstretched their necks to crop the scant blades of moist grass clumped about the heather.

"If I did not have the English, I could slip you into Skarra occasionally, but now we have a dance. . . ."

"A dance?"

"Aye, it's Lydia's notion, and I am sure she is right. Young Dorset and Fanny and Charles . . ."

"Oh, how I would love to come." Bollingale's voice had an urgent poignancy to it, the longing by a man of taste and breeding for all that he has lost.

"Your neck comes first," Bruce said. "Time for frivolity as long as you live." He spurred Bellsinger away, not annoyed, but clearly aware there was no helping Bollingale.

8

It seemed that a huge desire had sprung up in the midst of their family to be jolly and spontaneous in laughter, filling Skarra with a holiday pleasure. It was way beyond Bruce to understand, and so he kept to himself as preparations went forward for the young people's ball. Riders were sent to Fendrath, to Strathdone, to Deverne, and to Fovern—in fact to every country seat in the Highlands within a day's ride and containing young unmarried folk—inviting them to Skarra for the evening of dancing and visiting.

It was risky, in that word of the unfortunate loss of the Roundheads would reach Argyll in Edinburgh before it reached London, yet Skarra chose his messengers carefully, believing a festive gala its own testimony to innocence, whereas an anguished explanation would imply guilt. "You must play off the natural treachery between London and Edinburgh," Lydia had said when he woke in the night, gripped in a terror that he had unleashed a British army into the Highlands.

"I was a fool to give Bollingale asylum."

"You didn't. The Highlanders did."

"Aye." He sank back into his feather tick. "These disasters come from trifles."

"Go to sleep. We have the English nobles."

"I cannot hold them forever."

"After the ball we will all feel better."

"I wish I were as sure."

"You will see."

"I just do not know."

The next day he saw the young people arriving by horseback. There was an urgent rush about their bright faces as they seemed to tumble from their saddles onto resilient legs that sprang up the steps of the piazza, their voices clear in the delight of youth.

"Fanny, I could not believe it, that you have two English officers," little Sharon Hamilton fairly shouted, her two hands gripping Fanny's hands.

"From London."

"Truly, from London?"

"Yes."

"Oh, London, how I wish I could go there." Sharon closed her eyes and shivered her body as she breathed deeply.

"From the University."

"Oh, the University!"

"University men."

"Oh, Fanny!" She flung herself into Fanny's arms and they hugged each other in girlish exuberance and delight.

Bruce marveled at the breathless talk of the young people, especially those yet in their teen years, as they surged in and out the doors, along the galleries, and through the bedrooms, which were carpeted with eiderdown puffs and feather ticking, the pallets where they would sleep. But sleep was the last thing on their minds. They moved in clutches, voices agog with incredulous delight, always talking to one another and moving toward some other room, to see someone, who was just as eagerly searching some other young person, and like as not encountering each other in further pleasant outcries which delighted the adults, even if they could not understand what had pleased the young people. Around and around the two days went, and Bruce did indeed have to admit each generation had its own interest to be served, which was its life, and past misfortune was not a part of the hope of children.

Bruce smiled to himself as he sat at his ledger books in the Palladian office on the third floor of Skarra. He had been infected by the joy of the ball for the young people. Lydia was right. He even turned his mind to the management of the estate.

"Sheep may be grazed with cattle," he said, strumming his feathered quill against his fingers. "They graze in a different manner."

Ian McGregor leaned forward on his stool at Bruce's side, his brow knitted.

"It's a matter of how the cattle use their tongues to wrap about the grass stems, to chuck them off high, while sheep clip the grass close."

"My lord, the sheep will starve out the cattle."

"No, not if we do not overgraze."

"The sheep are a curse, my lord said so."

"Aye, so I said. 'Tis in moderation that we can keep the cattle, the deer, and also the sheep. If we could card and spin and weave the wool, we could employ the crofters. . . ." He searched out the sandy eyes of his bailiff. "Instead of poverty and banishment to the New World."

The bailiff sat back and stared at him. "Lord Bruce, for you it might succeed."

"I know," Bruce said pensively. "Greed is so pervasive, and men so rapacious, yet we might make Skarra a beacon of hope that men could live in purpose and harmony without fouling their nests."

"With a Puritan king in London?"

"Perhaps you are right." He glanced over at the stocky Scot. "At some later time, in peace, perhaps."

"The estates are solvent, and more . . ."

"Aye, we're not extravagant, and if we tend our garden it will keep us in health."

He heard a heavy coach on the cobbles, and they went to the Palladian windows to look down. It was a large wheeled vehicle drawn by six Shire horses and spattered with mud up to the driver's legs and streaked with branches dragged through the wet scum, and one window was broken.

"The Earl of Strathdone," McGregor said.

"Lord, what a fool to drive that damned coach through the Highlands."

"That coach means a lot to the gentleman."

"Yes, the coach is his vanity."

"If it snows we will have to put it on skids and drag it back to Strathdone with oxen."

"Good God, McGregor, don't even think of such misfortune."

The thought seemed to hit each man at the same instant, and they commenced to laugh, laughing until they were spent, and secure that they laughed alone, unheard by the household which swirled with jolly purpose from the kitchen wing to the bedrooms.

There was a rap at the door which McGregor rose and answered, speaking to a servant woman. "No, the lord is out on the moor, I don't care what you heard." He closed the door and came back with a grin.

"Who was it this time?" Bruce said.

"The laird of Fovern."

"Jamie Lundee."

"Aye."

"All wanting to jaw about the damned Roundheads."

"Aye, my lord," said McGregor, getting astride the leather-topped stool once more.

"They crave excitement, not knowing it is a curse, because it is easier than the ordinary."

McGregor stared at Bruce, not understanding the convolutions of Bruce's mind but absolutely loyal to his chief in the blind fidelity of the Highlands. "My lord has a plan, if the clans are not to rise?"

"Aye, a season for all things, Ian."

"I do not pry, my lord."

"I know you do not. Tonight it is the ball."

Bruce dressed quietly that evening, sliding long Scottish trews onto his legs and idling as the bustle moved through his large bedchamber. He had slipped into and out of Skarra by the hidden stairs, avoiding his guests, for he did not want to talk about the thing on everybody's mind, which was warfare with England. He was soldier enough to know he could never win, and diplomat enough to know he could win Cromwell with money, for only the money of commerce would bring peace. The insight filled him with confidence as he fiddled with his lace jabot at his throat. "The French are mad with reason, which is remarkable, considering their fashions," he said to himself, and smiled.

In his bedroom Charles brushed his long blond hair for the

thousandth time, it seemed, and studied his immature features, which were still molded by a layer of baby-fat even if his face was slender, a trait inherited from his mother. He felt the excitement of the very young, deluded with the apparent power and strength of an adult, but still protected from the rough world by the parents' home. He swung into the refrain of "Froggie Went A-Courtin' " and was surprised to hear his voice break out: "Missie Mouse, will you marry me, hmmhmm hmmhmm."

"Charles!" It was his twin sister. "Really! Will you marry me?" The blond girl came through the door from her bedroom, her hands clasped, and laughing. Charles felt himself flush.

"You should rap on the threshold."

"Oh, Charles." Fanny came up to him.

"I never have any privacy."

"You are so handsome." Her eyes lit with appreciation of his refined and symmetrical features.

"Oh, bother," he said.

"You are pleased. I have watched you look in the mirror."

"Go away." He gestured through her door. "To all those girls."

"I heard a compliment."

"You did?"

"So complimentary."

"Who?"

"Can't tell."

"Who was it?"

"You know it would spoil it. They all love you."

"Oh, bother."

"You sound just like Papa." Her voice was solemn and a grave look swept her eyes when he heard it and looked to her.

"Him!" he said harshly, and turned back to brushing his hair.

"Charles, why?"

"Nothing."

"No, tell me, why?" Her voice pressed in on him.

"He thinks he is God, with all that philosophy."

"But what has brought this on?" She put her hand on her brother's shoulder and turned him to face her, her eyes searching his, which looked away.

"He is never wrong."

"But Charles, he's our father."

"I know, and he is like a god."

"But not to us, to his children. To us, he is a quiet father who held us and petted us and consoled us and fed us. . . ."

"Aye, he was all that, but he is never wrong."

"Why, he's wrong all the time." Her voice had a sharp edge of reproof. "You can see it in his eyes, and you are blind to it?"

"Bother, he knows everything." Charles turned back to the mirror.

"Father, of all people, knows when he is wrong. No, it is us who are wrong. We won't let our father be wrong and be human, and so he suffers alone, in sorrow."

Charles shook his head, his eyes on his long hair.

"I am ashamed of you."

"Who can stand a man who is always right?" He leaned into the French glass to study the fall of a wisp of hair over his temple.

Fanny stared at him a moment, and felt the twinge of grief claw at her heart. "A woman." She spoke slowly.

"I am not a woman," her brother said.

"Nor are you a man."

"I do not want to quarrel." He glanced at her.

"Killing those Roundheads does not make you a man," she said, although she knew Charles' resentment of their father was deeper than any act of passion or reason.

"It was easy, killing them."

"Puffed up with a big head."

"It was easy." The boy smiled at his image in the glass. "He is always right. He always takes things under consideration. He talks about God as though he invented religion. He will not raise the clans. . . ."

"Charles!" She spun her twin brother about to face her. "He would not have married Mother if he had believed in religion, and even the Earl of Argyll said he had killed so many men he had scandalized both

God and man, and his wisdom keeps the Highlands Scottish, and you, his own son, talk this nonsense."

"Not nonsense."

"It's going to the University—to Oxford—that's what it is." She had a pensive note to her voice. "The common people love Papa, and the Oxford dons adore him—I do not understand."

"And everybody in between hates him."

"Those are the educated fools," Fanny said, turning away toward her bedroom door. "They are corrupted by their own brains, and of course they hate wisdom—it shows up their petty minds. Oh, Charles." She turned back, beginning to cry, and slipped her arms about her brother's neck and hugged his body into hers.

"I am sorry, oh really, I am sorry," she said.

The music filtered up through the house as the small French orchestra warmed up their Italian flutes and violins and tuned the harpsichord. Bruce was pleased to have discovered them traveling overland to Dundee from Inverness, and persuaded them to come to Skarra for the ball. Fanny could hear the stylized Continental melodies that demanded the elegant steps and gallantry of posing for one's partner as one danced. She felt her heart soar with delight, knowing George Seymour, son and heir to the Earl of Dorset, had smiled at her, had ridden with her, had chased her across the moor by horseback, and she had outraced him on her father's horse—she would have to be careful about not running too fast in future—and Teddy Wilton, the other young Englishman, had slipped her poetic notes, already, and pinned with shards of heather, and he was Sir Edward Wilton, but he still had freckles over the bridge of his nose that laughed when he smiled. Charles was forgotten as her heart surged toward life and the houseful of young people.

"I do not like it, my lady," Bea said, stepping back and running her eyes over Fanny's new French gown. "No, it will not do."

"Oh, it's stunning," Sharon Hamilton said while Fanny smiled in a flush of excitement that colored her neck. "Isn't it, Beth?"

"Absolutely," said the tall girl, leading two other girls to Bea, who stood cross-armed, her head and eyebrows cocked, staring at the bare tops of the girl's breasts.

"No, it will not do," Bea said, shaking her head. "If a man has got to have a naked tit to see before he is caught, he is not fit to catch."

"Oh, but it is high fashion in London," said Beth Lundee.

"It is not high fashion in the Highlands, my lady." The Highland woman did not take her eyes off Fanny's bare breasts. "I can see your titties and the cleft, it is not good. . . ."

"But Bea," Fanny said, her eyes shining, "everyone is tired of Cromwell."

"My lady will strip her body when there be no evil in her man's eyes, not before, this is no affair of any government."

"It is absolutely the abiding gasp," Sharon said, her ruddy but pretty face alive with the cunning of encouraging a rival to destroy herself by trying too hard.

" 'Tis gospel," said Mary McLean, sensing the delight of the destruction of a woman more beautiful than herself.

"No, Lady Fanny," Bea said, turning toward the door of the master chamber. "Penelope—come, woman!" She walked to the stooped old nurse, who was dressed in the bright colors of Finland. "Look"—she gestured at Fanny—"the girl has lost her mind, brazenly stripping to gain an advantage when she already be a lily among a bog of cabbages."

"Faw!" "Faw!" Penelope's cries were followed by loud Finnish oaths when she realized what the hubbub was about. She snatched the peasant shawl from about her shoulders and thrust it forward as a shield to cover the girl's bosom.

"My Lord Skarra," Bea said, going to the door. "Come, Lady Fanny has gone daft."

Bruce walked into the girls' chamber, Lydia not being present to settle whatever difficulty had arisen among the women, and was astounded to catch his daughter's eyes. He hesitated in his step and caught his breath when he saw his daughter's naked breasts, seeming to float out of the top of her gown, and felt a flush of horror on his neck. He realized she meant to bare herself to grief and sorrow and growth, and fearless in her commitment.

"Daughter." He walked to her and took her hands into his as Fanny looked up, her eyes aglow with innocent hope. "It is not necessary to show so much, though every woman would like to, to the man she loves."

"I do love, Father."

"Perhaps, but you do not know."

"I think I know, Father." The voice was earnest with credulity.

"But you do not know for certain, and to show your breasts, in our society, means true love."

"Papa, when will I know true love?"

"I do not know, but I do know you must go a lifetime with him, and in your naked breasts you will offer him all that you are, your whole life, and this is too much to offer a man until he is willing to offer you his whole life."

"In London, Father . . ."

"We are Scottish, daughter."

Fanny looked down and away. Bruce looked down from her fragile brow to the two small white breasts before him. Her beauty was more than he had realized. The fair shoulders and graceful neck were joined in a motion of milk-white skin that seemed to radiate beauty and innocence. He drew her into his chest and felt the gentle warmth of her through his evening dress.

"Daughter," he whispered, smelling her sweet hair tied loosely atop her head, "let life come to you, for the man can be fickle, but the woman is life's bondservant." He felt her nod. "Yet you delight your father in your gallantry toward living, but get you dressed and keep you dressed until you have true love." He turned her face up to kiss her, then smiled and released her, wishing not to embarrass her any more than she had been already. "Get Her Ladyship dressed, Bea."

"Aye, Lord Bruce."

"Faw, she's not too big to whip with birch rods, faw."

Bruce left the girls' bedchamber and came back into his own, where he found Lydia. "By God, she had her breasts bare, right down to the nipple."

"Who?" Lydia said.

"Our daughter."

"Oh, every woman has to grow through that notion."

"But you should tell her."

"She knows. It's just the fashion. . . ."

"I thought that went out with Queen Bess."

"Bruce, the breasts will never be out of fashion."

"Oh, God, I did not say that."

"No, but it is a family party, and the gown is truly French."

"This discussion makes no sense to me."

Lydia put her hand on his shoulder. "I would never have let her offend Scottish morality with a bare bosom."

"I should hope not."

"Aren't you proud of her courage?"

"Aye. She is, indeed, all woman."

"Our daughter. I'm so proud of her."

"Yes, we did right well." He smiled slowly at Lydia, who kissed his cheek.

Bruce stood on the flagstones outside the great hall of Skarra and was vaguely aware of the beautiful scene moving across the polished boards, as though in elegant ballet steps, to the French orchestra. Lovely young women who seemed to be half-nude flowers tipped upside-down were attended by young men in gallant gestures—it was an unreal pantomime. Close about him were the Scottish lairds and nobles, fairly seething to press their questions onto him. Lundee's bald head came up to his shoulder, and had an aged pixie look about it, with his two bushy white ear tufts of hair. "How could ye kill so many and not be present?"

Bruce sipped his drambuie and ignored his guests.

"Bruce—tell me, man—are we to rise? Is it to be Bannockburn?"

"The only time Scottish arms remained disciplined." It was a tall Scot with a carved red face who said this.

"Scotland needs only peace, gentlemen, for the battle is to him who endures." Bruce glanced at the men about him, men whom he had known since childhood, to all of whom he was blood-related. "What you call a victory over the Roundheads was a terrible mistake, a grievous unpleasantry of misunderstanding. . . ."

"Hoot, man!"

The men fell to laughing.

"A joyous misunderstanding."

"Lord have mercy, the Highlanders say this very hall and grounds were covered with English dead." It was the tall John Stevenson of Strathdone, the disciplinarian who had arrived in a coach, a man so stern he had never married, and had no children, yet who was invited because of nieces and nephews. "If a Scottish regiment can be disciplined, it will be invincible." He stared at Bruce.

"No doubt, John, but we have no need of anything save time."

"It takes blood to get attention."

"No, we will not take that route."

"Still the professor of reason."

"Hardly, Strathdone. Men worship their insanity," Bruce said, looking into the hall where he knew Lydia would be enlivening the ball, and where he knew he belonged. Since he had remained incommunicado to his peers and kinfolk, he felt obliged to share their company for a moment.

"I vow, if I knew I had ara an enemy, I would never talk as ye do, Brucie," Lundee said. " 'Tis blasphemy."

"Aye, blasphemy." Bruce sipped his drambuie, and smiled when he saw Sergei's face appear for a moment, showing the large eyes, which had the Oriental shape but were blue.

"The Star Chamber has hanged for far less," Glen McMillan said.

"I never heard a Presbyterian talk like that!"

Bruce enjoyed his friends, yet it was hopeless to expect any of them to fully understand him.

"Lundee, you never heard every Presbyterian talk," Bruce said. "And I can read the Bible as well as Professor Knox. Men do worship insanity, as long as it is their own, whether religion, politics, or women." He smiled tolerantly at his kinsmen, who stared at him, eyes goggled and mouths ajar. "Now, we have a ball to join, gentlemen—let us dance."

Bruce came into the large hall walking ahead of a score of Highland chiefs, most in kilts but some in breeches and silk stockings of London fashion. He saw Henry Seymour and Buckey Hailyham in velvet and lace and satin breeches with silver buckles on their shoes, and fairly dripping embroidery. He smiled and moved off to his left, along the wall of mirrors and under the Highland banners, noticing the Scottish chiefs diverted to their right, along the tables of meat and hot bread and the tankards of raw whiskey.

"Bruce, where have you hid?" Hailyham said, coming toward him, while Seymour stood at a small table set before a semicircle of Jacobean chairs, as the honored guest of Skarra.

"Abed and on the moor," Bruce said, taking the large red hand.

"Ah, you have taken it all much too hard—where's that champion drunkard of Balliol, eh?"

"I suppose I did drink then."

"Drink? You were never sober!"

"Not so loud." The old university chum filled Bruce with delight.

"You said you could never write an examination unless you were drunk."

"I must have been drunk to say that."

"Yes, you did blame your drunkenness on your professors." The Englishman fairly shouted with the enthusiasm of recollecting a boyhood thirty years gone by.

"Buckey, my people will hear."

"What people?"

"Good Lord, my servants and my family, my children . . ."

"Oh, they are dancing—ah, what a lovely girl is that daughter of yours, ten years younger and I would take her."

"No, Buckey, it would take twenty."

"Ah, these young whips don't know what a woman is; when I see a young man with a lovely girl I think of the awful waste of beauty."

"We were young once, ourselves, Buckey."

They were watching the roomful of graceful people stepping to the notes and rhapsody of the music, the brilliant eyes fixed on each other as the passion of life within their bodies excited them with concentration. Henry Seymour had come up, Bruce realized, when he heard the Earl say, "George can see nothing save that white skin and blond hair."

"Aye, they have no eyes save for life, my lord."

"As it should be," Seymour said.

"Aye." Bruce turned toward the chairs and saw Lydia.

"I have never seen such lush white beauty, Skarra." Seymour stared hard at Fanny and his son, who were circling and bowing and changing places in a minuet. "The girl has the ethereal quality of a wood sprite, one might say." He swallowed and looked to Bruce.

"Fanny is no wood sprite, Seymour."

"No, I can see that."

"You cannot tell a girl by her looks, and my daughter is all woman."

"All woman, eh?"

"Like her mother, as should be."

"Yes, sensible at that."

"Quite."

"Ah, Bruce, the warrior." Bruce recognized the voice of Wendy McTosh, a leader of Edinburgh society who spoke without a burr, showing her English blood and background. He was looking for Lydia, but the back of Wendy's hand came up under his face, pressed toward his nose, and he knew he was supposed to kiss it. His mind made an impression that Wendy's skin was dry and flaking, a bit like a dried fish's even under the French powder. Instinctively, he kissed at the wrist to get the foul thing past and done with, hoping to be rid of her. "Argyll has not heard—ooo, you bold man—alas, Edinburgh will be insane with excitement, and just think, I was visiting in the Highlands, right in the middle of the Scottish uprising. . . ."

"Woman, ye be out of y'r wits," Bruce said.

"On the contrary." The eyes glittered with pleasure at excitement and suffering, and delighted at the prospect of more to come. "It means war."

"There is no uprising."

"You killed—slew, shall we say—a regiment of English." She chuckled.

"I killed no one. You be daft."

"Lady Wendy's imagination is soaring," Seymour said.

"Aye, the English fly their worst bats up to Scotland," Bruce said, making everybody laugh, and he had the pleasure of seeing the cold pure hate show in the whites of Wendy McTosh's eyes—a vain middle-aged woman.

"Capital!"

"Isn't Lord Skarra jolly?" Lydia said, joining him.

"Quite," Seymour said.

"I cannot wait to return to Edinburgh," Wendy said.

"I am sure you will have to." Bruce turned away.

"The secretary to the Lord Deputy's Privy Council is coming to sup directly as I return, and we shall have a little chat—oh, indeed we shall."

"Poor man," Hailyham said.

"He's probably not a man, if he's a secretary."

"Lady Wendy, I must apologize for my husband's jolly nature. Excuse us, please."

They walked away, hearing the razor-sharp breath of an angry woman whose life was a burden to her, for she was beyond love and not yet beyond life.

"Lord Bruce," said a young man, holding a salver of wine goblets toward him.

"Thank you, Keith." Bruce took the fine stem into his fingers and sipped the refreshing chill of the French import. "It is nice with snow to cool it." He spoke idly.

"Have you watched them dance?" Lydia said.

"Aye."

"Never was there more grace in our home."

He nodded his head. " 'Tis beautiful." The great hall seemed to swim with music and swaying youth whose vitality was not concealed beneath the fine clothes and confined manners. He could see the sweat shine on the young men's faces, making their foreheads glisten above their insistent eyes, and along the upper lips of the girls, who watched intently as they circled and curtseyed and shifted their feet in unison, as though seeking to take a journey with the young men. It pleased him.

"Lydia, would you honor me by dancing?"

She looked into his eyes, and he saw the girl who had danced with him in desperation, on the frozen verges of Russia twenty years before, offering him her life and soul if he would take her away with him. He saw the soft look come over her eyes, of love, which had never changed.

"Yes, a dance forever."

He reached for her hand and led her out to where a reel was taking its position. He watched her dip her hands into the folds of her skirt and lift it so he could see her slippered feet, and watched the wide smile come slowly over her face as they waited for the piper to gather the sound in the pipes.

The Highland music seemed to swell in the hall, raising even them on its passion, and he was laughing as he watched Lydia dance. Her skirts were pulled up and her toes were skittering in furious motion as she glided toward him, then away, swaying her head and neck and sashaying her hips, alternating from side to side.

"That will get you into trouble." She was gone in a moment and he heard her clear bell-tone laugh, of defiance and joy in a middle-aged woman.

He was into the hand of a girl who smiled brilliantly at him every time her face was on him. He felt self-conscious and nodded, smiling a little foolishly and aware he was no longer laughing.

The reel of dancers came together and parted, and shifted and stamped and backed and circled, with the women swirling like fluttering wraiths about the men. He was delighted, and felt his lank frame and bony knees swirling and pirouetting, and he laughed outright to himself when he thought he had heard one of his leg-joints crack. He glimpsed the five pipers standing on the dais, playing their dashing melodies, and he saw the Frenchmen watching them in immobile silence, obviously unused to pipers.

"Papa, you are divine!"

"Oh, daughter"—he recognized Fanny in his hand—"do not frighten me."

"You are so handsome."

"That afears me worse."

She was laughing and he saw her hair down in loose strands which fell across the white shoulders, and occasionally a bare knee flashed into his sight.

"Daughter, you please me." He spoke the words into her ear as she came close when he drew her past him, and was gone.

The reel surged out and collapsed in on itself and expanded just as quickly, the dancers laughing and going faster and faster. He had trouble keeping up and was startled to see a diminutive, dark Russian face with the purest blue eyes staring up at him, smiling just like Lydia.

"Papa, you are in a trance!"

"Cassie. You imp!"

"You are so-o-o elegant." She gestured at him, and he saw the grace and quick motion of Lydia as she flung back her head and laughed wildly, the child's mouth and throat full of innocent joy.

"You imp! Cassie!" He was shouting as she went away, and laughing. Cassie was barely ten years old.

He saw that Henry Seymour and Buckey Hailyham had joined the reel, but they were too stiff and English, and were reaching here and there, not certain where the woman was to be led. He saw them laughing good-naturedly at their mistakes, in contrast to some of the Highland chiefs still glowering in a group about the keg of whiskey.

"Ahhee-EE-aaa!" He heard the wild cry of Scotland erupt in their midst, and was surprised to see it was Sergei, who was in kilts. The voice was boyish, not yet broken in manhood. It relieved Bruce, for some of the Highland chieftains were dancing, and the power of the reel and its wild elations often swept men into fierce cries, particularly if slightly drunk.

"Bruce, you are wonderful." Lydia was before him, and he had once more gone through every woman in the reel, the children, the over-plump girls, the youthful complexions, the ungainly, and the joyous, and now it was Lydia, his wife. He was glad the reel was to end.

"Divine, elegant, wonderful, my women have me foxed!" He was amazed as she bent and spun about before him, her knees flying in and out of sight, alternating with her heel and toe movements, her hands sometimes over her head and sometimes down to lift her skirts to clear her flying knees and elegant slippers.

"Ahhee-EE-aaa!" Bruce was elated to hear himself bellow the old Scottish cry, and of a sudden the curdling Highland yells and screams rose on every throat, drowning the pipers for an instant, who then seemed to spring out in response, and the din of the war pipes exploded upon them, until the halls and rooms and walls of Skarra echoed and re-echoed to skull-shaking joy and fury of ancient Scotland.

He glimpsed the wave of horror pass behind Lydia's eyes, her hand stopping as she wheeled under an elegant down-thrust finger. "No!" her mouth said. He stopped dancing and clapped his palms, his eyes onto the pipers, who shifted the pipes, breaking the beat. "No more!"

In a moment the hall was still, and he saw the five Englishmen staring at him, as though for deliverance from an unexpected and vengeful ghost or joyous savagery, their eyes being round and their mouths silent.

"A French minuet!" he called and began to laugh, shaking his head.

"A reel! A reel!"

"No more reels!" His voice was stern as he looked to the pipers.

"*Menuet de Louis*!" Lydia called to the Frenchmen, who jumped instantly to life at the familiar and consoling words of their own language, after the sudden appearance of Scottish barbarism in the great hall.

George Seymour's eyes seemed to glisten more intently as the evening wore on, Fanny thought. He seemed to enter a trance of desire. She had watched him run his eyes from her breasts to her neck and look back to her bosom, and she sensed a power over George, and all men, for their weakness and the pathetic confusion of them. She had watched George's dusty little mustache tilt upward on the corners of his lip, and she liked the taste of the fine hair of it when she had kissed him, and she had very carefully not touched his teeth with her tongue, as she felt urgently compelled to do, to not let him know she craved to touch him as much as he did her, lest it unsettle him with more passion than he could control.

Fanny smiled to herself as she realized that she wished to strip her body nude for love, for somebody, whoever would be gentle with her. She saw her father's grandness, for he saw her need to go honestly to the affairs at hand, to make life through her body, and that as a woman, to be fair to life, but only if the rules were played so that the players could live a whole lifetime together. She was right, and her father was right. And she would have either George Seymour or Teddy Wilton before another fortnight. She had decided she loved them both equally well.

The ball was at its genteel climax with the French court minuet. Bruce shook his head at the goblet of iced wine a gillie offered him. He noticed that Lydia drank nothing but water and tea, and he spoke. "To have never really liked whiskey, I have drunk a great deal."

"It seems your drinking is all your university friends can remember."

"Whiskey placates my anger, I think."

"Then everybody is angry," Lydia said, swooping into a slight dip as the two Englishmen came up. "My Lord Dorset."

"Skarra, you and Lady Lydia baffle me," Seymour said, watching the dancers once more. "Scotland is a fog-bound hell of rebellion, and you live in its midst more English than Oxford, and still Highland nobles."

"Living, Henry, living. The cure for life is living. Life must be served without the leisure to suck the sore gum of self-pity."

"Aye, some of our young do not know that."

"And their elders could also learn," Lydia said.

"It's never too late to prune the vine, I daresay," Seymour said, watching the minuet.

"Seymour, you mock the Bible by quoting it," Hailyham said, eating a mutton joint with one hand and wiping his moist full lips with a silk handkerchief far too fine for its use.

"Aye, the Bible does a nobleman little good. It is the common people who need God, while we have duty and that is all the god we need."

"God is a duty," Lydia said.

"Or duty a god," Hailyham said.

"An ambiguous god, one could say, yet I know of no better God." Seymour spoke idly, his eyes on the ball. "She is so pretty."

Bruce ignored the obvious fascination of the middle-aged Englishman with Fanny. "The mind is a burden which only the body can cool out through work."

"Seymour and his sprig are smitten with your daughter, and so am I"—Hailyham spoke expansively. "She belongs in London, in court."

Skarra felt Lydia stir at his side, and he flushed along his spine, aware of the brilliance of Lydia's plan, of its stunning success, and horrified at the appearance of that awful hour where he was to lose his daughter, whom he loved. He heard his voice speak as though a stranger's and was surprised at its control, when all he could feel was the storm raging inside his mind. "It is fortunate if men and women can balance their minds against the passion of their bodies, hold the balance, and as man and wife, live together always."

"And what if they are lovers, and not man and wife, Bruce?"

"If they are lovers, they are man and wife."

"Aye, 'tis common law," Seymour said, turning to them.

"And all people be common," Bruce said.

"You fox me with your riddles."

Bruce nodded, fatigued with the gala evening. He liked the Englishmen, particularly Hailyham. If four of the Englishmen liked his daughter, he was glad at the number, for the girl had to narrow down the admirers before any commitment could be made to one. He could see the sated dancers turning on legs not so elegant. "It was a huge success," he said to Lydia.

"One more dance. Breakfast, then bed," she said. "They are all so tired they will sleep without mischief on their own pallets."

"Lord, I should hope."

He was distracted by an eruption of strident voices and the appearance of rough men in wet tams and fog-mottled tartans wrapped about their thick bodies, shoving rudely through the double doors into the candlelit ballroom. He turned his head to see if he could not be mistaken, and heard Sarah's voice cackle in triumph. "A spy from Edinburgh."

He saw the dancers stop, though he heard the French orchestra play on. Every face was on the Highlanders piling onto the parquetry, and he saw McGregor and Duff and some of the older men holding a mud-spattered rider still in his jackboots and redingote. They were shoving the man toward him.

"My lord, he is from Argyll," McGregor said. "An officer."

"Unhand him."

"A spy, Lord Bruce." Sarah's bristling chin and puckering toothless mouth gave her a bizarre countenance which Hailyham and Henry Seymour could not tear their eyes from.

"Let him speak."

The man was obviously relieved to be free of his capturers. "I am seeking Lord Bruce of Skarra."

"You have found him."

"I have a warrant to arrest you from His Grace, the Earl of Argyll."

"Give it to me."

The man looked at Duff, then at Bruce, and then at the Englishmen. "You all be under arrest for rebellion to the Commonwealth," he said.

"And you are a witless knave," Bruce said, taking the parchment thrust from the man's belt.

"I'm not afraid of Highlanders." The officer dusted his elbows fitfully.

"That is why you are a fool," Bruce said, breaking the seal on the folio and unfolding it so Henry Seymour could see as well.

"It must be some mistake," Seymour said, holding a circular glass before his eye.

"No mistake, Henry."

"Sire," Lydia said, attracting the attention of the officer, "how was His Grace informed of the rebellion?"

"By messenger, my lady." The man's blue eyes were open, seemingly relieved at a simple question.

"I would say by rumor."

"No, my lord, 'twas a Highland chief."

The company fell silent, the kilted lairds darkening in their visages.

"So we have treachery again," Bruce said.

"And you Scots all be under arrest." The officer waved his arm across the assembled company.

"Hardly," Seymour said. "Your warrant is signed by Argyll in Edinburgh, while I represent Westminster in London."

"You all be arrested."

"I am the Earl of Dorset, and I am not under arrest, and I have been in Skarra for a week, and I have found no rebellion. Therefore, you are wrong." Seymour folded the warrant and handed it to the officer.

"Yes, capital, capital solution," Hailyham said.

"The sheep shame you Scots," Seymour said, speaking to the Scottish chiefs for the first time. "If you were half so eager to control your greed as you are to fight, Scotland would be a paradise, fog-bound hell or no."

"Perhaps we should have breakfast, Lydia."

"Yes, send the Frenchmen on to supper." Lydia looked to the orchestra, which had played on, the formal notes of a classical restraint seeming frail in the midst of unfettered human discord.

9

To send Fanny to Oliver Cromwell was a high adventure which could not fail. Not just Skarra, but the Highlands, the last of the ancient Celtic life—yes, even the Pictic heritage—lay prostrate before English and Lowland power and cunning, and the scramble for lucre. Even though all people decried greed, it never seemed to apply personally. Time and Lydia were Skarra's only allies, and neither was Scottish by birth. Yet he believed he could win because he could not afford to fail, and also, only he seemed to grasp the notion that victory belonged to time, and time alone. Bruce felt quietly assured, for he had no personal ambition, so he could not personally be defeated, and his weapon was absolute: time, which razes all dreams of pomp and insolence, leaving the field to those who live, whether man or wild beast.

"The Swedish pistols," Lydia said, holding a massive cavalry baldric in either hand.

"See that my claymore is slung behind my saddle," he said as Bea checked the bright metal buttons on his tunic and Penelope waited with a thick felted tartan. "I cannot draw my sword if it is slung from my shoulder."

"McGregor has slung it on Bellsinger."

He glanced up at Lydia.

"I have known for five years you could not draw your sword."

"My shoulder hurts," he said, turning his attention once more to the boots he hated.

"I know it hurts." She touched the graying thatch of hair at his crown. He looked up at her touch, and felt a great love for her. It seemed strange to him that so little, and what should be obvious to all, the love of a woman, could not only pacify him but sustain him as a man. It shamed him that he would so brazenly resort to his own cunning and wits, yet survival left him no choice. The confusion of orders and shouts along the halls of Skarra and out on the lawns as the expedition to England was got ready forced his introspective mood from his mind. Again, he felt life demand to be served, and if he had any right to be ennobled, it was because he was its chief servant.

He would meet Albain and Buchan, the Highland subchiefs on the moor, and escort Fanny and Hailyham and the two young Englishmen through Ang and Striveling and Louthian, into Northumberland. The plan turned around his emissaries reaching Westminster at London, with his daughter in the company of the English officers and troopers, as vivid proof of their loyalty to the Protector's Commonwealth in that Fanny would be the living hostage from his home and the Highlands, and proof that his fidelity was true, and that there was no Highland rebellion, only a dreadful mistake at dawn.

Bruce knew the English could see through it, and that he would fox nobody. Yet, he also knew he would confound the English at Westminster, where the United Kingdom was governed, with the obvious: a Highland war or graceful admission of Highland loyalty, secured in the person of a beautiful girl.

"Cromwell is no fool," Lydia had said. "He will jump at a way out."

"Perhaps."

"Fanny's innocence will do it."

"I do not like it. Using a girl."

"Tush, she's more than any man."

"I will not be easy."

"What is there to fear?"

"One girl?"

"And three Englishmen in her company who love her, and each trusted by London."

"Aye, 'tis better than risking Charles."

Her face clouded. "They would kill a man, but not a woman."

"They have before." He raised his eyebrows.

"Not this time. They are Protestant officers escorting her, and a Protestant Commonwealth, and you are known as a Protestant in Westminster."

"Aye, this notion of God prevails, except you have made Fanny Catholic."

"Only Voltoff knew."

He nodded his head vaguely. "I have admonished her to put her life ahead of religion, for one is a delusion and the other reality."

"She will."

"I like it not."

"England is afraid of a Highland war, such as you would fight. Our daughter will have no trouble, provided you can get her into England." The assurance in Lydia's voice eased his disquietude at the venture.

"But what if they hold her?"

"Hold her? Who?"

"Good Lord, the English."

"Let them. You cannot hold a pretty woman in your home without marrying her. She is brighter than either young Wilton or Seymour. Let them hold her." Lydia's eyes danced with certainty.

"I like it not."

"Bruce"—she slid her hand into his—"our daughter will trap the English, confound Scotland, and gain a husband, all at a single swoop."

"When you say it, it seems plausible."

"That is why I am your wife. Now get ready, and try to avoid a fight."

"Oh God, how I weary of death and turmoil."

"If you can slip past Edinburgh . . ."

"I will keep to the open moors." He stood and allowed Bea to help his tunic onto his shoulders.

They rode at a fast walk through the heavy mist which cloyed at their faces from time to time, traveling just under the crests of the Ang Hills. About him rode young Seymour and Wilton, and on one side rode Fanny and Bea, her nurse, and Buckey Hailyham on the other. The English troopers rode in front. He had seen the Scottish column strung through the trees behind him, occasionally out of view, and moving in a route step of silent, wool-wrapped men. They marched in whatever step pleased them, as Highlanders, and carried arms suitable for fast skirmishing. He wanted to sideslip past frontal conflict, and get Fanny and Bea and the Englishmen to the Roman Wall, and into England, before returning alone to Skarra.

The mist rose and he could see the rock scallops of Ben Macdhui looming against the clouds in massive vaults of slate stone over the skirt of gorse, and washed in skudding rain which hurried along the valley and lashed the Grampian mountain range.

"Only the deer and the wild cattle are abroad," he said, ducking his mouth and chin into his voluminous tartan.

"Aye, Bruce, mad Scots and sober Englishmen." Hailyham squinted his watering eyes against the sharp, moist wind they rode through.

"Not so awfully sober." Bruce spoke laconically. He could feel the easy tireless gait of Bellsinger between his knees, the muscled warmth of the beast's body rising like sap to restore him with vigor and confidence. He was pleased with his stallion, yet he had mounted his daughter on his fastest horse, his mare, Forest Witch.

"My lord," Albain said, nodding toward the squared sight of gray rock set in the forest.

Bruce watched the movement of men appear in the distant swale, this side of the river from Blair Castle.

"The laird, likely."

"Aye. Too few to make battle." Bruce nodded ahead to signal they were not to form for skirmishing.

In moments Moray Blair was in their company. He was volatile in his enthusiasm to hear from Bruce the "honest facts" about what he had heard about the "joyous calamity at Skarra."

" 'Tis nothing, Moray."

"With an army with ye?"

"An escort, nothing more."

"Perhaps for England, but not for Scotland."

"Perhaps." He spoke through wool wrapped about his neck and mouth.

"And why be ye in the hills, 'stead of on the King's Road?" He gestured at a faint trace of discolor in the valley floor four miles distant.

"I crave fresh air, Moray; now if ye have no further affairs to content ye at home, ye'd best seek to discover what ye overlooked." He glanced at the stoop-backed man, who slumped in his saddle.

"Damn ye, Bruce, ye don't know who your friends are!"

" 'Tis a fact, Moray."

The laird kicked his horse's flanks with his heels, cursing and rocking gaunt buttocks to set the animal moving.

"I am hated and loved at the same instant by both friends and enemies," Bruce said, speaking to Hailyham.

"I have no enemies save the Froggies."

"Give up soldiering and live, man."

"Nay, publicans and commoners are over-convoluted to please a soldier's honor."

"Keep your honor, Buckey. It is all a soldier ever has."

"No fear. Beyond honor, I am faithfully ignorant." The English colonel laughed good-naturedly, his breath coming in puffs of fog.

"You are a rogue."

"My honor is my shield against the treachery of knowledge."

Bruce found himself enjoying the wit of his university chum of thirty years before, easy in his company.

"Without knowledge, I have no enemies."

"True wisdom, there!" He basked in the bluff company of the English officer.

The march took them through the Grampian Mountains to the west of Cairnwell Pass and south toward Crieff, avoiding Perth. As he led them south, traversing Striveling and Louthian, he consoled them with one observation: "We have marched with the wind in our eyes and the rain on our necks, but we have walked on heather, and not in the mud." For five nights Bruce had gone amidst the wet camp, which bedded down under thatched lean-tos of bracken and dried out their unwashed wool socks and leggings before their cooking fires. The men nodded in quiet respect, not rising before him, knowing he would be offended if he had discommoded them. The last night he realized he would enter Northumberland at dawn, and reach the Roman Wall at noon. "You will be in Westminster in two days' riding," he said to Hailyham.

"Easy riding, I should say."

He stood on a low hill with Fanny at his side, staring out across the low swale at the Roman Wall which divided Scotland and England. The Englishmen and the troop of dragoons were reined up before them, waiting for his daughter, as he told her good-bye, while his column was ranged in a skirmishing crescent, well behind him. He felt very much alone with her, and he was awkward, holding the loose reins in his fingers.

"Father, I will be safe." She searched his eyes, and he was aware his daughter felt stronger than he did, because she knew he could help her no more.

"You look like your mother."

"Thank you, Father."

"I mean Geney."

"I know who you mean."

"You must be cautious with men," Bruce said, hearing his own voice sound strange, and looking at his booted toe.

"Yes, Father." Her voice was very soft, and encouraging.

"Never undress your body to lay with a man, unless you mean to have him a lifetime." He was aware of the movement of her head as she nodded. "Never bare your secrets to a man or woman, unless they are to love you forever, and this you will never know, unless they be a man who loves you."

"I know, Father." She lay her hand on his forearm, whispering.

"I cannot tell you what man will do, for each must discover this for himself; yet people, like all animals, breed true to their own blood, for evil or bliss, so get you to their parents to know the offspring."

"Thank you, Father."

"You will be not only a prisoner but emissary and hostage for myself and the Highlands, and as such, they will be extremely agreeable, to prove they are not holding you captive—for their fear of me and a Highland war."

"Mother explained the politics." He heard a note of impatience.

"If you lay with a man and wrap his body with your arms and legs, and feel him inside your body, and feel him tremble and die in your arms in love, you will believe he is the man for you, even if he is a rogue and a grievous sorrow, for it is a good woman's nature to believe for the best in life." He paused and glanced into her fair eyes, and saw the open soul of understanding as she searched his. "It is for this reason you must remain chaste until you have a good man, for you are the bondservant to life."

She nodded, her eyes fixed onto his. "I will get a good man, or none at all."

"Thank you." He pulled her into him and slipped the hood of her cloak off her face and kissed the lips of a fresh girl who in an instant reminded him he was kissing his mother, and kissing his wife, as well as his daughter, and he was stricken with confusion as she came away from his lips. "Father," she said, and he knew Fanny had seen it.

"Give me your foot, my love." He felt the boot brush his laced fingers and it seemed she was cantering down the swale, the mare's gathered hoofbeats thundering off toward the cavalcade of smiling Englishmen and the waiting nurse, as soon as he could focus his burning eyes and sort his addled mind. He watched the cavalcade gallop away in a rumble of soft noise on the moor, and toward the Roman Wall where the stones had been thrown down in centuries past to admit some long-forgotten adventure. They went through the wall, the horses picking their dainty steps over the tumbled rocks with their necks extended, and were gone.

He swung up into his saddle and signaled to form column for a quick march, as Albain galloped up. "The McDougels and Argyll will be out in force to catch the fox, my lord."

"Aye, and it is a wolf they will catch." Bruce was angry, and heard the rasp in his teeth as he spoke.

"West, Albain, up the Tweed River valley."

The column moved out handsomely. Ahead of him he had his outriders quartering as if they were spaniels to flush any ambuscade awaiting him. He knew it was now common knowledge in Scotland that he was out on the moors leading a small army, and thus fair game for all who could advance their cause by proving their "loyalty" in defeating him in battle.

It was while they were encamped on the edge of the Pentland Hills, his men having roasted an elk they had brought down, that a spy was captured and brought before him.

"Can he speak?" Bruce said, looking at Ruff. The spy was a large Scot, whose head had tufts of red hair pulled from it.

"Aye, he is afeared, my lord."

"Tell him to talk, and I will spare him."

Ruff thrust the point of his dirk against the man's windpipe until a fresh strain of blood ran through the coarse red neck hairs. "Speak for your life, and do not stop till ye fall dead or ye be pitied."

Bruce stood and watched the terrified blue eyes which no longer contained the ability to understand, nor could the mind grasp reality, so blind was the fear, as the mouth poured out a panic of jumbled information: "My lord, the Earl of Argyll and Lord Connok are north, through Perth, in position on the Grampian Mountains." The message was clear.

"Stop him, feed him, and keep him."

"Do you think it be a trap?" Albain said.

"No. They want to fight in the Highlands, not the Lowlands. The rebellion is no rebellion if it is not in the Highlands."

The Highlander smiled in understanding.

"Quick-march straight north, across the Clyde."

By divination he heard the column spring forward like a beast going home, the soft voices of the men sharing the good news, and in their midst he heard the war pipe gather its wind and songs of Scotland pour out upon the clan.

In two days of forced march he had crossed the Grampian Mountains at Drumochter Pass and had slipped into the Aviemore Wood by nightfall, thus flanking Argyll and the Lowlanders to the westward. He waited in the rain of a soggy dawn on the bald side of a spruce clearing, his column pressed into the rhododendron and broom, their fires filtering wet smoke into the low clouds. The Gaelic stragglers, who had been uprooted and driven from their rock huts and lean-tos in the Highlands by the Earl of Argyll's incursion into Banff and Moray, had come before him all night, having been rounded up by his scouts who were scouring the moors and valleys, seeking the enemy force. They were exhausted, blond people, smelling of the cattle they kept and sheep they drove, and wrapped in matted shaggy animal skins. The beauty of their children was a constant protest to Bruce of how a harsh life defiles what is fair. The innocence of the blue eyes and purity of their treble voices reminded him of his own family. One woman held a contented child to the milk-smeared nipple of a ponderous breast, which was beautiful in its round white grace, delighting the child, who sucked noisily and pushed its mouth away to belch, and again clambered greedily for milk, while the mother stared at Bruce for succor from darkened eyes. "We are less than beasts, my lord."

He nodded. Words were useless in the face of barbarism.

"We be filth to the strangers." The man spoke at her side, mixing Gaelic and Scottish.

"Feed them and shelter them," Bruce said to Albain and Buchan, his subchiefs.

"Ye'll have to shed blood to gain their respect, my lord." Albain stared evenly at him, a small bearded man with a deep voice and graceful hands.

"English gold and Scottish greed is a certain sickness for the Highlands." He ignored his chiefs and walked to his lean-to, where he flung himself onto his wool-felt blankets and closed his eyes. He could only wait until his scouts had located the enemy. Then he must decide if he would strike them to bleed them and compel respect. Or perhaps he would sideslip through them and on to Skarra, where the Earl of Dorset was his guest—"prisoner" was the truth of it. He longed to fight—his heartbeat thumped fast, even at the thought of it—yet he knew in his guts that victory lay in peace.

The day wore on with no firm news: Lowland foot soldiers had forded the River Dee; Edinburgh adventurers with English sappers were collecting boats on the Don; and heavy English cavalry were seen in Strathdone and Alford, but no main enemy force. The cavalry worried him, for if he were caught in the open on clear ground they could cut his column to pieces and destroy it with ease. "Nay, I shall wait in these woods until I am certain," he said to himself, hearing the desultory squish of his men's footsteps outside his shelter. His cook had brought him stew, but he had turned down whiskey. He wanted to read his Bible, but he wanted more to fight and his mind was full of a thousand alternate plans to assure victory and survival. Whiskey would have drugged his capacity to savor his mind, as well as impaired his ability to think.

In the evening John Bollingale was brought in, and Bruce rose and greeted the Englishman. "Still alive, eh, John?" He took the elegant hand of the Cambridge don.

"In Hell, one is condemned to eat haggis forever."

"Bring whiskey for Lord John!"

"They say Argyll is cutting a swath of rapine," Bollingale said, settling on a blanket and taking the whiskey. "Slaughtering cattle and scattering crofters."

"Aye. 'Tis to outrage me and draw me into open warfare."

Bollingale looked into Bruce's eyes and saw the mask he wore to hide his plans. He smiled and focused his eyes into his flagon of whiskey.

"I will not know what I will do until I find the enemy and his size and situation."

"He has English allies."

"And so have I English allies."

Bollingale nodded. "You are a canny Scot."

The darkness settled out of the rain and mist which clung through the forest. Bruce felt shut off from the world, and was glad when John Bollingale was bedded down in another shelter. He wanted his own kind, Scots, about him, the rough crude men of trust who were his blood and childhood memories, as he waited alone to gamble for his people.

"My lord," said a voice lifting the skin flap to his shelter and waking him.

"Aye." He rolled up on an elbow.

"No news yet, Lord Bruce, but ye have visitors."

"Visitors?" He started to wrap a tartan about his upper torso when a hairy fist gestured to what appeared to Bruce to be two young women, and into his shelter. "What the devil," he said, sitting upright as the flap fell and shut them in with him.

The two girls watched him, holding to each other in uncertainty, and fear showing in their blue eyes.

"What are you doing in my shelter?" He sounded annoyed and was about to call his bodyguards, yet he realized Ruff and Jamie had permitted their entrance, and he hesitated in order to hear them out. "Who are you?"

The larger girl's eyes sought his. "Do not you recall, my lord?"

"No, I never saw you before in my life."

"Nay, Lord Bruce, you saved me."

"Saved you? How?"

"On the lea of Ben Lawker, Lord Bruce." The girl's voice had a note of soft reproach in it.

"Oh, my word, yes!" He climbed to his feet, putting out his hand to the girl, who he now recognized had been raped by the Lowlanders when he had hunted with the Clan McDougel. Her eyes looked deep into his. "You are feeling better—yes, ah, yes, you look well, indeed. I am so glad." Bruce was aware of his own discomfiture, not at the girl's misfortune but at the open admiration burning in her eyes. "And who is this?" He gestured at a slightly smaller, fair-skinned girl, whose thick brushed hair fell below her waist.

"My sister, my lord."

"Oh, your sister."

"And you are out on the moor?"

"Aye, my lord, Meg and I."

"Meg, what a pretty name. Is there any reason to be loose on the moor that I do not know about?"

"No, my lord."

"Then why are you not bedded down in shelter, either at hearth or with your kin, if I may ask?"

"You, Lord Bruce."

"Pray God, why me?" He was slipping his bare arms into a shirt and reaching for his tunic.

"To sleep with you, my lord, to bear your child."

He looked quickly from one girl to the other, seeking to grasp the purpose beneath the deep blue Celtic eyes. He was too startled to even think of threatening to whip them.

"Meg is the virgin, betrothed to be wed in two months. . . ."

"That child!" His voice croaked as he gestured at the small girl whose level eyes never left his.

"I be a woman in my body, my lord," the girl said, speaking for the first time.

"Good God, I have a battle to fight tomorrow."

"Meg is the virgin, her purity untouched."

"My God, get out! Ruff!" He was shouting.

"My lord, would you dishonor us before our own kin?"

"What?"

"Yes, Lord Bruce?" Ruff and Jamie had their fog-wet faces at the upraised flap.

"These girls, get them out!"

"Nay, Lord Bruce, 'tis for ye to put outen, not us, for 'tis scorn to do." The flap fell and he was alone with the girls once more.

"My lord, you are the Bruce," the larger girl said.

"Who are they? Ruff?"

The face appeared at the flap for a moment. "Rhonda and Meggie McLawker, daughters of Ian McLawker, of your own clan." There was a note of finality, of approval in the Highlander's voice, with a sense of irritation that Bruce did not know his own people and their way of life.

"I do not hold to the ancient beliefs," he said, turning to the sisters.

"Lord Bruce, they are our beliefs, and you are our laird."

"Aye." He shook his head slowly. "I am an old man, I feel old and tired, my bones hurt and I cannot draw my sword. . . ."

"The clan knows that, Lord Bruce," Rhonda said, smiling purposefully, her voice assured.

"You love beauty, your house is full of children," the smaller sister said.

"You are not that tired."

"You are not being fair with your chief," he said, seeking not to offend the girls with rejection, yet honoring the role he played as Highland chief.

"You will not be tired if you hold me," the one called Meg said. She smiled and he saw the innocent blue eyes light with a willingness to accept life, while the freckles glinted over her nose. She slipped off her cloak and he saw she had the full body of a woman, and her fair shanks were mud-streaked. He watched her slip her feet out of her skin shoes and stand barefoot on his felt robes, while the older sister took into her own hands the garments as her sister disrobed.

"No, it is not possible. I love my wife."

"My father consulted the parson and the parson said it was right and fair, if you still loved your wife, the foreign lady." The older girl did not look at him as she took the final garments, and her sister was standing nude in the dim flame of a grease lamp, her hair falling down to her navel and her white shoulders quite lovely as they appeared in the glint of smooth skin and hair. Bruce was momentarily stunned with the grace and open purity of the girl.

"You're betrothed." He spoke quietly.

"He knows and he is honored," the girl said. "The parson said all life was from God, and it was God's gift, and if it is in you, and if you will give it to us, then you have honored us and honored God—that is what the parson said."

"Before the marriage," the older sister said, "for the parson said God had no favorites in children."

"Your child would be ours, and you will never die." The girl smiled for the first time after undressing.

"You will honor our people," Rhonda said, nodding to her sister, who stepped toward him, standing in the middle of his pallet.

"Lord Bruce, please." It was a child's voice speaking a woman's passion.

He leaned forward and touched her hair, and felt the shock of desire rage of a fiery instant throughout his body, so that his breath gasped. He felt her grasp his forearm into her bare breasts, which he had not dared to look at, and against the skin of the back of his hand he could feel the quick fluid passion of heat shatter his whole being.

"Come," the girl said, kneeling and drawing him down to his knees and into her full nude figure, her hair moist in his breath and strewn in his open mouth.

"Ah, the beauty," he said, whispering and dragging her into his body.

It seemed that the girl's resilient body and clear flesh was everywhere under his palms and that her mouth drew his breath as he struggled to kiss her. He drew her waist into him and felt the nude breasts against his cheek as she kissed his straining neck, and his hands gripped the muscles of her shoulders and along her spine, until he grasped her buttocks and felt his mind lost to all purpose except the wish to live with his body.

She had his hand in her hands as he pulled and loosened at his clothes—baffled, it seemed, at their immense complexity. "Pull them off," he said to the older girl, "and leave us."

It was more than he had dreamed, and perhaps it was not another woman but the same woman he had grasped to his body since childhood, in the long succession of women he had loved, always trying to reach a woman in one final moment of complete understanding with no impediment to divide the two of them as human beings, and always failing just as he felt he had reached the point of absolute insight.

He felt her arms and legs wrapped about his body and her face pressed against his, the lips swollen and urgent on his skin, and her knees up and her soft belly pressed against the need he felt drive him on, as though he had given over all his life, and in this fresh girl he had one more final grasp at the life he could feel slip through him. The exquisite nest of hair in her armpit filled his nose with an intoxicant and he pushed against the soft wet lips and gossamer at the pit of her belly and felt her gasp as he entered her in a sublime union.

He wanted to tell her not to be afraid when he had pushed inside her body, and shuddered in the delusion he had captured his youth once more. He was surprised to feel the girl's body twist beneath him into his loins. She seemed to kiss the breath from him as he whipped his passion into her, until he felt the ecstasy lunge up his body in an explosion of crashing waves, and he collapsed into her arms.

The night wore on and he slept in the girl's arms, warmed by her body. Before the dawn came of the long northern night, he woke with the stirring of the other sister, who had brought him hot porridge, and in waking, he awoke Meg. She turned her face to him. "You have done for us what only you can do. You have made us your equals and ladies."

"Eat, Lord Bruce," Rhonda said, holding the bowl to him.

"Ah, it was madness, all madness." He took the bowl and commenced to eat the unsweetened porridge. The younger sister slipped out from beneath the covers and took a second bowl set at the foot of the pallet and began to eat as she slipped on a thin camisole and pulled a loose frock over her head. "I had him only once." She spoke to her sister.

Bruce saw the older sister nod and slip out of her clothing, tossing it to Meg.

"Get out! Both of you!" He flung back the covers as the older girl pushed them back and slipped her nude figure into his pallet against him. He pulled away as she grasped his hand.

"Lord Bruce, they say I am damaged in the ill-use of rape."

He caught the desperate urgency of hope in her voice and saw the beauty of a naked woman in full bloom stretched out before him, pleading with her face and body.

"Lord Bruce, please, I beg of you."

He paused and looked at her strong fingers gripping his arm.

"You said I was not damaged, for I was ravished against my will."

"Aye, so you were."

"But I canna get a husband, for they say I am spoiled."

"Rubbish, lass, rubbish!"

"If you will lay with me, you be the laird, and all who follow will be honored."

He stared at the girl's face, the soft look of desperation in her eyes, and the naked commitment to life.

"Oh, my God, I am fifty years old—I do not have the strength."

"You slept, Lord Bruce." She drew him back into the covers. "I slept at the foot of the pallet, we slept all three throughout the night, and you slept like a child."

"God, I am one lonely man."

"Please, Lord Bruce, try. It is my only hope if I am to ever get an honorable man."

"Lay with her, Bruce," Meg said, her voice grave and commanding, startling Bruce from such a child. "She is my sister, and the parson said it was right in the book he reads."

"Please, if you did it once, it will do again, for you are fresh with love, I can feel it in your body." She was wrapped against him, and he lost all hope as he did indeed feel the sweeping passion rise on his skin and flood his sinews with a desire to drive himself deep into her, until he wove and exploded and died with his face full of the sweet nipples he sucked and the mouth that drew his passion from him in the confusion of long auburn hair strewn across his pallet.

10

Bruce dressed slowly, as the false dawn lifted and the gray light flooded his shelter. The cook brought him oatmeal cakes and a roast grouse, which he ate in silence. The sisters, who had dressed of an instant, helped him get into his field clothes and the hooded boots. He could see and hear his men moving about outside the entrance, where he saw Ruff and Jamie sharpening weapons and occasionally glancing in at them.

"A runner, Lord Bruce," Jamie said when he stood on his booted legs.

"Aye." He gestured at his heavy pistols at the head of his pallet, signaling to his bodyguards they were to enter his quarters and to prime them afresh, and stepped out into the bald clearing in the forest. "Where is the messenger?"

A Highlander in heavy wool leggings came before him.

"Is he true?" Bruce looked at Albain.

"Aye. Know his father and mother."

"What news?"

"That Campbell and Monck in Inverness seek ye, but fear ye are in England."

"Who would know this?" Bruce said.

"Oh, 'tis common gossip. . . ."

"Where are the forces afield?"

"English cavalry in Argyll's service, south of the River Don."

"How many?"

"Five hundred, and heavy war horses, unfit for the moor."

Bruce nodded. "Infantry? Of the foot?"

"Scattered between Crathie and Tarland."

"How many?"

"All plundering and not possible to count."

"Thank you. Eat and rest and return. Count the dragoons."

When he was alone with Albain he spoke quietly. "It is a mob that Argyll has, save for his cavalry, and they have to tend their horses else they would join the plunder."

"We be outnumbered, Lord Bruce."

"I will choose the ground to even the advantage."

"We fight?" Albain said, his blue eyes glittering and his beard quivering slightly as he tilted up his face to look at Bruce.

"Nay, but hide our camp and prepare the men for marching." Bruce turned back to Rhonda and Meg McLawker, and to Ruff and Jamie. John Bollingale was in their company and they were sitting on split logs and matted bracken, tying up their duffle. He noticed that the Englishman had an agitated glare about his usually unfocusing eyes. They had a piercing white look about them.

"Slept well, John?"

"Aye, and you?"

"Well enough."

"With these!" He gestured at the two sisters, who looked up.

"John, you are impudent."

"No, it is common knowledge among your men that you slept the night with two sisters—sisters!" The cultured voice faltered.

"It is not what you think."

"What should I think?"

"It is not possible for you to understand. . . ."

"Sodom and Gomorrah!"

"Rubbish." He took his riding gloves from his cook.

"And the men are proud of you. . . ."

"Have you talked to the men?"

"They have not mutinied at the disgrace of their commander."

"I am their chief and their kin and it is Celtic law we follow. . . ."

"The immorality of spending the night with two women who are sisters, under some pagan god who condones carnal gymnastics. . . ." The face turned pale and the eyes slipped out of focus onto the distance.

"John, all that dramatic nonsense—Lord, you are as bad as those damned Puritans. You each be the reverse of the other, and the ass is but a matter of personal opinion."

By divination he saw his column forming up in the shadowed woods. He looked at the sisters, whose eyes never left him. "Can you get to your men?"

"Easily," Rhonda said.

"Then go. We will soon have the intruder occupied with grim reality and he will lose his stomach for debauching the impoverished."

Rhonda slipped her hand out and touched his, her eyes searching his face. "Thank you, Lord Bruce. We are mere crofters, but you have made us ladies so that no man can ever deny us."

"Lord, forgive me."

"Nay, only a good man could do what ye did. Others would mock or rail or scorn. Ye are the Bruce."

He clasped their hands into his chest as the girls began to weep. "Now off to Ben Lawker with you!" He touched their fingers to his lips and turned them away. He walked to his stallion with Ruff and Jamie following, and told Buchan to get the Englishman back into hiding. John Bollingale was beginning to be an opinionated bore and an intellectual fanatic, and he had a glimpse of why he had never cared for the company of professors.

"We put the Englishman with as fine a lass as walked the Highlands, but he finds no peace in a woman," Ruff said in a burst of speech which surprised Bruce.

"I know."

"He is a troubled man."

"Aye, Ruff, without a woman it is trouble for a man."

"Too much education," said his cook, whose dark hairy forearms were bare in the fog, the rain, or while roasting an ox, and whose opinion was served as regularly as his meals. Bruce glanced where he was loading a Highland pony, but the cook ignored him with indifferent gravity.

Bruce had quick-marched around the north slope of the Cairngorm, had forded the headwaters of the River Don at night, and had climbed once more into the mists of the mountain ridges and wet bracken and evergreen forests. He bedded down in the lee of Morven Mountain and at dawn led his men onto the crests, where they could see the Roundhead cavalry patroling the River Dee. He could see them as a scattering of small bodies of tiny horsemen in bright armor and helmets who kept to the rich green of the fields along the river, with groups idling at the stone bridges and the fords.

It did not occur to Bruce that he would not fight the English before returning to Skarra, not because they were English, but because they had intruded, and they offered him his only target, for the Lowland Scots were plundering and too scattered to attack effectively. He signaled for Albain and Buchan to join him as he dismounted and walked to the edge of the woods, where a bright glaze of open light cleared his vision over the whole river valley.

"It must be a careful fight," he said.

"Oh, most careful, Lord Bruce."

"No, I do not mean that. We could lose easily, if we abandon discipline. I want them to attack us, to our advantage."

The two Highland chiefs looked from him to the valley and waited for his directions, each knowing Bruce was an educated man who knew how to conduct a battle, and it was a fight for which they and their company of Highlanders had borne near a fortnight's rough weather and privation.

"They have no idea we are within a hundred miles," Bruce said, watching the circular image in his spyglass of five dismounted troopers lolling on a bridge, talking to an old man leading a bullock cart. He saw the men smile and forget the cart when two barefoot girls appeared on the road, driving a gaggle of Toulouse geese ahead of them.

"It will be such a shock for them."

"Pardon us, Lord Bruce?"

Bruce shook his head. He did not want to talk. When he was a young man he had a great desire to talk, to explain, to understand, and to know everything. Then, as he had grown older, he did try to explain and to understand, and he knew far more than he ever wanted to know, until he no longer wanted to know anything else, for it was all a grief. His wisdom had brought him to sorrow, relieved only by the joy of youth in its innocence and the love of his wife. Years ago, perhaps when he had buried Geney in the snow, did he learn talk was all useless and reason a mockery of human life.

"They will ne'er respect us 'less we shed blood, Lord Bruce." Albain spoke quietly, sensing his torn soul as he prepared his battle plan.

He nodded. " 'Twill be a skirmish at Westminster, a rout in Edinburgh, and for us, a gory day." He snapped closed the glass and sighed and turned back to his men.

The two chiefs followed him.

"I cannot understand how men cannot know they be accountable." He spoke more to himself, yet he was as drawn to the fight as though propelled by the omnipotent arms of a god.

He led his column along the shadowed edge of the forest, preserving his concealment, while watching the green valley of the Dee. His men were particularly silent, picking their steps cautiously and all but noiseless in the woods with their thick wool tartans and kilts. He watched the misty valley that swooped in cheerful undulations to the North Sea on the horizon. Gradually he saw the village of Ballater come into prominence. It was a happy conglomeration of cottages strung about a bridge and a little church with a brave steeple.

" 'Tis the Lord's Day," Albain said as they heard the church bell peel hopefully across the valley.

Bruce nodded in silence. He could see the bundled villagers hurrying along footpaths and crossing stiles at the rock walls dividing the fields. It was a scene of absolute peace, and he regretted he would have to disturb it, but he saw a bivouac of Roundhead cavalry staked in the park of Lord Selkirk's manor on the hill beyond the village, and heavy patrols were moving along the roads as far as he could see. Before him lay a wide field of grazing, easing downward to the village and the Dee, two miles away, and affording him tactical advantage.

"I think we will fight here," he said, raising his hand and turning into the woods to face his men. He paused as his column pressed forward around him. He sat on Bellsinger, keeping his eyes on the backs of his gauntlets. About him the Highland chiefs were astride their ponies, gesturing for the men to crowd up to him.

"Men," he said, speaking just above a whisper, and smelling the rich odor of fog-wet bodies and unwashed wool engulf him. "Men, we will fight here."

He raised his eyes and looked at the Highlanders. They were young men, heavy-bearded and long-haired and strong in their limbs and clear, light eyes. Their eyes were fastened onto him as though gripping his soul and extracting his breath.

"There is no purpose to inflame the human heart; yet, our peace and our cottages and our land is despoiled at caprice, and 'less we chasten our enemies, we could not dissuade them even if we groveled before them." He glanced into the faces about his knees. All his kin and related clans were there, going back to ancient Celtic and Pictic migrations. They were quiet in their assent to his words.

"I want to fight in this manner." He heard them breathe and the faces pressed closer. He turned and gestured out of the forest shadow, down the long green field. "I want the English cavalry to charge up that long field. I want you to be in broad rank of battle, set below the forest in the open field as I place you. And pipers"—he looked to his three pipers—"I want the war pipes to scream across this whole valley, drawing every horseman and stranger before us, in response to the challenge."

He paused and looked to Albain and Buchan. "The column is to hold just before the wood, as the pipes scream their challenge, until the cavalry rallies, musters, and rides out to fight."

"How do ye know they will fight, Lord Bruce?" Albain said.

"Cromwell. It is heavy cavalry and his strength, all through the war."

"What if they be afeared?"

"We will be afeared, for it is us backed against the wall." He glanced about at his men, who all seemed to savor his every word and shade of meaning. "They must fight, for they can never dare to admit they are wrong and they have gone too far to ever turn back."

He looked down the translucent valley on the calm Sunday morning. "They will come rolling up that long green swale, their bugles and trumpets sounding, and their mouths full of war." He looked back to his men. "When I throw my bonnet into the air the pipers are to silence, the drums are to beat and the column is to break and run for the forest. . . ."

"Break and run, my lord?"

"Aye, break ranks and run to the cover of the trees, where ye will fight the horsemen under the cover of the tree limbs and among the tree trunks." He looked into each face his eyes could reach. "The forest will break up the shock of the cavalry charge, and ye can scurry about the isolated horsemen half-hid by the foliage and set your arrows and pics into them at will. Under no way are ye to fight in the open field, d'ye ken me?"

"Aye, Lord Bruce."

"Aye, aye, Brucie."

"Aye, ye be the Bruce."

The men stirred and looked to each other once they understood the plan of battle.

"Once the battle is committed to the forest, I will order the pipers to sound the war pipes and ye will rally about the pipes, and slay the horsemen as they gallop through the confusion." He caught the flicker of a smile brush across faces about him, as the men got the image of how victory was to be had and ten thousand outrages avenged.

"And ye will stay and fight until ye have victory or death." He looked down at his gauntlets, knowing the men understood. He glanced up at his chiefs. "Prepare for battle."

There was a delight in the woods where he discovered a tangle of windfalls and twisted roots at a thicket of cedars. "There!" he said, "there, fell a few more trees, not to make a fort, but to hem the flood and lead the crest of their charge." He pounded his open hand atop his pommel as he rode among his men, who were cutting long poles to set as pics against the horsemen. "Quick about it, men, but make no fort. I want them to ride into our midst." He smiled, nodding to himself. "Albain! Albain, where are you?!"

"Behind you, my lord."

"Oh, yes." He was confused by his own intoxication with the fight he prepared for, exultant at avenging the Highland Celts, who were considered vermin that had refused to die in starvation. "Albain!"

"My lord, I am here!"

"Albain, unhorse them!"

"Aye, unhorse them?"

"It is a sudden shock to throw down a man from his saddle, it upsets his delusions of power with a rude dislocation, and he can be pounced upon to advantage once he is stretched upon the earth."

"Aye, men! Did ye hear Lord Bruce?"

The men muttered, nodding and straining at the limbs they were sharpening into points and cleaning of bark.

"Unhorse them, and cut their throats, men, or jab them in the armpit!" Albain was riding among the sweating, bearded men, who showed an occasional naked white back or hairy thigh that muscled under a burden.

"The throats or armpits, men! They be armored." Buchan followed Albain, passing again the orders for battle.

"Can we knife them in their privy parts?" It was a gaunt man with wide shoulders.

"If that be your taste, man."

Bruce heard the men break into coarse laughter at the crudity, and he flushed at the reality of what he was doing. He saw the battle as a righteous blow to preserve an ancient race of people, which it was, but it would be fought out in gore and fury, by common men. He flushed deeply, feeling a chill run along his spine, and the woods seemed a foreboding gloom to him.

"Let me know when ready," he said, settling his face down into his tartan, gripped by the lonely truth that life can be served without honor or justice.

He rode out of the woods into the sunlight, which seemed to mist a radiance over the valley, followed by his three pipers. "Sound the war pipes."

In a moment he was lost in the wailing skirl of Scottish pipers hurling a death challenge down the mountain that echoed off the lea. He could actually see when the villagers of Ballater heard the pipes. Worshippers who were moving devoutly along the roads and some still in the churchyard looked abruptly up the mountain, as though struck by an apparition, and then commenced to point toward him, and some ran helter-skelter.

He watched the English cavalry in Lord Selkirk's park of chestnut trees, and heard the village dogs begin to bark and faint cries of alarm among the villagers. He could see the slender colonel of the dragoons in the circular field of his spyglass. The officer appeared on the terrace of the manor and did not look in their direction, though Bruce knew the whole valley had by now heard the war cry and its challenge to battle.

"A good officer," Bruce said, speaking to himself, and watching the calm motion of the nonchalant hand that returned salutes to officers who scampered up. Not once did the Colonel speak, but kept his ear tilted toward his subordinates. "He listens."

"Ahh." Bruce could see the sunlight reflect off the spyglass, which the Colonel turned toward them. It pleased him to know his adversary had him in sight, not just because he had drawn the singular attention of a proud man, but because that man would be forced into a battle at Bruce's choice.

"Dress the line, dress the line!"

Bruce glanced behind him and saw the Highland column moving out of the woods in a broad rank, each man stepping in independent resolution from his neighbor and moving down the swale toward him. It thrilled him to see them, pitifully few that they were, not over a hundred and a half. He saw their faces brighten and the war cry rise when they recognized the enemy. "Ahhee-EE-aaa!"

Bruce turned and looked at the English troopers, who were by now carrying saddles and blankets, and a loose horse galloped out of the park down the drive toward the village. He could see the village seem to spew out people who would dash into sight, then disappear only to reappear in a moment, dragging some other household member, to stand and stare at his pipers and column, then turn to look at the

English cavalry, which was sounding bugles and rolling its drums of alarm. The opposing forces were across the valley from each other, so that the villagers had to keep turning from one to the other to keep acquainted with the overture of the fight.

"Hold," Bruce said, nodding toward Albain, when he was satisfied his column was in full sight and clear of the woods by a quarter-mile.

"My lord!" called Buchan, gesturing to a troop of cavalry splashing through the River Dee and laboring in wet bounds to get to the dry ground to his right.

"Aye."

He watched the ensign riding at the head of seven troopers, coming unevenly through the gardens of the village and onto the long swale.

"Hold," he said to the pipers, and watched the young officer ride toward them. The troop split, and he saw a sergeant lead three horsemen to his left, toward Albain's flank. "No action unless they charge the line!"

"No action!"

Behind him the men shifted and were silent, and he gestured his pipers back toward the Scottish line, slowly reining Bellsinger to follow, but never taking his eyes off the cavalry.

"They come, my lord," said a young piper.

"Aye, thank ye."

He could hear the suction of the horses' hooves on the wet turf, and he knew he had chosen well.

"In the name of the Protector, who passes?" The young officer's voice was clear in the bell tone of youth.

"Lord Skarra of Skarra!"

"In war or peace?"

"In peace!"

The young officer rode slowly toward him as he reined backward toward his men, the troopers following.

"The war pipes are forbidden. . . ."

"Is breath forbidden?" Bruce laughed.

"An armed band of men." He rode straight up to Bruce, his fresh skin pink under his visored helmet.

"We are Scots in our homeland."

"Armed for war, I dare say." He craned his neck to look past Bellsinger at the Highlanders. "Five fusiliers and the rest bows. . . ."

"Sir, you be armed and in your neighbor's country, which you are blind to, but you count our pipes and breath and arrows." Bruce straightened in his saddle. "Go tell your colonel to depart in peace. . . ."

"Not likely, my lord. We have waited for you." The young man smiled without innocence. "Now we have found you."

"We will advance no further."

"The colonel will be delighted." He reined his horse about abruptly, signaling to his ratings. "The riffraff is at bay, praise God!" The troop went into a slow gallop toward the village.

"Pipers." Bruce was still as he watched the war pipes hurl a challenge once more down the lea and across the hills to where armed men were assembling. It was the usual lies and deceptions between men, about to start the fight. But the tree is still known by its fruit, and they are armed and in my homeland, Bruce thought.

He rode clear of his men by a few feet and watched the cavalry form up into squads and platoons and move purposefully down the roads and out of the parks, passing into the village to reach the broad field at the end of which he waited. He noticed that the English officers hardly deigned to look up the field at him and his pipers, and he counted three hundred and sixty-odd horsemen. They moved out into a front, two rows deep, and under their banners and sabers they were a bold sight. He set his heels to Bellsinger and felt the stallion leap into life beneath him, and he cantered across his front before his men, to assure them of his presence and to let the strangers know he had the audacity to confront them.

He was looking at the villagers who had climbed atop their roofs and chimneys to watch the battle when he saw the cavalry trot out, accompanied by bugles.

"Play!" He shouted at his pipers. He felt a great calm envelop him as he watched the Roundhead charge gather itself into a dashing trot, the banners snapping over the breastplates and the regiment in a single purpose. Yet he felt of an instant the incomprehension grip his ribs, that he was so utterly cautious, far more so than other men and devoted only to life's fair survival, that he felt an unfair advantage over them. Wherever he looked he saw little reason to men's endeavors beyond vanity, and that only in the love of a woman was there any purpose to life, yet even here he felt he had failed, honoring an ancient code that had seduced him.

The bugles sounded clearly across the wailing skirl of his pipers and his mind snapped back to what appalled him. He rose in his stirrups and bellowed the ancient war cry: "Ahhee-EE-aaa!" Behind him he heard his men pick up his scream and echo the lust for battle.

He watched the cavalry mount its charge. The dress was excellent and the front was straight, the officers galloping slightly to the fore. The men rode upright, their legs hanging in long stirrups, and he knew they would have difficulty in leaning down to strike. "It is the colonel's second mistake," he said to himself. His first was to underestimate his enemy. He noticed some of the horses begin to lag and saw the laboring motion of other horses in the line, and he knew the distance on the soft moor was beginning to tire them. "Committed to the attack too soon."

He glanced to his people. They were absorbed with the enemy, a long ragged tableau of unwashed men in kilts whose bare shoulders and arms were freed to hold bows and set arrows. He saw his eleven flintlocks level and aiming, the shooters' eyes a cold white behind the hammers.

The bugles were clear and he estimated a mile parted them, and he heard Buchan call, "Lord Bruce."

He watched the enemy, and gestured to the pipers to silence. In the gasp of air from the dying pipes he heard the thudding rumble of the oncoming horsemen, and he saw the colonel stand in his stirrups and wave his saber level, and the whole regiment lower its sabers. They are disciplined soldiers, he thought. He pulled his bonnet from his head and glanced at the rushing force, and flung his headgear high over the Highlanders, bellowing "Break for the forest!"

The men stared at him for an instant, rooted before disaster, held by some determination to stand and fight. "To the woods!" He drove Bellsinger into his people, scattering them. "To the woods, men!"

Men were running frantically for the cover of the trees as he waved them on, glancing back to hear the Roundheads break into thick cheering, the huzzahs echoing on the edge of the forest over his ears.

In the confusion he was at the woods; his men were everywhere among the trees, coming into and out of sight about the trunks, and some were still in the field, facing off cavalry who had deflected at the thick cover. He was amazed to see horses rush past him with empty saddles, their heads up and dragging reins from their bits which were held high to free their forelegs. Off the edge of the shade he saw several men on the green earth who wore bright armor and massive boots, and it seemed strange that they would be there where all had been clear and free a moment before. The pipes were screaming deeper in the woods.

"The redoubt! Bruce, the redoubt!" It was Albain on a gray pony, his eyes ablaze and his beard quivering on his jaw.

He hesitated when he saw a handful of his men run down by horsemen, one's skull hewn open and all dead or flopping on the earth when the troop reined about to attack again. The sabers were red and one stuck with hair.

Someone had Bellsinger's bit and was leading the horse into the woods, which Bruce seemed powerless to stop, as though he were in a silent nightmare full of screaming men, war pipes, and the thud of hooves, with all bent on their own fury while he was whipped in the face by fresh tree limbs.

"Get down, Bruce!" He looked down at the face and saw Ruff had drawn out a boot and someone had tipped him out of his saddle, and he fell into the rough arms of his bodyguard but struggled onto his legs.

The heavy Roundhead was looking down at him with a single eye that glared past the feathered fletching of the arrow stuck in the other eye as the horse smashed into limbs, breaking off the arrow, and the man screamed and was carried away.

"Get him in the redoubt!" He could hear Albain's voice above the rushing noise in the trees about him.

"A day of jubilation!" said a man pulling him into the shelter of a thwart of logs and turning away with his pic, crouching low to set the butt into some roots as he aimed it. "We are killing them fast, Lord Bruce!"

It was not clear who was doing what, except for the awful noise of breaking timber and over-rolling thunder, and an endless scream which was right at his feet, though he could see nothing. "What is that?" he said, but the Scots about him were oblivious to his words, totally absorbed in the battle. He saw he was in the half-open redoubt of upended trees and felled logs, and Roundhead cavalry troopers were pouring through the woods, not at a gallop but in confused dashes, pulling up and milling about, while his men were swarming everywhere he looked, like earth-gnomes crawling from the very roots of trees.

The awful scream came again and he said, "A horse, a horse, poor thing."

"Kill it!" He heard Albain.

"Oh, Albain."

"Kill it, men."

Bruce turned and saw Albain in the middle of the redoubt, astride the gray pony, the pipers perched on a thick root, the war cries on all sides and a thick body of men driving arrows into the enemy who swung into sight, and some working in pairs, running crouched-over to set the pics.

"Bellsinger," he said, aware he was terrified lest the animal had been wounded, and he saw a man leap over a log and slip a dirk around the soft gullet of a beautiful chestnut mare who stared at him with moist reproaching eyes, then bubbled blood out her throat in a wet scream and thrashed with her elegant forelegs, one of which was broken.

"The bastard rode his horse into the logs," the man said, leaping back over the snag and seeing the dismay in Bruce's face. "Cutting his throat was a pleasure, Brucie."

Bruce looked back for Albain, eased that his presence under fire was so commanding. He wanted his horse. Bellsinger, whom he had raised. He went to the horse and caught the bridle to mount.

"Nay, Lord Bruce, 'tis not the place for ye to be up," Albain said.

"Nonsense."

"Not now, 'tis not safe."

"It is my horse and I am the laird."

" 'Tis not the time."

Bruce shoved his toe into his stirrup, ready to swing up.

"Ruff, the strangers would kill the laird to pay us for their whipping in the body of one man," Albain said.

"Nay, Lord Bruce, ye canna mount." The toe was shoved out of the stirrup and the elderly man shoved in between him and the horse's flank.

He turned back to the battle, which was being fought with unceasing din. His claymore was unsheathed from the saddle and thrust into his right hand and a cavalry pistol slung over his shoulder on a thick baldric. "Ye can fight on foot, if ye're a mind to," said his bodyguard, who was directing the flintlocks. He heard the scattered gunfire and saw the smoke hanging like filaments of gauze on the limbs of the evergreens.

"The caracole of gunfire!"

He could hear the English commands and saw the dragoons had unholstered their pistols and were aiming and firing, but he could not see who they were shooting at, though men and horses were down and thrashing with each other all across the forest carpet, among the stately trees. He had trouble telling his own men from the helpless animals, for they were hide- and fur-covered, and seemed to spring up out of nowhere to stick knives into the bright-armored soldiers, all swarming about each other in a tumbling mass of pain wherever he looked.

"Shoot their officers!"

He looked to see a Midland accent from a coarse sergeant and felt a stunning blow in his chest, as though a horse had delivered a double kick into his bosom, and he fell backwards into the roots of a cedar tree. The repose of his body amazed him. He looked up and saw his pipers playing forcefully as ever, though one was drooling pink froth from his lips as he held his hand over a hole in his ribs to plug the gunshot wound. The tree limbs were feathery over his head, spread against a pure sky.

"Lord Bruce!" Ruff was kneeling.

"A gunshot."

"Mortal, Bruce?" The rough fingers were lifting clothing over his chest.

"I do not think so."

"The baldric! The bullet hit y'er buckle."

He touched over his heart and felt the hot lead molten on the buckle. "It must have slowed it."

"Aye, the bullet is in y'er ribs and not in y'er heart. I can feel it."

"Help me up."

He was onto his legs, swept with that ecstatic moment which comes in battle where he knew he could not only endure the fear but enjoy the holocaust and exult in the victory he could taste with his breath on the smoke and noise.

"Baalooom!"

He saw the concussion of a flintlock shake the leaves under a long streak of flame and saw the face of a Roundhead change into a red mass.

"Nothing like a stone," said the boy who was pouring another charge of powder down the barrel.

"No need to cut his throat, David," Ruff said. "Get the next one."

The flintlocks were being served by a group of men who had taken a steady toll of Roundheads, strewing the logs and near-forest floor with a thick carpeting of shiny, armored figures who sprawled in death like strange forest beetles.

"Carash!"

"He's off, man!"

Bruce saw the pic bowed into the earth, lifting a man out of the saddle, the point stuck in his groin as he waved a bland sword at the two footmen. He thumped onto his back on the other side of the horse, which galloped on, and Bruce saw a ragged figure pounce on his head and twist it backward, and he saw the man strangle in his own blood.

"It is well it is so terrible, 'else we would become addicted," he said, looking for a falling back of strangers, as a sign of the victory he tasted by divination. Dead Englishmen were stretched out in the quiet woods wherever he looked, and he saw some of his men leading horses, and in a moment he realized the field was theirs.

" 'Scotland the Brave,' " he said to his pipers, realizing the piper with the lung shot lay dead at his heels. "Let the men know we prevailed." He turned to his horse, which a boy was leading toward him.

"Lord Bruce!" a man said, and he recognized Eric McLean, "Your bonnet." McLean thrust out the bonnet.

"Thank you, Eric."

"My son died to retrieve it for ye."

Bruce caught his breath, almost not daring to touch the feathered Scottish bonnet.

"He ran back to retrieve his master's bonnet, dying gladly, my lord."

"McLean, oh, McLean." He clasped the man into his bosom, not daring to say what was on his lips, that no soiled apparel, no symbol, was worth a boy's life—no, no life—they would not understand. He closed his eyes, releasing the old Highlander, and reached for his horse, stunned by the battle.

He led the horse through the forest, stepping over the dead or going around them, until he got to the swale, where he mounted. The English cavalry was in a loose formation, a good mile away, with many riderless horses and much confusion of calling voices. He set his heels to Bellsinger and galloped half the distance, where he reined up and called, "Parley! Parley with the colonel!"

He sat easy, his spyglass to his eye, watching the English officer ride toward him. It was the same slender, elegant man he had watched on Lord Selkirk's piazza. The face was blanched white and the lips small compressions.

"I am Lord Skarra of Skarra," Bruce called out at earshot. "Send a detail to get your dead."

The Colonel looked surprised.

"I must hold the battlefield, and I do not want to touch your dead."

"My God, why?" The Colonel gestured up toward the woods. "My God, what a beating."

"I am sorry."

"But why, man?"

"You attacked me." Bruce looked into the uncertain confused eyes of a gentleman.

"But you killed so many."

"My God, Colonel, do not you know when you unleash men to fight, they do not know when nor how to stop? Good God!" Bruce's voice rose. "I wanted no battle, but this is Scotland, and I am Scottish and you are not, and you are in Scotland."

The Colonel shook his well-clipped head and grimaced with his refined mouth. "One law, one flag, one nation, one Protector."

"No, one God and one life, equally divine for all."

The English colonel was silent, looking hard into Bruce's eyes.

"If a law or a god or a nation or even a people cannot live without death, then that thing is dead, and does not deserve life."

Bruce watched him for a moment, each gaining a respect if not an agreement, and each embarrassed at their understanding of the other.

"I am truly sorry," Bruce said.

"I will send the burial detail."

"My word of safe passage."

"Aye, Skarra, you are well known for that, and I wish to God I had believed the rest of what they said about you."

"I am very, very sorry, Colonel."

"And I am more sorry. I lost." He reined his horse away and cantered back to his cavalry.

He marched along the crests over the River Dee and crossed the valley of the Don, leading his column and carrying his twenty-eight dead. He was cautious to keep to the mists and forests, but he was careful to expose his ranks in view of all villages and hamlets, where his war pipes could be heard and the victory shared. Bruce wanted the Scots to know of their invincible courage without the burden of having to govern a nation or defend an idea. He fought for time and the Scottish identity, for he knew anything else was certain to fail.

He led the column down the Firth of Skarra, disbanding his men into the swarming masses of women and children, noticing Lydia as he swung out of the saddle. He threw up his hands to dismiss his stallion to his grooms and walked to her. "Lord, I am tired, and I have a bullet in my chest."

"Can you walk?"

"Yes, how is Seymour?"

"Sympathetic, but restive."

"I want to lie down, and just our body servants and the children." They walked slowly up the stairs, her arm about his waist. "Talk to me first."

He lay in the master bed, with Lydia standing at his side, free of the weapons and thick clothing, in his nightgown. She held his hand and waited.

"Lydia, I was dishonest."

"And how?"

"Two girls, sisters, it is Celtic law that the king deflower their chastity."

"Did you?"

"Yes."

"Then you did what your station demands."

"No, I could have turned them down."

"You need not talk. I would like to have the bullet out of your ribs."

"I want to talk first."

"You will not die," Lydia said, speaking carefully as she watched his face, now deeply grimed in fatigue and dirt.

"Thank you. You know I love you."

"I know you do. And my life is you, alone."

"The girls were pretty, not in the sense of a beautiful woman but in their freshness for life. The younger one was a virgin, scarce more than a child, and in their innocence it was not vile, but had a rare beauty." He looked into her eyes and saw she understood him. "It was almost as though I saw in them every woman and hope I had ever known in life, and those two simple girls sensed it, and it was something I had to do, not just for myself, for actually it exhausted me, but for our race and our cause and our women who carry the purpose to life in their wombs."

"I'm glad you did."

"We fought a brisk action, but the two sisters unsettled my mind."

"I'm sorry you were alone."

"Aye, in the girls I could see my mother, and Geney and you, all the beauty I had ever known and every hope I ever loved."

"I followed you to Scotland for that reason." She kissed his temple and set her fingers over his lips.

He closed his eyes. "The lies a man has to live by, my greatest success has been my lies."

"Go to sleep," she said.

II

Forest Witch was a splendid black mare who galloped in a rocking gait of smooth springs. Fanny loved to feel the supple strength of the mare's back as she rode astride, the English officers cantering beside her and Bea clattering unevenly behind her on a tireless gelding, showing a face that seemed to wince at every hoofbeat. "Poor Bea," Fanny said to herself, delighted with her responsibility and her escape to freedom, away from her parents, yet aware of a new clutch of chilled uncertainty resting beneath her ribs as she breathed. It was fear, and Fanny had never before known the common anxiety which ages parents from their inability to protect themselves and what they love from the threat of an uncertain future.

"Pretty Witch," Fanny whispered to the perked ears of the mare, making them switch as she flicked her tail in response to the girl's voice. The beautiful horse's body galloping between her thighs reassured Fanny almost by instinct of the natural power of raw life they each shared, and gave her confidence she would prevail against fear and misfortune.

The English officers were silent as they passed through Lancashire and south into Darbyshire and Staffordshire. Fanny noted the florid wattles of flesh beneath the chilled ears of Colonel Buckey Hailyham. He was very much the English colonel, once away from her father. And Teddy Wilton and George Seymour would scarcely look at her. All was changed in the men about her, almost from the moment she rode away from her father, and by divination she knew her father's wisdom and humane tolerance of folly had sheltered the men from their own fleshly cravings and deceptions, and once her father was gone, the Englishmen very quickly fell back into a role of silence and guarded speech and rank.

Fanny could not know what was on the mind of Buckey Hailyham, the third son of an Elizabethan curate and younger brother of Sir Wendle Hailyham, who had married an estate and abandoned Charles for Cromwell before the Civil War. She could not know he was a middle-aged man returning alone to Westminster to confront Cromwell and the Protectorate after what to him was a delightful excursion into Scotland but to the Commonwealth would be a gross failure. Buckey Hailyham knew what he faced.

Though none of the Englishmen would openly acknowledge it, a Roundhead troop of cavalry had been crushed, the victorious Scottish laird whose domain they had come to subdue was afield with an armed column, lost in the mists and crags of the Highlands; and yet the rebel chief, for this is what Westminster would call him, was a cultured Oxford graduate, educated by England, beloved by scholars and professors as a student, a professor himself, more English than the English. And yet it was he alone who commanded the loyalty of the Highlanders, a people considered riffraff, a strange race of Celtic aborigines surviving primordial times, and fit for extermination, like the red deer and the shaggy cattle by the English merchants; and England was all commerce and money, and avarice was called a virtue. And if Hailyham knew Bruce McTaggart of Skarra, he knew the Scot would not get home before he slew another goodly number of Roundheads and Lowlanders. And Hailyham knew the fault would be on England, not Bruce, and yet Westminster would know they had been foxed, and blame and curse him, the messenger.

Buckey Hailyham was absorbed in his thoughts, hoping he could play the ignorant, bluff military officer to protect himself.

"How far, my lord?" Fanny said.

"The forenoon, my lady." He looked at the girl and was again struck by the fresh beauty about her teeth and lips and fragile mouth. He looked away, feeling a pang of longing stab him, of wanting the girl, of a craving to taste her teeth and breathe her breath, and he knew it was all gone from him forever, the true beauty of life that only a woman brought to a man. Now he was riding to Westminster with a lone girl of slender grace more Swedish than Scottish in appearance, the fair daughter of the Scottish chief, whose pathetic vulnerability was as audacious as her father's forays in the Highlands. And he knew Fanny would outrage the Puritans as well as captivate them. She was absolutely Protestant in her talk yet he knew her soul belonged to the Russian Catholic mother who had loved her. And the English would sense it, but never quite prove it.

"Get up!" Hailyham muttered to his gelding, while sinking his chin into the upturned collar of his redingote.

Fanny disturbed him. In her he saw the hope a middle-aged man sees in a young girl, who can once more fulfill the cycle of life as a woman, which a young man cannot see. A girl is a young man's triumph for his vanity, his trophy to be paraded as his success before his envious peers, but an old man knows better. An old man knows a girl is the willing slave to life, either young or old, and if he is gentle, an old man can woo and take any girl from any swain or buck, if he can raise his passion, because the girl has to have life inside her as well as outside her. "And that is the very devil of it," Buckey Hailyham muttered again, speaking to himself. "I've drunk too much wine and ale and ate pork and capon until my belly is all I feel. If I ever got a cock up to crow it might kill me." He kept his chin down in his collar, and he knew he hated the two young men beside him, not out of envy but for their ignorance. They could thrust a girl with a cock of life, but they would not know what they had done. "A pearl mouthed by swine," he muttered. "I wish to God I had the body and the time to love her, and by God, I would."

Teddy Wilton glanced over at Seymour and winked, hearing the Colonel talking to himself. Fanny rode erect, her face set in repose, isolating herself from the English officers, knowing she was to become more than a houseguest and willing to play the role her father had asked of her. Fanny knew by divination she would marry an Englishman, and make him a Scot, and bring him home to Skarra to live as a Highlander, loyal to her and her family, because she knew she belonged to her family first, not to England. England would come to her, for she saw life as her mother saw it, and as her father saw it, and life was Scotland and family. And Fanny knew she could never explain it to anybody, yet she also knew she would do it better if she kept her own counsel, with only Bea, her nurse, to share it.

Fanny was aghast at the smells of London, of the narrow streets which burst with squalor and ragged figures, through which elegant sedan chairs moved on disdaining legs and shoulders. Cursing and blasphemy fell off the shop walls, echoing the shrill lips of anger, more female than male, erupting on all sides of their cavalcade as they clattered through the City, enroute to Westminster.

"Puritan bastards!"

"Murderers!"

"Bloody Mary in breeches!"

Fanny looked to Colonel Hailyham, a quizzical expression sweeping her eyes.

"London is tired of virtues," Hailyham said.

"So it would seem."

"Not fitting for ye to hear," Bea clucked at her side.

Hailyham smiled tiredly, laying his hand atop hers to reassure her. "London is commerce and royalist. Cromwell's time is running out, he should have gone to America."

"Why America?"

"In America Englishmen are building a nation on all of England's faults."

"What a quaint way to build a nation," Fanny said, glad to ease the Colonel by encouraging him to talk.

"Yes, there is to be no heroic devotion to a noble ideal in America, just common greed with each man pitting his strength against his neighbor to sate his vanity, no more."

"Can you build such a nation?"

"I suppose you could build any sort of unnatural edifice, but it could never last a good blow."

"I should think not."

"No, lass, Cromwell is dying."

"Dying? Cromwell dying?"

"Aye, his dream came true." Hailyham chuckled deep in his throat. "His dream was a nightmare."

"Scotland, dear Scotland," Fanny said, gathering her reins and cantering ahead to clear the City. "I want no other."

They rode through the final miles to Hampton Court, the escort turning north to Saffron Walden, where the army maintained its camp, and they soon galloped onto the cobblestones of the Elizabethan manor house. Fanny glanced about at the yawning wings, which seemed to embrace her. "But the King is gone," she said.

"My orders," Hailyham said, nodding to an officer in a red tunic who met them with a bustle of servants.

"I do not like its empty windows, rather much like dead eyes staring onto the stone courts."

"It was the King's residence."

"I do not want to stay here."

"Perhaps just for a little while."

" 'Tis cold—no, I will not stay." Bea was at her side as they stared about at the vast facades of lifeless glass and silent quadrangles.

"The Lord Protector . . ."

"Cromwell?"

"Aye, the Lord Protector has a bleak apartment at Westminster. He does not want you there. You cannot go to Dorset."

"And why not?"

"Because you are a prisoner."

"It is the royal palace," young Wilton said, as if to encourage Fanny.

"I do not want it." She put her head down and felt the tears spring up behind her eyes, of frustration and terror, and the realization she had to play the role. She sniffed her nose on a kerchief Bea handed her. "Very well, I will go." She handed her reins to the groom and reached her hands to the officer.

"Be brave, young one, the battle is never to the strong," Hailyham said as the women dismounted.

"I want my horse kept here."

"Aye, my lady, I shall personally see your mare to her proper bedding."

"I want to ride her every morning."

"Name the hour and your horse will be waiting." The officer smiled and lifted his stiff hat, showing a close-cropped head that his clean neck softened in its fresh grace. "I am Captain Harold Jenkins, Captain of the Court."

"Our wants will be small," Fanny said.

"Lady Fanny, your whim is our command," the Captain said.

Fanny looked at Hailyham and Teddy Wilton and George Seymour, who had not dismounted. Their eyes were mute as if they had conspired to jail her and now were guilty of it at its fruition. "Tell the Lord Protector the Highlands of Scotland are at peace, and I am here to secure the peace with my body." She pressed her hand between her breasts and walked through the portals of Hampton Court.

Their bedroom and apartment were hung in splendid tapestries from Flanders, though they ate off pewter, because Charles I, the King, had melted down all his sterling to pay his army. They were without obvious guards, though their servants, in serving them, were their guards, so they were never free. Bea's absolute faith in Scotland and its superiority enabled her to dismiss their natural ills of confinement as incidentals. But Fanny understood the gravity of any imprisonment, and was not deluded into dismissing English strength and caprice, or to believing faith without action would prevail.

"My finest, absolutely my most elegant gown," Fanny said to Bea when the officer with heavy mutton-chop whiskers on his jowls arrived from Westminster to escort them to the "Puritan Court."

"We are a Commonwealth," the officer said, resting his hand on his saber bell.

"Of course, whatever it is, I will come," Fanny said, smiling at the officer and forcing him to look away as she searched his face.

The ride from Hampton Court to Westminster was a fine gallop and Fanny enjoyed the pleasure of Forest Witch and the mare's clear speed over the troopers' mounts. When they arrived at the seat of traditional rule in England, of the Parliament and the halls of discourse and contemplation, Fanny was shown into an anteroom, and a Puritan with a thin, shrewd face said, "The Lord Protector will see my lady."

"The Lord Cromwell?" Fanny said.

"Oliver Cromwell, with no title," the man said. "There be no monarchy."

"My lord, I am honored," Fanny said, noticing the man's cold blue eyes glare fixedly at the small pink eye of flesh in the center of her bosom, revealed by an open bodice pinned atop the plunge of her breasts.

"The Lord Protector."

"The Lord Protector, my lord." Fanny curtsied lightly.

She was alone with Bea for perhaps an hour, scarce daring to believe she would see Oliver Cromwell, eating fitfully at a tray of unleavened biscuits which were brought them and setting and resetting her long hair, which she wore tied with a ribbon at the crown and loose down over her shoulders to her waist, in the Scottish fashion, while Bea fretted and pinned and patted every fold of her gown and hair.

"Use the commode," Bea said.

"I have, just a minute ago."

"I did not hear you."

"You helped me pull up my dress."

"So I did."

"Bea, they are just men," Fanny said, taking her nurse by her wrists.

"Too pure for men."

"Perhaps, but men nonetheless."

The doors swung in with a rap, and three officers in red tunics and two clergymen in black surcoats to their thighs smiled stiffly at Fanny. "The Lady Fanny of Skarra?"

"My lords." Fanny sank into a curtsey.

"Come girl, the Lord Protector wouldst see thee."

"Thou hast the grace of God about thee, my maid." One of the clergymen put out a pale hand to raise her up.

"Thank you, my lord." Fanny gestured to Bea. "My nurse, I would have my nurse with me."

"This woman, your nurse?" It was an officer.

"It is altogether seemly for the maid to have her nurse," said the other clergyman, touching his fingertips together and tilting his head backward to eye the officers.

"By the grace of God, a maiden alone in a strange land, with no mother nor cousin, should have her nurse."

The two clergymen seemed to confront the Roundhead officers with the eagerness of the Spiritual world to limit the Temporal.

Oliver Cromwell was sitting at his desk when they entered a modest room with thick wood paneling. The officers stopped at the door and Fanny walked slowly ahead, unsure of how the great man would look. The secretary, who was writing with a goose quill at a small desk, stood as she walked up. Cromwell did not look up. Fanny paused and heard the room fill with the rich sound of her voluminous dress when she settled into a deep curtsey before the desk. She bowed her head and kept her neck bent down until she heard a discordant sound of a boot striking a wooden panel.

"In the bowels of Christ, girl, do not bow!" It was a harsh Midlands accent.

She looked up and saw a full-lipped face with an unhealthy white pallor, swollen about the protruding eyes which stared in reproach at her. "Up, girl."

"Yes, my lord." She rose to stand before the man.

"Dost thou know me?"

"No, my lord, though they said you were the Lord Protector."

"Hast thou been well cared for?"

"Most adequately, my lord, but I do not like a king's palace."

"What wouldst thou have, girl?" Cromwell got to his feet.

"The country, my lord. Dorset."

"Take her out of that moldy pile." Cromwell spoke to his secretary, who flourished the quill feather.

"I long for my home, my lord."

"Thou canst not have thy home, girl." Cromwell gestured at a chair at the corner of his desk.

"Thank you, my lord," Fanny said. "Only if my lord would be at his ease." She walked around the desk, as if in a dream where the two principals played out a courtly pantomime, saying things they did not mean, except that each was sorry they had inconvenienced the other.

"Thank you, girl." Cromwell sat down heavily. "My blood is thick."

"I am sorry, my lord."

"They have to bleed me every morning."

Fanny shook her head and sat on the edge of her chair.

"Thou art beautiful." He looked at the long hair which fell in a happy mass about her torso.

"Thank you, sire."

"Thy father is loyal to Britain, didst thou know that?"

"Aye, my lord."

"Then why does he kill my men?"

"He does not kill them, my lord. They kill themselves by attacking Highlanders." Fanny stared into the bulging eyes and saw the yellow bile of a sick man. He seemed tired of power and wise enough to know his virtue had been corrupted by his triumphs. "My father has never attacked the English."

"But he is there when they are killed, girl!"

"If he were not there, far more English would be killed, my lord, for my father strives every day to curb the passions of the Highlands."

"So I hear. And the case of Lord John Bollingale?"

"An Englishman." Fanny spoke emphatically.

"Aye, but he has refuge in Scotland."

"I have never seen him, but the Scots keep him as an odd specimen of Englishman, my lord, to prove the English are cruel."

"Hmmm." Cromwell cocked his head and stared at Fanny. "In one so young, thou art brave and thou hast thy wits about thee."

"My lord, I have to be brave, because I am terrified."

"Thou speakest well. Go." He sat back in his chair. "But first, button thy bosom, for the flesh is the carnal trap that debauches the soul to eternal perdition." The spiked fingers thrust out at her breasts.

Fanny clutched together the small opening over her bosom.

"Send the girl to Dorset, and tell thy father when thou writest him that the Protector expects him to keep the peace."

"My lord." Fanny rose and curtsied and withdrew from the side of the Lord Protector of Britain.

Cranborn Hall came into sight as fragments of stone appearing among the full trees off the drive they rode upon. It was typical of England: the spiral yew trees, the rhododendron-lined paths, the fuchsia, the hawthorn, and the oak, and the quiet manor house of the gentry, who preserved an uncertain allegiance over the common folk through a passion for fair play, despite occasional barbarities and considerable selfishness. It was the country seat of the Seymours and the Selfridges, in an age when the nobles had given up their castles, because cannon fire could knock down their defenses, and had surrendered to elegant country homes in yielding to the central authority of the king who owned the cannons.

The setting sun reflected off the glass of its windows in a bright moment that bathed the park and trees with a warm light. Fanny watched the glinting rays hold their intensity, then slowly fade into the twilight.

"Did you live here, always?" Fanny said to George Seymour, who rode with her.

"Yes, I was born here."

"Your mother . . . ?" Fanny wanted to ask but was afraid to be personal, lest his mother were dead.

"Alive, thank God." He smiled.

"I am so glad." She hunched her shoulders in a quick movement of warmth.

"The Lady Skarra is not your mother, is she?" They rode side by side at the head of a small cavalcade of retainers and a single troop of cavalry.

"No."

"Who was your mother?"

"A friend of the lady who raised me."

"Do you know nothing?"

"Why do you ask?"

"Your blood, your heritage . . ."

"Swedish and Scottish, and you saw the icons of Mother Russia."

"But you must know something."

She looked at George Seymour and saw him clearly for an instant for what he was, a very small man who was beautifully handsome in the youth and vanity of a boy but who would later know the price of everything and the value of nothing. She smiled and shook back her long hair.

"George, when you have parents like the man and woman who brought us up as their children, you never doubt your blood nor your heritage nor your purpose as men and women. It never comes up."

"But you must remember something."

"I do."

"Your mother?"

"Yes. Very blond and very frail and very Swedish. . . ."

"But her parents?"

"The clergy, they told me, killed by religion, how else?"

"Blood will tell, they say." Seymour sounded reproachful.

"Aye, Master George." Fanny looked momentarily at him. "Mine is Scottish, and 'tis gospel that my father, Lord Skarra, has made this point clear to the English on several unpleasant occasions." She smiled disarmingly.

"If a gentleman is to marry . . ."

"The woman must love him, and I do not know you, let alone love you." She drove her heels into the flanks of Forest Witch and reined the mare into the manicured park of hedges and flowerbeds composing the frontal aspect of Cranborn Hall, and galloped on the wet sod.

Cranborn Hall was full of people who were eager to please Fanny, both because she was young and pretty and unmarried and because they enjoyed holding something beautiful in captivity, and hurting it in so doing—and also, they were hedging their bets with Cromwell and the Commonwealth, or the Monarchy, should it be restored. Her quarters were the finest, reserved for royal progresses in the days of the Monarchy, and in keeping with her role among the English as a hostage of the Commonwealth for the safety of the Highlands. In the suite of small sitting rooms and dining room and her large bedroom,

Fanny had refused the servants who were assigned her and demanded only Bea. "No, it is bad enough to be in exile from home, and captive as well. Surely I have paid dear enough and deserve my nurse, alone," Fanny insisted, and she stood her ground until the English yielded, as she knew they would. It would demean them in their own eyes if they crushed her, and she knew the game well, as a woman.

"Tea, and then we shall ride to the Channel."

"Not again," Bea said, setting her napkin and serviette at the small table beside her canopied bed.

"Or the moor, how would you like the moor, Bea?"

"I like that better, my lady," Bea said. " 'Tis closer and less marsh underfoot. I still ache from our last ride."

"Bea, you shall never love horses."

"No, ma'm, I shall not. Horses should love horses, and humans should love humans, 'tis why the Lord made all things in pairs."

"I should love to be a horse. So free to run." Fanny yawned and stretched contentedly with stiff arms and arching spine, then bowed her neck to stretch her back muscles.

"Ye will outgrow it, my lady. Once ye meet the right man."

"Oh!" Fanny collapsed from her stiff, arched pose. "The common people all talk alike."

"The common people talk about life."

"I know, but you can talk about it, whilst I cannot, because I am so afraid of it, for I have mine yet to live."

"The right man, and ye will na' fear."

"The right man, and I will fear, likely." Fanny laughed nervously to herself.

"Never ye fear, lass, ye will know him, and I will tell ye."

"Good Lord, Bea, it is I who has to make the choice."

"Aye, ye must make the choice. Yet, I know the man who will stand aside to let a woman flourish as her due and right, and the man who is too vain to see a woman, because I am older, 'tis the reason."

"Older, older, older . . ." Fanny picked up her teacup and breathed atop it, savoring the steaming bouquet that moistened her face.

"How else can a body see more, 'cept in being older, and what was oncet done 'twill be done yet again, if a body can see and remember."

"Breakfast, Bea, I want to ride. Oh, I adore Forest Witch." She closed her eyes and inhaled deeply, in a shuddering motion.

"Age is just remembering and seeing ahead."

"I see a galloping mare chased by a Highland beast across the Dorset moor."

"Ye're not too old to whip, no ye're not." Bea sat down across the table from Fanny and wiped the back of her wrist across her red nose, and Fanny hid her eyes, not daring to look at her angry nurse.

They made a dashing picture galloping over the broad, wind-whipped moors, Forest Witch snorting and throwing her head from side to side with the pretty blond girl astride her, and followed by the resolute gelding in his stiff gait, ridden by a woman who jolted in a sidesaddle. "On, on!" Fanny shouted, ajoy with the fresh air and the exultation of youth.

Behind them, following on the horizon, were the two cavalry troopers who kept them in sight but did not approach. Fanny knew she could outride them, but her purpose in Dorset was not escape.

She had come at least seven miles from Cranborn Hall and had passed three stone cottages and their small farms when she saw a lonely spectacle on the distant sweep of the moor. It was a rickety two-wheeled cart piled high with household furniture and the white disarray of bedding, and which seemed to be overrunning the horse that struggled in shafts before it.

"Over there!" Fanny shouted, gesturing at the slow-moving figure.

"Not so fast, my lady," Bea said in a voice lost under the sound of hoofbeats.

As she galloped up onto the cart Fanny saw the scattering of children about its wheels, the larger ones heaving back on ropes tied to the cart-box to help retard the weight of the vehicle, which towered over the gaunt horse as they descended a long hill to a valley.

"Halloo!" Fanny called, and saw a man at the head of the horse turn to look. The horse's hipbones stood out like fans and its ribs made its body seem like a hair-covered accordion, beyond which was a swayed sheep neck and hammer head.

"Halloo," Fanny said, cantering up, her eyes on the man, whom she saw was young, wind-burnt over his knuckles and ruddy face, and had much thick dark hair on his forearms, face, and curling out of his shirt at his chest.

"Halloo, to you," the young man said, his eyes on his uncertain horse and teetering cart. "Easy, girl, easy." He had his hands on the point of the shaft, his shoulder under it, guiding and tugging and bearing weight with the horse. "Guide, Timothy, guide her!"

"I am, Jonathan, I am." A half-grown boy peered around the head of the horse to look at Fanny.

"Guide her, she's falling! Up! Hold her!"

Fanny saw the tall cartwheel catch against a stone, twisting the cart momentarily as it rolled downhill and throwing the horse off-stride and toward a bank. There was a scraping sound as the mare went to her knees and the shafts dug furrows aslant across the roadbed, and buried their points into the soft bank, pinning the fallen mare and stopping the cart suddenly, which tumbled some of its contents down over the head of an old woman in the cart, whom Fanny had overlooked.

"Oh, I am sorry," Fanny said, reining up Forest Witch.

About the cart appeared the clean startled faces of a family of children, all in stairsteps of size, and judging by the blue eyes and broad forehead, brothers and sisters of the strapping young man who struggled at the shafts, and who now looked up at her but still lifted to ease his aged and fallen bay mare.

"Oh, I am sorry, so sorry," Fanny said as the picture came clear to her of a family alone on the moor with their household goods, and now stranded at twilight without shelter and with a broken-down horse.

The young man's biceps showed corded muscles. He spoke when he saw Fanny staring at his straining position, the jaded mare thrashing its forelegs at his feet. "She was a childhood pet."

"Let me help!" Fanny jumped down off Forest Witch and grabbed hold of the other shaft, joining the blond boy.

"The shafts are buried and the weight of the cart is too much to push. . . ."

"Bea!"

"We need men," Bea said, joining the people strung along each shaft, heaving unevenly backward while the mare seemed to realize the hopelessness of her predicament and stretched out her full length before them.

"We are trying to lift the horse as well as push the cart," Fanny said.

"She's tired," the young man said.

"Bea, call the Roundheads."

"Roundheads!?" The young man recoiled. "Who are you?"

"Lady Fanny of Skarra. Bea, get those soldiers."

"We want no soldiers."

"Who are you? And Bea, call those preening bloods, I'm getting tired." Fanny looked up and smiled at the young man. He had clean white teeth and full dark lips, and the hair was thick on his chest and it was wiry on his neck where he had clipped it close.

"I am Jonathan Hogarth and our estates were taken by Cromwell, sequestered, they call it. . . ."

"Roundheads, Jonathan," said the boy at her side as the cavalry troopers cantered up in a clatter of stones and deep voices.

"They are harmless, truly. I am their captive, but they belong to me."

Jonathan knitted his brows at her words.

"I am the prisoner of the English, their hostage to force my father to keep the peace of Scotland."

"In Dorset?" Jonathan said.

"Aye, 'tis a long way from Scotland."

"Their prisoner?" He looked at the two strapping soldiers, one a sergeant, tying their horses and turning toward the cart.

"Not really. Cromwell is tired and dying and he fears the Highland war my father refuses to fight. They are really our prisoners."

"I do not understand, my lady."

"No Englishman does." She shook back the hair from her face. "Sergeant, get the cart off the horse, if you please."

The two soldiers shoved in among the children, glancing at Hogarth. There was an eruption of a flailing figure out of the cart, and they were surprised to hear a china pot explode in their midst as it struck the helmet of the soldier.

"Shameful men! Go!" The old lady had come suddenly to life. "Roundheads!" She was screaming. The soldiers drew back.

"Never mind her, get the horse up!"

"But she is attacking us, my lady," the Sergeant said.

"But she is not hurting you. You have the armor. Get the horse up."

"Easy, Mum, they take their orders from the lady," Hogarth said.

"I would rather be dead."

"No, she would not," Fanny said, glancing up at Hogarth. "Or you would not be struggling across this lifeless moor."

"Father was lost at Marston Moor."

"Nobody is lost as long as their children will live," Fanny said.

The young man smiled quickly at her, the crinkles in the corners of his eyes as quick as his upturned lips.

"Put my nurse's horse in the shafts."

"My horse?"

"You can ride in the cart," Fanny said.

"Where are we going?" Hogarth said, searching her eyes.

"To Cranborn Hall."

"Never."

"That, or death."

"Very well." He exhaled and looked down tiredly.

"Your brothers and sisters must have shelter."

"We have been five weeks on the road."

"At least we have family in Scotland."

"To the common folk we were intellectuals; to the Puritans we were corrupted monarchists; to our friends we were a reminder of what might befall them; to the Royalists we were a symbol of what had failed and what they owed us, and to the intellectuals we were farmers and clergymen. We are alone." The young man stepped back from the shaft to let the soldiers heave.

"In Scotland our only problem is vanity and treachery, and—oh, yes—insanity. My father says it is everywhere, though, the insanity."

"We have been so hungry we have no beliefs."

"My father would say you are better off that way."

"You love your father." Hogarth spoke quietly, looking down at his hands as he rolled down his sleeves.

"I adore him."

"You have mentioned him several times."

"I think of him often."

"Not often that a girl can love her father so."

"If she does not love her father, how can she ever know to love a man?"

"I do not know."

"Nor I," Fanny said.

Fanny enjoyed the slow walk along the limestone road which ran through the low and endless green moors. It rained twice, forcing her to sit close to Jonathan, under the bow of canvas over them, when he offered her shelter. It made quite a troop of walking horses and young people as they made their way toward Cranborn Hall.

"You have considered our plight?" Jonathan said, holding the reins to Bea's Norfolk cob as though his forearms were a part of the bit and horse's mouth.

"Yes, you must eat today if you are to live to see a restoration."

"Aye, three meals a day are a true solace, but we would settle for one."

"I will think of something."

They drove the cart along the peaceful road, the single movement of life on the broad moors, except for a band of wild Exmoor ponies that cut from a copse of hawthorn and galloped out of sight to the west. Fanny was pleased to be with the young man and his obvious misfortune, for she felt an uncertain tremble in her bosom as she spoke with him; and yet she knew it had more to do with a man who would not abandon his younger brothers or sisters and widowed mother than it had to do with his strong figure, but it was on his body and skin and limbs that her mind turned for pure joy. She had even forgotten his mother's name, the old lady who perched atop the cart in a nest of rags and glowered at the Roundhead troopers.

About the cart walked the five younger children, three girls and two boys, whose bright faces smiled up at them occasionally. Bea also walked, because, she said, the cart had no springs and unsettled her bile.

"Jonathan, she is pretty. Lord, she is pretty," the boy called Tim said several times. Fanny realized the children sensed help in her arrival, and in another person of their generation, on their own side in the nightmare of civil war, and so were openly drawn to her and did not hide their admiration.

"Sergeant," Fanny said to the soldier, "I shall walk, and Mister Hogarth will accompany me."

When they got down from the cart, she was able to walk alone with Jonathan through the moors while the cart followed the road, and they had their privacy to talk.

"That was clever of you," Jonathan said.

"Lord, with Bea and those soldiers, how could a body have any privacy?"

"Aye. I noticed they did what you said."

"I have no power, so I have all the authority a woman needs."

"I have never understood women."

"Nor I men, until I studied my father."

"Really? I mean study your father."

"Oh, yes." She caught the glance of dismay in Jonathan's eye, for he had seen she did love her father and felt as though he had invaded their sanctimony.

"Oh, I did not mean to pry."

"No, you did not. I owe my father a great debt."

"A debt?"

"Why, yes. I told you. I know what a man is from my father. And I have to have a man, and I shall know if that man will do when I measure him beside my father."

Jonathan looked away, then down at the wrapped toes of his tattered boots, feeling them sink in the turf of the damp moor at each step, and knowing the girl was measuring him against an unseen talent, and it made him very self-conscious, just at the time he was growing fond of the exquisite blond girl.

"Tell me about your own father," Fanny said, speaking softly. "He must have been a great man if you will take up his burden and go forward."

"I loved him." He did not look at Fanny.

"Tell me about him."

"He was full of illusions."

"My mother says all men are."

"Jonathan Hogarth, I was named for him. He was a farmer and a teacher and scholar and we supported the King." He stopped talking.

"There must be more."

"There is. It hurts to talk about your parents if you love them."

"You loved him." She spoke again.

Jonathan smiled. "Oh, indeed. He was a big man and he liked to sing. He sang all the time, in the house, in the garden working in the spring, and he liked to turn the earth with a fork, not a plough—he said he got to see the roots and the worms where all life started, he said." Jonathan breathed and laughed a deep chuckle and smiled at Fanny. "He hated the factories, because they shut off the people from the earth where he said they belonged, and he loved the rain, to have it run down his hair and over his face—why, his hair was thicker than feathers on a duck's belly, and oily, and he never caught cold in the rain and the winter."

"Like your hair?" Fanny said, looking at the rich crop of abundant hair falling to the top of Jonathan's shoulders.

"Yes, like mine." He breathed and went on. "Oh, he could do anything. He would invent furniture and then make it in his workshop behind the vicarage. . . ."

"Was he a clergyman?"

"Aye, if you are not the nobles, nor the gentry, nor the army, and still a part of them, then you are either a schoolmaster or a clergyman. . . ."

"Which happens to be the same thing," Fanny said to encourage him.

"And it got dangerous." He nodded his head. "Teaching is the deadly profession. Nobody is neutral."

"My father was a university don until he inherited the title."

"That was one advantage we had. No title, but we did inherit a farm, Ironwood Place, from a great-aunt, where the finest wool in Sussex grew—that, and my father's teaching, did us in."

"How was it so?"

"Simple. Father said man could not worship God and Mammon, and he preached his sermons like Old Testament proclamations. Mammon was the factories and money and the new power of commerce, and here we had that nice farm and the wrong politics." He paused.

Fanny shook her head slowly.

"It was simple. Father was branded a traitor to the new government and they sequestered our farm, and when Father resisted with a musket, they shot him."

Fanny nodded.

"I do not think the Commonwealth or Cromwell, or whatever it is gives a damn about God. It is a matter of land and wealth, and the vanity of power. And that is what it is all about. Owning our farm really ruined us."

Fanny nodded and looked into the faded sky, where the distant slate roofs of Cranborn Hall were coming into sight.

"What was your life like?" he said after they had walked in silence.

"Oh, the usual. Brothers and sisters and parents."

"Was it happy?"

"Oh, yes. Deliciously so."

"What was it like?"

"I do not know, except that we were a happy family. My mother and father were in love and they are virtuous people, and I grew up on the Highland moors in the midst of cousins without number and a family who loved me. I would not know how to be unhappy." She looked into the blue eyes, which seemed dark in their penetration of her.

"You are very beautiful," he said.

"Were you happy?" she said gravely.

"You saw me with my family."

"Yes. You are happy."

"Where else is there happiness except in love and with your family?" he said.

"I do not know," Fanny said. "It is all that I have ever known."

"That is all you need, girl."

She smiled at him, and in a moment she heard them both laugh spontaneously, their voices fresh in the glazing sunset which was settling across the moor, and in the distance, sheening on the wet tile roofs of Cranborn Hall.

12

Cranborn Hall and the Seymour family began to feel the full effect of unwanted guests the day Fanny came in off the moor with the Hogarth family and insisted they be sheltered in the stable. That night she had taken her supper with them and had joined them in evening family singing. She was pleased to know they sang only one hymn. She was too much like her father to enjoy any excess of zeal for anything except life. Two days later Fanny had used the Roundhead guards in a clever ploy to cajole the gamekeeper out of the hunting lodge called Claygate, situated two miles away on the verge of Pearson's Woods. She had the Hogarths settled in and spread out before the Dowager Marchioness of Dorset, the Lady Rebecca Seymour, knew about it.

It caused the first open breach with Fanny's hosts, and she sensed that old Becky Seymour's ire was raised mainly by the handsome Jonathan Hogarth, whom, as a woman, she saw Fanny attracted to, instead of her grandson, George Seymour. Of course Fanny had ridden out on Forest Witch and ordered the Sergeant to tell the gamekeeper that Claygate Lodge, since it was vacant, was now to house guests. And the Hogarth children had swarmed in, delighted at the single vast beamed room and the huge fireplace and warm oven for heating and baking. And Fanny had spent an enchanting afternoon in her bare arms, baking Scotch bread and starting a mutton stew, again using the two soldiers to steal and butcher the sheep, and, of course, feeding everybody until they groaned with contentment. Fanny knew it was a complete success when Mother Hogarth sat down at the table to eat with the two Puritan soldiers, saying, "One must not judge, even the mistakes of the Lord." She glared at the cowed troopers, who were ill at ease at their end of the boards, until Fanny personally served them and told them they would offend her if they did not eat, for she had fixed it with her own hands, upon which they dived into their pewter plates and ate like hungry men, with bare fingers and sweating foreheads.

"What a perfect afternoon," Fanny said, sitting beside Jonathan at the table. "We have food and shelter."

"Aye, 'tis cheerful."

"And there is a grand well, and tubs to do the washing, and straw and ticking for dry pallets for all." She threw out her arms expansively.

"Fanny, you have done too much."

"I could not have done less, not when friends are hungry and vagrant."

"Yes, but I do worry."

"Worry? Why worry?"

"We are not the ascendancy. In short, we lost."

"No, one woman is a majority—at least I hope so." She laughed, and heard a giddy note of fright strike through her voice, causing Bea to look at her and Jonathan to frown.

"My lady, I think we play a dangerous game," he said.

"But I have no choice." Fanny touched her bosom with her hand.

As the weeks went by, Fanny spent as much time as possible riding out to Claygate Lodge. She had seemed to find in the Hogarth family a substitute for her own family at Skarra, and her lively presence sparked their days with joy. They all shared the common gravity of a mutual enemy and their survival of its assault. Bea joined her in throwing herself into the ordinary duties of housekeeping, mending, and cooking food brought from Cranborn, which gave them both a deep satisfaction and which inspired the three younger sisters, Emma, Catherine, and Beth, to join them in the youthful exuberance of knowing a female slightly older than themselves, whom they might love and emulate, especially since they had undergone the total wreck and dispossession of all they had known, save their lives.

Though Fanny was filled with the delight of these tasks, the thought of Jonathan Hogarth—his deep voice, assured laughter, and the rich thick hair on his arms and his heavy beard—made her dizzy when he was near her, and he worked at Claygate Lodge like a sweating laborer, to put things right for them. He even had the Roundhead troopers down off their horses and working at his side, out of their armor and eager to join a university graduate who liked hard manual work. "We's soldiered 'nough for the Protector. 'Tis time we worked our trades oncet more." Cranborn Hall was forgotten when Fanny was at Claygate Lodge.

However, at evening Fanny and Bea would ride back to Cranborn, followed by the Puritan soldiers, who had taken to not donning their cuirasses and breastplates and steel helmets, but rather tying them to the backs of their saddles. In this fashion the four of them would come galloping in from the moor at dusk, the swords clanking against the empty armor and making a great din in the stableyard at Cranborn.

George Seymour had been on duty with his regiment, north of London, when he appeared one evening in the courtyard. He was accompanied by his father, Henry Seymour, who had just returned from Scotland.

"My lord," Fanny said, handing her reins to a groom and turning to the elder Seymour, "what news of my family?"

"Fine, all flourishing in the mists, and all have written."

"Letters?"

"A royal pouchful, and waiting on your bed."

"Oh, thank you!"

"And dinner this evening?"

"Yes, my lord."

"You will sit at my right side." The middle-aged man smiled warmly at her, and Fanny saw through him in an instant, and felt a pang of warmth in her heart for his open love of simple grace.

"You honor me, my lord."

"No, Lady Fanny. 'Tis you who shame us with your courage and honor us with your guileless being." He patted the back of her hand while his son watched and smiled uncertainly.

It was a gala dinner party in honor of Henry Seymour's return. Fanny was at his right; his mother, Becky Seymour, was across the long table from him; and at his left was seated his wife, Leslie Seymour, a slight woman who seldom looked up, having been cowed by her mother-in-law. Beyond Fanny to her right sat a tall man dressed in black, with a gaunt body but muscular shoulders, who had been introduced as "our resident conscience, the Puritan Reverend Miles Proctor." Fanny had smiled in brief recognition, but had supposed he might be better suited to working at some trade rather than the clergy, for there was a stolid air of achievement, not contemplation, about him.

The dinner was an exquisite success of French cuisine, with Portuguese wine and Moorish coffee. It lacked something to Fanny, however; then she realized it was the warm steaming gusto of Scottish appetites and the naked sheep's belly stuffed with stew, the haggis.

Something else was missing as well, and it took Fanny most of the dinner to realize only she and Henry Seymour seemed to be enjoying themselves. George was to his mother's left, and he smiled self-consciously every time their eyes met, though she saw him brighten once when the Puritan clergyman caught his eye with some signal. Otherwise, George was so ill at ease with her that he was unable to put his eyes upon her neck, or bare shoulders, or bosom without flushing and looking down at his plate. Fanny put it out of mind as a result of his having had no close family life with brothers and sisters, and so his feelings for a woman were foreign to him.

"How is the army?" Fanny said to encourage him.

"Marvelous fun."

"If I were a man I would love to be a soldier, but only in peace." She smiled at George.

"War is the test of manhood," George said.

"We must not talk about unpleasantries," the Dowager Marchioness said.

"Yes, Mother," Henry said, nodding down the table.

"My father would disagree," Fanny said.

There was a visible silence around the table, and Fanny caught a shared look of a secret passing among the eyes of her hosts at the mention of her father. It stunned her momentarily, for her letters in the handwriting of both her mother and her father, sealed with the rampant phoenix of Skarra, told her all was well, and thrilled her to touch, to see, to smell, and she had even licked the ink on both her mother's and father's letters, to reassure herself by taste of their being and love. The silence about the table arrested her. She knew her parents were too cautious to ever write of misfortune—where their enemies might take advantage of them. And in a second her warmth for the pathos of Henry Seymour changed to a guarded approach to sound him out. "But, of course, Lord Dorset understands my father better than a woman."

"Oh, I would not know," Seymour said, his voice easing.

"You knew him in London."

"Aye, but it is hard to ever know a man, thoroughly."

"How is that, my lord?"

"Oh, you never know what he will do."

"My father always does the same thing."

"Eh?"

"Loves peace," Fanny said blandly.

"A man of hypocrisy, I dare say." The stentorian voice of Miles Proctor rolled down the bright table at them, even arresting the step of the liveried servants behind each chair.

Fanny looked uneasily into the two fierce eyes which seemed to merge into a single glare of conviction, dominating the white angular face.

"My lord . . ."

"I be no nobleman, good woman," Proctor cut her off.

"He is the disseminator of news and instructions from the Commonwealth and our Lord Protector," Henry Seymour said, speaking affably. "And the enemy of iniquity."

"Good man, you must be busy," Fanny said.

"Aye, sin is everywhere."

"The sin keeps him happy," Lady Leslie said without looking up.

"To serve the Lord through the state is a rare honor," said Proctor.

"I should never dare to know what the Lord wanted," Fanny said.

"The flesh is weak."

"And the flesh is exciting, eh, Brother Proctor?" Henry Seymour said, obviously unafraid of the Puritan clergyman assigned to Cranborn Hall to watch over the morals of the nobility as well as to spy.

"The flesh is corrupt," Proctor said, seeming to shrink away from the mention of carnal lusts.

"Come, come, Puritan. No flesh, no temptation, and no salvation. Blessed be the name of the flesh." Seymour smiled tolerantly about the table, pleased with his remarks. Only Fanny smiled, delighted in a champion, for she had an intuitive glimpse that Miles Proctor hated women, and she feared him.

"Your father destroyed an English regiment on the Don. . . ." Proctor spoke sullenly.

"He did no such thing!" Fanny said. She looked to Henry Seymour.

"Aye," Seymour nodded sadly. "The regiment attacked him in a woods, at the orders of Archibald Campbell, the Earl of Argyll."

"All Scotland knows Campbell is a traitor."

"Aye, that is what every Scot says about his neighbor," the Englishman said.

"So my father did not destroy an English regiment. It destroyed itself. I know my father loves peace."

"But the regiment was decimated!" George said.

"I think you must understand," Seymour said to his son, "that Lady Fanny sees the destruction of an English regiment in Scotland as a natural phenomenon, whereas we in England find such an event a public outrage. It is a matter of personal view. . . ."

"Henry, you sound like a fool," Becky Seymour said, her blue eyes glittering from the thick paste of French powder on her face. "The girl is a traitor, and you have been fawning over her all evening, whilst Cromwell's agents are everywhere."

"Oh, Mother, the Protectorate is tired and sick."

"An old dog bites meaner."

"England is tired of salvation, Mother."

"Let us not burden our guests with vexatious talk," Leslie Seymour said, her black-blue eyes searching across the table. "Fanny is not here at her will, and England wants her lawful king, and we at Cranborn must do our duty as bidden and mind our manners as hosts to whatever fortune brings."

Fanny was still for a moment, looking into the eyes of the woman with whose husband she had flirted throughout the dinner, and she saw the woman understood and forgave her. "Thank you, ma'am," Fanny said, and felt herself blush with being discovered.

Leslie put her hand across the table, setting it atop Fanny's. "I am sure your family loves peace as much as our family."

"Thank you, my lady. May I be excused?"

"Yes, child, of course."

Fanny rose suddenly, and pushed back her chair and faced the Englishwoman and curtsied before her, without showing her face, and turned and walked quickly from the dinner party.

The days came and went, spring giving way to the rich warmth of an English summer. The hawthorn thickets and the nightingale which sang its notes of lamenting joy were a thrill to Fanny when she swung open her leaded casement windows overlooking the garden. There was an especial rustic self-containment in the countryside of England, much like Scotland, and in the free and random growth of trees and singing birds was a constant buoyance to her in her captivity.

After she had leaned against the sill, drinking of the wet dawn air and feeling its exultant taste throughout her body, Bea would join her, tucking the eiderdown puff about her body so she did not chill, and gently remind her, "We will be for Scotland, bye and bye."

"Bye and bye, for Scotland, yes." Yet she would not leave the window. "The same air I breathe is breathed in Scotland and in Claygate, by Jonathan. Oh, Bea, I want to breathe what my loved ones breathe."

"Someday, yes, but not now."

"I think I love him, Bea."

"He has a family to support, and has no prospects."

"He is educated and he likes to work."

"I am not faulting him. Time for tea." The tea was an addiction

Fanny had succumbed to after she had left Scotland, as though it were one way she could keep in touch with her mother, by being like her. The tea steamed before her face, and she was startled to see it waft away from the paneled oak wall of her bedchamber toward the open window.

"Bea, look at the steam."

Bea was helping pour the large kettles of hot water into the wooden tub serving girls had brought for Fanny's bath.

" 'Tis from your bath, my lady," said one of the girls.

"Hot, just as you like it," Bea said, thrusting her bare wrist into the tub of water, which was steaming heavily in the chill air of the bedchamber. "Come." She raised her hands to slip off the nightclothes as Fanny walked up, still swaddled in the puff.

"Look at the steam," Fanny said, letting go the puff and feeling Bea strip her body naked in a deft shucking motion that left her tingling with surprise, even though Bea had done this a thousand times before. "The steam is going the wrong way."

"Steam always goes up off water," Bea said, dipping the sponge ahead of the girl's bare knee and thigh, as if enticing a child into its bath.

" 'Tis the chill," said a maidservant, holding a towel and watching.

"No, neither of you understand," Fanny said, stepping into the tub and involuntarily raising her hands to reassure herself her hair had been pinned up, well off her neck. She felt the steam and hot water envelop her naked body in warmth as Bea sponged the length of her torso and legs in long vertical sweeps and a maid handed her a heavy sponge to wash her face and bosom. It was a delight to be lost in the wet heat of her bath.

"It takes no time to bathe," Bea said as she completed the toilette, the water and sponges and scented French soap having swept over and through the secret and bare places of her body. "Now rub."

Fanny took the towel and wrapped her head and wiped her face as she stepped out of the tub, feeling Bea's rough hands go vigorously over her body once more to dry her.

Fanny watched idly as the girls carried the tub from the bedchamber, and saw the steam blow away from the wall, toward the open window, as though a secret vent were open. She felt herself crinkle in goose flesh in the same instant she realized somebody was watching her bathe, spying on her in her privacy. "The steam," she said to Bea. "Oh, wrap me!"

"Of course, lass."

"Now." She clutched a towel to her breasts. "Somebody is spying on me."

Bea's face shifted from its bland unconfused servant assurance to a look of whitish dismay, with the eyes going a hard blue with a streak of fire showing somewhere deep, as the anger upset the ordinary good nature. "Wrap yourself, my lady." The eiderdown puff was about her once more.

Fanny shook her head, and took her teacup once more, and noticed the steam was rising with the air currents off the open window. "They have gone," she said, nodding at the wall.

Bea turned to the wall, her nose and eyes sweeping the paneling, her hands feeling it like a spaniel quartering open brush, seeking the spy-port. Fanny watched from her bath rug, and was pleased to see Bea was able to understand the devilish annoyance of being peeped upon in their intimate privacy.

"I canna find it, lass," Bea said.

"Use a candle. The flame will waver."

Bea had a candle lit and was moving it slowly across the front of the woodwork. Their four eyes followed it as though transfixed, knowing that behind the wall was a passage. Fanny was not alarmed for her safety, for she had carefully avoided knowing any state secrets, and her parents were too wise to confide any secrets to her, to spare her.

Fanny felt a great annoyance as she waited. It was not just that somebody had watched her in her private moments, had seen her body, which she realized was exactly like every other woman's body; it was the demeaning of her purpose as a woman and human being. To spy on her as a woman denied her right as a woman to give away her privacy willingly, in passion, and further, it was a dismissal of the mystique that sustained her identity as a woman, the feminine elixir of her self-respect that brings the man and the marriage and the family to fruition. It was a denigration of life, to spy. And Fanny did not like it.

"I have found it, my lady," Bea said, gesturing to her to come forward.

"Do not break it," Fanny said, seeing the strong Highland fingers wedging open the small hinged slot in the woodwork, which had been discovered by the wavering candle flame. "Surely there is a door which can be sprung open from within the room, for escape purposes."

"Aye, there should be."

"We will wait until my next bath, then we will spring open the door and flush the culprit."

The Highland woman's face darkened. "You would face the wicked?"

"Lord, yes."

"Aye, the good book says to speak your anger." Bea sounded pensive.

"I was thinking more as a woman."

It took Bea just over three hours of feeling the paneled wall, ridge and denticle piece by piece, before the trigger board dropped back and a large section of paneling swung away. Behind it was a passage with a stairway going both up and down and filled with a dank odor. They agreed that they would tell nobody, not even Jonathan, for he already had enough vexations, and would spring the surprise alone.

At her next bath Fanny could scarcely concentrate on her morning tea while she waited for the maids to fill the tub. She kept her eyes on the steam rising in billowing sweeps off the water, and watched it drift away from the wall.

"Your bath, my lady," Bea said in a grave voice.

"The morning is beautiful." Fanny walked up and raised her arms over her head so her nurse could shed her nightgown from her body. "I do adore the dawn." She felt the clothes sweep off her flesh and bare her to the chill, and she stepped into the tub.

"I like it not, my lady," Bea said, grimly avoiding Fanny's eyes.

Fanny raised her arms and placed her hands behind her neck, and closed her eyes and turned back her head and let Bea slosh the wet sponges over her flesh, facing the spy-loop.

"I think now." She spoke above a whisper.

"As you will, my lady," Bea said, sloughing aside so Fanny could pass.

Fanny stepped quickly from the tub and ran naked across the bedchamber to the paneled oak wall and tripped the false slot. She stepped aside and stood before the wide oak panel which seemed to disassociate itself from the wall and swing outward in a ponderous motion.

"For shame," Bea said.

The two men were dumbfounded as they faced the roomful of women and the naked girl, still dripping from her bath.

"George," Fanny said, seeing George Seymour turning red as a flushing vegetable and as limp, his mouth slack and his eyes appalled. A glance at George was enough to dismiss him. The man in black was different. He was a full man, and not pretty. He looked cadaverous and was thin.

"Who be ye?" Bea shouldered in to her side.

"Oh, my Lord, the Puritan Miles Proctor!" One of the maidservants shouted and ran from the bedchamber. "It's the Reverend Proctor!"

"The Puritan watchman!"

"The Midlands stranger and Lord George!"

Around Fanny the women spoke. The man was dressed in black with a touch of white about his throat and a double white starched bib.

"You, in my room?" Fanny said.

"You are naked." The man spoke, his eyes glittering to life as they swept over Fanny.

"I am in my bedchamber at my bath."

"You are naked, brazen hussy."

"You are in my chamber among my women." Fanny stared into the glittering blue eyes sunk deep on each side of the high thin nose, and felt a great outrage rise, at the insolence of his trespass upon her right of privacy as a woman.

"Your flesh . . ."

"How dare you!" Fanny swung her open palm with a fury of passionate anger and felt the ecstasy of fire burn her open hand, "Slappt!" She saw the finger marks, lying parallel up the jaw and along the cheek, rise white as welts then swell in red grooves. The eyes seemed to sink and then rise outward as the sparse hair fell out of place.

"My God, she has slapped the Lord Protector's man! God save us!"

The serving women were screaming, dropping their towels, and running for the door.

"Jezebel, you have bewitched me with your vile flesh."

"You beast!" Fanny turned from the man who had stood his ground, refusing to be cowed or to apologize. "Lord Henry! I want the Earl of Dorset!" Fanny ran through the apartment, and out into the hall. "Lady Becky! Where is the Marchioness of Dorset?"

She ran the length of the hall and skittered down the broad stairs of Cranborn Hall, shouting every step of the way. The man had frightened her.

"Fanny, put this on you!" It was Bea tearing along behind her, the eiderdown puff in her hands, and passing the household staff who had commenced to appear out of the rooms, to stare in disbelief at the sight and cries which now could be heard throughout the mansion. "She slapped Cromwell's preacher!" "We are done for!"

There was a frantic rush in Fanny's lungs, of the panic she felt at confronting a man who would pervert morality to invade her bath and bedroom. She was screaming for Henry Seymour and the dowager mother and Lady Leslie when she was surprised to find herself in the main hall, surrounded with the family and the household. "Fanny, what is it?" The Earl had her by her arm, holding her.

"Get her some port," Becky Seymour said.

"Bailiff, what is it about?" Seymour said.

" 'Tis the Reverend Proctor," a woman said.

"Clothe her and give her port."

"Fanny, you are naked," Seymour said, reaching over her shoulders and drawing the heavy puff around her body.

"A man, and he's dressed all in black and he is in my room!" She gulped the port. "More, please! Oh, dear God, I slapped him."

"You slapped him? The Puritan?" Henry Seymour's face was swept in waves of alternating pleasure and dismay. "You slapped him, Fanny?"

"Almos' tuk his 'ead off, she did," a heavy woman said.

"I told you she was trouble," Becky said to her son.

"He had no shame," Fanny said.

"He was no man," Bea said.

The hubbub quieted in a few moments, as individual comments were exchanged between family members and their servants, everybody unburdening themselves without regard to rank or polite words.

"Obviously, I must have a talk with Mister Proctor," Seymour said, commanding the quiet.

"Ye won't 'ave long ter wait, me lord," said an elderly bald-headed man dressed in pantry livery. "Yon comes our Puritan friend."

Miles Proctor was a stoic product of the English reformation, contemptuous of human venality and weakness, as well as kindness, in all civilizations following that of Solomon's. His deity was on his side, and he was oblivious to other men, as he did his duty to his truth, and he approached the group in the flagged hallway with a measured tread, his hat on, absolutely sure he was the keeper of the sole key to salvation.

"What is this nonsense you are about?" Seymour said as he walked up.

"A wanton . . ."

"No more of that talk!" Seymour's voice was sharp, and he was aware his mother would rather sacrifice the girl than risk their estates to confiscation by the Commonwealth, but he was clever enough to know Cromwell was dying and could not afford incurring more ill-will.

"She stripped her body naked."

"But I was bathing!" Fanny said, incredulity hot on her words. "How else was I to bathe?"

" 'E peeps, me lord," said the buxom woman with char-worn knuckles.

"Take your hat off in this company," Seymour said to Proctor.

"We take off our hats only for the Lord, not for men."

"I'll not tolerate confusing bad manners with God. Take your hat off!"

"Only before God."

"Off, you bastard!" Seymour knocked the tall conical black hat with the wide brim from the lean head.

" 'E peeps at women, me lord," said the buxom washerwoman in a monotonous voice.

"Proctor, back to your quarters in the garden," Seymour said. "And where is George?"

"George is your fault," Leslie said.

"He will outgrow it," the grandmother said.

" 'Tis about time, but she is pretty."

"What about *him?*" Fanny gestured at the clergyman.

"I am charged with instructing the errant in ways spiritual and political." Proctor seemed unruffled, as though he were unable to experience or comprehend the subtlest human feelings, that fragile bond by which men and women sustain each other. There was an assured intellectual purpose to him, of no depth but much appearance, even in the movement of his large hands. "The enemies of the people must be rooted out. . . ."

"Go!" Seymour gestured toward the open front door where the two Roundhead cavalrymen were standing, looking confused. "By God's teeth, England has had her surfeit of instructing sinners."

"You should go to America," said Leslie Seymour.

"Go!"

The tall Puritan clergyman stared calmly at them, then nodded slightly, stooped and picked up his hat and departed for his small cottage on the grounds.

" 'E peeps, me lord."

"For God's sake, shut her up before I lose my mind!" the nobleman shouted.

"Please return to the second floor," Leslie said.

"Thank 'e mum, but 'e peeps."

"Yes, Belinda, we know he peeps."

Fanny was not sure what time of night it was or how long Bea had been out of their apartment, having received a message from the kitchen, but she had bolted the door herself, and Henry Seymour had personally seen the carpenters close the passage with heavy timbers. Yet the cloying fear persisted that she was not alone in her darkened bedchamber. "Bea?" she said, rising on one elbow to look into the dark, then toward the casement window. She thought it was shut, but she did not remember bolting it. "The cool air, yes, the window." She spoke to herself and half rose, reaching for a wrap to either go out into the hall or assure herself the window was truly bolted. "Oh, what a frightened ninny," she said, knowing she was safe, and dropped back and closed her eyes.

She felt her hair drawn across the pillow and she knew a strange hand was at her face, yet she knew she should not scream. "Yes?" she said, trying to rise and feeling her hair hold her head in a vise locked into the pillow.

"Who is it, prithee speak?"

The hand was at her breasts and in a blinding fear she heard her nightgown torn from her bosom to her knees, and snapped from beneath her shoulders and buttocks, making her suddenly naked atop the open bed, shocking her with her nude vulnerability that had been so comfortably snug under covers but a second before.

"Please, sire," she said raising her hands and opening her eyes, finally forcing herself to look at the ultimate nightmare. Her hands rushed over the hard lean body of a strong man, whose black clothes concealed his form but whose face gleamed white behind his panting breath. The eyes, the cold white eyes of hard passion flamed in silence. "Reverend Proctor, please." She felt herself flung down into the bed by a hand of fingers which fumbled like oak pegs across her breasts and her nipples.

"Please, you are hurting me," Fanny said, not wanting to threaten to scream, for in that very act, of screaming, she would admit her panic to her assailant and perhaps trigger even greater violence, and she would be finally accepting the psychic imbalance of rape and lose any chance she had to reason the man to his senses.

"Wanton!" Proctor's voice croaked in a thick passion.

"I beg of you."

His fist balled her hair about his hand and buried itself into the feather tick, pinning her head by her hair into the bed, and she felt a pillow over her face. "If ye cry, I will smother ye!"

Fanny tried to kick her body sideways across the bed, and knew for the first time Proctor had stripped his body naked as he held her. She felt his iron-muscled knee, of bare flesh and rough-bristled hair, thrust between her knees, holding her, and driven upward to spread her thighs, jamming hard against her soft crotch. "Please!" she cried, and she screamed, screaming a long agonizing passion of hopeless frustration and terror as she heard her voice spent in the muffle of a million feathers, and unable to breathe again as he pressed her, she knew it was her life or rape. Her lungs exploded against her ribs in agonies of empty spasms as he smothered her. She yielded.

"Wanton, seductress!" The voice came in from a great distance, as she felt her knees rise and her legs spread, and her private parts upraised and easy prey. The pillow lifted, and her lungs fought for air.

"Strike thy keeper, wouldst thee?"

She felt the cold stiff appendage at his loins plunge at her life place, the dry foreign stick blind in its insane lunging, first into the fold of her buttock, then into her thigh, then upthrust through the hair, then too low, into her vent which she felt cringe taut, and suddenly she felt a sense of power. He could not get the penis into her, in the dark, in the passion, in the confusion, at least for just the moment. She still would fight.

"Bastard!" she shouted, digging her fingernails into his eyes and down his cheeks, feeling the grooves of flesh peel clear of his face.

"Wham!" Her face exploded in lights as he hit her with his fist, but he had lost the compulsion of his rhythm in his hips, and her vitals were spared.

"Bea!" she screamed.

"Wham!" The blows landed into her temples and into her skull, stunning her with their concussions. But since she was so much smaller than Proctor, the fists missed her face.

"Lady Frances?" the hoarse voice asked uncertainly in a moment of stillness.

"You bastard!" She came back to life, and raked again with her fingernails, digging bloody streaks over his shoulders and lean flanks.

"Wanton!" He crammed his hot iron-dry body against her with renewed vigor, and Fanny knew she had lost a momentary psychic advantage by hurting him once more. The ecstasy brought him back to life and the attack. She felt his breath change from a dry pant to a gulping musky stench, as though the act of savage passion had stirred up and broken loose a lifetime of stagnant, festering lusts, locked deep in Proctor's body.

"Wanton!"

She spat into the cold dry skin, into the eyes and across the white, leathered lips and nose, spitting again and again, covering the gulping hole, the mouth and putrid tongue, that fouled her hair and face and pillow.

"Filth!" she said, sitting upright to face the gaunt naked specter who had sat back to stare at her in horror.

"You do not like me, Lady Frances?"

"My God, what a question!" She sat upright and reached for a taper. In a moment she had a candle lit and was facing the Puritan, who still sat on the edge of the vast bed, seemingly stunned. His gaunt white body and slack muscles stretched long on his big frame gave him a look of ridiculous sorrow as much as corruption, like a forlorn seabird standing in the surf with a broken wing trailing in the white scud.

"You do not like me," the voice said.

"Rape me, and I should like you?"

"You are a woman. . . ."

"You fool, you mock me."

"Nay, my lady. You are a wanton hussy. . . ."

"Who told you that?" She saw the baffled look of a man who has lost his way at the precipice of a great inner awareness.

"You are so pretty you must be evil."

"If I were dowdy, I would be pure?"

"Yes, perhaps that would be so."

"My God, have you ever seen a whore—a bundle of gawdy colors and stink atop a pathetic woman on fallen arches?"

"I have never seen a whore."

"Then go look at a whore and forgive her, now get dressed and get out." She could hear Bea pounding on her door.

She held the candle, lighting the way for the addled, middle-aged virgin to dress, fearless in her strength over him. She saw him to the window and walked naked to the door, throwing back the bolt. "Bea, he tried to rape me." She wept convulsively in her nurse's arms.

In the morning it was the place of Cranborn Hall to send the Reverend Miles Proctor packing to Westminster. Henry Seymour was glad to use the escapade in Fanny's quarters as a pretext of supreme indignation to rid his household of a Commonwealth spy.

Seymour and the ladies assured themselves that Fanny had not been "damaged," and were abashed when Fanny said, "No, when I could breathe I could squirm and he could not get it in."

To herself Fanny was more than a graceful body with pleasant curves of flesh, and she saw herself as something much more than her skin and flesh and hair. She was a woman first, and deep in her soul she wanted to be what her mother was, although she, as yet, was unfulfilled. In this light, an attempted rape upon her was certainly to be avoided and fought off; still, it was a small thing, even—ugly as it was—a natural thing for any woman to face, but nothing compared to the courage demanded of a woman in daily living.

When she galloped across the summer fields of Cranborn, her heart sang in her throat at the sight of Claygate Lodge and the happy Hogarth band. She dropped into Jonathan's arms.

"We want to be alone," Fanny said, dismissing the Roundhead soldiers, who had by now become so intimately involved in the lives of the Hogarths and the Seymour family and its servants that they withdrew to the dovecote they were building at Claygate.

"Why the urgency?" Jonathan said as she walked along the lea bordering a hedgerow with him.

"I want to marry."

"You know I cannot. No prospects."

"With the restoration you would have your farm once more."

" 'Tis small, and we are six."

"There is Skarra," Fanny said, her voice unsure as she considered her estate, and how it was to be divided, if at all.

"Your dowry." He smiled at her, a merry light in his eyes.

"Our lives should do."

"Life itself should be dowry enough, but 'tis not thought so. One lives on money, not on life."

"It seems so unfair."

"It is unfair."

She walked hand in hand with him, crossing the cotters' fields with the quick-stepping flocks of sheep, and past barnyards with burnished fowl and an occasional sniffing dog. It was hot, in the peak of a late summer, and she noticed that she and Jonathan were carrying their topcoats and hats.

"You can teach and you could preach, and you have read law at Saint Paul's."

"Aye, all that I could do, but we are not in the ascendancy, just yet, and as of tonight I have to snare a rabbit to flavor a turnip stew to feed seven bellies."

He grinned at her. "But we are alive, and we have no complaints."

"We could embark for America."

"Man's last great chance, Eden incarnate, a fresh unspoiled paradise, that blessed continent." He looked away into a distant sky. "Who would not want to live in America, but if we be no better men and women in that blessed land than now, then that last chance will be no advantage."

"They are driving out the Highlanders to run sheep, and sending them to America."

"Angry immigrants they will be."

"Already an angry Eden, I suppose," Fanny said pensively.

"We will stay," Jonathan said.

"I love Scotland, anyway."

"The sins of the fathers will pass unredeemed to the children. There is no reality in Eden, and America is Eden."

"I want you, I don't care where I have you." She pulled up and looked into Jonathan's face, seeking his complete understanding.

"Yes, and I you."

"Now."

He shook his head ruefully, and looked away down a distant rolling swale, and back into the hedgerow they were walking past.

"If we yield the body, we have committed the soul," he said.

"I know."

"I am willing to commit the flesh but the soul is a universe all to itself, and essential to human survival."

"That is why I want to commit it."

"To life?"

"I want your body because I cannot live without your soul." She spoke quietly.

"Are you afraid?"

"Yes, and you?"

"Lord, yes. I, the man, must carry it off."

She looked at him.

"Are you chaste?"

"I think so, yes."

" 'Tis of small import."

"Jonathan, hear me out. That degenerate man almost ravished me, and it would have been nothing to him if he had, except some signal to his insanity, but to me, it would have been a fool mocking my life."

He nodded his head and searched her eyes and saw a woman without illusions.

"I love you, ever since the moment you rode up and put your horse into our cart. . . ."

"If a knave can deceive a woman or a cruel savage rape her, then why may not her lover take her at his will?"

He shook his head and avoided her eyes. "I love you too much."

"To be like an animal?"

"Yes," he said vaguely.

"Are we not all animal, and some of us human?"

"You are too much woman." He pulled her into him and loosened the pin that let her hair fall out over his arm. "I am mad to smell your hair, since I first laid eyes on you that jolly afternoon." He smiled gently and commenced to help her undress.

In a moment she was nude, her hair streaming over her shoulders, wisping about her breasts and feathery over her waist to the swell of her hips. Their clothing lay scant on the grass about them, and looked so sparse to do so much. Fanny felt herself seem to expand in her nakedness.

"I cannot stay in this condition without either dressing or loving, for I have never felt so naked before."

" 'Tis better in bed," he said.

"No. We could not see each other then, and I want to see you." She placed the flat of her hand into the thick carpet of short dark hair on his chest which ran up over his shoulders and onto his back, and down his arms, all the way to his fingers. "Oh," she said.

The hair was coarse between her slender white fingers which slid through it, and her hands went over his shoulders where she gripped her fingers into the strong muscles and twisted the hair, feeling Jonathan sweep her into his massive chest, bend her down and backward.

"Jonathan," she whispered, kissing his sweet tongue. She sought to wrap her body into and about the hair and strong body she loved.

In a moment she felt herself down, her thighs slid apart on his smooth hair-covered thigh where she felt him jam her, bending her body as he took her. The passion was a scourging liquid of fire that sloshed through her thighs and flooded her belly from her loins, until she was mad. "Oh, Jonathan," she murmured, seeking to wrap him into her body at her thighs and womb, and she felt her arms circle and grasp and circle again the great hairy chest and beard she kissed with all loss of senses, save the rampant fire in her body.

Speech was beyond her as she caught his beard and lips in her teeth and bit and kissed him, and all that she could touch and hold with her hands, and tear at with her fingers, feeling the ecstasy of pulling out small wavelets of short hair from his flanks.

She heard him groan and crush her into the earth, smelling the musk of crushed grass amidst the tart flavor of his rich armpits, as she licked the wonderful bunches of hair that curled out into her face.

In the sweat which dripped from his forehead and ran under his eyes, she breathed his breath, and instinctively raised her hips and clung about his waist with her knees and locked feet, seeking the life force of his loins in an elemental need to live.

In moments she felt the intimate thrust of persistent flesh which cut past her lips, tearing and burning, past the instant of fear, to a fulfilled sense of bleeding triumph, to a joy that flooded her hips and belly, and was stifled as she felt him trembling in her arms and ebbing his massive strength between her thighs, and she heard him sob for life as his head fell away from her mouth into the earth at her shoulder.

She waited a moment, hearing him struggle for his breath, momentarily frightened by what she had done to him, for he seemed to have died in his ecstasy. "Jonathan?" she whispered.

He shifted his face and she felt his rough hand caress aimlessly, without strength, at her cheek. She kissed the strong fingers which were cupped like a child's. He sighed and she felt his massive strength relax as he drifted into sleep, sprawled across her and into the warm earth of the summer. She listened dimly to the rhythm of his sleeping breath and the faint hum of a summer beetle, each seeming to ebb and flow with life as she slipped out of thought in her contentment.

13

For Fanny it was a time of bliss without end. She had found her purpose in life. It was Jonathan. Her mind revolved inward and toward her love, and his breath and voice and body, and nowhere else. Forest Witch galloped wildly up the long swale leading to Turner's Hill, atop which sat Claygate Lodge, as delighted she could run as Fanny was to see the Hogarths. The whole family of them entranced her. She saw Jonathan in each of their faces, and she loved them all as extensions of him.

They would leave Bea and Forest Witch and the soldiers each day for long walks on the moors, picnicking out of a wicker hamper, sometimes overlooking the River Avon, or walking toward Poole, delicious in their solitary union, never able to talk enough of what they sought to say, mad with love.

Too much love was an indulgence, yet it seemed fair to yield her body in abandonment to seek a fulfillment for all the years she had remained continent, as though she had lived out an impatient lifetime which flowered in a sudden passion, and she could not get enough of it. That Jonathan would respond with the same rapture was all the proof she needed to assure herself the life was true.

To have his lips at her nipples and feel his beard and hair brush her naked belly and crinkle her flesh with delight as she felt his hot breath about her neck when she writhed her limbs before him, seeking to kiss his elbow or his knee or taste his hair in her mouth, tart after his tongue, and see his eyes glitter, then glaze, as she drew the sap from his loins and he died in her arms and body—this was life. It was Jonathan, and she had him in every way she could reach out and hold him. The English summer was her enchantment.

It came as such a surprise when they saw Timothy galloping along a distant road, mounted on Forest Witch.

"What is he doing on my horse?" Fanny said, each knowing the mare was hers alone to ride.

"Remarkable," Jonathan said, instinctively gathering up their picnic paraphernalia. "It must be serious."

"Serious?"

"Let us hear him out."

Timothy was with them in less than five minutes, jumping down off a lathered horse. "Galloped all the way."

"Leave her blow while we walk her," Fanny said, loosening the saddle's girth, and they walked in a large circle, cooling out the horse.

"A certain Sir Harry Vane with a warrant for Fanny . . ."

"A warrant for Fanny?"

"Aye, I took the horse so she could escape. . . ."

"Who told you?" Jonathan said.

"The Roundhead troopers. He cursed them for letting you both out of sight."

"I am already a prisoner."

"They are to try you for treason at Westminster."

"Westminster!" Fanny said. "No, I will not go!"

"You must ride for Henry Seymour."

"Aye, Mother said the same. The Earl of Dorset, Lord Henry himself . . ."

"Treason?" Fanny said, her voice baffled.

"Oh, he has a flock of parsons with him, all in black with big hats and white bibs."

"Sir Harry Vane, an American I believe," Jonathan said, musing to himself. "Both friend and foe of Cromwell." In the distance they saw come into sight a small cavalcade of diminutive figures. "You have been followed."

" 'Tis common knowledge you two picnic on the Avon," Timothy said.

"No matter. Fanny, can you outrace them to Cranborn Hall, if you all start even?"

"Easily," Fanny said, stroking the jaw of her mare, who had got her breath and was snatching at tussocks of grass, seeking to graze.

"When I give the word, you mount and fly, and I shall fling myself bodily into them, as a distraction."

"Would you dare?" Fanny said.

"Oh, Jonathan, do not!" the adolescent boy said.

"I will stumble and knock him down, and then sit on him to apologize." Jonathan laughed good-naturedly. Then he frowned and said, "Men without women are trouble, and Sir Harry Vane has a bad legal name, even among Puritans. He hangs witches. . . ."

"Oh, is he the man, at Salem?"

"I thought witches were old hags," Fanny said, cinching up the girth and setting the reins over Forest Witch's forelock.

"Witches are women whom men must silence."

"Oh," Fanny said, understanding.

"History is full of female martyrs."

"I do not want to be a martyr."

"Nobody expects you to."

"I want to live."

"We will." He took her hand into his as she looked fearfully at the black-clad cavalcade which was approaching in a broad flank, as though they expected her to escape. "Tim, you hold her horse; and Fanny, you stand at my side."

"Who comes?!" Jonathan hailed.

"A warrant for the Lady Frances McTaggart of Skarra," called out a tall man riding a gaunt horse, and whose knees flapped at the saddle roll with each step.

"Whose signature?" Jonathan called out, his hands on Fanny's forearms to steady her.

The man laughed loudly.

" 'Tis illegal without the Lord Protector's signature!" Jonathan bellowed, sensing an edge of advantage.

"Sir Harry Vane!" the man said, annoyed, for the other horsemen exchanged glances at the assertion of illegality.

"Sir Harry Vane, eh?"

"And who are you?" The tall thin man with a jaw-beard and high hat swung his off-leg awkwardly to dismount without listening to Jonathan.

"Jonathan Hogarth, squire of Ironwood and King's Counselor of Saint Paul's and the Court."

"Squatters at Claygate, I dare say," Vane said affably while running his eyes over Fanny, "and a lawyer."

"I have heard of your ecclesiastical triumphs in America, hanging women as witches," Jonathan said, speaking jovially. "Remarkable achievement in that you even revolted the Americans."

"Yes, you talk much." The voice was a high-pitched whine of reproach.

"Your fame precedes you, Sir Harry. You should be proud."

Fanny listened aghast to the exchange of insults, thrilled with Jonathan's courage and yet terrified for their lives.

"Do you identify this woman, Proctor?" Vane glanced up at one of the horsemen who had not dismounted.

" 'Tis the woman."

Jonathan looked at the semicircle of horsemen drawn up about them, then back to Harry Vane, a wily man with a shrewd mind so closed even Cromwell had quarreled with him.

"The Lady Frances is under house arrest at Cranborn Hall," Jonathan said. "As a ward of Cranborn, I shall insist you take the lady before the Earl, as a lieutenant of the Commonwealth . . ."

"Rubbish! Take her, men!"

Jonathan was surprised at the flash of his closed fist and ecstatic to feel the thin cartilage of Sir Harry's nose crush like parchment under the blow. It filled him with a joy of lustful power, and he drove his fist a second time into Sir Harry's belly and thrilled to see the man collapse onto the turf, bleeding in a gush through his fingers, which were cupped over his nose.

"Ride to Cranborn!" He lunged onto the back of a clergyman in a long black cloak, dragging him down as he reached for Fanny. "Run!" he shouted as the figure struggled with its arms and legs unevenly under the broad cloak which spread over the body like a web. "Be still, damn you!" Jonathan bellowed, driving his balled fist into the back of the fellow's neck and silencing him with a crunching noise.

Fanny was at the side of Forest Witch in a sprint, while the horsemen kicked up to stop her.

"Run!" Jonathan had snatched the cloak off the clergyman's back and had fanned it suddenly in the face of the horses, causing them to rear and wheel. "Run!" Tim shouted.

"High on!" Fanny screamed and slashed the Witch with her crop, and Jonathan saw the mare leap through the muddling band, scattering horses and men. "Run, Fanny!" screamed Timothy.

"Stop her, brothers!"

"Head her!"

The cries were lost in the scrambling thud of the flying hooves and the wild calls of the girl who dashed away.

"Damn you, lawyer," said Harry Vane, getting to his feet. "That was treason."

"Why do not you go back to Massachusetts where you were Governor and leave England alone?"

"I'll have you hanged."

"After Lady Fanny, and you have a long way to go." He laughed, rubbing his skinned knuckles and using a foot to roll over the quiet form of the man he had slugged on the turf.

The whole body of them watched Fanny ride past the distant guards who struggled to turn her, to catch her, or to head her, their stiff-legged mounts like jolting scarecrows in pursuit of the nimble Forest Witch. She rode straight at hedges, collecting her gait and soaring over them, leaping canals, thundering down into and out of cottage yards in an explosion of chickens and flapping geese, vanishing to reappear, leaving far behind her panting pursuers, who were barked at by all the dogs in the countryside, having been first aroused by the nimble flight of Fanny and her thoroughbred mare.

"By God, look at the bastards," Jonathan said, laughing uproariously as he swung his arm about Timothy's slender shoulders. "She is leading a desultory mob to Cranborn!"

Henry Seymour was an immensely sophisticated man who had supported the Monarchy, the nobility, the Church, and the yeomanry or the common people. God was never any problem to him—in fact God rarely occurred to him—because God was the land and farming and all things which lived off and loved the land, and the land was England. That he was the Earl of Dorset was no reason why he and the most common, ordinary Englishman could not and did not see eye to eye on all things. They were both sprung of the same earth, and molded of the land that formed them. To suppose a difference between man and man, or man and woman, was as impossible to Henry Seymour as to question the existence of God. Further, as a gentleman, it was bad taste to think too much on God, and certainly, no gentleman would discuss Him.

Yet, Seymour was a realist. The power of mercantile London was more than the old country families could thwart. The yeomanry was to be swept into cities, as a rootless mob; the factories and capital wealth were invincible.

What Henry Seymour could not understand was the messianic zealotry of the Puritans. They had won the civil war, they had the power, but there was something unstable in their minds. Fanny's warrant charged "witchcraft, having been seduced by the devil and diabolical forces to debauch the Lord's minister, Miles Proctor, divine agent of God . . ." To Henry Seymour, if a man sought to ravish a woman and she fought him off, it would be best to say nothing, and pass it off as a bad joke. To blame the woman and involve God while about it was to him absolute blasphemy and cowardice. To have such an affair under his roof was revolting, and to have it followed by the "Interrogation for Witchcraft" was an outrage that frightened him.

The trial was to be held in the large hall of Cranborn, and the judges were five clergymen down from Westminster, who had debated the dream of an English Utopia under the Cromwellian Protectorate, obeying their atavism of the Great Rebellion of the 1300's and Sir Thomas More, and now with the power to bring the dream to fact. Sir Harry Vane, former Governor of Massachusetts, was selected as chief justice, because of the success Englishmen had achieved in finding a Utopia in America.

"But how do I know if I have been debauched as a witch?" Fanny said to Jonathan as they planned her defense in the great library of Cranborn. Henry Seymour, Lady Leslie, Buckey Hailyham, and a Scottish officer, who had been assigned to her defense to ensure "fair play" but who appeared dumfounded at the proceedings, sought to help, but all seemed at a loss except for Jonathan.

"Thank God we had a change of venue," Jonathan said, gesturing to a book of canon law.

"Venue?" Timothy said, reaching to fetch it.

"I do not think it is fair to say a person is a witch," Fanny said.

"I have known some ghastly hags," Seymour mused before the fireplace.

"Change of place for the trial." Jonathan took the book from his younger brother. "For fair play."

"It is not fair," Fanny said.

"We have them on the moors, away from Westminster in the midst of monarchists."

"No," said Hailyham, his jovial red face and sparkling blue eyes somber, "no, only force will do, or the threat of it. A Highland rising strikes terror into the nation."

"Scotland is secure," Seymour said.

"No conquered nation is ever secure," Hailyham said. "You cannot conquer a man by force. Eventually you must face his children, and his cause is theirs."

"You could get married," Fanny said.

"Ah, leave it to a woman." Hailyham's voice was jovial once more.

"Witches come from the insane longings of the unbalanced mind," Jonathan said, his eyes fixed on his goose quill.

"Hmm, flimflam talk, as the Danes say," Seymour said.

"My lord, one answers the charge of witchcraft with flimflam." Jonathan looked steadily into the eyes of the nobleman. "To defend oneself against witchcraft demands one prove one is not a witch, which one cannot do without one's having knowledge of what a witch is, else one cannot know what to prove what one is not."

There was silence in the room while all faces looked at Jonathan. "And if one knows what a witch is, then one is obviously a witch, or has been a witch."

"Only a damned lawyer would say that."

"Thank God he is a lawyer," Leslie said.

"If I am to defend Fanny I have to attack the bias of the judges and appeal to the soul of England."

"What soul is there in a civil war?"

"Something endures, my lord."

"Not that I have noticed."

"People can stand the blows struck them by their illusions until the illusions triumph."

"My God, man, at the price of the girl's life!" Seymour bellowed at Jonathan, who sat back in his Jacobean chair.

"If Fanny were on trial in London in the reign of Queen Bess or Bloody Mary, we would jeopardize our lives in defending her. Or in Massachusetts today. But this is England, and our nightmare came true. They have not yet learned this in America."

"Aye, this blessed isle," Seymour said.

"This blessed land, my lord." Jonathan's voice was tinged with satisfaction of having gently made a point.

"But how do you get her free?"

"It depends on Sir Harry Vane's mode of attack. He is brilliant, and so he will offend the other judges, and I shall be waiting."

"Oh, Jonathan." Fanny set her hand atop his. "How would we ever know about these things without you?"

"Lady Frances," he said quite formally, "I cannot see my law books with your hand atop them," and he lifted Fanny's hand and squeezed it by compulsion.

Jonathan Hogarth was a good lawyer. He never had a thought nor said a word without considering its effects. In confronting Star Chamber proceedings he was in truth grappling with a court-martial, without the protection of a jury of equals, commoners or peers. Without a judge steeped in common law and Parliamentary Acts, he could establish no certain premise of common belief which they all agreed upon. With an adversary whom he considered politically opportunistic, versed in a quasi-religion of force, justified from Old Testament dogmatism and mixed with the physical excitement of a girl's body and the ecstasy of rape or death to appease suppressed lust, Jonathan was troubled and unsure. But in his demeanor he remained confident.

The first morning started late, after the judges settled themselves along the broad table placed athwart the fire, warming their backs and whispering as they turned their pale faces across the gloomy hall.

"They look like crows with skinned beaks," Timothy said, speaking at Fanny and Jonathan's table, while behind them were chairs and benches Sir Harry Vane had insisted be provided for "the servants and the yeomanry."

"He has no case, he has no proceedings, and he has no law, but he has power," Jonathan said, speaking to his brother.

"That is bad?" Fanny said.

"The worst. If a man has nothing but power he overuses it."

The Scottish officer assigned to Fanny's defense watched the judges, stared at his companions at Fanny's table, occasionally glanced behind him at the Seymour family and members of the gentry who had ridden over to see if it was actually true, that a trial for witchcraft was to be conducted at Cranborn Hall. He would occasionally get up to join Bea at a chair behind their table, where he would whisper, then rejoin them.

"Are there other allegations, quite aside from witchcraft?" Jonathan's voice rolled across the parqueted floor and enveloped the whispering figures. "We have waited all morning to attend justice, yet we have found none."

The five black-robed men shuffled, glancing at each other.

"The Lord in His time grinds true, but only in His time, not ours," Sir Harry said, his blue eyes merry with assurance.

"You have no writ of *habeas corpus,* my lord."

"Crimes against God and the State do not warrant the accommodation of *habeas corpus.*"

"Crimes, my lord? What crimes?"

"Hogarth, we wrangle with our mouths, true in our hearts as Englishmen, when a fine young woman has been debauched in her mind with wrong thoughts, thoughts seditious to the nation, and to God, for God ordained the nation."

"If we but wrangle with our mouths, I shall be content, my lord."

"A confession of guilt would require only a purging. . . ."

"No confession." Jonathan was emphatic.

"As you will. The effusion of blood will not be on our hands."

The chilled words gripped the hall in silence, and Fanny caught her breath. Beside her she saw Timothy's face turn scarlet under waves of color as the boy realized the cultured words revealed a desire to murder a girl whom he loved as only a younger brother can love.

"Bloodshed, my lord?"

"Only in the purging by blood can there be a rebirth kindled in the heart."

"So it is reasoned, but falsely," Jonathan said.

" 'Tis history," Vane said affably.

"Aye, and remembered for its injustice."

Harry Vane smiled knowledgeably, obviously enjoying himself as he matched wits with Jonathan, and displayed a complete assurance. "Who has power needs only to rationalize to strike, so history records."

"No, my lord, power is the illusion men can escape retribution for their scorn of living."

"We have not found it so in New England. . . ."

"Aye, so it was told. You slew the Indians who welcomed you to Massachusetts."

"A wondrous celebration, Thanksgiving."

"The Indians, my lord?"

"Savages. All savages."

"If you become what you love or you hate, your intemperance has commenced your own prison in America."

The judges fixed their eyes on Jonathan, obviously impressed with the bearded figure of a man who had matched his mind against Sir Harry Vane.

"Why, 'tis a free land, America, with no prisons. All men are equal in America. . . ."

"With notable exceptions, my lord," Jonathan said. They noticed the suppressed smiles here and there in the room, amidst a small note of laughter behind them.

"Clever young man." Harry Vane spoke easily. "America could use a good man."

"No, my lord, it is better to die a peasant in your own land than be a prince in a strange land."

"As you will."

"Thank you, my lord."

"If you wish to remain a peasant . . ."

"Aye, no flower is better than the manure pile that grows it."

"There are no classes in America. We are all equal. No manure pile. . . ."

"A nation of flowers? My lord, how rank the scent must be with the body unable to decompose."

There was a stunning moment while Harry Vane's face clouded white, then got very red. "By God, sire!" He lunged across the broad table, pounding it with his fist. "Mock me if you dare! I'll have that strumpet's private parts hanging on the Tower keep!"

"Sire!" said the judge at his left. "Sire, you speak intemperately."

"No, by God, sire, I'll have his wench! Tits and cunt!"

"Composure, Vane, this body should not lack decorum." The judges were arguing among themselves.

"How did you get him so angry?" Fanny said.

"Johnny, he means to kill Fanny," Timothy said, his face utterly white as his blue eyes stared in terror across the parqueted floor where death stalked them.

"I know."

"Oh, Johnny, ye terrify me."

"I terrify myself, but I have to fight."

"Do not bait him."

"I seek to unmask him before human decency. He is insane. The flower is an indivisible part of the manure pile."

"Oh, it scares me," Fanny said as the five judges huddled.

Jonathan waited, sipping a pewter mug of water and gently laying his hand atop Fanny's, his eyes never off his adversary, while feeling the whole hall of nobles, yeomen, and servants gripped in a hush behind him. Harry Vane's anger had frightened them all.

"My Lords Justice," Jonathan said, drawing the court's attention, "since capital punishment has been supposed, the 'effusion of blood,' as it was put, and since any such sentence might precipitate an armed rising of a dissident portion of the public, it would seem prudent that this investigation be suspended and the prisoner remanded to a duly constituted court. . . ."

"A duly constituted court cannot try a witch," Vane said, "for what crime can a witch commit, except her craft, which is not of this world."

Jonathan was dumfounded by the skill of Harry Vane, and his bland hypocrisy.

"And if the culprit is a witch, and brought to the stake, she will vanish in the flame, for a witch has no blood. . . ."

"Oooo. . . ." Behind them they heard the hall of ignorant tenants and yeomanry, recalling their imaginings of witchcraft and the occult.

"Therefore, if burnt, she will shed no blood, and as a point of fact, feel no pain." Harry Vane sat back, smiling slightly in his triumph after his outburst and loss of respect.

"Fanny!" Jonathan said, standing up and seizing Fanny by the arm and dragging her to her feet, and swinging her out before the court and assembled spectators. "I will prove she be no witch, here and now, before God and man." He glanced at the Scottish officer. "Your dirk, man, and quick about it!"

"Your dirk," Bea said, snatching the Highland dirk from the Scot's knee and handing it to Jonathan.

Jonathan held the dirk before them, then drove the point of it into the palm of Fanny's hand, avoiding the veins but making her scream. She did not jerk back her hand. The blood puddled in a moment and ran up the fair wrist.

"Blood! It is blood!" Jonathan raised her bleeding hand and

gore-slick forearm before the judges and wheeled her to face the spectators.

"She bleeds!"

"A noble lady!"

"For shame!"

Fanny's eyes were a fragmenting blue when he caught sight of them, of incomprehending horror, first glancing at the deep, bleeding wound, then at the obviously sympathetic, yet delighted audience, and to the floor where the dirk lay.

"You beast!" Leslie Seymour shouted, rushing toward Fanny, who was crying, and Jonathan, who was swinging her hand in an arc before the judges, shouting, "Blood, do ye see!" and spreading a small patter of red drops.

In a moment the hall of Cranborn was in uproar as rude tenants, yeomen, and gentry stood, uttering cries of dismay at the rough treatment of the girl, or ecstatic with suffering and delightful fantasies of witchcraft, either revealed or suppressed, but now free to express emotion. Oaths and cursing rose on all sides as the servants took the liberty to run wild.

"My God, man, did you have to be so rough?" Henry Seymour said to Jonathan as the swirling figures of the angry throng drove the judges from their table and into the main hall.

"It was her blood or her life."

"My God, to stab her?" Seymour spoke incredulously, without his usual urban polish and witty contentment.

"I needed blood, and fast."

"Do you suppose this is the end of it?"

"Not likely. He has quarreled with Cromwell and he was hateful in Boston, so he has no place to go, except repeat the crime that undid him."

"Brilliant, I must say."

"I am not sure of that," Jonathan said, turning back to their table and aware the staff of Cranborn were hustling the crowd out of the manor house. "I may have saved her life, but I also made a fool of a very angry man. We shall wait and see."

"Good boy," Seymour said, clapping him on the shoulder. "I never knew law could be so exciting."

Jonathan turned his attention to Fanny, who was in the midst of her women and the Seymours. She was pale, even including her lips, but her eyes were searching for his as he walked up. A brief smile flickered across her face. "I am glad you did not tell me what you were going to do."

"Fanny, forgive me."

"I was so astonished. You frightened me."

"I am sorry."

"You did not plan it, did you?"

"No. He made a slip and he wanted blood, and he was playing to the mob, so I caught the slip, and made a fool of him and won the mob by a drop or two of blood instead of a whole life."

"Oh, Jonathan, did you think of all that, that fast?"

"Aye, that fast."

"You are a great lawyer."

"No, I love you." He drew her into his bosom and held her. "We were each fighting for your life."

That evening Jonathan walked with Fanny in the formal gardens of Cranborn. He held her swaddled fist, scarcely touching her to assure himself as well as her that he had done something utterly foreign to him.

"No, I think it was wonderful," Fanny said. "You stabbed me to prove I bleed."

"Absolutely foolish." He shook his head.

"Bea blames it all on the English." The remark made them laugh in the long English twilight. "We shall be calm. His passion will undo him and our muddling stride will carry through."

He searched her eyes, and in so doing he saw the childlike beauty of a young woman he loved. There was an aura of innocence about her, and he felt a twinge of shame rise in his heart that he could understand the need to publicly hurt her, to appease the public cruelty.

"You saved me," she said, sensing his mood. "Like I found you on the moor."

"What a happy day that was."

"I shan't let you go."

After the uproar in the main hall at Cranborn all antagonists seemed to withdraw from each other, into their several apartments, cottages, and grace-and-favor houses about the estate. They still saw each other, however, nodding like mandarins when they met in the courtyard or gardens, even smiling at dinner when Henry Seymour sought to bring some elemental wisdom to his angry guests by simply feeding them well. "Feed their bellies, Henry," Leslie Seymour had said. "If there is any charity in a man, it takes a full belly before it can emerge." The supper party did not seem to do any good, though; Harry Vane still insisted on a trial, and again in public. "To instruct the common people as well as call them to their patriotism."

The trial opened as before, five days after Jonathan had won the first tilt. This time, however, it seemed more crowded. The gentry were there from miles around, and they had brought their servants, who with the staff of Cranborn thronged the hall.

"He has to have a coup," Jonathan said as he idled at their table. "His vanity demands it, and it is all illusion, and so I fight pure madness."

"I do not understand," Timothy said.

"He has to win, no matter who loses, even himself."

"Would he kill Fanny?"

"Lord, yes, Timothy. Fanny is just an incidental."

"I do not think he feels that way," Fanny said.

"If I were the witch I would doubtless feel differently." Jonathan's voice was pensive as he watched the judges settle themselves.

They sat at their table while the Reverend Miles Proctor was sworn to tell the truth as God ordained and to eschew the devil and all his wily seductions whilst he spoke the truth and none but the truth.

"I met her on the estate and was drawn to her comely skin, to what seemed pure to all of us who saw her," he said, staring moodily at Fanny.

"Did you have an inkling something was amiss?" Vane asked,

prompting the witness, who stood to the side, between the judges and Jonathan's table.

"Aye."

"And what inkling did you have, Brother Miles?"

"Such beauty must hide the vile."

"Hmm." Vane rubbed his chin.

"If a thing be excessively lovely, then it must follow that it be deeply vile in its secret places."

"Oh, rubbish," Jonathan said, his deep voice rolling through the hall, yet he did not stir his body nor look up where he slouched.

"If the Honorable Mister Hogarth will hold his peace . . ."

"Is a child lovely?" Jonathan looked up. "Ask the poor demented fool. Is a child lovely?"

Harry Vane hammered a heavy wooden mallet on the table to silence the hubbub in the hall. Jonathan eased back into his seat, satisfied he had struck back and won the crowd in his exchange, even if temporarily silenced.

"I meant a lovely woman," Proctor said, unabashed and apparently unable to see Jonathan's point.

"What did you see?"

"She bathed her nude body." He paused, as though such a thing was the end proof.

"Ahah, I see," Vane said.

"How does one bathe one's body except in the nude?" Jonathan said.

"She was not ashamed," Proctor said, turning to them.

"Shame implies guilt—obviously she has neither guilt nor shame."

"Unless she be shameless." The eyes flared in the aggressive assertion.

"And the innocent are as bold as a lion," Jonathan said, getting to his feet to address the witness and the court.

"The woman exulted in her bath, happy in her body—zounds, I could see it!"

"Did it bother you?" Jonathan said.

"Aye, the flesh is full of corruption."

"How do you know corruption if you are a good man?" Jonathan searched his face.

"Those of us who serve humanity give our lives to knowing and understanding the corruption of humanity and healing the corruption of those we love, even if we sometimes have to punish them. . . ."

"Could you not forgive the corruption of humanity, without having to punish?"

"God's law clearly states it is the duty of the nation to root out evil. . . ."

"Vengeance is mine, saith the Lord!" Jonathan's voice crashed out, filling the hall. "Are you suffering from that most insane of delusions that you are God, Brother Proctor?"

The spectators were caught up in the puzzling train of thoughts Jonathan hurled at the witness. There was a long pause as the judges whispered among themselves, and Harry Vane's beard bobbed along on his jaw as he talked to Miles Proctor.

Jonathan sat down and waited, never taking his eyes off Sir Harry Vane. "I have stopped him every time, and I think I have half the judges on my side, maybe more." He shook his head slowly. "When they lose the argument they either ridicule or attack the personal credibility of the culprit."

"Would the Lady Frances stand and be sworn?"

"As I feared," Jonathan said, nodding to Fanny, who clenched her fists and showed white about her lips. "No," she whispered.

"My Lords, no *prima facie* case exists," Jonathan said, standing. "You have no case."

"But we have a witness accused of witchcraft." Sir Harry Vane smiled with patronizing assurance. "And witchcraft does not have to be proven. Let her renounce her accusers, for all to hear, or does the lady have something to hide?"

Fanny stood and walked to the place where Proctor had stood and was sworn to the truth.

"Child, this is an interrogation, not a trial," Vane said, leaning forward on his elbows. "All you must do is to confess and ask for absolution. . . ."

"I did not know English jurisprudence demanded a confession and absolution," said one of the judges, a gaunt old Puritan, his eyes piercing Sir Harry Vane's. "Such doings smack of the Spanish Inquisition and our unlamented reign of Mary Tudor."

"Brother, in our Puritan nation, all the girl must do is confess and she is free," Miles said.

"And what if she be no witch?"

"Let her confess she is not a witch."

"I like it not," the old man said. "We got rid of the confessional, not because confession is not good, but because we had to confess, even when we had nothing to confess."

"Nobody is perfect, my brother. We can always improve ourselves."

"Aye, that is what they always say. Nay, I like it not." The old Puritan smacked his lips.

"I am no witch," Fanny said, drawing their attention.

"Good, lass, good," Harry Vane said, leaning forward, the jawbeard moving every time he spoke. "But you love life, do you not?"

"Aye, my lord," Fanny said.

"The sweet breath of life, the fields you gallop upon with your fine horse, and the young man—you love him?" He gestured at Jonathan.

"I love to be alive, my lord."

"No doubt, 'tis good to live." He smiled at Fanny.

Fanny nodded.

"And you love your body?"

"My body?" Fanny searched the blue eyes, which pierced her in a brittle line.

"If you love, girl, then you must use your senses, your body to love—am I right?" The voice swept her mind off balance.

"You are personal," Jonathan said.

"Answer! Do you love your body?"

"But how else is a woman to live?" Fanny said, raising her eyes to meet Sir Harry Vane's. "Except with her body. A woman's body serves whatever she loves."

"Then you admit the corruption!"

"What corruption?!" Jonathan said, his voice echoing in the hall.

"She admits her body is corrupt."

"Everybody defecates," Jonathan said, "and every flower blooms with its roots in a manure pile—no manure, no flower!"

"If she loved her body, then she could use it to corrupt a good man to his seduction. She bewitched his weakness."

"I have never before heard insanity defended in court," Jonathan said.

"Mister Hogarth, you have alluded to a manure pile in her defense. Are you suggesting the corruption of the young woman is so profound it contaminates her like a cesspool?"

"Nay, your worship. The divinity of the flower's life springs from the compost of decay."

"Yet you used the manure pile to defend Lady Frances' corruption," Vane said, leaning over the bench toward Jonathan, who had walked to Fanny's side.

"Nay, you have corrupted the words and thoughts out of your own corruption."

Sir Harry Vane smiled in pleasure at turning the images to defame Fanny.

"Your worship, if I may clarify the image for the court, if the lily blooms with its roots in the manure, none but a fool would seek to say where the lily ends and where the roots begin—to damn the smell of the roots mocks the bliss of the flower."

Jonathan turned to Miles Proctor. "The one of you has perverted God, the other the law, and it is the blood of a girl you crave."

The hall was silent while the judges stared at Jonathan and Fanny. Jonathan turned back to face Vane, who breathed through the teeth of his clamped jaw. "My lord, you have said you would have the girl's life, to what purpose you did not say, save her corruption."

"A corrupt woman." Proctor was unruffled.

"So you have said: 'corrupted.' "

"Her body had the unmistakable smell of corruption about it," Proctor said.

"The girl smelled bad?" Jonathan said.

"Aye, stank. Her privy parts."

Sir Harry Vane's eyes gleamed while he listened to Jonathan and Miles Proctor.

"The woman stank?"

"She stank."

"Corruption," Vane said, his voice soft as a sponge.

"I thought you said you saw her naked body when she bathed."

"Aye," Proctor said.

"I have smelt a woman, and I find the smell intoxicating." Jonathan spoke affably.

"Sickening," Vane said.

"A matter of opinion."

"When I smelt her I knew she was corrupted." Proctor was resolute.

"How could you smell this girl if she bathed?" Jonathan's voice was sudden.

"What?" Proctor looked addled.

"Did you smell her?"

"Yes."

"When?"

The table of judges watched the tall man whose balled fists sought out each other in the silence that settled through the hall.

"Fanny, did this man rape you?" Jonathan said.

"He tried." Fanny spoke quietly. "But he failed."

"The smell between her legs deranged me."

"Oh, it was the woman's fault?" Jonathan said.

"I was drawn to attack the corruption of her."

"But you did not penetrate her body with your privy stick?"

"No, she fought me. . . ."

"Then she is no witch, for you remain a virgin." Jonathan turned from the judges to the spectators. "The Reverend Proctor was not defiled. Lady Frances is no witch."

"But the smell of her!" Vane shouted.

"He did not stick it into me," Fanny said as Lord Henry Seymour stood and bellowed, "Lady Frances is a virgin! My women can attest it!"

"I like the smell of women," Jonathan said, dropping his chin onto his chest and wagging a finger at Sir Harry Vane. "It is the smell of the earth and of pure life." He waved his arm back to Miles Proctor. "Keep that fool in Westminster with the other divines. One of these old Devonshire harridans will kill him if he touches another girl."

"I was not told he had raped her," said the old Puritan at the end of the table.

"Sought to rape," Jonathan said.

"Lust is lust, young man." The old man's voice was like edged steel. "This trial is a mockery of England." He stood. "For shame, ye have raped a girl, then tried her in public for your own sorry mischief." He fumbled away from the table, clutching at his robes. "I want my horse. In the bowels of Christ, the Lord Protector must be apprised. Where is my horse? My horse!"

About Jonathan the people were moving in subdued voices, as though they had seen a brilliant man they did not understand do something they could understand.

"You foxed me," Henry Seymour said. Jonathan was looking at Sir Harry Vane, who was standing between the three remaining judges, whose brows were knit in quandary.

"Sir Harry Vane," Jonathan said, speaking firmly. "Your time has come and gone, and the hate is all you have to live on, and if you do not leave England they will hang you, just as you hanged the Salem witches in America, and your hate will be your death."

Sir Harry Vane's fingers dropped his goose quill and he turned away and went through the door.

"By God, you foxed me, Jonathan," Seymour said.

" 'E peeps, me lord," Belinda said, her ruddy face calm as her untroubled eyes.

"I'll geld him if he is not clear of Cranborn within the hour." He put his arm about the servant woman.

"Thank ye, me lord. A man should take a woman, not peep, me lord."

"Well spoken, Belinda!" Seymour grasped the buxom woman in his arms and kissed her cheek.

"For shame, my lord." She broke into giggles and rushed away among the people shifting through the great hall.

14

All was joy at Skarra. Fanny had come home, bringing Jonathan with her. To the Scots he was burly and short, yet actually he was tall and well muscled. Bruce was overjoyed with his daughter's choice for a husband. Bruce was not satisfied with the nobles. They were forever believing the role they played was real. "Drunk as the lord," was a way of life to make the nobles' dream come true. And Bruce was also chary of the middle class and its acquisitive notion that God sanctioned riches, which was why the rich got richer, and were guilt-stricken and became cruel. "Their wives and children turn hard like gold, no happier than King Midas." He had hugged both Fanny and Jonathan to his lank frame and said, "Bless you, my children. A gentleman who works with his hands as well as his head is all a man can hope for in a son."

Jonathan walked unafraid and unannounced through the large household of Scottish servants and retainers, hiking and visiting across the moors, his coarse black beard as confident and reassuring to the slender taciturn Celtic races as it was to the English.

Bea came into her own after an occluded lifetime. She spent hours each evening relating to the servants the lurid details of English barbarism and carnal pleasures, which Mister Jonathan alone knew how to disfever.

In his heart Jonathan grew to love the Scots. Their philosophy already had won England, but the pathos and sorrow of their human insights and their abiding personal courage gave him a keen sense of elation. "I doubt that I could spend a lifetime on the moors of Skarra," he told Fanny, "but if I could not live some of my life among the Scots I would not consider my life to be lived."

"We shall do a little bit at a time," Fanny said. "I want to bear our child at Skarra."

"Aye, you need your mother at birth." He took and pressed her hand to his waist. He sensed the merit in Bruce's inflexible regimen of cleanliness and use of mountain snow to freeze wounds, both for the beasts and flocks of Skarra and for the women of his household.

Bruce was at ease in his heart. He had lived long enough to see both ends of the spectrum of life—was young enough to savor the simple fact of living and old enough to sorrow that it would not last. Bruce tolerated the unsettled political union with England. He had never opposed it, only the exploitative greed which a union seemed to cultivate in Scotland, due to the riches of England. He accepted the continuing wars with Holland, France, and Spain as extensions of rivalry in commerce and to be chosen as substitutes for the war of extermination motivated by Old Testament certainty. Now they fought by day and got drunk together at night.

Yet he deeply regretted he had never fought Cromwell in battle, because he knew he could defeat any army on earth with a Scottish line, if he could discipline it.

A love for fighting seemed to have grown insensibly within him as he had matured and then aged, perhaps out of the hope he still harbored that life could be innocent, and that a struggle might regain this lost innocence.

Now old Oliver Cromwell was coming to Scotland, to make a final peace, and Bruce was going to meet him at Perth Castle. Bruce knew Cromwell wanted peace when he declared he would enter the Highlands.

"I always knew my waiting game with England would win," he said to Lydia.

"And now that you have won, it wasn't the battles, was it?" She put her hands to his temples.

"No. It was for the children. There is no other purpose to life."

"Yes, the children and Voltoff; that is all that kept me alive."

He shook his head and held her.

"And I did love you," she whispered. "To love you is all I've ever had."

Behind him he could hear his servants and retainers galloping across the moors. Lydia was riding sidesaddle beside him, her eyes well pleased as she watched the thin trace of a road they galloped along. He smiled with the contentment that he had been fair to her, in bringing her to Scotland, and had been true to his promise, for insensibly he measured all women by Lydia, and lived from her purpose. She rode the saddle with grace and in perfect harmony with the horse's body.

"You always rode like the wind."

She glanced at him, then back to her mount.

"You never changed," Bruce said.

"No, no purpose to that." The trace brushed through the rhododendron.

Bruce had left the Highland chieftains among their clans on the moors. If he had brought armed troops, or chieftains, it might be not only construed as a threat, but might also tempt the English to capture them for what could be rationalized as an act of treachery. If Bruce trusted Cromwell, he still knew the Independents of the English Parliament had toyed with the notion of proclaiming a major general as ruler, after Cromwell's death, thus continuing the Protectorate. Bruce knew these men feared for their lives, at the death of Cromwell, and would not stop at any deception or violence.

To ease the wounded pride of the Puritans and to remove their source of anger, Bruce had slipped John Bollingale onto a Dutch ship bound for Virginia. It had the mollifying effect he had hoped it might, for if the English could forgive the Scots, they could not forgive each other.

They rode through the streets of Perth and to the castle, escorted by a considerable troop of cavalry. Major George Atkinson, who had recovered from his wounds received at Skarra, was among the English, and he was beside himself to shout "Halloo!"

Hailyham and Seymour were in the court with greetings and drinks and giving orders to grooms.

"Thank you for protecting my daughter," Bruce said, taking Seymour's hand.

"We all adored her, some too much." The elegant Englishman shoved a tankard into his hand.

"She would have none of a soldier," Hailyham said.

"The lawyer got her," Seymour said.

"Sly fox, that one. I thought he was an Anglican rector."

"I think she made the right choice," Bruce said. "Each year's swallows surprise their parents when they fly home."

"We are to have peace," Seymour said.

"Cromwell is that sick?"

"Dying."

"He hangs on to satisfy his following, for 'tis now their death they face, for they slew the king."

"Bad show all this killing, and it must run its course in retribution. Such a sorrow." Bruce handed his tankard to a servant and looked for Lydia, who was at his side.

At dinner that night they met the Lord Protector. Oliver Cromwell was dressed in black, which gave his bloated skin a severe, deathly assertion, and his eyes were yellow-flecked, of bile unable to pass out of his body as urine. The food came immediately and was spartan in its simplicity, and Bruce wondered that such a healthy diet could produce such a sick man.

"I trust no man in Scotland," Cromwell said, eating his thin gruel.

"I came without guards or arms," Bruce said, sitting to the right.

The bloated eyes lifted to glance at Bruce. "Thou didst, I know. But thou slew my men."

"My lord, we were assaulted. . . ."

"I know, I know. Bad as a lawyer. They hated me at Oxford," Cromwell said.

Bruce waited in silence.

"The intellectuals always grow to hate whatever it is they once supported." He stared at Bruce.

"Could you not say, my lord, that all men grow to hate and love whatever they learn to know?" Bruce said.

Cromwell looked down into his plate. "Not much hope there."

"My lord, life is hope," Lydia said, her voice breaking over them like a fresh summer sunset.

"Thy daughter is a beautiful girl, Lady Skarra. I am ashamed of how we English treated her."

"She came home betrothed, my lord." Lydia spoke comfortingly.

"I sent that fool to Massachusetts Bay. They say they have found God in Massachusetts."

"And I sent Bollingale to Virginia."

"He was a bad one, prayed with John Milton, like a maiden." Cromwell spoke musingly. "Yes, rotting flowers smell far worse than hay."

"Hay smells clean, my lord," Seymour said.

"Work makes it smell good. Work. All men should work."

"Aye, even the American Indian works to chase his deer, they say."

Cromwell laughed, the swollen shoulders hunching unnaturally.

"It is peace I want," Cromwell said, looking at Bruce.

"You have peace—my word on it, my lord."

"Richard lacks strength and Argyll wouldst be king. . . ."

"Scotland is Stuart forever."

"Aye, a dead Stuart is more of a menace than a live Parliament."

"Scotland is herself."

"Just a name, man, what be the difference between one Scot and another, whenst thy be the same breed o' man." Cromwell stared petulantly at Bruce, then around the table.

"My lord, 'tis the greed that unsettled the Highlands, not the politics of England and Scotland. The clans are naught but families who cling to an uncertain life on the moor, and who have no quarrel with ara man or beast. Yet with our union of England and Scotland, bringing English law and the Enclosure Acts, the clans are driven from their common lands and rock communes to make way for sheep and commerce."

"The law is the law, and the majority is the law," Cromwell said, the harshness shredding his voice.

"My lord, the law is what men make it, and no law is beyond judgment." Bruce looked quietly into the bilious eyes. "Time is on the side of Scotland and against the law."

"Scotland will be banished beyond the seas."

"A dangerous place to continue our discord, my lord."

"Aye, all our folly has emigrated to America." Cromwell settled back into his chair. "What dost thou want?"

"Nothing, my lord, save directions to Archibald Campbell in Edinburgh that he is to keep to the Lowlands and leave the Highlands in tranquility."

"Done!" Cromwell shoved back his chair, turning to Lydia. "My lady, thou art a fortunate woman. Thou hast a brave husband whose word is gold, and a daughter who is chaste in her body and true in her tongue. A pity thou art not English and Puritan." He put his hand to his belly and belched a sour note, his eyes watering. "*Excusez-moi*, my dyspepsia."

Bruce and Lydia rose as the table stood, while the secretary and body servants withdrew with England's dying Lord Protector, a man who had obvious regrets for his own harsh view of life and the pathos to understand he lacked the grace of a king in the role thrust upon him.

At Skarra that fall there was the expectant elation which grips a home when a new child is due to be born. The women seemed to scurry with a quickened step, through the kitchen and up and down the stairs and along the halls, their faces bright with hope. Three midwives, as well as Lydia, had decided that Fanny's hips were wide and that unlike Geney she would have no trouble bearing the child. With that fact clear in his mind, Bruce rather much stayed out of the way, conferring endlessly with McGregor about the estate books and the cattle, as well as instituting a trial plan for industry among the cotters in weaving their wool.

When his mind fell back to his daughter, he was content that he had kept the faith with Geney, and that his daughter would pay back the man and woman who bore her with another generation. "The child will return a life to its parents and pay the debt for its own life."

Cromwell was as good as his word. Archibald Campbell, the Earl of Argyll, kept his forays out of the Highlands, and the discord between England and Scotland shifted to the Lowlands, and rivalry between their nation's capitals, London and Edinburgh. Bruce often wondered if he would have had the audacity and wisdom of playing off his enemies without the guidance of Lydia. "That Russian intuition which accepts horror as normal and still prays to God and loves children." Yet Lydia had always dismissed his gratitude. "What good is advice if you lack the wisdom to use it?" she had often said, sometimes kissing him.

He had been on the piazza of Skarra when the Highland boy burst across the grounds and fell exhausted into their midst with the news of Charles' capture by a hunting party of McDougels.

Bruce had broken from the family and retainers and leaped on the first saddled mount he had found, and had galloped through the gorse and over the Scottish moors until the pony had fallen, and he had run on foot until his chest ached and his breath made him sick to his stomach. He ran all the way to where his clan had encircled the Lowland party against a gray stone escarpment on Ben Lawker, and where they now held Charles hostage, his life for their escape.

"Depart in peace!" Bruce shouted, "and send us our man!"

He had seen the dozen men shift among themselves, knowing they had won, for Bruce had yielded.

Bruce saw Charles break from their midst and come hurtling into view, cutting from side to side, his long hair flying, his face full of despair and hope. "Father, I was betrayed!"

Bruce stood, openly showing himself, and held his breath. He saw the gunshots blossom in puffs of white against the stone and over the bracken. "No, dear God, spare him."

He heard the bullet strike flesh in a wet whop, and saw his son catapult onto his face and tumble in a mass of loose arms and legs.

"My God, my son," he said, stepping forward amidst a dull, eternal ringing in his stomach that made his ears dizzy. He was blind to the wave of screaming Highlanders who swept over Charles' body in their passion for vengeance.

He had Charles into his arms, his bosom to the boy's chest. "My son." He raised his tear-blind eyes to say "Quarter" to Ruff.

Charles was alive, the bullet deep into his ribs, but how fatal, Bruce did not know. His hand was dark with Charles' blood.

He crossed the moors with Charles slung on a tartan between four Highlanders. Charles was bright when his eyes caught Bruce's face. "Father, I was hunting, and I thought it inhospitable to not let them approach."

"Do not talk. I know. So you did what any boy would do." He put his hand onto Charles' fingers and squeezed them.

"No, Father, I was glad. I was sure you were wrong and I thought I could be a friend to the McDougels."

"No, hush, now."

"And they betrayed me." Charlies' chin dimpled. "I am sorry," the lips said.

Charles was still alive. Bruce had sent for the surgeon from Edinburgh, who had arrived in four days. The surgeon was a lean man who could not keep his eyes from Bruce nor from the interior of Skarra and the servants who bustled past them on skin slippers.

"We should bleed him," the surgeon said. "The putrid blood must be drained before the purified blood can rise to reach the wound and cleanse it." Bruce looked at the physician in silence, while Lydia and the women were at his side and McGregor and the men behind. "It is an exact analogy to pumping out the putrified water of a pool to let the fresh spring water bubble up." He searched Bruce's face.

"Thank you, not yet, physician."

"I cannot be responsible."

"It is my decision," Bruce said.

"As long as I am paid, my lord."

"You were paid."

"If I am detained . . . ?"

"You will be paid more." Bruce returned to the sickroom. Charles was lying on a stiff pallet atop his bed. He had not bled from his mouth, nor had he frothed pink as he coughed, and his breath lacked that foul odor which was a certain sign of rot within the chest, of a wound draining inward and making death but a matter of time. Still Charles hovered toward death, as though drawn by an invisible urge.

When Bruce had seen into the boy's eyes he saw the gray web of death fading the eyeball from within, a look he had seen appear in the eyes of all men as they died. Charles' fever had risen and Bruce had sent a stream of runners to the mountains for snow to keep the forehead and temples cool.

"It is a sickness of the soul," he said. "The death is there, but the wound is not fatal."

He remembered when he and Lydia had crept into the nursery to hear the breathing of their babies. They had each of them listened in dread for the breath which signaled the baby was still alive, and had not died in the quiet of the night. He remembered that he and Lydia had each refused to let the other see the awful thought they shared. He knew Lydia had caught the sight again. She put her hand atop his.

"I am very much afraid," he said.

"His body is trying. It's him that's failing," she said.

The wound had crusted into a scabbed crater, with a putrified pus blob under a thick clot, and it drained outward, staining the sheets with a rotted smell that showed the body was fighting for its life.

"Bruce, you must reach him," Lydia said. "He was our first-born and we made our mistakes with him."

"Aye, but I was gentle with him."

"You were, but you learned with him." Lydia was at his side in the vigil.

Bruce waited until Charles was conscious after sleeping a fitful set of hours. The Lady Sharon Hamilton had been at his bedside and had wept those easy tears of the romantic young, who fancy death as a dramatic interlude among lovers and have no full understanding of relentless grief.

"Keep that girl out of his room," Lydia said, and Bea had nodded and followed the girl.

Bruce stood at the boy's bedside.

"Can you hear me, son?"

"Yes, Father."

"Your wound is not fatal, or you would be dead by now."

The blue eyes moved over to him. "I do not think you could understand, Father."

"I would like to listen."

"I am mortified. I would gladly die. I hope I can die. Father, you see, I hated you." The drained eyes found his.

"Perhaps you did, and perhaps you only fancied you did."

"Whatever, real or fancy, I thought it was true, so it was true."

"Why did you hate me?"

"Because you were right."

"Me?"

"A god. Lord, I was a fool in your presence."

"I pulled you from your mother's womb, with these hands." He held up a veined, bone-limbed hand before Charles. "Her blood and feces all over you and her screaming and Lydia sucking the phlegm out your mouth, and you no more than a wet blob of flesh that breathed. I thought you no fool then, and I think you no fool now."

"Father, when you tell me that, do you not know I want to die?"

Bruce heard life in Charles' voice, and caught a light of anger behind the eye.

"I may have hated you, but I am mortified for my misconduct."

"You judge yourself?"

"Yes."

"And how qualified are you, to judge yourself?"

The eyes searched his.

"Your mother judged herself by the cruelty of a society that judged her, and she did it to make a way for you children, and it killed her. And I swore I would never let that demented code judge another that I loved, nor would I again respect it. Son, would you accept what is manifest death as your judge for being?"

"I do not understand you, Father."

"Charles, none of us has to die to atone, and youth is, in its way, always wrong, for youth is a time of illusions, of action inspired by a hope of perfection on earth, of immediacy as eternal, when in fact, the eternal is known only by enduring time, by sufferance and forbearance. . . ."

"I am disgusted with myself, Father. I betrayed us all."

"Son, nothing is ever right for a boy. It is why we change the rules for the young, for a young man is the prey to the cunning of clever men, the plunder of iniquitous folk who exploit the illusion of an abiding hope without which the young cannot live nor grow to adulthood."

Charles' hand reached toward him.

"To be a man you have to know evil and not accept it as true, to understand the inherent iniquity of the human species and still not judge them. You must grow, and brighten, and finally expand to some place as a man or woman where you can reach the toe bone of God."

"Toe bone, Father?" A faint trace of a smile flickered behind Charles' lips.

"Oh, I would not want to offend the Lord by climbing into His bosom. The toe bone will do."

"Father." The boy began to cry. "I love you."

"I know," Bruce whispered, taking Charles' face into his chest. "Will you live?"

"Yes, I will live."

"Thank you."

"I promise."

Bruce held his son to his body for a long time, and felt a strength rise in the boy's torso, a deepening breath and a flexing of arms and movement of legs. The boy stopped crying and his head settled purposefully into Bruce's bosom, and the breathing was measured and strong.

The gloom of the day settled over them, and Bruce watched the women who crept on tiptoe about the room throw up the fire, and he remembered how he had held Geney to his body many years ago while she died. To feel his son move in his arms, in life, filled him with a great peace, but the sorrow of Geney came flooding back, so close was death.

"I love you, Geney," he said.

Charles' breath changed, giving him a momentary fright, then came rhythmically deep. Bruce breathed and closed his eyes. There was a God. The life that was before it is must return to where it came and be itself when it is no more. What lives before it was must be before it is, and if it cannot be comprehended, it must be accepted, for life is before death can be. It is the hand of God, but a God I can never see nor truly understand.

"Lydia, our son will live."

"Yes." She touched his arm and he knew solace.